PRAISE FOR

The Thursday MURDER Club

'As the bodies pile up and more is revealed of the lives and loves of Joyce, Ibrahim, Ron and Elizabeth, you can't help cheering them on – and hoping to meet them again soon'
THE TIMES

'Elegant and witty . . . It is delightful' **DAILY MAIL**

'A gripping read and rather moving' **SUNDAY TIMES**

'One of the most enjoyable books of the year . . .
Well written, hilarious and joyously big-hearted'
DAILY EXPRESS

'Pure escapism' **GUARDIAN**

'As gripping as it is funny' **EVENING STANDARD**

'Christie-style sleuthing with brilliant skill'
WOMAN & HOME

'Just brilliant: smart, charming and wryly funny'
GOOD HOUSEKEEPING

'Quirky, joyful and oh-so British' **HEAT**

'Witty, warm and wise with irresistible characters.
This is one of the most delightful novels of the year'
DAILY MIRROR

'Funny and original' **SUN**

'A witty and poignant tale' **DAILY TELEGRAPH**

'Keenly observed, drily funny . . .
Delight after delight from first page to last' **RED**

RiCHARD OSMAN

The Man Who Died TWICE

PENGUIN BOOKS

PENGUIN BOOKS

UK | USA | Canada | Ireland | Australia
India | New Zealand | South Africa

Penguin Books is part of the Penguin Random House group of companies
whose addresses can be found at global.penguinrandomhouse.com.

First published by Viking 2021
Published in Penguin Books 2022

007

Copyright © Richard Osman, 2021

The moral right of the author has been asserted

Typeset by Jouve (UK), Milton Keynes
Printed and bound in Great Britain by Clays Ltd, Elcograf S.p.A.

The authorized representative in the EEA is Penguin Random House Ireland,
Morrison Chambers, 32 Nassau Street, Dublin D02 YH68

A CIP catalogue record for this book is available from the British Library

ISBN: 978–0–241–98824–4

www.greenpenguin.co.uk

Penguin Random House is committed to a
sustainable future for our business, our readers
and our planet. This book is made from Forest
Stewardship Council® certified paper.

To Ruby and Sonny – I'm so proud and so lucky to be your dad.

Sylvia Finch wonders how much longer she can do this.

One foot in front of the other, her suede shoes darkening in the autumn puddles.

Death hangs about her like a fine mist. It is in her hair and in her clothes. Surely everyone she passes can tell?

Will she ever be rid of it? Sylvia hopes so, and she also hopes not.

When was the last time something truly good happened? Something that gave her some hope?

As Sylvia keys in the security code for the door, the sun breaks through the clouds.

In she goes.

PART ONE

Your Friends are Sure to Visit

1

The following Thursday . . .

'I was talking to a woman in Ruskin Court and she said she's on a diet,' says Joyce, finishing her glass of wine. 'She's eighty-two!'

'Zimmer frames make you look fat,' says Ron. 'It's the thin legs.'

'Why diet at eighty-two?' says Joyce. 'What's a sausage roll going to do to you? Kill you? Well, join the queue.'

The Thursday Murder Club has concluded its latest meeting. This week they have been looking at the cold case of a Hastings newsagent who murdered an intruder with a crossbow. He'd been arrested, but then the media had got involved, and the consensus was that a man should be allowed to protect his own shop with a crossbow, for goodness' sake. He walked free, head held high.

A month or so later police had discovered that the intruder was dating the newsagent's teenage daughter, and the newsagent had a long record of GBH, but at that point everybody had moved on. It was 1975, after all. No CCTV, and no one wanting to make a fuss.

'Do you think a dog might be good company?' asks

Joyce. 'I thought I might either get a dog or join Instagram.'

'I would advise against it,' says Ibrahim.

'Oh, you'd advise against everything,' says Ron.

'Broadly, yes,' agrees Ibrahim.

'Not a big dog, of course,' says Joyce. 'I haven't got the hoover for a big dog.'

Joyce, Ron, Ibrahim and Elizabeth are enjoying lunch at the restaurant that sits at the heart of the Coopers Chase community. There is a bottle of red and a bottle of white on their table. It is around a quarter to twelve.

'Don't get a small dog though, Joyce,' says Ron. 'Small dogs are like small men: always got a point to prove. Yapping it up, barking at cars.'

Joyce nods. 'Perhaps a medium dog, then? Elizabeth?'

'Mmm, good idea,' replies Elizabeth, though she is not really listening. How could she be, after the letter she has just received?

She's picking up the main points, of course. Elizabeth always stays alert, because you never know what might fall into your lap. She has heard all sorts over the years. A snippet of conversation in a Berlin bar, a loose-lipped Russian sailor on shore leave in Tripoli. In this instance, on a Thursday lunchtime in a sleepy Kent retirement village, it seems that Joyce wants a dog, there is a discussion about sizes and Ibrahim has doubts. But her mind is elsewhere.

The letter was slipped under Elizabeth's door, by unseen hand.

Dear Elizabeth,

I wonder if you remember me? Perhaps you don't, but without blowing my own trumpet, I imagine you might.

Life has worked its magic once more, and I discover, upon moving in this week, that we are now neighbours. What company I keep! You must be thinking they let in any old riff-raff these days.

I know it has been some while since you last saw me, but I think it would be wonderful to renew our acquaintance after all these years.

Would you like to join me at 14 Ruskin Court for a drink? A little housewarming? If so, how would 3 p.m. tomorrow suit? No need to reply, I shall await with a bottle of wine regardless.

It really would be lovely to see you. So much to catch up on. An awful lot of water under the bridge and so on.

I do hope you remember me, and I do hope to see you tomorrow.

Your old friend,
Marcus Carmichael

Elizabeth has been mulling it over ever since.

The last time she had seen Marcus Carmichael would have been late November 1981, a very dark, very cold night by Lambeth Bridge, the Thames at low tide, her breath clouding in the freezing air. There had been a team of them, each one a specialist, and Elizabeth was in charge. They arrived in a white Transit van, shabby on the outside, seemingly owned by 'G. Procter – Windows, Gutters, All Jobs Considered', but, on the inside, gleaming, full of buttons and screens. A young constable had cordoned off an area of the foreshore and the pavement on the Albert Embankment had been closed.

Elizabeth and her team clambered down a flight of stone steps, lethal with slick moss. The low tide had left behind a corpse, propped, almost sitting, against the nearest stone pillar under the bridge. Everything had been done properly, Elizabeth had made sure of that. One of her team had examined the clothing and rifled through the pockets of his heavy overcoat, a young woman from Highgate had taken photographs and the doctor had recorded the death. It was clear the man had jumped into the Thames further upstream, or been pushed. That was for the coroner to decide. It would all be typed into a report by somebody or other and Elizabeth would simply add her initials at the bottom. Neat and tidy.

The journey back up those slick steps with the corpse on a military stretcher had taken some time. The young constable, thrilled to have been called to help, had fallen and broken an ankle, which was all they needed. They explained they wouldn't be able to call an ambulance for the time being, and he took it in fairly good part. He received an unwarranted promotion several months later, so no lasting harm was done.

Her little unit eventually reached the Embankment, and the body was loaded into the white Transit van. 'All jobs considered'.

The team dispersed, save for Elizabeth and the doctor, who stayed in the van with the corpse as it was driven to a morgue in Hampshire. She hadn't worked with this particular doctor before – broad, red-faced, a dark moustache turning grey – but he was interesting enough. A man you would remember. They'd discussed euthanasia and cricket until the doctor had dozed off.

Ibrahim is making a point with his wine glass. 'I'm afraid I would advise against a dog altogether, Joyce, small, medium, or large. At your time in life.'

'Oh, here he comes,' says Ron.

'A medium dog,' says Ibrahim, 'say a terrier, or a Jack Russell perhaps, would have a life expectancy of around fourteen years.'

'Says who?' asks Ron.

'Says the Kennel Club, in case you want to take it up with them, Ron. Would you like to take it up with them?'

'No, you're all right.'

'Now, Joyce,' Ibrahim continues, 'you are seventy-seven years old?'

Joyce nods, 'Seventy-eight next year.'

'Well, that goes without saying, yes,' agrees Ibrahim. 'So, at seventy-seven years old, we have to take a look at your life expectancy.'

'Ooh, yes!' says Joyce. 'I love this sort of thing. I had my Tarot done on the pier once. She said I was going to come into money.'

'Specifically, we have to look at the chances of your life expectancy exceeding the life expectancy of a medium dog.'

'It's a mystery to me why you never got married, old son,' says Ron to Ibrahim, and takes the bottle of white wine from the cooler on the table. 'With that silver tongue of yours. Top-up, anyone?'

'Thank you, Ron,' says Joyce. 'Fill it to the brim to save having to do it again.'

Ibrahim continues. 'A woman of seventy-seven has a fifty-one per cent chance of living for another fifteen years.'

'This is jolly,' says Joyce. 'I didn't come into money, by the way.'

'So if you were to get a dog now, Joyce, would you outlive it? That's the question.'

'I'd outlive a dog through pure spite,' says Ron. 'We'd just sit in opposite corners of the room, staring each other out, and see who went first. Not me. It's like when we were negotiating with British Leyland in 'seventy-eight. The moment one of their lot went to the loo first, I knew we had 'em.' Ron knocks back more wine. 'Never go to the loo first. Tie a knot in it if you have to.'

'The truth is, Joyce,' says Ibrahim. 'Maybe you would, and maybe you wouldn't. Fifty-one per cent. It's the toss of a coin, and I don't believe that is a risk worth taking. You must never die before your dog.'

'And is that an old Egyptian saying, or an old psychiatrist's saying?' asks Joyce. 'Or something you just made up?'

Ibrahim tips his glass towards Joyce again, an indication of more wisdom to come. 'You must die before your children, of course, because you have taught them to live without you. But not your dog. You teach your dog only to live *with* you.'

'Well, that is certainly food for thought, Ibrahim; thank you,' says Joyce. 'A bit soulless perhaps. Don't you think, Elizabeth?'

Elizabeth hears, but her mind is still in the back of the speeding Transit van, with the corpse and the doctor with the moustache. Not the only such occasion in Elizabeth's career, but unusual enough to be memorable – anyone who knew Marcus Carmichael would have known that.

'Beat Ibrahim's system,' Elizabeth says. 'Get a dog that's old already.'

And here was Carmichael again, years later. Looking for what? A friendly chat? Cosy reminiscence by an open fire? Who knew?

Their bill is brought to the table by a new member of the serving staff. Her name is Poppy and she has a tattoo of a daisy on her forearm. Poppy has been at the restaurant for nearly two weeks now and, thus far, the reviews have not been good.

'You've brought us table twelve, Poppy,' says Ron.

Poppy nods. 'Oh, yes, that's . . . silly me . . . what table is this?'

'Fifteen,' says Ron. 'You can tell because of the big number fifteen written on the candle.'

'Sorry,' says Poppy. 'It's just remembering the food, and carrying it, and then the numbers. I'll get the hang of it eventually.' She walks back to the kitchens.

'She is very well meaning,' says Ibrahim. 'But ill suited to this role.'

'She has lovely nails, though,' says Joyce. 'Immaculate. Immaculate, aren't they, Elizabeth?'

Elizabeth nods. 'Immaculate.' Not the only thing she has noticed about Poppy, who seems to have sprung from nowhere, with her nails and her incompetence. But she has other things on her mind for now, and the mystery of Poppy can wait for another day.

She is going through the text of the letter again in her head. *I wonder if you remember me? An awful lot of water under the bridge . . .*

Did Elizabeth remember Marcus Carmichael? What a ridiculous question. She had found Marcus Carmichael's dead body slumped against a Thames bridge at low tide. She had helped to carry that body up those slick stone steps in the dead of night. She had sat feet away from his corpse in a white Transit van advertising window-cleaning services. She had broken the news of his death to his young wife and she had stood beside the grave at his funeral, as an appropriate mark of respect.

So, yes, Elizabeth remembers Marcus Carmichael very well indeed. Time to be back in the room though. One thing at a time.

Elizabeth reaches for the white wine. 'Ibrahim, not everything is about numbers. Ron, you would die long before the dog, male life expectancy is far lower than female life expectancy, and you know what your GP has said about your blood sugar. And Joyce, we both know you've already made up your mind. You'll get a rescue dog. It'll be sitting somewhere right now, all alone with big eyes, just waiting for you. You will be powerless, and, besides, it'll be fun for all of us, so let's stop even discussing it.'

Job done.

'And how about Instagram?' says Joyce.

'I don't even know what that is, so feel free,' says Elizabeth, and finishes her wine.

An invitation from a dead man? On reflection, she will be accepting.

2

'We were watching *Antiques Roadshow* the other night,' says DCI Chris Hudson, drumming his fingers on the steering wheel. 'And this woman comes on, and she's got these jugs, and your mum leans over to me and says –'

PC Donna De Freitas slams her head against the dashboard. 'Sir, I am begging you. I am literally begging you. Please stop talking about my mum for ten minutes.'

Chris Hudson is supposed to be mentoring her, smoothing her eventual path into CID, but you wouldn't know it from the almost total disrespect with which they treat each other, or, indeed, from their friendship, which had blossomed the moment they met.

Donna had recently introduced Chris, her boss, to Patrice, her mum. She thought they might get along. As it turned out, they are getting along a little bit too well for her liking.

Stakeouts with Chris Hudson used to be more fun. There would be crisps, there would be quizzes, there would be gossip about the new DS who'd just started at Fairhaven and had accidentally sent a picture of his penis to a local shopkeeper who was asking for advice on security grilles.

They'd laugh, they'd eat, they'd put the world to rights.

But now? Sitting in Chris's Ford Focus on a late-autumn evening, keeping a watchful eye on Connie Johnson's lock-up? Now Chris has a Tupperware container filled with olives, carrot batons and hummus. The Tupperware container bought by her mum, the hummus made by her mum and the carrot batons sliced by her mum. When Donna had suggested buying a KitKat he'd looked at her and said 'empty calories'.

Connie Johnson was their friendly local drug dealer. Well, Connie was more a drug *wholesaler* these days. The two Antonio brothers from St Leonards had controlled the local drug trade for some years, but they had gone missing around a year ago and Connie Johnson had stepped into the breach. Whether she was just a drug wholesaler, or whether she was a murderer too, was open to question, but, either way, that's why they were spending their week sitting in a Ford Focus, training binoculars on a Fairhaven lock-up.

Chris has lost a bit of weight, he has had a nice haircut, and is now wearing a pair of age-appropriate trainers – everything Donna had ever told him to do. She had used all the tricks in the book to encourage him, to convince him, to cajole him into looking after himself. But it turned out that, all along, the only real motivation he needed to change was to start having sex with her mum. You have to be so careful what you wish for.

Donna sinks back into her seat and puffs out her cheeks. She would kill for a KitKat.

'Fair enough, fair enough,' says Chris. 'OK, I spy, with my little eye, something beginning with Y.'

Donna looks out of the window. Far below she sees the line of lock-up garages, one of which belongs to Connie Johnson, the new drugs kingpin of Fairhaven. Queenpin? Beyond the lock-ups is the sea. The English Channel, inky black, moonlight picking out gentle waves. There is a light on the horizon, far out to sea.

'Yacht?' says Donna.

'Nope,' says Chris, shaking his head.

Donna stretches and looks back towards the row of garages. A hooded figure on a BMX bike rides up to Connie's lock-up and bangs on the door. They can hear the faint metallic thunder even up on the hill.

'Youth on bicycle?' says Donna.

'Nope,' says Chris.

Donna watches as the door opens and the boy walks inside. All day, every day, this was happening. Couriers in and out. Leaving with coke, Es and hash, coming back with cash. It was non-stop. Donna knows they could raid the place right now and find a nice little haul of drugs, a bored middleman sitting at a table and a youth on a bicycle. But, instead, the team were biding their time, taking photographs of whoever walked in or out, following them wherever they were going, trying to build up a full picture of Connie Johnson's operation. Gathering enough evidence to take the whole thing down in one go. With any luck there would be a series of dawn raids. With a bit more luck they would have a tactical support group armed with pneumatic battering rams to smash a few doors down and one of the tactical support officers would be single.

'Yellow jacket?' says Donna, seeing a woman walking along the high path towards the car park.

'Nope,' says Chris.

The big prize was Connie Johnson herself. That's why she and Chris were there. Had Connie murdered two rivals and got away with it?

Occasionally, among the youths on bicycles they would see more familiar faces. Senior figures from the Fairhaven drug scene. Every name was noted. If Connie had murdered the Antonio brothers, then she hadn't done it by herself. She was no fool. Sooner or later, in fact, she would notice she was being watched. Then things would become less blatant, harder to track. So they were getting all their evidence lined up while they could.

Donna jumps as a knuckle raps on her side window. She turns and sees the yellow jacket of the woman who had been walking along the path. A smiling face appears at the window and holds up two cups of coffee. Donna registers the shock of blonde hair and the smear of red lipstick. She winds down her window.

The woman crouches, then smiles. 'Now, we haven't been introduced, but I think you're Donna and Chris. I bought you coffees from the garage.'

She hands the coffees over, and Donna and Chris look at each other and take them.

'I'm Connie Johnson, but I think you know that,' says the woman. She pats the pockets of her jacket. 'I also bought sausage rolls, if you'd like one?'

'No, thank you,' says Chris.

'Yes, please,' says Donna.

Connie hands Donna a sausage roll in a paper bag. 'I'm afraid I didn't buy anything for the policewoman hiding behind the bins, taking all the photographs.'

'She's vegan anyway,' says Donna. 'From Brighton.'

'Anyway, just wanted to introduce myself,' says Connie. 'Feel free to arrest me any time.'

'We will,' says Chris.

'What's your eye-shadow?' Connie asks Donna.

'Pat McGrath, Gold Standard,' says Donna.

'It's lush,' says Connie. 'Anyway, business all done for today if you wanted to go home. And you haven't seen anything I didn't want you to see for the last two weeks.'

Chris sips his coffee. 'Is this really from the garage? It's very good.'

'They've got a new machine,' says Connie. She reaches into an inside pocket, takes out an envelope and hands it to Donna. 'You can have these. There's photographs of you in there, photographs of all the other officers you've had crawling around, too. Two can play at that game. Bet you didn't see anyone take them, eh? Followed a few of you home too. They took a nice one of you on a date the other day, Donna. You can do better, that's my opinion.'

'Yep,' says Donna.

'I'll be on my way, but nice to finally say hello in person. I've been dying to meet you.' Connie blows them a kiss. 'Don't be strangers.'

Connie straightens up and walks away from the Ford Focus. Behind them a Range Rover appears. The passenger door is opened and Connie climbs in and is driven away.

'Well,' says Chris.

'Well,' agrees Donna. 'What now?'

Chris shrugs.

'Great plan, boss,' says Donna. 'What was your I spy? Something beginning with Y?'

Chris turns his key in the ignition and puts on his seat-belt. 'It was your mother's beautiful face. I see it every time I close my eyes.'

'Oh, Christ,' says Donna. 'I'm asking for a transfer.'

'Good idea,' says Chris. 'Not until we've nicked Connie Johnson though, eh?'

3

Joyce

I do wish something exciting would happen again. I don't mind what.

Perhaps a fire, but where no one gets hurt? Just flames and fire engines. We can all stand around watching, with flasks, and Ron can shout advice to the firefighters. Or an affair, that would be fun. Preferably mine, but I'm not greedy, so long as there's a bit of scandal, like a big age difference, or someone suddenly needing a replacement hip. Perhaps a gay affair? We haven't had one of those at Coopers Chase yet, and I think everyone would enjoy it. Maybe someone's grandson could go to prison? Or a flood that doesn't affect us? You know the sort of thing I mean.

When you think of how many people have died around here recently, it is quite hard to just go back to pottering around the garden centre and watching old episodes of *Taggart*. Although I do like *Taggart*.

When I was a nurse, patients would die all the time. They were popping off left, right and centre. Don't get the wrong idea, I never killed anyone, although it would have been very easy to. Easier than a doctor. They used to check up on doctors a lot. They probably check up on everyone these days, but I bet you could still do it if the mood took you.

Ibrahim doesn't want me to get a dog, but I am sure I can change his mind. Before you know it, he'll be dog this and dog that. You can bet he'll be first in line to walk it, too. I wish I'd got my hands on Ibrahim thirty years ago.

There is an animal rescue centre just across the border in Sussex, and they have all sorts there. The usual cats and dogs, but then also donkeys and rabbits and guinea pigs. I've never thought that a guinea pig might need rescuing before, but I suppose they do. We all need it once in a while, and I don't see why guinea pigs would be any different. They eat guinea pigs in Peru, did you know? It was on *MasterChef* the other day. They just mentioned it, they didn't actually eat one.

Lots of the dogs are from Romania; they save them and bring them over. I don't know how they bring them over, that's something I will ask. I don't imagine they have a plane full of dogs. In a big van? They will have worked out a way. Ron says they will bark in a foreign accent, but that's Ron.

We looked on the rescue centre website and you should see the dogs, honestly. There is one called Alan I have got my eye on. 'Indeterminate terrier', according to his profile. You and me both, I thought when I saw that. Alan is six years old, and they say you mustn't change their names, because they get used to them, but I won't call a dog Alan, whatever pressure I am put under.

Maybe I can persuade Ibrahim to drive me over next week. He's gone car mad recently. He's even driving into

Fairhaven tomorrow. He has really come out of his shell since everyone started getting murdered. Driving here, there and everywhere like he's Murray Walker.

I'm still wondering why Elizabeth was in a funny mood at lunch. Listening but not listening. Perhaps something is wrong with Stephen? You remember, her husband? Or perhaps she's still not over Penny. Either way, she has something on her mind, and she walked away from lunch with a purpose. That's always bad news for someone. Your only real hope is that it's not you.

I am also knitting. I know, can you imagine?

I got talking to Deirdre at Knit & Natter. Her husband was French but died some time ago – I think he fell off a ladder, but it might have been cancer, I can't remember. Deirdre has been knitting little friendship bracelets for charity and has given me the pattern. You make them in different colours, depending on who you make them for. People pay you whatever they choose and all the money goes to charity. I also put sequins on mine. The pattern doesn't say to put sequins on, but I've had some in a drawer for ages.

I made a red, white and blue bracelet for Elizabeth. It was my first go and was rather ragged but she was very good about it. I asked her what charity she wanted the money to go to and she said Living With Dementia and that's the closest we have got to talking about Stephen. I don't think she can keep him to herself for much longer, though; dementia just ploughs on through the woods and never turns back. Poor Elizabeth. Poor Stephen as well, obviously.

I also made a friendship bracelet for Bogdan. It was yellow and blue, which I had mistakenly thought were the colours of the Polish flag. According to Bogdan, the colours of the Polish flag are red and white, and, to give him his due, he would know. He thought that perhaps I had been thinking of Sweden, and perhaps I had. Gerry would have put me right. Like all good husbands, Gerry knew all the flags.

I saw Bogdan wearing his bracelet the other day. He was on his way up to work at the building site at the top of the hill, and he gave me a little wave and there it was on his wrist, wrapped around his tattoos of goodness knows what. I know it's silly, but I couldn't stop smiling. The sequins were sparkling in the sunshine and so was I.

Elizabeth hasn't worn hers yet, and I can't say I blame her. I am getting better at it though, and, besides, Elizabeth and I don't need a bracelet to show we are friends.

Last night I dreamt of the house Gerry and I lived in when we were first married. We opened a door and found a new room we hadn't ever seen before, and we were full of schemes as to what to do with it.

I don't know what age Gerry was, he was just Gerry, but I was me now. Two people who never met, touching and laughing and making plans. A pot plant here, a coffee table there. The stuff of love.

When I woke up, and realized Gerry had gone, my heart broke once again, and I sobbed and sobbed. I imagine if you could hear all the morning tears in this place it would sound like birdsong.

4

It is another glorious autumn day, but there is a bite in the air that tells you there won't be too many left. Winter is waiting impatiently round the corner.

It is 3 p.m., and Elizabeth is carrying flowers for Marcus Carmichael. The dead man. That drowned body, suddenly alive as you like and living at 14 Ruskin Court. The man she saw lowered into a grave in a Hampshire churchyard, now unpacking boxes and struggling with his new Wi-Fi.

She walks past Willows, the nursing home at the heart of Coopers Chase. The place Elizabeth would visit every day while Penny was there, just to sit and chat to her old friend, to plot and to gossip, not knowing whether Penny could hear her or not.

No more Penny now, of course.

The nights are beginning to draw in a little, and the sun is sinking behind the trees on top of the hill as Elizabeth reaches Ruskin Court and rings the bell for number 14. Here goes nothing. There is a brief wait and she is buzzed up.

There are lifts in all the buildings, but Elizabeth will use the stairs while she still can. Stairs are good for hip and knee flexibility. Also, it is very easy to kill someone in a lift when the doors open. Nowhere to run, nowhere to hide, and a *ping* to announce you're about to appear. Not that she's worried about being killed, it doesn't feel to her like that's what is happening here, but it's always important to remember best practice. Elizabeth has never killed anyone in a lift. She once saw someone pushed down an empty lift shaft in Essen, but that was different.

She turns left at the top of the stairs, transfers the flowers to her left hand and knocks on the door of number 14. Who will answer the door? What is the story here? Should she be worried?

The door opens, and she sees a very familiar face.

It's not Marcus Carmichael, how could it have been? But it is certainly someone who knew the name Marcus Carmichael. And who knew it would get her attention.

And it turns out that, yes, she should be worried.

The man is handsome and tanned, strands of sandy grey hair still gamely holding on. She might have known he would never go bald.

How to play this one?

'Marcus Carmichael, I assume?' says Elizabeth.

'Well, I assume so, too,' says the man. 'Good to see you, Elizabeth. Are those flowers for me?'

'No, I have taken to carrying flowers around with me as an affectation,' says Elizabeth, handing them over as she is ushered in.

'Quite right, quite right, I'll put them in water, nonetheless. Come in, sit down, make yourself at home.' He disappears into the kitchen.

Elizabeth takes in the flat: bare, not a picture, not an

ornament, not a single frill to be seen. No sign of any-one 'moving in'. Two armchairs, both ready for the skip, a pile of books on the floor, a reading lamp.

'I like what you've done with the place,' says Elizabeth in the direction of the kitchen.

'Not my choice, dear,' says the man, re-entering the room with the flowers in a kettle. 'I daresay I'll grow into it, though I hope I shan't be here for long. Can I get you a glass of wine?' He sets the kettle on a windowsill.

'Yes, please,' says Elizabeth, settling into an armchair. What was happening? Why was he here? And what did he want from her after all this time? Whatever it was looked like trouble to her. A room barely furnished, blinds drawn, a padlocked bedroom. Number 14 Ruskin Court had the look of a safe house.

But safe from what?

The man walks back in, with two glasses of red wine. 'A Malbec for you, if I'm not mistaken?'

Elizabeth takes her glass as the man sits in the arm-chair opposite her. 'You seem to think that's a stunning feat of memory, to remember the wine I drank for the twenty-odd years we knew each other?'

'I'm nearly seventy, darling, everything is a stunning feat of memory these days. Cheers!' He raises his glass.

'And to you,' says Elizabeth, raising hers. 'Long time.'

'Very long time. But you remembered Marcus Carmichael?'

'That was very neat.'

Marcus Carmichael had been a ghost, invented by Elizabeth. She was an expert in it. A man who never existed, concocted entirely to pass secrets to the Russians. A man with a past created from false documents and staged photographs. An agent who never existed, passing secrets that never existed, to the enemy. And when the Russians got a bit closer, and wanted a bit more from their new source, it was time to kill Marcus Carmichael off, to 'borrow' an unclaimed cadaver from one of the London teaching hospitals and bury it in a Hampshire churchyard, with a young typist from the pool bawling her eyes out as the grieving widow. And bury the lie with him. So Marcus Carmichael was a dead man who had never lived.

'Thank you, I thought it might amuse you. You look very well. Very well. How is ... remind me ... is it Stephen? The current husband?'

'Shall we not do this?' sighs Elizabeth. 'Shall we cut to you telling me why you're here?'

The man nods. 'Certainly, Liz. Plenty of time to catch up when everything is out in the open. I believe it is Stephen, though?'

Elizabeth thinks about Stephen, back at home. She left him with the television on, so hopefully he is dozing. She wants to be back with him, to sit with him, to have his arms around her. She does not want to be here, in this empty flat with this dangerous man. A man she has seen kill before. This is not the adventure she was hoping for today. Give her Stephen and his kisses. Give her Joyce and her dogs.

Elizabeth takes another sip of wine. 'I'm assuming you want something from me? As ever.'

The man sits back in his armchair. 'Well, yes, I suppose

I do. But nothing too taxing – in fact, something you might think is rather fun. You remember fun, Elizabeth?'

'I'm already having my fair share of fun around here, but thank you.'

'Well, yes, so I hear. Dead bodies and so on. Read the whole file.'

'File?' asks Elizabeth. A sinking feeling.

'Oh yes, you've caused quite a stir in London, asking for all kinds of favours over the last couple of months. Financial records, forensics reports, I believe you even had a retired pathologist down here, digging up bones? You thought that might go unnoticed?'

Elizabeth realizes she has been short-sighted. She had certainly called in favours while she and the Thursday Murder Club were investigating the deaths of Tony Curran and Ian Ventham. And when they were identifying the other corpse they'd found, buried in the graveyard up on the hill. She should have known that somebody, somewhere was taking notes. You can't expect favours without being asked to repay them. So what was it to be?

'What do you need from me?' she asks.

'Just some babysitting.'

'Babysitting who?'

'Babysitting me.'

'And why would someone need to babysit you?'

The man nods, takes a sip of his wine and leans forward. 'The thing is, Elizabeth, I'm afraid I've got myself in a spot of bother.'

'Some things never change, do they? Why don't you tell me about it?'

There is the sound of a key in the lock and the door swings open.

'Bang on time for once,' says the man. 'Here's just the woman to help me tell the story. Meet my handler.'

Into the room walks Poppy, the new waitress from the restaurant. She nods to them both. 'Sir, ma'am.'

'Well, that explains an awful lot,' says Elizabeth. 'Poppy, I hope you're a better operative than you are a waitress.'

Poppy blushes. 'To be honest, I'm not sure I am, I'm afraid. But between the three of us I expect we can muddle through it all and stay safe.'

Safe houses, in Elizabeth's experience, rarely stayed safe for long. Poppy moves the flowers in the kettle to one side. 'Lovely flowers.' She perches on the windowsill.

'Safe from what, exactly?' asks Elizabeth.

'Well, let me start at the beginning,' says the man.

'I wish you would, Douglas,' says Elizabeth, and downs her glass of wine. 'You were an awful husband, but you always knew how to tell a good story.'

5

Ibrahim has just finished lunch with Ron. He had tried to persuade Ron to try hummus, but Ron was intractable. Ron would eat ham, eggs and chips every day if you let him. And to be fair, he was seventy-five and still going strong, so who's to say he was wrong? Ibrahim pulls the car door shut and buckles his seatbelt.

Ron had been excited because his grandson, Kendrick, is coming to stay next week, and Ibrahim is excited too.

Ibrahim would have made a wonderful father, a wonderful grandfather, too. But it wasn't to be, like so much else in his life. You silly old man, he thinks, as he turns the key in the ignition, you made the biggest mistake of them all. You forgot to live, you just hid away, safe and sound.

What good has it done him, though? Those decisions he had been too cautious to make? The loves he had been too timid to pursue? Ibrahim thinks of the many lives he has missed, somewhere along the way.

Ibrahim has always been good at 'thinking things through', but, now, he is choosing to take the proverbial bull by the horns. He has decided to live in the moment a little more. He is choosing to learn a lesson from Ron's chaotic freedom, from Joyce's joyful optimism and from the forensic wrecking ball that is Elizabeth.

Don't buy a dog, Joyce. That's what he had said. But of course she should. He will tell her when he gets back. Will she let him walk it? Surely she will. Terrific cardiovascular exercise. Everyone should buy dogs. Men should marry the women they loved, and not run away to England in fear. Ibrahim has had a lifetime to think about that decision. Has never even discussed it with his friends. Perhaps one day he should?

He turns left out of the gate of Coopers Chase. After checking, and then checking again, naturally.

There is a whole world out here, and, however frightened it makes him feel, he has decided he needs to get out of Coopers Chase every now and again. So here he is, out among the noise and the traffic and the people.

He has decided, once a week, to take Ron's Daihatsu out for a spin and visit Fairhaven. He passes the town sign. It is quite a buzz. Just him, by himself. He's going to do a bit of shopping, sit in a Starbucks with a coffee and read the paper. And while he's here, he's going to look and listen. What are people saying these days? Do they look unhappy?

Ibrahim is anxious that he won't be able to find anywhere to park, but he finds a space easily. He worries that he won't be able to work out how to pay for the parking, but that is a cinch too.

What sort of psychiatrist is frightened of life? All psychiatrists he supposes, I mean, that's why they became psychiatrists. Even so, it wouldn't do any harm to let the world in. A mind could calcify at Coopers Chase, if you let it. The same people, the same conversations, the same grumbles and gripes. Investigating the murders has done Ibrahim a world of good.

He quickly discovers both self-service checkouts and contactless payments. The absolute minimum of human interaction. You don't have to nod hello to someone you have never met. To think he might have missed out on all this!

He finds a lovely independent bookshop where no one minds if you sit in an armchair and read for an hour. Of course, he buys the book he has been reading. It is called *You*, and is about a psychopath called Joe, for whom Ibrahim has a great deal of sympathy. He buys three other books too, because he wants the bookshop still to be here when he comes back next week. There was a sign behind the till saying 'Your Local Bookshop – Use It Or Lose It'.

Use It Or Lose It. That was quite right. That is why he is here. Out in the noise, with cars speeding by, with teenagers shouting and builders swearing. He feels good. He feels less frightened. His brain feels alive. Use it or lose it.

He looks at his watch. Three hours have gone by in a rush and it is time to head home, his head full of adventure. After telling Joyce that she should get a dog, he will tell her all about contactless payments. She will know about them already, but perhaps she won't have looked into the technology behind them, which he just has. Time flies when you are living it.

He has parked Ron's Daihatsu near Fairhaven Police Station, because surely that's the safest place to park.

Perhaps one week he will pop in and see Chris and Donna. Are you allowed to visit police officers at work? He is sure they would be delighted to see him, but he wouldn't want to hold up, say, an arson investigation while they felt they had to make small talk. But those worries were old Ibrahim. New Ibrahim would just take the chance. You want to see someone? Just go and see them. That's what Ron would do. Though Ron would also go to the bathroom and leave the door open, so Ibrahim must remember there are limits.

He passes three teenagers on a corner near the police station, all on bikes, and all three with hoods up. He smells cannabis. A lot of people at Coopers Chase smoke cannabis. Supposedly to relieve glaucoma, but statistically not that many people can have glaucoma, surely? As a young man, Ibrahim had been persuaded by some of his richer friends to smoke opium. He had been too much of a coward ever to try it again, but perhaps that was another thing he should put on his list? He wonders where you can buy opium. Chris and Donna would know. It was very useful, knowing police officers.

These three youths are exactly the sort of people that Ibrahim should be scared of, he knows that. But they don't frighten him at all. Young men had always hung around on street corners on bicycles, and they always would. In Fairhaven, in London, in Cairo.

Ibrahim sees the Daihatsu up ahead. He will take it through the car wash on the way back. Firstly, to say thank you to Ron, but also because he likes car washes. He takes out his phone. This was the first thing he learned today.

You can pay for your parking on a mobile phone app, which is short for application. Perhaps it's OK that everyone is looking at their phones? Perhaps if you have the entire history of human knowledge and achievement in your pocket it's OK to spend your time looking at –

Ibrahim doesn't hear the bicycle approach, but he feels it rushing past him, sees the hand grabbing his phone, ripping it from his grasp with a jerk that sends him tumbling to the ground.

Ibrahim lands on his side and rolls until he hits the kerb. The pain is immediate, in his arm, in his ribs. His jacket sleeve is torn. Will he be able to get it mended? He hopes so – it is a favourite jacket, but the rip looks bad, the white lining shining through like bone. He hears footsteps, running, and teenage laughter. As the footsteps reach him, he feels two kicks. One in the back and one to the back of the head. His head hits the kerb once more.

'Ryan, come on!'

This is very bad, Ibrahim understands that. Something serious has happened. He wants to move, but he is unable to. The damp of the gutter is seeping through the wool of his trousers, and he tastes blood.

There are more footsteps running, but Ibrahim has no way of protecting himself. He feels the cold of the kerb against his face. The footsteps stop, but no kick this time, instead he feels hands on shoulders.

'Mate? Mate? Jesus! Christine, call an ambulance.'

Yes, the adventure always ends with an ambulance, it doesn't matter who you are. What was the damage here?

Just broken bones? Bad enough at his age. Or worse? He had taken a kick to the back of the head. Whatever happened next he knew one thing was certain. He had made a mistake. He should have stayed safe. So now there will be no more trips to Fairhaven, no more sitting in the armchair in the bookshop. Where were his new books? In the street, getting wet? He is being shaken.

'Mate, open your eyes, stay awake!'

But my eyes are open, thinks Ibrahim, before realizing they are not.

6

Elizabeth is sipping her second Malbec, and listening to her ex-husband, Douglas Middlemiss, talking about international money laundering. Explaining the story of why a man of his age might need babysitting.

'We'd been looking at him for a while, this chap Martin Lomax, lovely big old house, plenty of money, but with the paperwork to prove where everything came from. The financial boys couldn't touch him. But when you know, you know, don't you?'

'You do,' agrees Elizabeth.

'There would be all sorts turning up at his house, at all hours. Russians, Serbians, the Turkish mafia. All coming to this secluded house outside a sleepy village. Hambledon, if you know it? They invented cricket there.'

'I'm sorry to hear that,' says Elizabeth.

'Range Rovers, Bentleys, up and down the country lanes. Arabs in helicopters, the full works. An Irish Republican commander once parachuted out of a light aircraft and landed in his garden.'

'What's his business?' asks Elizabeth. 'Unofficially?'

'Insurance,' says Poppy.

'Insurance?'

'He acts as a bank for major crime gangs,' says Douglas, leaning forward. 'Say the Turks are buying a hundred million pounds' worth of heroin from the Afghans. They won't pay the full amount.'

'Just as you don't have to pay the full amount for a freezer until it's delivered,' says Poppy.

'Thank you, Poppy,' says Elizabeth. 'I'd be lost without you.'

'So they'll give a security deposit of, say, ten million to a trusted middleman,' says Douglas. 'As a gesture of good faith.'

'And Martin Lomax is the middleman?'

'Well, they all trust him. You'd trust him if you met him. He's a peculiar fellow, quite evil, but solid. It is hard to find evil people who are also reliable. As you know.'

Elizabeth nods. 'So he has a house stuffed with cash?'

'Sometimes cash, sometimes far more exotic things. Priceless paintings, gold, diamonds,' says Douglas.

'An Uzbek drug dealer once brought in a first edition of *The Canterbury Tales*,' adds Poppy.

'Anything with a value,' says Douglas. 'And these things sit in a strongroom at our chap's house. If all goes well with a deal, he returns the down payment, often to be used again. And if things go wrong, then the down payment is paid in compensation.'

'So this strongroom is quite the place?' asks Elizabeth.

'I suspect at any one time you might find half a billion in cash, the same again in gold and stones, stolen Rembrandts, Chinese jade worth millions. Just sitting there, a few miles from Winchester if you please.'

'And how do you know all of this?'

'We've been in the house a number of times,' says

Poppy. 'We have microphones drilled into walls, cameras in light switches.'

'All the tricks you'd know,' says Douglas.

'Even in the strongroom?'

Poppy shakes her head. 'We've never made it into the strongroom.'

'But there's plenty enough just lying about elsewhere,' says Douglas. 'When I broke in, there was a Van Eyck on a pool table.'

'When you broke in?'

'I had help, naturally. Poppy and one of the boys from the Special Boat Service.'

'You're a housebreaker, too, Poppy?' says Elizabeth to the young woman sitting on the windowsill, legs dangling.

'I just dressed in black and did what I was told,' says Poppy, shifting to get comfortable.

'Well, that sums up a career in the security services,' says Elizabeth. 'So the two of you and some interested friends break into this house, stuffed to the gills with treasure?'

'Precisely,' says Douglas. 'Just for a little look around, you know? Scope it out, take a few piccies, dash off with no one any the wiser. Nothing you and I haven't done a hundred times before.'

'I see, and does this have anything to do with why you're in a flat with two armchairs and a padlocked bedroom, looking for your very happily ex-wife to babysit you?'

'It's fair to say it's where my little problem began, yes. Are you ready?'

'Fire away, Douglas,' says Elizabeth, looking straight at him. That twinkle in his eye was undimmed. The twinkle that gave an entirely undeserved suggestion of wisdom and charm. The twinkle that could make you walk down the aisle with a man almost ten years your junior, and regret it within months. The twinkle you soon realize is actually the beam of a lighthouse, warning you off the rocks.

'Can I ask you a question first?' says Poppy from the windowsill. 'Before we tell you everything?'

'Of course, dear,' says Elizabeth.

'How much do they know about you around here? Quite a lot, I suppose, given what's in the file?'

'They know a thing or two about me, yes,' says Elizabeth. 'My close friends.'

'And your close friends would be Joyce Meadowcroft, Ron Ritchie and Ibrahim Arif?'

'They would. That's quite a file you have, Poppy. Joyce will be thrilled when I tell her she's in a file.'

'Could I ask – I've been asked to ask – before we go any further. Have you at any point in the last four months broken the Official Secrets Act?'

Elizabeth laughs. 'Oh, goodness me, yes. Over and over.'

'OK, I'll make a note of that. It's very important that none of your friends learn about Douglas or me. Can you guarantee that at least?'

'Certainly not. I shall tell them the moment I'm out of the door.'

'I'm afraid I can't allow that.'

'I don't see that you have a choice, Poppy.'

'You will understand, ma'am, better than most people, that I have orders.'

'Poppy – firstly, call me Elizabeth. Secondly, I haven't seen you get an order right in two weeks, so why change now? Now, let's hear this story, and I'll tell you if I accept the job. And then I'll tell my friends, but you mustn't worry yourself.'

Douglas is chuckling. 'So your friends know everything about you?'

'Everything they need to, yes,' says Elizabeth.

'Do they know that you're Dame Elizabeth?'

'Of course not.'

'So not everything?'

'Not everything.'

'When was the last time you used your title, Elizabeth?'

'When I needed to borrow a motorcycle to get out of Kosovo in a hurry. When was the last time you used yours, Sir Douglas?'

'When I tried to get tickets for *Hamilton*.'

Elizabeth's phone rings. Which is rare. She looks down. Joyce is calling her. Which is rarer still.

'Forgive me, I have to take this.'

7

In a way, you had to admire Connie Johnson's confidence. She did things with a bit of style. But the stakeout had been a colossal waste of time, and if they were going to catch Connie, they were going to have to think of something a great deal cleverer. Though quite what that clever thing might be is eluding DCI Chris Hudson for the moment. And, to add insult to injury, he is now on an exercise bike.

Of all the machines at the gym, the bike suits him best. For a start you're sitting down, and you can look at your phone while you're using it. You can take things at your own pace – sedate in Chris's case – but you can also speed up to look more impressive any time a muscled man in a singlet or a muscled woman in Lycra walks by. A lot of Chris's colleagues from Fairhaven Police Station use this same gym. He sees them sometimes, and his rank doesn't seem to count for anything here. The other day a PC slapped him on the back and said, 'Keep going, mate, you'll get there.' Mate? Next time Chris needs someone to sit through three days' worth of CCTV from a twenty-four-hour garage, that young constable will see just who his mate is.

Right now Chris can see his DI, Terry Hallet, doing pull-ups with his top off. For the love of God.

But still Chris pedals in his loose-fitting T-shirt and baggy shorts. Shorts? That is what it has come to. And, of course, he pedals because of Patrice. Because for the first time in nearly two years a woman is regularly seeing him naked. Admittedly usually in as low a light as he can get away with, but still. And so far, so good, Chris is happy, Patrice *seems* happy, although what would she say if she wasn't? Well, Chris supposes that she wouldn't keep sleeping with him, but, even so, there is no harm in trying to eat better, trying to lose some weight and trying to echo-locate some muscles under his spongy surface.

It was still early days for Chris and Patrice, the days of lust and art galleries. Perhaps in six months they would be in love and he could safely put the weight back on. But for now here he was.

The exercise bike is a work of art, full of dials and buttons to increase resistance, to replicate hilly ground, to measure heart rate, to measure distance travelled, time elapsed and calories burned. Chris has most of the displays switched off. The heart-rate monitor was terrifying; Chris had seen numbers that surely couldn't be right. The calorie counter was worst of all. Six miles of cycling to burn off a hundred calories? Six miles? For half a Twix? It didn't bear thinking about.

So instead, he's watching an antiques programme on the TV screen and glancing up at the clock on the gym wall roughly every forty-five seconds, praying for the hour to be up.

As an elderly man on the TV hides a look of disappointment that his ship in a bottle is only worth sixty pounds, Chris's phone rings. He generally tries not to answer his phone in the gym, but he sees that Donna is calling. Something about Connie Johnson? Fingers crossed.

Chris slows his already slow pace and picks up the call.

'Donna, I'm on the bike. I'm like Lance Armstrong but without the –'

'Sir, can you get to the hospital?'

Donna had called him 'Sir'. So it was a case.

'Of course, what's up?'

'A mugging. A nasty one.'

'Gotcha. Why me though?'

'Chris,' says Donna. 'It's Ibrahim.'

Chris is running before he hangs up.

8

Joyce is holding Ibrahim's left hand. She squeezes it as he talks. Elizabeth is holding the other hand. Ron has propped himself against the far wall, putting as much distance as possible between him and his friend in the bed. But Ron has tears in his eyes, and Joyce has never seen that before, so he can stand where he wants.

Ibrahim has tubes in his nose, heavy bandages around his torso, a neck brace and a drip in his arm. He is entirely drained of colour. He looks broken. He looks frightened. He looks, Joyce realizes, old.

But he is conscious; he is sitting, propped up, and he is talking. Slowly and quietly, and clearly in pain, but talking.

Joyce leans in to catch what Ibrahim is saying.

'You can pay for the parking on your phone, you see. It's very convenient.'

'Whatever next?' asks Joyce, and squeezes his hand again.

'Ibrahim?' says Elizabeth, her voice as gentle as Joyce has ever heard it. 'With respect, we don't want to hear about the parking. We want to know who did this.'

Ibrahim nods as best he can and takes a shallow breath against the pain. He releases his hand from Elizabeth's grasp and tries to raise a finger but gives up. 'OK, but the app is really very clever. You just –'

The door flies open and Chris and Donna rush in, and make straight for the bed.

'Ibrahim!' cries Donna.

Joyce lets Donna take Ibrahim's hand. They've all had a turn. Chris walks over to the other side of the bed and taps the headboard. He looks down at Ibrahim and attempts a smile.

'You had us worried there for a moment.'

Ibrahim gives Chris a weak thumbs-up.

'We should see the other guy, right?' says Donna.

'You should catch the other guy, certainly,' says Elizabeth.

'Yes, forgive us, Elizabeth,' says Chris. 'We haven't managed to crack the case in the nine seconds we've been in the room.'

'Don't row,' says Joyce. 'Not in a hospital.'

'Can you speak, Ibrahim?' asks Donna, and Ibrahim nods. 'Whoever did this, we'll find them, and we'll get them in a room with the cameras off and they'll regret it.'

'That's my girl,' says Elizabeth. 'That's a proper police officer.'

'Hundred yards from your station,' says Ron, jabbing a finger at Chris. 'That's what it's come to. While you're off arresting someone for putting the recycling in the wrong bin.'

'All right, Ron,' says Joyce.

'I was at the gym,' says Chris.

'Well, that says it all,' says Ron.

'It doesn't say anything, Ron,' says Elizabeth. 'So be quiet and let Chris and Donna do their job.'

Chris nods to Elizabeth, then perches on the bed and looks at Ibrahim. 'Mate, if there's anything you remember, anything at all, then it all helps us. I know it must have been a blur, but even a small detail.'

'Only if you can,' says Joyce.

Ibrahim nods again and begins to speak, slowly, with the occasional pause when the pain gets too much.

'I don't remember much, Chris. You know I'm normally good with details.'

'Of course, mate, that's fine. Just anything.'

'There were three of them. Two white, one Asian – Bangladeshi, I would say.'

'That's great, Ibrahim,' says Chris. 'Anything else?'

'All on bikes. One of the bicycles was a Carrera Vulcan, one was a Norco Storm 4, and I'm afraid I'm not quite certain of the make of the third, but probably a Voodoo Bantu.'

'Right . . .' says Chris.

'All three wore hooded garments, one a burgundy Nike top with a white drawstring, and the other two in black Adidas. Their trainers were white Reebok, white Adidas, and I have forgotten the third.' Ibrahim looks to Chris in apology.

'Yes, I see,' says Chris.

'I do remember that one of the white boys had a watch with a beige strap and a blue face, and the other white boy had a tattoo of three stars on his left hand. The Bangladeshi boy had acne scars down the right side of his face. One of the other boys had a shaving rash, but that is moot, as I don't imagine it will last longer than a day. One had a rip in his jeans, and on his thigh you could see the bottom of a tattoo, which looked to me like a football crest, Brighton and Hove Albion, I think, and I could make out the letters "r-e-v-e-r" which I took to be the end of the word "forever", but of course I couldn't swear to it. That's all I remember, I'm afraid. It's a bit of a haze.'

Joyce smiles. That's her Ibrahim.

'I mean, I'll be honest,' says Chris, 'that was more than I expected. We'll find them on CCTV somewhere, and then we'll find those bikes. We'll get them for you.'

'Thank you,' says Ibrahim. 'And also, I know the first name of the one who attacked me, if that helps?'

'You know his name?'

'As I was lying there, they shouted, "Ryan, come on!"'

'Come on, Ryan?' says Donna.

'There's your man,' says Ron. 'Right there. Stop pillocking around and go and arrest Ryan.'

'If I arrested every Ryan with a criminal record in Fairhaven, we'd need more cells,' says Chris.

A nurse walks in and Joyce recognizes the look on her face. Joyce stands.

'Time to go, everyone, let the nurses get on with their jobs.'

Ibrahim gets gentle hugs and kisses from everyone in turn, and they start to file out. Only Ron remains.

'Come on, Ron,' says Joyce. 'Let's get you home.'

Ron shuffles from foot to foot.

'Um, I'm staying.'

'You're staying here?'

'Yeah, I just . . . Well, they're going to make me up a camp bed, and they said I could stay.' Ron shrugs; he looks a little awkward. 'Keep him company. Got my iPad, might watch a film.'

'There is a Korean film I have been looking forward to,' says Ibrahim.

'Not that,' says Ron.

Joyce walks over to Ron and gives him a hug, feeling his embarrassment as she does. 'You look after our boy.' Joyce then walks out of the door, letting it close behind her, and sees Chris and Donna in conference with Elizabeth.

'The phone was just snatched, so there'll be no forensics,' says Chris, 'and from what I've heard we don't have witnesses. There's no CCTV there either, they'll have known that. We can find them for sure, with Ibrahim's description, but they'll laugh in our faces in an interview.'

'And off they'll trot, to do the same thing to someone else,' says Donna.

'You're going to let them get away with this?' says Elizabeth. 'After doing that to Ibrahim?'

Chris looks around him, just to make sure he's among friends. 'Of course we're not going to let them get away with it.'

'Oh, good,' says Joyce.

'We'll bring them in, I promise you that. We'll waste a bit of their time. But other than that, there's nothing me and Donna can do.'

Elizabeth looks at him. 'Donna and I, Chris. How many times are we going to go through this?'

Chris ignores her. 'But I know you well enough to reckon there's probably something you could do, Elizabeth? You and Joyce and Ron?'

'Go on,' says Elizabeth. 'I'm listening.'

Chris turns to Donna. 'Who did it sound like Ibrahim was describing, Donna? From the name, to the clothes, right down to the tattoo.'

'It sounded like Ryan Baird to me, sir.'

Chris nods, and turns to face Elizabeth. 'It sounded like Ryan Baird to me, too.'

'Ryan Baird,' says Elizabeth. A statement, not a question. Locked into the vault, never to escape.

'So we'll nip off now and arrest him, and question him, and get a string of "no comments", and then we'll have to let him go, a little smirk on his face, knowing he's got away with it again.'

'Oh, he hasn't got away with it this time,' says Elizabeth. 'No one gets away with hurting Ibrahim.'

'I was hoping you'd say that,' says Chris. 'You know how much the four of you mean to us, don't you?'

'I do,' says Elizabeth. 'And I hope you both know the same.'

'We do,' says Donna. 'Now let's go and arrest Ryan Baird, and may God have mercy on his soul.'

'I don't think even God will be able to help him,' says Joyce, as she sees a hospital porter wheeling a camp bed into Ibrahim's room.

9

Elizabeth is finding it hard to focus. After seeing Ibrahim in the bed yesterday evening, hooked up to tubes, just as Penny had been. She doesn't want to lose anyone else.

She has to keep her wits about her though. She is walking through the woods, high above Coopers Chase, with Douglas Middlemiss. Her ex-husband and her new responsibility. A job she never asked for. People died around Douglas. Too many people.

Why had she married him? Well, he had asked at around about the time she felt she ought to get married. And, dangerous though he was, he could also be kind. Pretend to be, at least. And it wasn't as if she hadn't killed a few people in her time, too. If Ryan Baird were in front of her now she would probably add another one to her list.

Trailing quite happily behind them is Poppy, headphones on. That had been the compromise. Poppy would need to keep Douglas in her sight, but Douglas would be able to speak freely to Elizabeth.

'It was as routine as these things can be,' says Douglas. 'We took our photos, broke into whatever we could break into, and off we toddled. Couldn't have been in Lomax's house more than half an hour. He rarely goes out, so we had to be quick.'

Elizabeth stops for a moment to take in the view, Coopers Chase below her, the buildings, the lakes, the rolling fields. Above her, the cemetery where the nuns, who had previously called this place home for centuries, were buried. Still behind them, Poppy halts too and takes in the same view.

'And you messed up somehow?'

'I don't know about messed up exactly, but two days later we get a message, through certain channels. Martin Lomax has been in touch.'

'Has he now?' says Elizabeth, as they resume their walk. 'Do go on.'

'Effing and blinding, they say. You broke into my property, human rights, flagrant disregard, the whole shooting match. Guts for garters, you know the routine.'

'And how did he know it was MI5?'

'Well, a hundred ways, I suppose. You never really leave things exactly where you found them, do you? If someone knows what they're looking for. And who breaks in without stealing anything? Only us, dear, in this day and age.'

There is construction noise from further up the hill, where the final part of the Coopers Chase development is being built. Douglas stops by an old oak with a hollow pocket in its trunk. He pats it.

'Perfect dead-letter drop, this, eh?' he says.

Elizabeth looks at the oak and agrees. She has had dead-letter drops all over the world. Behind loose bricks in low walls, hooks under park benches, obscure books in old shops, anywhere one agent could hide something completely, and another could pick it up without suspicion. This tree would be perfect, were it in Warsaw or Beirut.

'You remember the tree we used in East Berlin? In the park?' asks Douglas.

'West Berlin, but yes, I remember,' says Elizabeth. Almost ten years older, but memory sharper, she would take that victory.

They stop admiring the tree and Douglas continues.

'So Lomax is shouting the odds, and he's got us buggered all ways to Wednesday because we shouldn't have been in there, and he knows that and we know that, and then he drops the bomb.'

'The bomb?'

'The bomb.'

'And this bomb is why you're here?'

Douglas nods. 'There he is, Martin Lomax, firing both barrels and reloading, and then he says, "Where are my diamonds?"'

'Diamonds?'

'Stop just repeating what I said last, Elizabeth, it's a terrible habit of yours. That and adultery.'

'So these diamonds, Douglas?' says Elizabeth, not breaking stride.

'Says he had twenty million pounds' worth of diamonds in the house. Uncut. Down payment from a businessman in New York to a Colombian cartel.'

'And they disappeared after your visit?'

'Thin air, says our man. Accusing us of I don't know what, seeking reparation, yelling the ceilings off. So I get hauled in – quite right too, protocol, no complaint from me – and I take them through the operation, me and another chap, Lance, Special Boat Service, trustworthy, MI5 likes him. Poppy outside on lookout duty, waiting for the hunters to emerge. No diamonds seen, no diamonds taken, chap must be bluffing.'

'And they believed you?'

'No reason not to. We could all see the game he was playing. Getting a bit of leverage over us. So back they go to Martin Lomax, sorry we broke in, just doing our job, but come off it with the diamonds old boy, and let's find a way to be friends.'

'And he is unamenable to this?'

'The definition of it. Swears this is no bluff, tells us he's got Colombians ready to break this leg and that leg if they don't get their diamonds back, and what are we going to do about it?'

'And what did you do?'

'Nothing we can do. They kept at me and the rest of the team for a couple of days, just to make sure we were telling the truth, then they report back and tell Martin Lomax, look, friend, if the diamonds ever existed at all, which frankly we doubt, then someone else has them. There's a bit of back and forth, and then he drops another bomb.'

'Goodness me, Douglas,' says Elizabeth. 'Two bombs.'

'Martin Lomax says, "I'm sending over a photograph," and through it comes, CCTV, a shot from the side of his house, it's yours truly, full face, clear as a bell, mask off.'

'You took your mask off?'

'I was hot, it was itchy, you know me, Elizabeth, and the balaclavas are synthetic these days. Whatever happened to wool is something I would like to know. So there's my face, and he's done his research, knows who I am, and under the photograph he writes "Tell Douglas Middlemiss he has two weeks to return my diamonds. If the diamonds haven't been returned within two weeks then I will tell the Americans and the Colombians that he has them." Kind regards, and so on.'

'And when was this?'

Douglas stops, looks around and nods to himself. He then looks at Elizabeth.

'Well, this was two weeks ago.'

Elizabeth purses her lips. They have broken through the cover of the trees now, and find themselves by the path leading to the nuns' cemetery. She motions to a bench up ahead.

'Shall we?'

Elizabeth and Douglas walk over to the bench and take a seat.

'So you are now being hunted by the New York mafia and by a Colombian drug cartel?'

'Never rains but it pours, eh, darling?'

'And the Service have sent you here to keep you safe?'

'Well, if I may be honest, that was my bright idea. I'd been reading about you, about your recent escapades, and about this place, Coopers Chase, and it struck me as the perfect place to hide.'

'Well, depends what you're hiding,' says Elizabeth, looking up at the cemetery. 'But yes.'

'So you'll help look after me? Mobilize some of the troops around here? Keep them alert to stranger danger, but don't tell them why? I'll only be here until this sorts itself out.'

'Douglas, you have no incentive to give me an honest answer to this, but, just so I've asked, did you steal the diamonds?'

'Of course I did, darling. They were just sitting there. Couldn't resist.'

Elizabeth nods.

'And I need you to keep me safe long enough so I can pick them up, take them to Antwerp and cash them in. Thought I'd stumbled across the perfect crime, didn't I? If I hadn't taken that stupid mask off I'd be in Bermuda already, I assure you.'

'I see,' says Elizabeth. 'And where are the diamonds now, Douglas?'

'Keep me alive, my darling, and I'll tell you,' says Douglas. 'Ah, here's our friend Hermione Granger.'

Poppy has reached the bench. She motions to her headphones, asking if it's safe to take them off. Elizabeth gives her a nod.

'I hope you enjoyed the walk, dear?' asks Elizabeth.

'Very much,' says Poppy. 'We used to do hiking at uni.'

'What were you listening to? Grime music?'

'A podcast about bees,' says Poppy. 'If they die, we're doomed, I'm afraid.'

'Then I shall be more careful in future,' says Elizabeth. 'Now, Poppy, Douglas has persuaded me to accept the position you are offering. I imagine I can be helpful.'

'Oh, terrific,' says Poppy. 'That's a relief.'

'I have two caveats, however. Firstly, this task, keeping an eye out and so on, will be so much easier to perform with my three friends to help me.'

'That's impossible, I'm afraid,' says Poppy.

'Oh, my dear, as you get older you'll realize very few things are impossible. Certainly not this.'

'And the second thing?' asks Douglas.

'Well, the second thing is very important. More important than diamonds, and more important than Douglas. If I'm to accept this job, then I need a favour from MI5. A simple favour, but one that will mean a great deal to me.'

'Go on?' says Poppy.

'I need all the information you have on a teenager from Fairhaven named Ryan Baird.'

'Ryan Baird?' says Douglas.

'Oh, Douglas, stop repeating what I last said, it's a terrible habit of yours. That and adultery.'

Elizabeth stands and crooks an elbow so Poppy can take her arm.

'Could you do that for me, dear?'

'I mean I suppose I *could*,' says Poppy. 'Can I ask what it's for?'

'I'm afraid not, no,' says Elizabeth.

'Then can you promise me this Ryan Baird won't come to any harm?'

'Oh "promise" is such a big word, isn't it? Let's all have a nice walk home. I don't want you to be late for your lunch shift.'

10

Joyce

So I have joined Instagram, if you know it?

Joanna persuaded me. She said you can see all sorts of photos from all sorts of people. Nigella, Fiona Bruce, everyone.

I joined this morning. It asked me for a 'username' so I put in my name and it said '@JoyceMeadowcroft has already been taken' and I thought 'I should be so lucky'. Then I tried @JoyceMeadowcroft2, but that was gone as well.

Then I thought about nicknames, but really most people just call me Joyce. Then I remembered a nickname from back in my nursing days. There was one consultant who would always call me 'Great Joy'. Whenever our paths crossed, he would say, 'Ah, here she is, Great Joy, her beautiful smile spreading happiness.' Which was lovely, but not when you're changing a catheter.

Looking back, I realize he wanted to get into my apron, and I would have let him, had I caught on. The paths not taken.

So I tried '@GreatJoy', but nothing doing. I added my year of birth so I was '@GreatJoy44' but still no luck. Then I added Joanna's year of birth and, bingo! So I'm all set up and registered as '@GreatJoy69', and am looking forward to having lots of fun. I've already followed the Hairy Bikers and the National Trust.

It was a nice thing to do, to be honest, because today is Sunday, and I sometimes get blue on Sundays. Time seems to go a little slower. I think because lots of people are spending it with their families. The restaurant is always full of fidgeting nieces and disappointing sons-in-law. Also on Sunday the daytime TV is not as good, the *Bargain Hunts* are always repeats, there's no *Homes Under the Hammer*, nothing. Joanna says I can watch something on catch-up, and I'm sure she's right, but that feels even lonelier somehow. I'd honestly rather she just came down for lunch with her mum. She does come sometimes, to be fair. She was here an awful lot more during the murders, and who can blame her? Not me.

In the absence of any more murders, though, I imagine a dog would be a draw. Though Joanna's probably allergic. She never was as a child, but people seem to get allergic to all sorts as soon as they move to London.

Today I am going to get a taxi down to Fairhaven with Ron and Elizabeth to visit Ibrahim, so that will cheer me up at least. I love hospitals, they're like airports.

I have bought Ibrahim a *Sunday Times*, because I once saw one at his place. Goodness me, it weighs a ton. To lighten the load I have taken out any sections I think won't interest him, but that's only fashion, and a special pull-out report about Estonia, so it has made very little difference. I have also bought him some flowers, a big Dairy Milk, and a can of Red Bull because of the adverts.

I know the others were shaken to see him bruised and bandaged, but I was grateful to see it was only that. I was certainly relieved to hear him talking. Relieved, and then a bit bored, because you know Ibrahim, but the boredom was a lovely feeling.

I have seen worse is all I'm saying. A great deal worse. I won't go into details.

On our way there on Friday I was reassuring Ron and Elizabeth, nothing to worry about, he's in good hands, they found him so quickly. But I had feared the worst. There are some injuries you don't recover from. Ron and Elizabeth are no fools, of course, so they will have known I was just being reassuring, but that doesn't make it any less important. At any given time, somebody has to be calm, and it was my turn.

When I got home I had a cry, and I'm sure they both did too. But when we were together, we were as good as gold.

I know I'm only talking about the immediate injuries, by the way. I realize there is an awful road ahead for Ibrahim when what has happened sinks in. He is very wise, but he is also very vulnerable. Perhaps he is wise because he is vulnerable? Because he lets everything in? Now I'm the one who sounds like a psychiatrist! I think I would talk too much to be a psychiatrist. You wouldn't get your hour's worth.

Is it psychiatrist or psychotherapist, by the way? I can't remember which one Ibrahim calls himself. I'll ask him today. I am looking forward to seeing him ever so much. One thing I know is that it will be important to have good friends around him when he gets home, and I can guarantee that.

Another thing I can guarantee? The boy who decided to steal my friend's phone, and aim a kick at my friend's head, and race off leaving him for dead? He will wish he was never born.

I don't think psychiatrists really encourage revenge. I don't know, but I imagine they might preach forgiveness, like Buddhists? There was a quote on Facebook about it. Either way, psychiatrists and I are going to have to disagree on this one.

Perhaps Ryan Baird has had a difficult upbringing? Perhaps his dad left or his mum left, or they both left, or he's hooked on drugs, or he was bullied, or he didn't fit in. Perhaps all of these things are true, and perhaps there are places Ryan Baird might find a sympathetic hearing. But he won't find one with me, he won't find one with Ron and he won't find one with Elizabeth. Ryan is out of whatever luck he may ever have had.

I can't tell you how tempted I am to have some of this Dairy Milk. I know Ibrahim will let me have some as soon as I hand it over, but you know what it's like when it's just staring you straight in the face? I should have bought him grapes, then I wouldn't have been tempted.

I will have a bit of the chocolate now. Don't you think? I'll just nip up to the shop and buy him a new one before the taxi arrives. Then everyone's happy, aren't they?

I see that @GreatJoy69 has already had a few private messages on Instagram. That was quick! I will take a look at them when I get back. How very exciting!

11

The woman from the *Sunday Telegraph* is very friendly, but Martin Lomax supposes that's all part of her job. She is cooing over his Japanese anemones and stroking one of his ornamental box hedges as they wander.

'I mean, I've seen some beautiful private gardens, Mr Lomax, but really this tops them all. It tops them all. Where has this been hiding?'

Martin Lomax nods, and they keep walking. She seems quite happy talking. It is a beautiful garden, he knows that. It really should be for the money. But the best? The very best? Come now. But that's her job, of course.

'The use of symmetry is fascinating. It unfurls, doesn't it? It reveals itself. Do you know the famous William Blake poem, Mr Lomax?'

Martin Lomax shakes his head. He once killed a poet, but that's as far as he and poetry go.

'Tyger tyger in the night, burning very very bright. What immortal symmetry. Have thee.'

Martin Lomax nods again and thinks he should probably say something like 'beautiful'. In case she starts to think he might be a sociopath. He has read *The Psychopath Test*.

'Beautiful.'

He has wanted to be in the *Sunday Telegraph*'s 'Britain's

Best Gardens' supplement for a long time. In the distance he sees the photographer under a hedge, shooting upwards into the cloudless sky. That will be a beautiful photograph. There is a box containing half a million emergency dollars buried under that hedge, because you should never keep all your money in one place.

'And you're having your first ever Open Garden event this week?' asks the journalist.

Martin Lomax nods. He was looking forward to it. To showing off what he had created. He could watch from an upstairs window as people enjoyed themselves. If anyone decided to take a liberty, he would have them killed. But everybody else would be very welcome.

'For the piece, we were going to describe you as a "businessman". Does that suit? I read all about you — private insurance services, was that it? I wonder if that would just confuse people. "Businessman" usually does the trick, or if it's a woman, "mum and entrepreneur". Sometimes we'll say "heir to the something fortune". But you're happy with "businessman"?'

Martin Lomax nods. He had a Ukrainian coming to the house this afternoon. The Ukrainian has just agreed to buy some decommissioned Saudi anti-aircraft missiles for twelve million dollars and is planning to kidnap a racehorse as down payment.

'The chrysanthemums are beautiful,' says the woman. 'Exquisite.'

A kidnapped racehorse was not ideal, as far as Martin Lomax was concerned, but if both sides were happy with the arrangement he has ample stabling by the paddock. He has done business with the Ukrainians before and found them violent but trustworthy. Martin Lomax will get the local Scout troop to run a refreshment stall on one of the Open Garden days. Water and so on. People need water, he has noticed. They go crazy for the stuff.

'Dawn,' calls the journalist to the photographer. 'Can you get some shots of this mulch? It's imported from Crete.'

No plastic water bottles, though; people would complain, and he wouldn't want anything to spoil the experience. Thinking it through now, he realizes he will have to keep people away from the stables, just in case. And, of course, away from the house, that goes without saying. And away from the bodies in the cesspit, though who would go near that, anyway? And no digging. There are grenades somewhere. For the life of him he can't remember where they are buried, but he knows they are in a safe location, and he has written it down somewhere. Under the Venetian gazebo? On reflection, he can't even remember whose grenades they were, or why he had agreed to bury them, but that comes with age.

'We don't need any biographical detail, Mr Lomax, but people like it sometimes. Can I mention a wife? Children?'

Martin Lomax shakes his head. 'One-man band.'

'That's absolutely fine. It's all about the gardens, really.'

Martin Lomax nods. After the Ukrainian, he would

have to deal with that other matter. The break-in. He had handled it very nicely so far. You shouldn't really mess with MI5, he knows that, and he would far rather be friend than foe. But twenty million is twenty million when all's said and done. He is certain that somebody will end up dead, and he just needs to make sure it's not him.

'Do you think, I wonder, that I might use your bathroom?' asks the journalist. 'Long trip here, long trip back.'

'Of course,' says Martin Lomax. 'There's one in the equipment shed. You see it? Behind the fountain? I don't think there's paper, so use whatever's at hand.'

'Oh, yes, certainly, certainly,' says the journalist. 'Don't suppose I could be cheeky and go in the house?'

Martin Lomax shakes his head again. 'The equipment shed is nearer.'

No one ever comes in the house unless it's business. No one. First it's toilets, and then you never know what. MI5 think they can just break in? We'll see about that. Martin Lomax has many friends. Saudi princes, a one-eyed Kazakh with a one-eyed Rottweiler. Both the Kazakh and the Rottweiler would rip you apart without hesitation. No one comes into the house without his invitation.

Martin Lomax looks around the gardens once more. How lucky he is to live among such beauty. It was a wonderful world when you thought about it. But enough reflection for the moment, he had anti-aircraft missiles to worry about. And maybe he should bake some biscuits for the Open Garden too? Perhaps some brownies?

He hears an ancient toilet flush and, in the distance, the first vibrations of an approaching helicopter.

White chocolate and raspberry? People would like them, he's sure of it.

12

'And that's it in a nutshell. No need for drama, and no need to look at me, jaws agape.'

Elizabeth finishes her story and sits back in the low chair. For a moment the only sound is Ibrahim's heart monitor.

'But diamonds?' says Ibrahim, pushing himself up in his hospital bed.

'Yes,' says Elizabeth.

'Twenty million quid's worth of diamonds?' says Ron, who had stood still throughout the story, but is now pacing. Joyce had brought him fresh underwear from home, and he had dutifully changed in the disabled toilet, even though his present underwear easily had another day in it.

'Yes,' says Elizabeth, rolling her eyes. 'Any more obvious questions?'

Ibrahim, Joyce and Ron look at each other.

'He's your ex-husband?' says Ibrahim.

'He is, yes,' says Elizabeth. 'With respect to the three of you, this is tiresome. Any questions about anything I haven't covered?'

'And we'll get to meet him?' asks Ron. 'In the flesh?'

'Unfortunately, yes,' says Elizabeth.

Ron and Ibrahim are shaking their heads in wonder. Elizabeth turns to Joyce.

'Joyce, you're very quiet. Nothing to ask about the diamonds or the ex-husband? Or the mafia? Or the Colombians?'

Joyce shifts forward in her seat. 'Well, I have plenty to say about it all, and I'm excited to meet Douglas. I bet he's handsome. Is he handsome?'

'A bit too obviously handsome,' says Elizabeth. 'If you know the sort of thing.'

'Ooh, I do know that sort of thing,' says Joyce. 'You can't be obvious enough for me.'

'Not as handsome as Stephen, though,' says Elizabeth.

'Oh, no one's as handsome as Stephen,' says Joyce. 'But, honestly, all I was really thinking, all the way through, was that it explains Poppy's nails.'

'Yes, I could see the penny drop,' says Elizabeth.

A nurse walks into the room to fill Ibrahim's water jug and the friends fall silent and nod their thanks. She leaves.

'I am conventionally handsome,' says Ibrahim.

'Not at the moment you're not,' says Ron.

'So you need us to look out for him?' asks Joyce. 'Like bodyguards?'

'Hardly bodyguards, Joyce,' says Elizabeth.

'We're guarding his body,' says Ron.

'All right, bodyguards then, Ron, as you wish.'

Ron nods. 'Yep, I do wish.'

'Well, the invitation is there,' says Elizabeth. 'If you're too busy, then don't.'

'I can fit it in,' says Ron. 'We getting paid?'

'After a fashion, yes,' says Elizabeth. 'Douglas and Poppy have agreed to give us information on Ryan Baird.'

'Ryan Baird?' asks Ron.

'That's the name of the boy who stole Ibrahim's phone,' says Joyce.

'Oh,' says Ibrahim.

'Ryan Baird,' says Ron. 'Ryan Baird.'

'I didn't . . . I don't think I like him having a surname,' says Ibrahim. 'I think it's harder to pretend it never happened when he has a surname. I don't . . . sorry, I'm not sure about this at all.'

'I know,' says Elizabeth. 'I understand. We're taking care of it.'

'Revenge is what you need,' says Ron. 'Beaten up, locked up, whatever Elizabeth's got in store.'

'I don't really believe in revenge,' says Ibrahim.

'I knew it,' says Joyce quietly.

'Well, I do,' says Ron.

'As do I,' says Elizabeth. 'So the matter is decided, I'm afraid. Now, let's agree to speak his name no more.'

The room falls quiet. Ibrahim tilts his head back. He grimaces slightly.

'What do you think Douglas has done with the diamonds?' asks Ibrahim.

'I don't know,' says Elizabeth. 'But it feels like it might be fun to find out.'

'Let's find them and sell 'em,' says Ron.

'Ooh yes!' says Joyce. 'Twenty million between the four of us!'

'What do we know about Martin Lomax?' asks Ibrahim.

'Very little,' says Elizabeth. 'But if we're protecting Douglas then I think we should find out a bit more.'

'Ron and I can use the iPad this evening,' says Ibrahim. 'Do a little research.'

'You're staying again, Ron?' asks Joyce.

'Well, just another night, you know. I can flirt with the nurses, and they make a nice cup of tea.'

'I'll bring you more pants,' says Joyce.

'Honestly, no need,' says Ron.

13

PC Donna De Freitas is sitting with DCI Chris Hudson in Interview Suite B. Opposite them is Ryan Baird, wearing a look of poorly attempted nonchalance, and his solicitor, wearing a suit that should be in a dry cleaner's rather than Fairhaven Police Station. What was he thinking when he put it on? He even has a wedding ring. How did that happen? Being a man was such an easy gig. The work Donna puts into herself and she's still single. And here's this guy. Anyway.

'Where were you on Friday, Ryan?' asks Chris. 'Between about five and five fifteen?'

'I've forgotten,' says Ryan.

His solicitor makes a note. Or pretends to. It's hard to know what the note might be.

'How's your cup of tea?' asks Donna.

'How's *your* cup of tea?' replies Ryan.

'It's actually not bad,' says Donna.

'Well done,' says Ryan.

Look at him, acne and bravado. A child, really. A lost boy.

'You own a bicycle, Ryan,' says Chris. 'A Norco Storm 4?'

Ryan Baird shrugs.

'Are you shrugging because I said it wrong, or shrugging because you don't know if you own one?'

'I don't own one. No comment,' says Ryan.

'You have to pick one or the other, Ryan,' says Donna. 'You can't answer the question *and* say no comment.'

'No comment,' says Ryan Baird.

'That's better,' says Donna. 'Not so hard, is it?'

'A man was mugged, Ryan, on Appleby Street,' says Chris. 'Phone stolen, then kicked in the head while he was lying on the ground.'

'No comment,' says Ryan.

'I didn't ask you a question,' says Chris.

'No comment.'

'Again, no question.'

'He was eighty years old,' says Donna. 'He could have died. He'll live, if you're interested?'

Ryan Baird says nothing.

'Now that was a question,' says Chris. 'Are you interested?'

'No,' says Ryan.

'Well, that's some honesty, finally. Now, cameras pick you and a couple of your buddies up on Theodore Street, that's a couple of minutes away from the mugging. That's at five seventeen, and we can see you here on a Norco Storm bike that may or may not be yours.'

Chris passes a photograph over to Ryan. 'I am showing Ryan Baird photograph P19.'

'Is that you, Ryan?' asks Donna.

'No comment.'

'In either case,' says Ryan's solicitor, 'it's not illegal to be near a crime.'

This hangs in the air for a moment. Chris taps his pen on his pad a few times, thinking.

'OK, that's us done,' says Chris, standing suddenly. Donna sees the surprise in the solicitor's eyes. 'Interview terminated at four fifty-seven p.m.'

Chris walks over to the door, opens it and motions for Ryan and his solicitor to leave. Ryan is first through the door, but the solicitor holds back.

'Just wait in the corridor, Ryan,' says the solicitor. 'I won't be a moment.'

Ryan shuffles off and, as soon as he's out of earshot, the solicitor speaks to Chris in a low voice.

'That's all you have? You must have more than just CCTV?'

'We've got more,' says Chris.

The solicitor cocks his head to the side. 'So what's this? A trap? You know if you're going to call him back in and show him more footage, or introduce a witness, then I need to see it now.'

'I know,' says Chris. 'I'm not going to show him any more footage.'

'You're not going to search his flat?'

'Nope,' says Chris.

'You're not looking for the other two boys?'

Now that Donna is standing at the solicitor's shoulder she notices a tidemark of dirt on his shirt collar. Donna is delighted that Chris has started taking a bit more care of his appearance since he's started dating her mum. There were certain men you could allow to dress themselves and certain men you couldn't. Chris was on the cusp. Soon he would be able to run free.

'What's the point?' asks Chris.

'The point?' asks the solicitor.

'Yep, what's the point? You know we won't get enough to convict him, we know we won't get enough, and God knows what Ryan thinks about anything, but I'm guessing he knows too, the little scumbag.'

'The what, sorry?' says the solicitor.

'We won't be bringing Ryan back in,' says Donna. 'That's all you need to worry about.'

'We're not going to sit through another interview like that,' says Chris. 'Not this time. You can go and break the good news to him.'

'Am I missing something here?' asks the solicitor, looking from Chris to Donna and back again. 'I really feel like I'm missing something. You're going to let him walk free? Can I ask why?'

Donna looks him straight in the eye. 'No comment.'

She walks out through the open doorway. Chris looks at the solicitor and gives him a shrug.

Donna pops her head back round the door. 'Look, this isn't a judgement at all, but with suits you need to dry clean them once a month or so. Honestly, it'll make a big difference.'

14

'It was an accident, really,' says Poppy, wiping the crumbs of a coconut macaroon from the corner of her mouth.

'Oh, it often is,' says Elizabeth.

'I was at Warwick, studying English and Media. A woman from the Foreign Office came along and gave a talk, and there were drinks afterwards so we all went. Anyway, she said the starting salary at the Foreign Office was £24,000 and so I applied.'

'Not very cloak and dagger,' says Joyce, walking in with more tea.

'No,' agrees Poppy. 'I had an interview with the Foreign Office; that was in London so I went down with my student railcard, and I'd prepared all sorts of things, reading up about Russia and China and whatever they might talk about, but it was just a chat, really.'

'It always was,' says Elizabeth.

'They asked me who my favourite author is and I said Boris Pasternak, even though it's really Marian Keyes. But they liked that, and I was invited back for a second interview. I told them I couldn't really afford to come down to London twice, and they said, "Don't worry, we'll pay the fare, we'll put you up somewhere," and I said, "Honestly, I'm happier just going home, I don't need to stay over," and they said, "We insist," and on the next interview they told me who they were, and they took me out and got me hammered and put me up in rooms in a club in Mayfair, and the next morning that was that. They sent me home with my own laptop and told me they'd be seeing me when I graduated.'

Joyce is pouring tea. 'I remember Joanna, that's my daughter, leaving university. She was at the LSE in London, if you know it, and I was terribly worried when she left because I didn't know what she was going to do. She said she was going to be a DJ, and I said, well, I knew one of the people who did the hospital radio where I worked, Derek Whiting, and I could put in a word and get her some work experience, but she said it wasn't that sort of DJ – apparently there was another sort – and she'd be travelling round the world, that was the plan. Then two days later she rang me and said she had an interview at Goldman Sachs, and could I lend her some money for smart clothes for the interview? And that was that.'

'She sounds a character,' says Poppy.

'She has her moments,' agrees Joyce. 'Derek Whiting eventually died falling off a cruise ship. You never know what's round the corner, do you?'

'And you enjoy it, Poppy?' asks Elizabeth.

Poppy takes a sip of tea, considering her answer. 'Not really. Do you mind if I say that?'

'Not at all,' says Elizabeth. 'It's not for everyone.'

'I just fell into it. I needed a job and it seemed exciting, and I'd never had any money before. But I don't have the temperament for it. Do you like keeping secrets, Elizabeth?'

'Very much so,' says Elizabeth.

'Well, I don't,' says Poppy. 'I don't like telling one thing to person A and one thing to person B.'

'I'm the same,' says Joyce. 'Even if someone has a haircut that doesn't suit them, I can't keep quiet.'

'But that's the job,' says Elizabeth.

'Oh, I know,' says Poppy. 'It's absolutely what I signed up for. The problem is me, it's just the wrong job for me. I hate the drama of it. Meetings you're invited to, meetings you're not invited to.'

'What would you rather do?' asks Joyce.

'Well,' starts Poppy, then pauses.

'Go on,' says Joyce. 'We won't tell anyone.'

'I write poetry.'

'I don't have time for poetry,' says Elizabeth. 'Never have, never will. Do you mind if we get on to Ryan Baird?'

'Oh, yes,' says Poppy, and reaches over the side of her chair for her bag. She pulls out a file and hands it to Elizabeth. 'Name, address, email, mobile number and recent call log, national insurance, NHS records, browser history, mobile numbers of close associates. I'm afraid that's all I could get at short notice.'

'That will do for starters, thank you, Poppy,' says Elizabeth.

'Don't thank me,' says Poppy, 'thank Douglas. If it was up to me you wouldn't have them. I'm sorry to say it doesn't feel entirely legal.'

'Oh, nothing's legal any more, you can barely walk down the street these days. You have to bend the rules sometimes,' says Elizabeth.

'But that's just it, isn't it?' says Poppy. 'I don't want to bend the rules. It doesn't give me a thrill. It gives you a thrill, doesn't it?'

'Yes,' agrees Elizabeth.

'Well, not me. It makes me anxious. And my whole job is bending rules.'

'I'd be the same,' says Joyce.

'Oh, Joyce, get over yourself,' says Elizabeth. 'You would have made the perfect spy.'

'I still think Poppy should do her poetry.'

'Thank you,' says Poppy. 'That's what my mum says too. And she's usually right.'

'Don't get me wrong, I think you should too,' says Elizabeth. 'I don't want to *hear* it, but you should certainly do it. First, though, we have this job to do. To protect Douglas.'

'I can't wait to meet him,' says Joyce. 'Are you worried I'll fall in love with him?'

'Joyce, you will find him very handsome, but you will see through him in a moment.'

'We'll see,' says Joyce. 'Poppy, can I ask why you have a tattoo of a daisy on your wrist? I would have thought you'd have a tattoo of a poppy?'

Poppy smiles and strokes the small tattoo. 'Daisy is my grandmother. I told her once I wanted a tattoo and she said over her dead body, anchors and mermaids and so on. So I went away, had this done and showed it to her the next time I visited. I said, "Daisy, meet daisy," and there wasn't a lot she could say about it then, was there?'

'Clever girl,' says Joyce.

'Then two weeks later I went round again, and she rolled up her sleeve and said, "Poppy, meet poppy." A great big poppy tattoo all the way up her forearm. She said if I was going to be an idiot, then she was, too.'

Elizabeth laughs, and Joyce claps her hands.

'Well, she sounds just our type,' says Elizabeth. 'Poppy, if this is your last job with the Service, so be it, but I promise we'll do everything we can to make it a fun one for you.'

'We will,' says Joyce. 'Another macaroon, Poppy? You enjoyed the last one.'

Poppy raises a hand to decline the offer.

'We won't let anyone in here who shouldn't be here. Douglas will be quite safe, which, of course, means you will be quite safe, too,' says Elizabeth.

'Unless they show up this evening while we're eating macaroons,' says Poppy.

'And, while we all sit around with nothing to do, I'm sure we can crack the mystery of what Douglas has done with the diamonds.'

'Well, he denies stealing them, as you know. And, besides, that's not our job,' says Poppy. 'Our job is to protect Douglas.'

'Poppy, I honestly don't mind you being anxious, I don't mind you being conflicted, I don't even mind you being arty, but I absolutely won't tolerate you being boring, because I can tell you are not a boring human being. Do we have a deal?'

'Don't be boring?'

'If it's not too much to ask?'

'You both really think I should write poetry?'

'Oh, yes,' says Joyce. 'What's that poem I like?'

Poppy and Elizabeth look at each other. They don't know.

While she is looking at Elizabeth, Poppy says, 'In the interest of not being boring, can I ask you a question?'

'Up to a point, yes,' says Elizabeth.

'How did you end up in the Service? Did you follow your dream? And I need the non-boring answer, please. I'm not a tourist.'

Elizabeth nods.

'I had a professor; I was studying French and Italian at Edinburgh. Anyway, he had friends who had friends who were always on the lookout, and he floated the idea and it wasn't for me, but then he'd float it again and again.'

'And why did you finally sign up?'

'Well, he was desperate to sleep with me, this professor – people were in those days. So I knew he wanted to sleep with me, and I knew he wanted me to interview for the Service. And I honestly felt I should probably do one or the other – you know how men can be with rejection. So I had to either sleep with him or interview with the Service, and I chose the lesser of two evils. And once the Service has its hooks in you, they don't like to let go, as you will find out.'

'So your career was just to avoid sleeping with some-one?' asks Poppy.

Elizabeth nods.

'What do you think you would have done otherwise?'

'I know you don't like to keep secrets, Poppy, but you have been very helpful with Ryan Baird. So here's something I don't think I've ever told anyone before. Not my family, none of my husbands, not even Joyce. I always fancied being a marine biologist.'

Poppy nods.

'Marine biologist?' says Joyce. 'What is that? Dolphins and so on?'

Elizabeth nods.

Joyce reaches over and places her hand on her friend's arm. 'I think you would have made a wonderful marine biologist.'

Elizabeth nods again. 'Thank you, Joyce, I might have, mightn't I?'

15

Douglas Middlemiss is in bed, reading a book about Nazis, largely anti, when he hears the noise. It is the door to the flat opening, very slowly and very quietly. It isn't Poppy; she came back an hour or so ago. Where had she been? Collared by Elizabeth, perhaps? That would be Elizabeth's style, killing the new girl with kindness.

Speaking of killing, the door being opened quite so softly is bad news for Douglas. Only he and Poppy have keys, and the only other way to open a door that quietly is to be a professional. So what was this? A burglar or an assassin?

He would find out soon enough.

Douglas wishes he had a gun. In the old days he would have done. Once, in Jakarta, he accidentally shot a cultural attaché from the Japanese embassy through the arm during a bout of vigorous love-making. She was terrifically good about it. The National Gallery was persuaded to lend a Rembrandt to a Tokyo museum and nothing more was said about it. But from that day on he would tape his gun under the bed rather than leave it under the pillow.

He thought all this as he took off his reading glasses, did up the button fly on his pyjama bottoms and slipped out of bed. Poppy had a gun. She didn't seem the type to ever use it, but she must have had the training, surely? Had she heard the front door open? Perhaps not. Douglas had grown alert to danger over the years, but Poppy would not have. Perhaps never would. He'd met Poppy's type many times before, and she would be out of the Service and having babies before you knew it. Not that you're allowed to say that these days. World gone mad etc.

As Douglas starts to straighten the bedclothes he hears the rattle of the padlock on his bedroom door. So, an assassin rather than a burglar? Douglas had suspected as much. Sent by Martin Lomax, perhaps? The Americans? The Colombians? It seemed ridiculous, really, but Douglas would prefer to be shot by someone British. English ideally, but beggars can't be choosers.

Bolt cutters would get through the padlock within a minute. But not without making a noise. Not without waking Poppy. He just needs Poppy to reach the intruder before the intruder reaches him.

The bed is straightened, and it now looks untouched, as if no one has slept there, as if the occupant is still out enjoying the night air. Douglas walks quietly over to the wardrobe, opens the doors and steps in. This will probably buy him only ten or fifteen seconds, but that might be enough. He closes the wardrobe doors behind him and stands in the dark.

You always wonder, in this job, where it might end for you. Douglas might have died, variously, on a glacier in Norway, in a car boot on the Iran–Iraq border, or in a missile attack on an American base in Kinshasa. But perhaps it was all going to end in a tatty wardrobe, in his pyjamas, in an old people's home? Douglas was interested to find out. Scared too, certainly, but still interested. Of all the things that were to happen to you in life, death was one of the very biggest. Douglas hears the padlock give way. Surely Poppy heard *that*?

Through the thin crack between the wardrobe doors, Douglas can make out a man walking into the room, gun raised and pointed at the bed. A pale light from a street lamp shines a single thin column through the curtains.

He watches the man turn and look around him, having seen the bed is empty. Douglas is not breathing. Might never breathe again, he realizes, as the man turns to face the wardrobe. If someone is hiding, then this is the only conceivable place. And anyone who can silently open a door without a key and cut through an MI5 padlock within a minute will know that.

The man takes two steps towards the wardrobe, gun still raised. White, Douglas thinks, maybe forty? So hard in this light. What was his name, Douglas wondered. It felt like that was information he should be allowed to know. Had they ever met? Passed on a street like future lovers?

Poppy wasn't coming. How had she not heard? Unless? Oh, of course. Of course. Perhaps Poppy had not been with Elizabeth this evening at all. Perhaps there had been a briefing? Orders handed down. We want this problem to go away. Just turn a blind eye, no one's to know. We'll send in one of our men. Douglas doesn't have any relatives, no kids to be asking questions. Poppy was junior enough to fall in line. She would be in her room now, cowering. When they found his body, would Elizabeth work out what had happened? A ridiculous thought, no one would find his body. A Special Ops group would be on hand to clear everything up. A military coroner would be waiting for him somewhere. All the paperwork done right. Probably a suicide. Elizabeth would never get close enough to know any different. Elizabeth really was looking good, Douglas had to admit it. He would have loved another crack at her. Will she find his other letter? Of course she will.

The man hooks an outstretched foot under one of the wardrobe doors and pulls them open. He smiles to himself as he sees Douglas standing there.

The man looks English. The gun isn't Service issue, but sometimes they employed freelancers. 'Worth a go,' says Douglas, his hands indicating the inside of the wardrobe.

The man nods. Douglas waits for an epiphany, a sudden flash of clarity about his life. Something to take with him on whatever journey he is about to embark upon. But there is nothing. Just a man with a gun, and the label of his pyjama top itching against the back of his neck. What a way to go.

'Where are the diamonds?' asks the man. An English accent. That brings Douglas some peace.

'Afraid not, old boy,' says Douglas. 'You're going to kill me anyway, and I'd rather someone else ended up with the diamonds.'

'I might not kill you,' says the man.

Douglas smiles and raises a dubious eyebrow at the man with the gun. The man with the gun nods in concession.

'This will sound ridiculous,' says Douglas. 'But let me solve one final mystery. I'd love to know who sent you?'

The man shakes his head and Douglas watches as he squeezes the trigger.

16

Ibrahim can't sleep.

The air around him is still. How many people have died in this hospital room? In this bed? In these sheets?

How many final breaths still hung in this air?

When his eyes close he is back in the gutter. He feels the water, he hears the footsteps, he tastes the blood.

The kick to the head now has a name. Ryan Baird. Where was Ryan Baird, he wonders. Where was Ibrahim's phone? Who bought stolen phones? Ibrahim had a *Tetris* app on his phone. There were 200 levels, and he was on level 127 after playing for a considerable amount of time. All of that progress was lost.

He looks at the red plastic tag on his wrist. The admin of death. There will be a drawer full of them somewhere.

He has finally persuaded Ron to go home. Not that he isn't grateful for the company. Each night so far Ron has stayed up with him and talked about West Ham and the problem with the Labour Party. And then, even later in the night, about his ex-wife and daughter, his son, Jason, and about leaving school at fourteen and never knowing his dad. Anything, really, other than talk about what had happened. They watched *Die Hard*, but only the first one. No point watching the others, apparently. Ibrahim has never had a friend like Ron before, and Ron has never had a friend like Ibrahim before. Ron will fill his water jug when it needs filling, will get him Frazzles from the machine, but will never make physical contact, no hand on his arm. Which is just fine by Ibrahim. It must be harder being a man these days, he thinks, being expected to hug.

Ibrahim wants to go home, which he knows is a positive thing. It was positive to have a home in which he felt safe. To be surrounded by people who made him feel safer still.

But he knows he will then never want to leave home again.

Things would get back to normal. The brain is tremendously clever, one of the reasons Ibrahim likes it so much. Your foot was your foot and would remain your foot through thick and thin. But the brain changes, in form and in function. Ibrahim has respect for podiatrists, but really, looking at feet all day?

The brain. That magnificent, dumb beast. He knows that alien chemicals are currently racing around his brain, protecting him in this moment of crisis. In time these chemicals would fade, leaving nothing but a faint stain. When they say that time heals, that's what they mean. Like most things, when you really drill down into them, it is neuroscience, not poetry.

Yes, time heals, time heals. But what if time is the one thing Ibrahim doesn't have?

I don't really believe in revenge. That's what he had said to the others when they talked about Ryan Baird. And in theory he didn't. Revenge is not a straight line, it's a circle. It's a grenade that goes off while you're still in the room, and you can't help but be caught in the blast.

Ibrahim had once had a client, Eric Mason, who had bought a used BMW from a dealer, an old school friend, in Gillingham. He soon discovered that the car had a faulty clutch. His friend at the dealership refused to accept liability and Eric Mason, who, it should be said, had issues around emotional control and anger management, had replaced the clutch at his own expense and then driven the BMW straight through the window of the dealership in the dead of night.

The car had then stalled – understandably, as it had just been driven through a large window – so Eric Mason was forced to abandon it and flee as alarms blared all around him. Unfortunately, he fell and impaled himself on a large shard of glass, and was saved from bleeding to death only by the arrival of the police.

Recovering in hospital, Eric Mason received a huge bouquet of flowers from the dealership, but, upon opening the card, discovered they had attached a court summons and a bill for £14,000. A spell of community service and bankruptcy followed. His fury grew.

Eric's daughter and the son of the car dealer had also been friends at school. Eric forbade his daughter from ever talking to the boy again and so, as winter follows summer, they had got married two years later, with Eric refusing to attend the wedding. Another year later and Eric's grandson was born. Neither side would give ground, so Eric was unable to see his first grandchild. All because of a faulty clutch.

It was at this point that Eric felt perhaps he should take responsibility for his own actions, and decided to see a psychotherapist.

Twelve months later, on his final visit to Ibrahim, Eric Mason had brought in his daughter and his son-in-law to say thank you in person. He had also brought in his infant grandson, and they had posed together for a photograph, smiles all round.

Ibrahim could feel himself drifting off and decided to stop fighting it. Whatever was waiting for him in his dreams, it was best to just face it unafraid. Accept the damage Ryan Baird had inflicted on him without thinking. Not the ribs, not the face — they would heal soon enough — but his freedom and his peace of mind, snatched away for a phone.

They say a man who desires revenge should dig two graves, and this is surely right. Then again, Ibrahim feels like his own grave has already been dug, so would there really be much harm in digging another for Ryan Baird? He wonders what his friends have in store for Ryan. Nothing physical, Ibrahim is sure of that. But freedom and peace of mind? Ryan might have a little surprise coming.

The photograph of Ibrahim, Eric Mason and Eric's grandson was in a special file Ibrahim kept at home. A file filled with a few mementos, not too many, all reminding Ibrahim why he loved his job. The file is the only one on Ibrahim's shelves that isn't kept in strict alphabetical order. Because sometimes you had to remember that life wasn't always arranged in alphabetical order, however much you would like it to be.

Eric Mason, years later, discovered that nothing had been wrong with the clutch at all. He simply hadn't understood the electronic controls, and pressing a reset button for five seconds would have cleared it up. So you do have to be careful with revenge, but, in all honesty, Ibrahim has spent most of his life being careful, and sometimes you had to do things differently if you wanted to grow as a human being.

Ibrahim is certain that he could just press his own reset button for five seconds, and he could go on with forgiveness in his heart, go on doing the right thing, the correct thing, the boring thing. The cruise control.

But he still remembers Eric Mason, for all of his regrets, talking about the sheer ecstatic thrill of driving his car through that dealership window.

And it is that image, not the kick to the head, not Ryan Baird's footsteps and not the taste of blood, that Ibrahim is thinking about as he falls into his first peaceful sleep since the attack.

17

Joyce

It is two in the morning, but I want to write this all down while it is still fresh.

My phone rang at midnight, and of course I thought Ibrahim had died. What else would you have thought, in the circumstances? Nobody rings at midnight. He had looked well when we left him, but I've seen all sorts. I must have reached the phone within two rings.

It was Elizabeth, and the first thing she said was, 'It's not Ibrahim,' so that was a relief. She can be sensitive when she tries. She said she knew that it was midnight, but I was to throw on some clothes and meet her at 14 Ruskin Court as soon as I was able. I wondered if I needed to bring a flask, but I was told there was already a kettle, and just to bring myself. It would have been quick to fill a flask, but you try telling Elizabeth that at midnight.

I walked over to Ruskin, and it really is very pretty here in the dark. There are a few lamps lighting the paths, and you can hear the animals in the bushes. I could just imagine the foxes thinking, What's this old woman up to? and I was thinking the same. It was cold, but I have just bought a cardigan from Marks, which was perfect for the job. They delivered a few bits yesterday. I didn't mention it, because I don't mention everything. For example, yesterday I was defrosting a lasagne and completely forgot about it. And that's the first you've heard of it.

At the door I was buzzed upstairs, heart pounding if I'm honest, not knowing what I was going to see. I pushed the door open and saw poor Poppy sitting in an armchair, shaking. Opposite her was Elizabeth, in another armchair, but not shaking. That was the only furniture in the whole place. The flat was where Douglas was hiding, I worked that much out. 'Put the kettle on, Joyce,' Elizabeth said, 'Poppy's had a shock.' She sounded bossy, but I know she didn't mean it; she was just being professional.

You wouldn't believe the kitchen, by the way. Two mugs, two plates, two glasses, two bowls, some Frosties, some white Mother's Pride, then, in the fridge, some tofu and some almond milk. There was tea and coffee in one of the cupboards and I poked my head back round and Elizabeth and Poppy stopped their conversation, and I asked Poppy if she wanted milk and sugar and she said could she have a cardamom and lychee infusion and I nodded as if this was quite normal, which I understand it is these days, and ducked back into the kitchen. Goodness me, that was a long sentence to write. In a book they would tell me to put a full stop in there somewhere. After 'infusion'?

I filled and boiled the kettle, anxious to get back to the living room and find out what was happening. If this was Douglas's flat, then where was he? I poured the water over the teabag, which was made of grey cloth, but each to their own, and was just thinking about whether you're supposed to leave the bag in or take it out with herbal tea? If I left it in then I could be out there quicker, but what if that wasn't the right thing to do? Joanna, like all daughters, would know. Anyway, that's when I heard the toilet flush, so, to hell with protocol, I left the bag in and went into the living room.

I knew it was Douglas straight away, you could just tell. Very handsome, if I do say so myself. I could see in an instant why Elizabeth had married him, and also why she had divorced him. I bet it was fun while it lasted though.

He was straight up to me and, 'Oh you must be Joyce, I've heard all about you,' and, really, I almost curtsied, and then I caught Elizabeth rolling her eyes, so I said, 'Yes, and you must be Douglas,' and he said, 'I imagine you've heard all about me too,' and I said, 'Not really, no,' and I could see that Elizabeth liked that.

I said let me go into the bedroom and find another chair but Elizabeth said to try Poppy's room, as there was a dead body on Douglas's floor.

Well, that was more like it.

I got a hard-backed chair from Poppy's room and Elizabeth let Douglas tell me the story.

He had been hiding in a wardrobe, which wasn't cowardly, but basic training, and some chap had a gun aimed at his head. He took some time over this bit of the story, discussing death and perspective, and man's moral duty and a life well lived. I wished Ron had been there, he would have told him to wind his neck in, but it was me, so I listened politely. He was ready to meet his maker, that was the gist of it, but as the mystery man reached for the trigger, his head was blown clean off, and there was Poppy, like the cavalry, gun in hand, cool as you like.

Cool according to Douglas, but you could see she wasn't cool at all, still shaking, still quiet, both hands around her tea. She had said nothing about the bag still being in, so maybe it's OK? Though I don't think she was really in any state to, so it wasn't a proper test.

I went and sat on the arm of Poppy's chair and put my arm around her, and she put her head on my shoulder and started to sob quietly. I don't think Douglas or Elizabeth had put their arm around her, and that's when I realized, of course, that was why Elizabeth had asked me there. Ron would have done just as well, but I bet Elizabeth isn't ready for Ron to meet Douglas yet. Douglas is so obvious, Ron would have a field day.

I told Poppy she had been very brave, and Elizabeth told her she had been a terrific shot too, and Douglas said amen to that. But Poppy was having none of it, just silently weeping.

Elizabeth did her best to be comforting, saying it was hard to kill someone, but sometimes that was the job, and then Poppy finally spoke and said, 'That's not a job I want,' and I had some sympathy with that. It must be fun doing all the training, I suppose, and creeping around with no one knowing, but blowing a man's head off from four feet away probably doesn't suit everyone. It wouldn't suit me, and it doesn't suit Poppy. Actually, perhaps it would suit me? You never know until you try, do you? I never thought I would like dark chocolate, for example.

I asked what was next, and had the police been called, and Elizabeth said, 'Well, after a fashion.' I was hoping Chris and Donna might make an appearance, but apparently in these cases, national security and so on, these things take a different route. So Elizabeth, Douglas and Poppy were waiting for some spies to come down from London and the case would be theirs. Which is a shame because Donna, in particular, would have enjoyed the whole scene.

Elizabeth asked if I would like to see the body, and even though I really wanted to, I felt I should stay with my arm around Poppy and so I said no, I was fine, but thank you.

We only had to wait twenty minutes or so until the door buzzed and a woman and a man arrived. Sue and Lance. MI5, according to Elizabeth. Sue was in charge.

They were both no-nonsense. Sue reminded me an awful lot of Elizabeth. The manner. She must be nearly sixty and would have been pretty if she wasn't so angry. I know it doesn't matter if she's pretty or not, I'm just giving you an idea of her. Her hair was a lovely chestnut colour. Dyed, but very nicely. I kept trying to make conversation, but I got nowhere.

I could tell even Elizabeth was being respectful, so I followed her lead. They turned down my offer of a cup of tea, however. They both barged past me as I stood in the kitchen doorway. Not rude, as I say, they just had a job to do. Sue knew exactly what had gone on, and told Douglas and Poppy to pack whatever they needed. She was surly with them both, especially Douglas. I ended up feeling quite sorry for him.

Lance was dealing with the corpse. Taking photos and so on. He looked like someone you would see in a DIY show on TV. Rugged, and good with his hands, but never quite the star of the show. Just sawing some wood in the background. I asked if I could take a look at his camera, because I am thinking of getting one for Joanna for Christmas. He said he would show me when he was finished up, but in the end he didn't.

Sue told Elizabeth they would need to speak to her in due course, and she said well naturally, but quiet as a mouse, not so much scared as knowing not to cause trouble. Sue looked at me at one point and said, 'Is this Joyce?' She told Elizabeth to ensure I told no one about the shooting and the body and so on. I said, 'Sue, you're safe with me,' but she didn't even look in my direction, just at Elizabeth. Elizabeth reassured Sue I wouldn't tell a soul, and she nodded, unconvinced. To be honest, I think she had bigger fish to fry.

MI5 know who I am now though, so that's one for the Christmas newsletter.

Presently there was another buzz at the door, and two men in overalls arrived with a stretcher. Paramedics wear green, of course, but these two were head to toe in black. They went into the bedroom and loaded the body onto the stretcher. Fortunately, I was able to get a quick peek before they zipped up the body bag and, yes, Poppy really had blown his head off. Or most of it at least. It took me right back to my days in A&E.

As Elizabeth and I were leading the stretcher down the corridor, a couple of doors opened, neighbours wondering about the noise, and Elizabeth was able to tell them not to worry. If you worried about every stretcher you saw at Coopers Chase you'd need one yourself soon enough.

As we got outside, into the open air, you could see a few lights on around the place, and a few curtains opened, but, again, they were used to seeing ambulances at the dead of night. I said to Elizabeth that I was surprised it was just a normal ambulance, and she said it wasn't a normal ambulance, it just looked like one.

As we went back in, Sue and Lance were leading Poppy and Douglas out. They had to be questioned, Elizabeth explained. Even in MI5 you can't just shoot someone without being asked a few questions about it. Elizabeth gave Poppy a hug, which was nice, and told her not to worry, she'd done everything right. Then I gave her a hug too, and told her not to worry. I very nearly asked about the teabag, but I will ask next time I see her instead.

I gave Sue and Lance a friendship bracelet each. Sue looked like I'd just given her a parking ticket, but Lance said, 'Thank you, I could use a bit of friendship.' I didn't ask them for money.

Douglas came out next, with a book called *Megastructures of the Third Reich* and a toothbrush.

Sue told Elizabeth to secure the flat and make sure no

one could gain entry. Elizabeth just nodded back to Sue and told her to take care of Poppy.

Elizabeth then told me to go home and sleep, and so I went home, but I haven't slept. Listen to this.

As soon as my door was shut, I took off my cardigan, to hang over the back of the chair. As I was taking it off I felt something in the pocket, and I fished out a folded piece of paper, which hadn't been there when I put it on.

On the piece of paper was a message which simply said 'RING MY MUM' followed by a phone number.

Poppy must have slipped it into my pocket while we were hugging.

So Poppy wants her mum, poor love. I will ring her in the morning.

I've put the television on. On BBC2 they are showing normal programmes from the day, but with someone doing sign language in the corner. Isn't that clever? I was just thinking it was unfair to make deaf people stay up so late, but then realized they could tape them. What a nice thing. I'm watching a programme about the coast of Britain called *Coast*. Someone is digging up whelks. No thanks, to be honest, but the lady doing the sign language has a lovely top.

I still haven't quite worked out how my Instagram works, which is very frustrating, as @GreatJoy69 now has over two hundred private messages.

I wonder if anyone else is awake?

18

Ryan Baird is awake. He is currently playing *Call of Duty* online. He is spraying machine-gun fire at full volume while his neighbours bang on the walls. Ryan made £150 today, selling a couple of laptops, a debit card and a watch to Connie Johnson, who runs the whole of Fairhaven from the lock-up garages by the seafront. She trusts him, even gives him a package now and then to deliver to one of the estates. Drugs? That's the thing to get into. Stealing phones is for kids.

Ryan has been called stupid his whole life. But who's stupid now? He's got cash in his pocket; Connie Johnson clearly likes him. He's making more money than any eighteen-year-old he knows, probably making more money than his old teachers. The police had him in yesterday for nicking a phone and giving someone a shove, but they can't touch him, because Ryan is smart. Too smart for the teachers, too smart for the cops, too smart for his neighbours now pressing on his door buzzer. Ryan Baird has got all the answers.

Ryan lights one last spliff before bedtime, then curses as his lapse in concentration sees him shot by a sniper. Lucky video games aren't real life. Ryan reloads and starts again. He's invincible.

*

Martin Lomax is awake, too. A Saudi lawyer has a bee in his bonnet about a powerboat. Martin Lomax is on the phone, trying to placate him. The long and short of it was, he had received the powerboat as agreed compensation from the Cartagena Cartel when the FDA had raided one of their Bolivian drugs labs, costing them all a great deal of money. The issue at hand was that the powerboat had arrived full of bullet holes, and the Saudi lawyer was of the opinion that this was aesthetically unpleasing, and also a hazard to seaworthiness.

Martin Lomax's other line rings, and he promises he will talk to the Cartagena Cartel as soon as possible.

MI5 are on the other line. Does he know an Andrew Hastings? He does. Does Andrew Hastings work for him? He does, no use lying, this is MI5 and they know already. Was Mr Hastings working for him this evening? No, he was not. We regret to inform you that Mr Hastings has been shot dead while trying to murder a member of the British Security Services, condolences for your loss, but I wonder if you would have any comment on that. No, no comment, no comment at all. Would you know Mr Hastings's next of kin? No. Was he married? I think he was. Who to? No idea, never asked. Sorry to disturb you so late at night. No, no, not at all, just doing your job.

Martin Lomax puts down the phone. Hastings dead. Well, that was inconvenient. But he would deal with the powerboat first. And he still needed to order some trestle tables for the Open Garden.

*

Poppy and Douglas are also awake. They are being interviewed in separate rooms inside a large country house near Godalming, just to get the facts straight. Poppy has coffee in front of her and a union rep beside her. Lance James is asking her to talk through what happened.

Douglas has no coffee and no union rep. It's just him and Sue Reardon. The way things should be done. Did he recognize the man who tried to kill him? Never seen him before. Would it surprise him to know the gunman worked for Martin Lomax? Well, yes and no. Yes and no how? Well, he must be working for someone, surely? And Martin Lomax has threatened him, so it's not outside the realms of possibility. But why would Martin Lomax want Douglas dead if he hadn't stolen the diamonds, answer us that? No idea, Martin Lomax is playing some sort of game, that's for certain, and I'm stuck in the middle of it, nearly getting my head blown off. Take us through the break-in at Martin Lomax's house again, step-by-step.

It is three in the morning by the time Poppy's union rep suggests it might be time to allow Poppy some sleep. As she walks down a long corridor, she can hear Sue Reardon still questioning Douglas Middlemiss.

19

Ron has skipped breakfast for this, and is even more furious than usual. He has spent some time looking at the large bloodstain on the bedroom carpet, and he now inspects the bullet hole in the bedroom wall.

'I've seen liberties taken,' says Ron. 'God knows, they've all tried it on with me over the years, but this takes the whassname. When did you find the body? Half eleven? I was probably still up. I could have slipped on my shoes and been straight over. I swear, it's not often I'm speechless, but I'm speechless. I wish I could speak, I wish I had words.'

Ron has had all the fun he's going to have with the bullet hole, and starts pacing.

'Ron, don't pace over the bloodstains, please,' says Elizabeth.

'But no, who gets the call? Joyce. Of course, Joyce. Everybody loves Joyce.'

'I don't know about that,' calls Joyce from the living room.

'Including you, Ron,' says Elizabeth.

'I haven't interrupted the two of you, so don't interrupt me,' says Ron. 'There's a dead body. A dead body, geezer shot in the head, and what do you do? You ring Joyce. You don't ring Ron, dear me, no. Why would you ring Ron? He wouldn't want to see a corpse, would he? Old Ron? Last thing he'd want to see. A bloodstain and a bullet hole will be enough for Ron. I've heard it all now.'

'Are you finished?' says Elizabeth, looking into her bag.

'Take a guess, Elizabeth? Take a guess if I'm finished. Use those powers of deduction. No, I'm not finished. I would have loved it. *Loved* it.'

'Come with me,' says Elizabeth.

Elizabeth walks into the living room and takes the armchair opposite Joyce. Ron follows her through. Elizabeth takes a folder from her bag and places it on her lap. Ron has a speech to make.

'Here's my promise to you,' he begins. 'With Joyce as my witness – and it's not a promise friends should have to make – if I *ever* find someone shot, I will call you. I will call you because you're my mate, and that's what mates do. Two in the morning, I don't care, I find a corpse, I pick up the phone, "Elizabeth, there's a corpse on the landing, on the bowls lawn, doesn't matter where, slip on a pair of shoes and come and take a look." I am absolutely *fuming.*'

'Are you finished *now*, Ron?' asks Elizabeth. 'I've got something I need to talk to you about.'

'Oh yeah? Well, what if I've got something to talk to you about? About friendship?'

'As you wish,' says Elizabeth. 'But we don't have an awful lot of time. We have a job to do.'

'I've made you both a cup of tea,' says Joyce. 'Don't be angry, but it's herbal.'

Ron hasn't finished though. 'No apology, no "Sorry,

Ron, spur of the moment, I panicked." You think I see corpses every day of the week? Is that it? I've been in the hospital three nights, I get home, and this is my reward. You see a dead body, Joyce sees a dead body and I'm sat at home, watching some documentary with Portillo on a train. That is insult to injury, I'm sorry but it is. I thought we were friends.'

Elizabeth sighs. 'Ron, I like you. It is a huge surprise to me, but I do. I respect you, too, in a number of areas. But listen to me, dear. I was in an operational situation. I had a man who had been seconds from death, a young girl who had just shot someone for the first time, I had a crime scene, and I had MI5 arriving any time. So I felt I needed another pair of hands. I knew that both of you would want to see the corpse, that was a given. So I was left with a simple choice between a woman with forty years of nursing experience and a man in a football top who would bang on about Michael Foot the moment MI5 arrived. Granted, thirty-odd years ago the job would still have gone to the man, but times change and I rang Joyce. Now, what can we do to calm you down?'

'I'm already calm,' shouts Ron.

'My mistake,' says Elizabeth.

'Drink your tea,' says Joyce.

Ron stops for a moment. 'What do you mean, we've got a job to do?'

'That's better,' says Elizabeth. 'Ron, I took a folder out of my bag. Midway through your rant.'

'It wasn't a rant, but let me ring the Queen and get you a medal for taking a folder out of a bag.'

'I did it quite slowly and deliberately. A buff-coloured folder, not the sort of thing I would normally carry in my bag. I thought you might notice.'

'Joyce noticed, I suppose?' says Ron. 'Clever old Joyce?'

'Well, yes she did, but the point is moot. Joyce hasn't seen this folder yet. It's just for me and you.'

'Joyce hasn't seen it?' asks Ron.

'Not yet, she can see it eventually,' says Elizabeth. 'But you and I have a job to do first.'

'I'm not sure about this,' says Joyce.

'Oh, don't you start,' says Elizabeth. 'I'm placating Ron.'

Ron nods. 'OK. Sorry if I lost my rag there.'

'You didn't at all, dear. You voiced your frustrations, perfectly understandable.'

'So what's the job? What's in the file?'

'Don't think it's gone unnoticed that you stayed by Ibrahim's side when he needed you,' says Elizabeth. 'And I think this is the reward you've earned.'

Elizabeth holds out the file and Ron reaches over and takes it.

'It has Ryan Baird's address, mobile telephone number, anything else you might need.'

Ron flicks through it, nodding. 'So we're going after him?' he asks. 'Straight away?'

'You're going after him, yes.'

'I'm going after him?'

Joyce beams. 'Wonderful.'

'Yes, I thought you'd like to?' says Elizabeth.

'I would like to, yes,' says Ron. 'You got a plan?'

'I do. I just need to see Bogdan about something first. Then you'll get your instructions.'

Ron nods. He taps the file against one of his big hands. 'Poppy get you this, did she?'

Elizabeth nods.

'What's going to happen to her? After blowing this geezer's head off?'

'She'll be fine,' says Elizabeth. 'She did the right thing in the right way. They'll question her today, get everything straight, then probably back to work.'

'Will they let her see her mum, do you think?' asks Joyce.

'Goodness no,' says Elizabeth. 'Why would they let her see her mother?'

'I think I'd want to see my mum if I'd just shot someone, wouldn't you?'

'It's not kindergarten, Joyce; you're always so sentimental,' says Elizabeth.

Ron, still leafing through the file, looks up. 'And your ex-husband? Dougie boy? What'll happen to him?'

'Much the same thing. They've had to move him out of here, of course. It's compromised.'

'So we're done with the whole thing?'

'We're done with it. Our babysitting days are officially over.'

'We can still look for the diamonds, though?'

'Of course.'

'Good. You want to know what I think, by the way?' says Ron.

'Not really, Ron,' replies Elizabeth.

'I think you could easily have made two phone calls last night, could have had me and Joyce both here. But I think you didn't want me to meet your ex-husband.'

Joyce nods as Elizabeth responds.

'Well, I've always wished I'd never met him, so I like to extend the same courtesy to my friends.'

'Handsome, Joyce says?'

'Very,' agrees Joyce.

Elizabeth shrugs. 'What is it with men and handsome? Wouldn't you rather be kind and clever and funny and brave than handsome?'

'No,' says Ron.

'Can I ask you both something?' says Joyce.

Her friends both nod.

'In your teas, I've left one bag in and one bag out. Could you try them both and let me know which you prefer?'

20

Something happened last night, Bogdan Jankowski can just tell.

He is on his way to the building site on top of the hill, but has popped into the shop at Coopers Chase to buy some Lilt Zero and twenty Rothmans.

A man he doesn't know has just got out of a van he doesn't recognize and headed over to Ruskin Court.

Bogdan watches as the man lets himself into Ruskin Court using a key he shouldn't have.

Something is up here. Bogdan approaches the van. As he peers through the passenger side window he sees a newspaper, which is usual in a van, but then notes it is the *Daily Telegraph*, which is not. He looks at the side of the van, 'F. Walker Roofing – All Jobs Considered'.

From the corner of his eye, Bogdan sees Elizabeth, Ron and Joyce emerging from Ruskin Court. What are they all doing in Ruskin Court? Trouble, always trouble. And if there is trouble to be had, then Bogdan would like a piece of it.

Elizabeth waves goodbye to Ron and Joyce, hurries over to him and, hooking her arm through his, leads him away from the van.

'What's the van?' asks Bogdan.

'How should I know?' says Elizabeth, who makes it

her business to know everything. 'Good morning, though.'

'Good morning to you. Who are you seeing in Ruskin Court so early?'

'I borrowed a book from Margery Scholes,' says Elizabeth.

'What book?' asks Bogdan.

'A Jeffery Deaver,' says Elizabeth. 'It's terrific.'

'Which one?' asks Bogdan. They are now approaching Elizabeth's home in Larkin Court.

'The most recent one. Thank you for walking me home. Will you be coming to see Stephen later?'

Bogdan nods. 'We got a big crane going up this morning, but nothing special after lunch so I come down.' Bogdan is in charge of the new Hillcrest development currently taking shape high up above them. He has had a series of rapid promotions due to the recent events, but is taking everything in his stride. Bogdan always takes everything in his stride.

'Who was the guy who went into Ruskin Court? Wearing gloves?'

'No idea, darling. Drains? Drains would wear gloves, wouldn't they?'

'He walked in thirty seconds before you walked out. And you walked out ten seconds after I start to look at the van?'

'I think you're being a little paranoid, Bogdan. Are you getting enough sleep?'

'I get eight hours and twenty minutes every night,' says Bogdan. 'You promise me something, though?'

'If I can, of course. If I can't, then no.'

'You tell me why you're lying eventually? About the van and the man? And I just saw Margery Scholes in the shop, so how did you get into Ruskin? You tell me sooner or later?'

'Oh, Bogdan, we all have our secrets. I'll see you later, I hope?'

Bogdan nods and Elizabeth goes inside. Bogdan retraces his steps, but the van has gone.

He walks up the hill thinking about men with gloves, and keys they shouldn't have.

The Hillcrest development is running according to plan. Of course it is. He is making plenty of money too. Half goes into the building society, and half goes into Bitcoin. He is not tempted to buy a house, because buying a house meant you were staying, and you could never really predict if you were staying, could you? Bogdan spends the morning checking the works, supervising the installation of the crane and smoking his Rothmans. He then makes his way back down the hill, to play chess with Elizabeth's husband, Stephen.

He passes the graveyard where the nuns are buried. What do they make of the steam hammers sinking foundation posts further up the hill? Bogdan finds the noise soothing, and he hopes they do, too. No one wants silence for eternity.

He passes Bernard's bench. It was strange not to see the old man there, keeping guard. People here came and went, they came and went. Knowing they were here to live out their days made them vital. They moved slowly, but their time ran fast. Bogdan liked to be among them. They will die, but so will we all. We are all gone in the blink of an eye, and there is nothing to do but live while you're waiting. Cause trouble, play chess, whatever suits you.

He and Stephen try to play at least three times a week. It gives Elizabeth a bit of time off to go shopping, visit friends, solve murders. Stephen forgets most people's names now, but he has never forgotten Bogdan's.

Inside Elizabeth's flat, the game is twelve moves old, and Bogdan has Stephen in something of a bind. Bogdan is not counting his chickens, of course – you must never do that with Stephen – but he is happy with his position. He doesn't see that Stephen has many options for his next move.

That next move may take a while, as Stephen has fallen asleep. It is happening more and more often these days as he shuts down further and further still. But so long as Stephen is here, Bogdan will play chess with him.

And whenever Stephen's eyes pop back open, Bogdan knows he will still be in for a brutal game. Exactly the way he likes it. Stephen has forgotten many things, but he hasn't forgotten how to win a game of chess. He also hasn't forgotten Bogdan's big secret, the part he played in the recent murders, and is happy to bring it up whenever a game is particularly tight.

Bogdan has no fear though. He trusts Stephen absolutely. And who would Stephen tell anyway? Only Elizabeth, and Bogdan trusts Elizabeth completely too.

And speak of the devil, Bogdan hears the key in the door, and sees Elizabeth walk in. She is carrying a large sports holdall. Which is unusual.

'Hello, dear,' says Elizabeth. 'Is he asleep?'

'Maybe. I think he's faking it though. He knows I've got him beaten.'

'Let me make you both a cup of tea. Could I ask you a favour, Bogdan?'

'Who was the man with the gloves?' asks Bogdan.

'An MI5 risk-assessment underwriter,' says Elizabeth. 'Happy?'

'Yes, thank you,' says Bogdan. 'What favour do you need?'

Elizabeth puts the holdall down on the dining table, next to the chess board. She unzips it to reveal bundles of money.

'Money,' says Bogdan.

'Nothing gets past you, does it, dear?' says Elizabeth.

'And what for?' asks Bogdan.

Elizabeth double-checks that Stephen is still asleep. 'Could you buy me ten thousand pounds' worth of cocaine?'

Bogdan looks at the money and nods. 'Sure.'

Elizabeth smiles. 'Thank you, I knew I could rely on you. Wholesale though, not street price.'

'Of course,' says Bogdan. 'Is this to do with the man and the van?'

'No, this is something different.'

'When do you need it by?'

'Tomorrow lunchtime?'

'No problem,' says Bogdan.

'Lovely, you're such a help, you really are. I'll flick the kettle on.'

Bogdan takes another look at the holdall as Elizabeth disappears into the kitchen. Who would have that much cocaine at this short notice? There was a woman in St Leonards who used to be a teaching assistant at a primary school and now works out of a row of lock-up garages by the seafront. He would try her first. She had once asked him on a date, and he had told her that he wasn't attracted to her, and that he worried about her career, because it is very important to be honest in romantic endeavours. No one will ever thank you for dishonesty. She had thrown a pint glass at him, but it was some months ago now, and he's sure she'll still do him a favour. Bogdan takes out his phone, but before he can text, Stephen wakes, looks at the board as if there has been no delay, and moves his bishop. Bogdan puts down his phone and processes what Stephen has done. He had not seen that coming at all. What a move. Bogdan smiles.

Elizabeth's ten thousand pounds. Stephen's bishop. No wonder they got married. You had to hand it to these two.

Bogdan has a job to do, and some thinking to do. Which is just how he likes it.

21

Douglas Middlemiss now has a view of the sea, which is some consolation at least.

The house is in Hove. Officially an 'executive let' but used exclusively by MI5. Douglas was in the big bedroom at the front, with the diagonal view of the sea. They had told him to stay away from the windows but, really, give a man a sea view and what do you expect? He is currently sitting in an armchair angled to catch the sun coming up behind the spidery ruins of Brighton's West Pier in the distance. If somebody shoots him through the window then there are worse ways to go.

Poppy is in a bedroom at the back of the house, with a view of a council car park and some bins. To get to his door, someone would have to go past Poppy's. And she had proved surprisingly effective last time. Shooting Andrew Hastings. One of Martin Lomax's close-protection officers, sent to kill him, but, instead, killed himself by a small woman with a nose ring and an Ottolenghi cookbook.

Moving to Coopers Chase had seemed like such a terrific idea at the time, the perfect hiding place. Also a chance to see Elizabeth again. To impose himself on her. But Martin Lomax had breached security somehow.

Which meant somebody had told him where he was hiding. But who?

Douglas has his suspicions. He had messed up, that was for sure, showing his face on the security cameras. He had put the Service in a very bad position. Perhaps someone felt a debt needed to be repaid? Would they really sacrifice one of their own? He'd seen it done. Rarely, but he'd seen it. Could he trust Sue and Lance? Sue he was sure of. But Lance? The man he broke into Lomax's house with? What did he really know about him?

Poppy knocks on the door and asks Douglas if he would like a cup of tea. He tells her that would be lovely and he'll be down in a moment. What on earth does someone like Poppy make of someone like him, he wonders.

Douglas was no longer a popular man. He knew that, and he could see why. My God, he used to be popular. But now? Now he was the type of man to take his mask off during a robbery, and the type of man to make a joke about a gay colleague in a briefing. He meant no harm by either, but he saw he was out of step, and he knew, deep down, that a man less self-regarding than himself would have the ability to act more professionally and kindly. He had hoped to reach the end of his service without having to change one bit. Afraid not, old boy.

The diamonds were his way out. A lucky break, at a good time. Sitting there on Lomax's dining-room table. But had his luck run out? How to get out of this one?

What has changed, he wonders. Twenty years ago and you could make jokes about whoever you liked, couldn't you? Never to be mean, a joke was a joke was a joke. At school there had been a boy, Peter something, who they teased because he had ginger hair. Nothing mean, just jokes. He left after a few terms, too sensitive, and that was still the problem, wasn't it? If people took offence then weren't they just being like Peter, who had wasted a perfectly good education because he couldn't take a bit of teasing?

Douglas had mentioned this when he was sent on a Gender and Sexuality Awareness course a few years ago. They had asked him to leave, and he was given one-on-one coaching instead. He passed with flying colours as it was run by an old friend who told him exactly what he needed to say if he wanted his certificate signed.

So perhaps the Service has finally had enough of him? Perhaps Sue thinks he is no longer useful? That life would be better with him out of the way? Perhaps she has persuaded everyone it would be a small price to pay for peace with Martin Lomax. Had Sue done a deal with Lomax, and disclosed his location?

How many other people had known that Douglas was at Coopers Chase? Five or six? Including Poppy, of course. Was she more than she appeared, with her podcasts and her poetry and her Gregorian chant music? Was that an act? He'd seen it all, to be honest, so perhaps there was more to her, perhaps she was in league with the others against him? But then why shoot the intruder?

Elizabeth? That was a bigger question. Would Elizabeth have disclosed where he was? Surely not. He had told her about Martin Lomax, though, hadn't he? Had she tracked him down? Elizabeth could track anyone down. Douglas had had four affairs during their marriage, and Elizabeth had discovered all of them. The final one, a junior analyst named Sally Montague, had ended the marriage for ever. He had gone on to marry Sally Montague at least. Though she was twenty years his junior and that marriage only lasted until his next affair. They fired her, very discreetly, after the divorce. Where was Sally now? He knows he should probably care, but sometimes it is all too much for him.

Heaven knows how many affairs Elizabeth had had. Plenty. But Douglas had never caught her once.

You only marry one Elizabeth in your life. If Douglas was any sort of a man he could have kept hold of her. But Douglas was just a boy, he knows that. He was charming and funny, and life came easily to him. Whatever Douglas wanted, he got; everybody fell for him, everybody fell for the act. Although he supposes that people who didn't fall for his act had probably just given him a wide berth over the years.

He had once asked Elizabeth when she had seen through him. She had said she'd known from the moment she'd met him. And she'd wondered what small, frightened boy must be hiding behind such an obvious act. She had fallen in love with that frightened boy, but was yet to meet him. Douglas could have taken that moment to turn his life round, to become real and live in honesty. But instead he threw a whisky glass against a wall and stormed out, staying the night with Sally Montague in West Kensington. The next day, when he returned, Elizabeth had said nothing, but that was the day she gave up trying.

So he has lived on his charm ever since. There were worse lives. But he has lost touch with what charming is. He sees new generations of men, who know what to say and how to say it, and he is left with the tools of a different age. Jokes he can't tell, passes he can't make. And without them, what has he got?

The diamonds. That's what Douglas has got. His great escape.

Douglas gets up from his chair and pulls a comb through his hair. Some careful combing and it still stood up to cursory scrutiny, which is all that matters for most people. Cursory scrutiny had got him through most of his career. But a new generation saw right through him. Which was very annoying.

The silly thing is, Douglas knows they are right. He knows he is only being asked to be respectful, and he knows people just want to turn up to work and do their job and not be reminded every five minutes of what they look like, or who they slept with. Douglas knows they are right and he is wrong. He doesn't miss the good old days, he misses *his* good old days. He doesn't suppose they were good for most people.

But to really admit that to himself would be to admit to a lifetime of wearing his comfortable blinkers. It would be admitting that he still wonders what happened to Peter. To Peter Whittock. Of course Douglas remembers his name. Bullied out of school by children who were also young and scared.

How many other Peter Whittocks had he left in his trail? How many more Elizabeths? Sally Montagues?

Twenty years ago you could leave your mask off and the whole thing would have been one big laugh, a bit of ribbing, a message to Martin Lomax to go and boil his head, and Douglas would have to buy the drinks that evening. But that had been the big mistake.

One way or another, things catch up with you.

There is no point moping, however – you get the life you deserve. Douglas resolves to think his way out of this particular spot of bother. Time to deal with the task at hand. Time to deal with the threat of Martin Lomax, and possibly a threat from inside the Service itself. Then disappear with the diamonds. New identity, maybe a farm in New Zealand, or Canada. Somewhere they spoke English.

He has to assume now that he is compromised. He has to assume that he is on his own. He can trust no one. He steps out onto the landing, hearing the kettle whistle from the kitchen.

Not true. He can trust Elizabeth. Of that he is sure.

This thought brings him some cheer. He has made it to another sunrise, and, descending the stairs, he decides he will have some marmalade on toast while he still can.

22

Joyce

So I rang Poppy's mum, and she could not have been nicer. She is called Siobhan, and, yes, I did just have to look up how to spell it. She must have been Irish at some point, but it doesn't seem like she is now.

I filled her in on what had happened. I thought that must be what Poppy meant, because perhaps when you're a spy you don't always tell your mum everything that's going on. Or perhaps that's just daughters in general? I'm lucky if I find out Joanna has had a haircut, for example. She once had a week in Crete and the first I knew about it was from Facebook. I reminded her that we had once had a week in Crete when she was little, but apparently this was a very different part of Crete, which she took delight in telling me. So I have been in Siobhan's shoes in some ways.

This is how it went. There were pleasantries, and I told her that Poppy had asked me to ring her, and that she was quite safe, but there had been an incident.

I actually said, 'Don't worry, no one has died,' before I realized that, of course, somebody had.

It became apparent, and I suppose I shouldn't have been surprised, that Siobhan wasn't fully on top of what her daughter does for a living. The way she had been told it,

Poppy worked for the Passport Office. They had done some checks on Siobhan when Poppy got the job, and she thought that unusual at the time, but hadn't really questioned it. There's always something with children, isn't there? Dressing them up for World Book Day and the like.

Really, I should have broken things to her in stages, but in nursing you get the sense of when it's better to come straight out with it. I said something along the lines of your daughter works for MI5 or MI6 and she's looking after a man who used to be married to my friend Elizabeth, and who has been accused of stealing diamonds (her: '*MI5?*' '*Elizabeth?*' '*Diamonds?*'). An intruder had tried to shoot the man last night, and Poppy had shot the intruder. That was as short as I could get it.

Siobhan was taken aback, and I thought perhaps she thought it was a prank, so I added, 'This isn't a prank, it really happened, she really did shoot him, and I even saw the body.'

I told her that Poppy had given me her number, and she asked where Poppy was now, and I said I didn't know, and that MI5 had taken her away, but that Elizabeth had said that was nothing to worry about, and that Poppy had done the right thing in the right way and had saved someone's life.

Siobhan asked where it happened and I told her all about Coopers Chase. She said it sounded lovely and I said, 'Well, why don't you come and visit? Meet me and Elizabeth?'

Siobhan said she would like that, and then she started to cry, which was for the best in my opinion. Let it out. Imagine if your daughter had just shot a man and been taken away by MI5? You couldn't help but feel emotional. I asked for her address, so I could pop a friendship bracelet straight in the post for her. I'll get the money when I see her.

We had a nice chat after that. She apologized for crying and I said not at all, then I asked if she liked Poppy's nose ring, and she thought for a while and said not really, she thought Poppy was prettier without it. I said Poppy was still very pretty with it, but I sympathized because Joanna once had three piercings in the same ear, one at the very top, and it was awful. You can still see a tiny scar there now, where it didn't properly heal over. You wouldn't notice it, but I always do. I think Siobhan and I are going to get along.

So Siobhan is going to come and see us, that's the big news. I hope Elizabeth won't mind. Poppy had slipped the phone number into my cardigan pocket, not Elizabeth's, so perhaps she knew this wasn't the done thing in these circumstances. Will Elizabeth object? Well, if she does, then that's her problem and not mine.

She lives in Wadhurst, by the way. Siobhan. I've been through it on the train, but that's about it. I'm sure it is very nice, if Poppy and her mum are anything to go by.

Just as I hung up, my door buzzer went, and it was Yvonne, my old neighbour, wanting a cup of tea and a chat. She was the first person I know to get a video recorder, I've never forgotten it. I remember they invited Joanna round to watch *ET*. Honestly, the look on Joanna's face. Anyway, she lives in Tunbridge Wells now, of course she does, so I asked her to pop the bracelet through Siobhan's letterbox on her way home. Saves a stamp, doesn't it?

What else then? Ryan Baird, of course. Ron has really

got the wind between his legs with that one. I am looking forward to hearing the plan. And Ibrahim should be home tomorrow. He told us not to visit him again, and that's for the best as Elizabeth wants us to take a trip to Hove, for reasons she kept to herself.

I'm baking for Siobhan now. I have no idea what she likes, and I couldn't find a place in our conversation to ask her. So I'm playing it very safe with a Victoria sponge, some brownies with no nuts and a coconut and raspberry slice in case she's adventurous.

I do keep thinking about the diamonds. Twenty million pounds would turn most people's heads, wouldn't it? It would turn mine. On *Deal or No Deal* they would say that £25,000 was 'life-changing money', but I don't know about that, once you'd paid off your credit cards and been to Portugal, perhaps a couple of replacement windows. But twenty million? Someone is going to get their hands on it, I suppose, even if they have to murder a few people along the way.

I realize I didn't mean that Ron has 'really got the wind between his legs' by the way. What's the right expression? It's something like that, isn't it? I'll leave it for now, though, because it actually rather suits Ron.

So, Hove with Elizabeth tomorrow, which will be fun. We're getting the 2.30 bus into Brighton, and we'll get out by the big M&S and walk into Hove. Elizabeth has said, 'Strictly no shopping, Joyce,' so we're certainly on business of some sort.

What sort of business though? Diamonds? Murder? Perhaps a bit of both? That would be nice.

23

Elizabeth looks at her watch and sighs. She speeds up a touch.

They are about twenty minutes behind schedule, because Joyce had insisted on stopping for a coffee. Joyce loves to sit in coffee shops and look out of the window at the people passing by. She would sit there all day if you let her, saying, 'Ooh, umbrellas are going up,' or, 'Do you think I would suit that coat, Elizabeth?' She doesn't even particularly like coffee, she just feels too awkward asking for tea in a coffee shop.

Douglas has asked to see her, and it's the least she can do in the circumstances. He was very nearly killed on her watch. She hadn't officially started looking after him, but even so.

They are on their way to the new safe house in Hove. Number 38 St Albans Avenue, one of many parallel streets leading down from the cafés of Church Road to the ice-cream parlours of the seafront.

'Isn't the sea air lovely?' says Joyce.

'A tonic,' agrees Elizabeth, as a large lorry drives past them.

Something wasn't right with Joyce. Elizabeth has learned to read her pretty well by now, and she is definitely being over-jolly. That was Joyce's trick. It worked on everybody else, but it didn't work on Elizabeth. Elizabeth stops outside the Nando's on Church Road, and puts her hand on Joyce's arm.

'Before we see Douglas and Poppy, why don't you let me know what you're hiding?'

Joyce looks up at her, those bright eyes so innocent, that halo of snow-white hair.

'I'm sure I don't know what you mean?'

'Joyce, you've held us up for twenty minutes already. I really don't want to stand here for another twenty minutes trying to get it out of you.'

'Sometimes, Elizabeth, you act as if you're my boss. And you're not.'

Elizabeth sighs. 'Please, I'm begging of you, don't be tiresome. Just tell me.'

Joyce looks at the Nando's. 'Do you know, I've never been to a Nando's?'

'You're clearly keeping something from me. Is it to do with Douglas, perhaps?'

'I might bring Ibrahim. He'd like a Nando's, don't you think? And we need to make sure he gets out.'

'Something to do with Poppy, then?'

'Sometimes, Elizabeth, you just have to accept that you don't know everything. And there it is, I'm afraid.'

Elizabeth stares into Joyce's eyes and nods. 'So, it *is* something to do with Poppy? You're good, Joyce, but you're not that good.'

Joyce smiles. 'This is just making us later, dear. We'll look rude. I haven't even brought anything for them. Do we have time to pick up some fudge?'

Elizabeth is thinking. 'Well, we know it's Poppy, that's written all over your face. Perhaps Poppy asked you something? But you weren't alone with her, were you?'

'I'm afraid you're barking up the wrong tree. There's a lovely bookshop further up, City Books? I could pick up a John Grisham for Douglas?'

'So Poppy gave you something? Is that it? On her way out, she slipped you something?'

'I think someone's slipped *you* something, Elizabeth. I'm right about Ibrahim, aren't I? We need to make sure he gets out. He won't want to. I think Nando's is mainly chicken, but they must do puddings and things.'

'What could she possibly have given you? And why you and not me?'

'I was thinking of going to the dog rescue centre. I might ask Ibrahim to drive me as soon as he's back.'

'A message, perhaps? Did Poppy give you a message? Slipped it into your hand as she was leaving?' Elizabeth looks long and hard at Joyce.

'He'll object, you know Ibrahim. But we'll talk him round. And dogs are very healing. I'm not telling you anything you don't already know, but his mental injuries will last far longer than his physical injuries.'

'Something personal.' Elizabeth steps aside as a group of youths barrels into the Nando's. 'That's why she chose you. An errand. Something she knew she could trust you with?'

'I checked on the website. Alan is still there. That's the dog. Though I'm going to call him Rusty; you're the first person I've told that. I wrote it in my diary, but I haven't said it out loud.'

'You were wearing your new cardigan, of course. Which suits you a great deal, by the way. So perhaps she just slipped it into your pocket?'

'Thank you about the cardigan. When I was a child the neighbours had a dog called Rusty, you see.'

'I wonder, Joyce, if she wanted you to contact someone for her? Just to let them know she was all right? That's the sort of thing I would absolutely trust you with.'

'He was a retriever, I think, though I get them mixed up with Labradors. We're all a bit of everything, though, aren't we? When you start looking into it?'

'Who does Poppy trust?' asks Elizabeth. 'That's the question.'

'Everyone loves John Grisham, don't they? He's a safe bet.'

Elizabeth puts her hands on Joyce's shoulders, nods and looks her directly in the eye.

'I wonder, Joyce. Did Poppy give you her mother's phone number?'

Joyce throws her hands up. 'Oh, for goodness' sake, Elizabeth. I can't have anything, can I?'

'You held out longer than most. Did you ring her?'

Joyce nods. 'Is that OK?'

'It's fine, I'm not surprised someone would want to talk to their mum the first time they killed someone. I mean, I didn't, but I'm me.'

'She seems lovely. I've invited her down, I'm afraid.'

'That's a nice idea. Now, shall we get on?'

Joyce smiles and the two friends walk towards St Albans Avenue.

'You're not cross?' asks Joyce.

'Not a bit,' says Elizabeth. 'Although I will say this: They don't like you to change the names of the dogs.'

'I know, but *Alan*,' says Joyce.

'Well, why don't you let Ibrahim decide? That's the sort of thing he's good at.'

'I can't wait to have him back, can you?'

Elizabeth slips her arm through Joyce's and they continue walking.

'Where was Ron off to, by the way?' asks Joyce. 'I saw him driving off before we left. He never drives these days.'

Elizabeth looks at her watch. 'Ron has a plumbing job. He was very keen to get to it.'

'A plumbing job?'

'You know Ron, he can turn his hand to anything.'

24

Selling cocaine is less glamorous than people imagine, and Connie Johnson is thinking that it is nice to have the opportunity to dress up for once.

It's not every day that Bogdan Jankowski wants to buy ten grand's worth of prime Colombian blow and Connie has been excited all day. The lock-up next door sells fake perfume, and she had dabbed some on earlier, only to have to wash it off immediately as the smell overpowered her. She has even had to reapply her mascara after the tears streamed down her face. She thinks she has got rid of the worst of it.

Why did Bogdan want coke all of a sudden? He wasn't the type at all. Perhaps he had developed a drug problem, and needed to fund his habit? Connie hopes so; it would certainly mean she would see more of him.

What was it about him? The sense of extreme danger and absolute safety in the same man? Or just the looks?

There is a rattling knock on the metal lock-up door. Connie adjusts her hair, spits her gum into an old filing cabinet and lights a menthol cigarette. Here we go.

She opens the door, sunshine floods into her dark world and there he is. Bogdan. Shaven-headed, tattoos snaking up both arms, deep blue eyes and an expression of total indifference. The full package. He shuts the door behind him and it is just the two of them. How should she play this? Nice and cool? She had tried flirting with Bogdan before and it had got her nowhere. But she suspects he had just been playing hard to get. Is he undressing her with his eyes? Connie thinks so. He's certainly doing something with his eyes. She nods down at his sports bag.

'That the money?'

Bogdan nods. 'Yes.'

Connie takes a long drag on her menthol cigarette, savouring the fresh minty taste.

'Ten grand?'

'Yes,' says Bogdan.

'Do I need to count it?'

'No,' says Bogdan, and puts the bag down on Connie's large, wooden desk.

When Connie's old secondary school closed they auctioned off the contents, and Connie bid on, and bought, the desk of her old headmistress. The desk she had stood across from so many times, being reprimanded for this, that and the other. For a while she delighted in using it to weigh out cocaine and to have sex. What would Mrs Gilbert have to say about that? Now business has expanded, however, she uses it mainly for admin. She has to admit, it is a good desk.

'So you'll be wanting your coke, then?' asks Connie.

'Yes,' says Bogdan, before adding, 'please.'

Connie senses this is going well. Is there a connection here? Electricity? My God, just look at him.

'It's out the back, Bogdan. Give me a minute, make

yourself at home, there's magazines. Mainly *Ultimate Fighting*.'

Connie opens a padlocked door and walks into a small storage room. There is no mirror here, so she checks herself in the reflection of an old CD-ROM. She is glad she does, as she has a little lipstick on her teeth. Had Bogdan noticed? She kneels in front of a safe and keys in the combination with one hand while rubbing her front teeth with the other. What if he had noticed the lipstick, and now notices she's rubbed it away? She takes out a kilo of cocaine from the safe, wrapped in brown paper and stamped 'Fragile – This Way Up'. If he notices then he'll know she's checked herself out in the mirror. Will that look too needy? She locks the safe again and heads back out. Too late now, if he notices, he notices. Best foot forward.

Connie padlocks the storage door once again and puts the package on her headmistress's desk next to the money. Bogdan is looking straight at her. At her teeth?

'You need to check it?' asks Connie.

'No,' says Bogdan. He takes the money from the sports holdall, and replaces it with the package.

'This going to be a regular thing, is it?' asks Connie. 'There's special treatment for regulars.'

'No, just this once,' says Bogdan.

'Special treatment' was too far, thinks Connie. Too flirty. Idiot. She decides to shrug.

'Well, you know your own business.'

Bogdan nods. 'Yes.'

'Let me get the door for you.' Connie walks over and opens the door. That sunshine again. Bogdan walks through, ducking his head slightly as he does.

'Thank you, Connie.'

Connie shrugs again – perfect – and shuts the door behind him. She falls back against the closed door and lets out a huge breath.

Christ, that was intense. She's going to have to take the rest of the day off.

Bogdan doesn't have far to walk. He is meeting Ron by the pier. It had gone OK with Connie, there didn't seem to be any hard feelings. He had felt for her because she had lipstick on her teeth. He was going to mention it, because it looked like she was going on a date later. But she had obviously noticed herself as it was gone when she came back with the cocaine. He was relieved he didn't have to mention it, as she didn't seem in a very good mood with him.

He is glad to be outside, not least because there was an awful smell.

Bogdan spots Ron and walks up to him. Ron is dressed as a plumber.

'All right, Bogdan,' says Ron.

'Hello, Ron,' says Bogdan.

'That it, then?' says Ron, indicating the bag.

'Yep, that's it,' says Bogdan.

'Good lad. I bet you're wondering why I'm dressed like a plumber?'

Bogdan shakes his head. 'Not really. Nothing with you

lot surprises me. I'd be more surprised if you weren't dressed like a plumber.'

Ron nods, agreeing that's a fair point.

'How is Ibrahim?' asks Bogdan. 'When is he back?'

'He's all right, old son. Knocked about a bit, you know? Nasty.'

Bogdan nods. 'You need help with the guy who did it?'

Ron takes the bag. 'You're already helping.'

'I thought so,' says Bogdan. 'Good, I am pleased. You know you just ask, and I do whatever.'

'You're a good lad.' Ron sniffs. 'Jesus, Bogdan, what's that smell?'

25

Elizabeth and Joyce are on St Albans Avenue. It is a road full of small hotels and retirement homes. You could walk the whole length of it without once feeling the need to look up from your phone, and that was perfect. They reach number 38. Blinds drawn in all the rooms facing the street, and a four-year-old 'Vote Lib Dem' poster in the front window. Absolutely textbook.

There is a Virgin Media van parked across the road and Elizabeth knocks on the window. She is expected.

The driver folds her newspaper, lowers her window and raises an eyebrow.

Elizabeth repeats exactly what she has been told to say. 'My reception is on the blink and I don't want to miss *Love Island.*' Someone in MI5 will have enjoyed thinking that one up for her.

The driver replies, as expected. 'You number 42?'

Elizabeth nods.

'That's Sky, not Virgin.'

'Sorry to trouble you,' says Elizabeth, and reaches in to shake the driver's hand. As they shake, she feels the key being pressed into her hand. The driver raises her window again and returns to her paper. A very boring job. Elizabeth sympathizes. At least the driver has a paper. There were times in eastern Europe, on twelve-hour watches, where Elizabeth would have killed for a *Daily Telegraph*. Even a *Daily Mirror*.

They cross the road towards the house.

'Was that spy talk?' asks Joyce. 'Code?'

'Very basic code, yes. Just an identifier.'

'Joanna watches *Love Island*. She says I'd love it. Men, and what have you.'

There is a 'No Junk Mail' sticker on the front door. The door looks normal from the outside, but Elizabeth knows it will have steel reinforcements behind it, should anyone get any ideas. The key looks perfectly normal, but is electronic, and the moment it is slipped into the lock there are a series of noises from inside the house, faint enough that they wouldn't be heard from the street.

The door opens and Elizabeth looks at her watch: 5.25. Ron should have picked up the package by now.

Douglas had said to meet them at five, but it wouldn't do any harm for Douglas to be kept waiting every now and again. Quite what she was doing there was a mystery. It was odd enough that Douglas had chosen to hide at Coopers Chase. Odder still that he wanted to see Elizabeth again, now that Coopers Chase was no longer an option.

Elizabeth could have said no, but something was going on here, and she wouldn't at all mind finding out what it was. It was one of Douglas's games, no doubt, but sometimes Douglas's games had been fun. Certainly worth seeing if he had one good one left in him.

Especially with twenty million pounds at the end of the rainbow. Think what you could do with twenty million pounds? But Elizabeth doesn't need to think. She knows exactly what she would do with it.

They walk over the threshold.

'I like their hall carpet,' says Joyce. Her voice echoes around the silent house. 'We nearly had similar.'

It shouldn't be silent, of course, with two people living here. Were they both sleeping? At 5.25? Unlikely.

Elizabeth feels a breeze. A breeze in a house where every door and window is shut. Bolted and sealed shut.

'Douglas?' calls Elizabeth. 'Poppy?'

Elizabeth steps into the kitchen. It is neat. There is a small table and two wooden chairs. There are two bowls and two mugs by the sink. An old calendar on the wall, British castles.

There is a back door, which leads onto a courtyard garden. Barbed wire atop a brick back wall.

The back door is wide open.

26

'And he kicked you in the back of the head?'

'I'm afraid he did, Anthony, yes.'

Ibrahim had not told the others what time he was coming back today. He knew they would make a fuss, and he didn't want a reception committee when he was unshaven. Instead he managed to get the final appointment of the day with Anthony, the hairdresser so in demand he now visits Coopers Chase three times a week. Ibrahim hasn't been at all happy with his hospital hair.

'You wouldn't be able to tell, honestly,' says Anthony, running a comb through Ibrahim's hair. 'No footprint, nothing.'

'Well, it's a skull,' says Ibrahim.

'You said it,' agrees Anthony. 'Tell me if I'm pressing too hard, though. We'll get you feeling better in no time. That's my job.'

'Thank you, Anthony.'

'You'll bounce back, I know you will.'

'Bouncing back is for younger men.'

'Nonsense, what doesn't kill you makes you stronger.'

'Well, I disagree at my age.'

'I'll give you a for example. I once had a two-day acid trip, in Kavos. You know Kavos?'

'Is that Greece?'

'Ooh, I wouldn't know, somewhere hot. Anyway, at the time it was terrifying, you know? I thought the walls of the villa were bleeding. I stood on the roof trying to grab hold of the aeroplanes as they were flying over. My mate Gav put it on Insta, 30,000 likes, and now I can see the funny side. But I thought I was going to die, and I didn't, and the experience has made me a stronger man.'

'In what way?'

'Well, I don't know. I mean, I do less acid these days? So that's something, isn't it? And I got about four hundred new followers on Insta. That's my point, really. I don't know what they did to your hair in hospital. I'm guessing no conditioner?'

'I asked Ron to get me some, but he said he wasn't sure what to ask for.'

'Well, you've got me now.'

'Anyway, I don't think this has made me stronger. I am rattled, Anthony.'

'Of course,' says Anthony. 'Post-traumatic whatever.'

'But I will get over it eventually.'

'Of course you will. Look at what Oprah's been through over the years.'

'Unless I die before I get over it. And then I will never get over it. That's how I feel right now. Perhaps I will never heal.'

'I'll tell Joyce you were being morose if you keep this up.'

'It is fine to say "what doesn't kill you makes you stronger". It is admirable. But it no longer applies when you're eighty. When you are eighty whatever doesn't kill you just ushers you through the next door, and the next door and the next, and all of these doors lock behind you. No bouncing back. The gravitational pull of youth disappears, and you just float up and up.'

'Well,' says Anthony, putting his palms on Ibrahim's temples and lifting his head to look into the mirror, 'I've just knocked ten years off you, so I'm doing the best I can to help. Do they know who mugged you?'

Ibrahim nods. 'They have a name, yes. But no evidence.'

'And what'll happen?'

'I suspect Elizabeth will happen.'

'Well, let's hope so,' says Anthony, holding up a mirror behind Ibrahim's head and getting another nod. 'No one touches my friends and gets away with it. You tell Elizabeth if she needs any help, just ask.'

'I will pass that on.'

'For what it's worth, and I do listen sometimes, you won't die before you get better, I promise.'

'Impossible to say.'

'Ibrahim, you're talking to someone who once dreamt the lottery numbers. Four of them. Three hundred and sixty quid. If I tell you you won't die yet, you won't die yet.'

'That is a comfort, thank you.'

Anthony is packing up his kit. 'We all know the order you lot will die. Ron first . . .'

Ibrahim nods.

'Then Elizabeth, probably shot. Then it's tough to call between you and Joyce.'

'I wouldn't want to be the last one left,' says Ibrahim.

'I have always tried to never get attached to people, but I have got attached to these three.'

'Well, let's say you third and Joyce last then.'

'I wouldn't want Joyce to be on her own either,' says Ibrahim.

'Oh, I don't think Joyce would be on her own for long, do you?'

'Well, I suppose not,' smiles Ibrahim.

'Such a naughty girl, that one.'

Ibrahim reaches into the pocket of his jacket, hanging behind the door, and pulls out his wallet. 'Card, I'm afraid, Anthony – I used my last cash for the taxi.' Ibrahim frowns as he opens the wallet. 'Well, that's peculiar, my card isn't in here.'

'I've heard it all now,' chuckles Anthony.

'I must have mislaid it, I'm ever so sorry. Can I owe you?'

Anthony walks over to Ibrahim and gives him a hug. 'This one's on me. Now, off you pop, handsome, they'll all be dropping like flies when they see you.'

Ibrahim looks at his reflection, moving his head to see both profiles. He nods. 'Thank you, Anthony. I rather think they will.'

Elizabeth walks out of the kitchen. If someone has been in the house, Elizabeth is sure they have gone. That's her instinct, but she still puts a finger to her lips and motions for Joyce to stay exactly where she is. She nudges open the living-room door with her foot. Nothing. Two armchairs, two side tables, a sideboard with a radio and a vase of flowers on it. No body, no blood – that was something. That gave Elizabeth some hope. She knows she will have to climb the stairs. If anyone is here then she knows how vulnerable she will be. No weapon. She turns back into the hallway and sees that Joyce is no longer there. There is a momentary panic until she sees Joyce emerge silently from the kitchen, a knife in either hand. Elizabeth nods.

Joyce hands over the bigger knife to Elizabeth. As she is handing it over she whispers, 'Careful, handle first.'

Elizabeth feels her heart thumping against her ribcage. Fast, but strong. How lucky she is.

Is there someone in the house? Has she walked into a trap? Worse than that, has she brought Joyce into the trap with her?

She motions for Joyce to stay downstairs and she begins to climb.

Say what you like about Ron, but you can't say he doesn't look like a plumber. Ryan Baird had let him in without a second glance. Housing Association sent me round, water pressure. Hold up the bag, here's my tools. It's all free, don't worry.

So this was Ryan Baird?

This was the kid who kicked Ron's best friend in the back of the head and left him for dead?

What was he? Seventeen? Eighteen? Skinny, hair dyed blond, electric-blue tracksuit bottoms and bare top. He'd had a games controller in his hand, and had gone straight back to playing a game after Ron had asked him where the bathroom was. A few years ago Ron would have decked him there and then. But sometimes Elizabeth's way was the best way, so he'll do what he's told. And perhaps he'll still get his chance to smack Ryan Baird right in that gaping mouth before this is all over. Ron hopes so. He has a lot of respect for Gandhi and his ilk, but sometimes you have to cross the line.

Ron lifts the lid from the cistern and takes the brown package from his sports holdall. He wedges it down as far as it will go. Ten grand really doesn't buy you that much coke, he thinks. He'll talk to his son, Jason, about it when he next sees him.

Ron checks that the lid will fit back on the cistern, then removes it again. He puts his hand into the pocket of his overalls. He doesn't know where Elizabeth got hold of the overalls, but boy were they comfortable. He wonders if he's allowed to keep them. Wearing overalls every day would be a slippery slope though. There's a thin line between wearing overalls and going to the shop in your pyjamas.

He pulls out Ibrahim's debit card and places it carefully inside the cistern.

Lid back on, Ron zips his bag back up. He realizes he actually needs to use the loo, but decides to wait. Who knows what happens when you flush a loo with a kilo of cocaine in the cistern?

Ron goes back into the hallway, calls out, 'All done, mate!' to no response from Ryan Baird and leaves the flat.

He gives it a minute or so, as you never know who's listening, before pulling out his phone. It is a burner phone, untraceable. Jason had lots of them and hadn't batted an eyelid when his dad had asked for one. He rings the number of PC Donna De Freitas. She answers on the third ring.

'Hello?'

'Hello, is that Donna De Freitas?'

'Hi, Ron, is that you?'

'No, no, I don't know a Ron. I just got some information.'

'Well, OK, I'll play along. But quick, I'm watching CCTV of someone driving a Renault into a Greggs.'

'It's just I'm a plumber . . .'

'Right.'

'And I've just been doing a job, flat eighteen, Hazeldene Gardens.'

'Eighteen Hazeldene Gardens?'

'Yep, only I found something when I was there. It's in the toilet cistern, first door off the hallway when you break your way in.'

'I see . . . sir. And is the resident of the flat at home right now?'

'He is. He's not even wearing a top, Donna. Jesus. I was going to deck him.'

'Well, Fairhaven Police would like to thank you for your help, sir. But we can't break into a private residence without due cause.'

'What sort of thing?'

'Like, someone being attacked.'

'Oh yeah, and someone was being attacked. Screams, the lot.'

'OK. We'll be right over.'

'Good, take Chris with you, too.'

'Could I take your name, then?'

'I prefer to remain anonymous.'

'Make one up, just for me.'

Ron thinks. 'Jonathan Ovaltine.'

'Thank you, Mr Ovaltine.'

'Thanks, darling, you go get him. See you soon.'

Ron ends the call and walks out of the estate, whistling as he goes.

Job done. Elizabeth will be pleased. Perhaps he'll give her a ring, too. A pint first, though.

29

Elizabeth is grasping the handle of the knife firmly with an overhand grip, the way she was taught more than fifty years before. An underhand grip, favoured by the Soviets, was briefly fashionable in the seventies, but overhand was back now. It allowed for much greater force, particularly if your assailant was bigger than you.

Elizabeth has still not heard a sound. This was very bad news. Should she alert the driver outside? Would she have a gun? She continues to climb the stairs. No sign of a disturbance anywhere. It all looked so staged, the silence, the open back door. Was Douglas playing a little trick? Ask Elizabeth to come and meet him and give her the fright of her life?

Elizabeth reaches the landing. She looks down and sees Joyce at the bottom of the stairs. Knife in an overhand grip. What a natural that woman is.

There are three doors leading off the landing. A bathroom door is half open. Elizabeth gives it a nudge and it swings further open. Nothing there. Underwear hanging on an airer. Toilet seat up, so she knows who used it last.

The two bedroom doors are shut. She slowly turns the handle of the first door, knife poised and ready. Won't she look a fool if Douglas and Poppy are hiding behind the door giggling away? Why is she thinking this is all a trick? All so neat? It doesn't look like a crime scene, it looks like an exercise. Was that it? Was this a test? See if the old girl has still got it?

She flings the door open and jumps into the room, flattening her back against the nearest wall. Nothing but a perfectly made bed, a Philip Larkin poetry book and a Jo Malone candle. Poppy's room. But no Poppy. There is a bookmark in the middle of the Philip Larkin, ready for Poppy to return.

Elizabeth turns back onto the landing. Only one more room to go. The bedroom at the front of the house. Douglas's room. The last remaining option.

She tightens her grip on the knife, and then has a thought. Poppy had been upset at shooting Andrew Hastings; it was traumatic, and she had even asked Joyce to contact her mother. What if Poppy had decided she'd had enough? Waited for Douglas to fall asleep. You could always tell when Douglas had fallen asleep. My God, the snoring. Perhaps she decided to make a run for it, and left the back door open as she went? All too much for her? She would know there was still an officer stationed outside the house to keep Douglas safe.

Her hand is on the door knob. She starts to turn it.

Elizabeth opens the door. She freezes. Just for a second. It wasn't an exercise, and it wasn't a trick. Of course Poppy would never have left the back door open. And, of course, Douglas could never be silently asleep.

Poppy's body is slumped in the armchair, a bullet having made a mess of her face and turned that beautiful blonde hair red. One arm lies across her body, no doubt her attempt to shield herself from the bullet. The other arm lies limply by her side. Blood has run down the arm and dried. The white daisy, which had so secretly thrilled her grandmother, is now a crimson red.

Douglas is propped up on the bed. His bullet wound has caused even more damage than Poppy's. He would be unrecognizable if you hadn't once been married to him. The wall behind his head is black with blood.

Whatever Douglas had wanted her to see, surely it wasn't this?

Elizabeth breathes deeply. She has to remain calm. This will not be her crime scene for long, so she takes out her phone and photographs it from every possible angle.

Elizabeth hears a noise behind her. She turns, knife raised, to see Joyce in the doorway. Joyce looks from Poppy's body to Douglas's body and back again.

'Oh, Poppy,' says Joyce. 'Oh, Elizabeth.'

Elizabeth nods. 'Don't touch a thing. Downstairs, let's go.'

Elizabeth ushers Joyce in front of her. She is glad that Joyce is not weak-minded; the last thing they need now is tears. Elizabeth opens the front door, telling Joyce to stay where she is. She rushes down the path and across to the Virgin Media van. Realizing she is still carrying her knife, she slips it into her handbag and knocks on the window. The bored driver winds it down once again.

'You done, are you? That was quick.'

Elizabeth takes out her phone and shows her a photograph. 'Both dead. While you're sitting here reading.'

The driver is out of the van in a shot and races to the house. No doubt thinking about her once-promising career every step of the way.

Holding her phone, Elizabeth realizes she will be straight off for questioning as soon as the troops arrive, and that won't be long. Her phone will be taken off her, the photographs deleted. She scans the front garden walls of St Albans Avenue until she sees what she needs two houses up. The driver has run into the house, so Elizabeth takes a brisk walk, dislodges a loose brick from the low wall, slides her mobile phone into the gap and then replaces the brick. The perfect dead-letter drop.

So now there are diamonds *and* killers to be found.

PART TWO

At Times, You Won't Believe Your Eyes

30

Patrice is on half-term and is staying with Chris. Chris still can't quite get used to it. He is pretending to eat healthily, which, after a couple of days, he realizes is the same as actually eating healthily. An apple is an apple whether you are eating it because you like to take care of yourself or you are eating it to impress a new girlfriend. The nutrients are the same. Chris hasn't had a Snickers since Monday.

Tonight they had been due to go to Le Pont Noir for dinner. Formerly a dive called the Black Bridge, it is now Fairhaven's leading, if only, gastropub. On Tuesdays they have a jazz trio playing in the dining room. Chris has never enjoyed jazz, never even quite worked out which bit he was supposed to be enjoying, but he does know that people who like jazz seem to enjoy life, and that he needs to pretend to enjoy life a bit more than he does. And what if it's the same as apples? What if pretending to enjoy life is the same as actually enjoying it? He has been smiling from the moment Patrice arrived, so perhaps there was something in it.

Patrice got things from him too, he knew that. He could objectively see that he was kind and funny. He had a proper job, catching criminals. Anything else? He had been told he had nice eyes. He was a good kisser.

Everything else could be covered up for now. Don't run before you can walk, Chris. And do all women tell all men they are good kissers? Chris supposes so. What does it cost them?

The call from Donna came at around six thirty. Ryan Baird had been arrested and was on his way to Fairhaven Police Station. No jazz for Chris, which was a relief; that new leaf could wait.

Patrice had been very understanding. Suspiciously understanding, in fact. What if Patrice didn't like jazz either? What if they were both pretending? That was something to explore. It would certainly be an enormous relief.

Chris had driven to the station, interviewed Ryan Baird, who had screamed blue murder about being framed by a plumber, and had eventually been charged with possession with intent to supply as well as robbery and led to a cell. His solicitor looked a little perkier than last time, too, so either he enjoyed seeing Ryan being sent down, or he too had escaped an evening of jazz.

Chris had texted Patrice, and they are now sitting in the snug of Le Pont Noir, the only evidence of the evening's jazz a solitary drumstick on a walnut barstool.

Chris and Patrice are together on a leather sofa, and opposite them, legs tucked underneath her in a deep armchair, is Donna. Chris's partner, Patrice's daughter.

'The Thursday Murder Club?' asks Patrice.

'There's four of them,' says Donna. 'Ibrahim was the one who had his phone stolen. Ron was the plumber.'

'And who got hold of ten grand's worth of coke?'

Donna looks at Chris. 'I'm guessing Elizabeth?'

Chris nods. 'I'd have thought so. I mean, never rule out Joyce.'

'But isn't it all illegal?'

'Very.'

'And wouldn't you get in trouble if it came out?'

'Mum,' says Donna, 'I got a call from a plumber saying he'd found cocaine and a stolen bank card at a flat. There were screams. I went to the flat and found the cocaine and the bank card. I arrested the youth present at the scene. Chris and I questioned him. He denied all charges . . .'

'Which they often do,' says Chris.

'Which they often do. We felt there was sufficient evidence to charge him, and so we charged him.'

'And what about when it comes to court? When they call this plumber as a witness and he isn't a plumber?'

Donna shrugs. 'I'm guessing Elizabeth will have thought of that.'

Patrice raises her whisky glass and the ice cubes tinkle in salute. 'They sound like a hell of a gang. I'd love to meet them.'

'We're keeping you a secret for now,' says Chris.

'Are we?' says Patrice, stretching a leg across Chris's lap.

'I'm involved about as much as I want to be with the Thursday Murder Club. If they can plant cocaine in someone's cistern, I don't want to think about what they'd do with my love life.'

'Cute you said "love life" and not "sex life",' says Patrice.

'Don't say "sex", Mum,' says Donna. 'Stop showing off.'

'I meant my personal life,' says Chris.

'Too late, you said it now,' says Patrice.

'That lot would have us married in weeks,' says Chris.

'How awful,' says Patrice with an eyebrow raised.

'Mum, stop pretending you want to marry Chris just because you've had two whiskies. Don't make me regret introducing you two.'

'Have you heard from Elizabeth, by the way?' Chris asks Donna.

'Not a peep,' says Donna, checking her phone. 'You'd think she'd be loving this. Ryan Baird in custody.'

Chris looks at his watch. 'Well, it's half ten, you know that lot. She'll be tucked up in bed by now.'

'Talking of which,' says Patrice, looking straight at Chris and playing with her necklace.

'Oh God, Mum, puke,' says Donna, and finishes her whisky with a shake of the head.

31

So let's see what Elizabeth Best has got, shall we? The great hero of the Service. Is she all she's cracked up to be?

Sue Reardon can't help but compare herself to the woman sitting directly across from her. Elizabeth Best. Silver hair and tweed jacket. Face impassive. What does she know? Or what is she willing to tell?

They have both killed people in their time. For good reasons, of course, but they've still done it. That creates a kinship and a respect. But also a suspicion. Elizabeth has every trick in the book, and Sue Reardon will need a few of her own to get what she needs. So be it.

The room is small, as they so often are.

Claustrophobia, that's the idea. The walls are metal-plated up to waist height, and concrete above that. It has no windows, but cameras in each corner. The thick walls muffle the conversation. It looks like it would survive a nuclear explosion, and, indeed, that's exactly what it has been designed to do. Lance James is pacing at the far wall.

'Keep still, for goodness' sake, it's not helping anyone,' says Elizabeth.

'Sorry,' says Lance.

Lance James is not the sort of man to sit still when he can stand and pace instead. He was seconded to Sue from the Special Boat Service, but she knows little else about him. He's quiet and he's hard-working, and that will do Sue just fine. He is in his early forties, and clinging on gamely to his medium-to-good looks. The already thinning blond hair, however, will soon thin further and grey, and then disappear altogether. A life of small rooms, stakeouts, late nights and stress; Sue has seen many a handsome man go south over the years. She gives Lance five years at most.

She had sat with Elizabeth and her friend Joyce in the back of a windowless van for the whole journey here. They had then been blindfolded as they were walked to this room. This was all to disguise their destination, but Elizabeth would know exactly where they were. Godalming. 'The House', they called it, in the isolation cells three floors below ground. She knows Elizabeth will have interviewed people in this very room during her time at MI5. She would have been sitting in Sue's seat. It had been given a spruce-up since then, some new grey paint on the ceiling. No cameras in those days either, which was probably best for all concerned.

'You don't hear of many Lances these days,' says Joyce. 'Is it a family name?'

'Afraid so,' says Lance.

Sue can see that Joyce has been thrilled by the whole experience. She had nodded off in the van, while Elizabeth was, no doubt, keeping track of time and direction, but she had particularly enjoyed the blindfolding. 'Well, I can tell we're going up in a lift, now,' she had said on their way down to this subterranean floor.

Lance leans back against the wall and folds his arms across his muscular chest.

'So you received a message from Douglas Middlemiss?' says Sue. 'Let's start there, shall we? What time would that have been, exactly?'

'I don't know,' says Elizabeth. She won't want to give everything away. Or anything away, if she can help it. That's fine. Softly, softly.

'And can you show us the message?' asks Sue, politeness itself. Sue is always polite in interrogations. The angry ones run out of patience long before you do.

'I'm afraid not. It's on my phone.'

'And where is your phone?' asks Sue. 'It wasn't in your bag, which we found strange.'

'Oh, we don't carry our phones everywhere, Sue,' says Joyce. 'Purse, keys, a bit of make-up just in case, and a bag for life, that's all you really need.'

Sue nods at Joyce. It's a double-act, is it? I need to keep an eye on this Joyce, too? What a tiny, formidable woman. Exactly the sort of woman you'd want parachuted behind enemy lines with a gun and a cipher machine. She turns back to Elizabeth. 'I wonder where it is then, Elizabeth?'

'Well, I wish I could remember,' says Elizabeth.

'You don't remember where your phone is?' says Lance from behind her. About time he piped up.

'I'm afraid not. It comes to us all, dear,' says Elizabeth.

'I once searched the whole flat for mine,' says Joyce. 'Honestly, twenty minutes it must have taken. And it was in my hand all along.'

'I wouldn't wish it on you, Lance,' says Elizabeth. 'Cherish your youth.'

Lance finally leaves the wall. He walks over and takes a seat next to Sue Reardon. Sue leans forward and addresses Elizabeth directly. 'I'm guessing it's at your flat?'

'One would imagine so,' agrees Elizabeth.

Sue gives a satisfied nod. 'That does sound the most likely, doesn't it? So you'll be comfortable with me sending a team over to search for it?'

'Aren't the rules these days that everything has to be left immaculate after a search?' asks Elizabeth.

'Those were always the rules,' says Lance.

'Yes, but now you actually have to abide by them? European Court of Justice sticking their oar in?'

'Everything will be left immaculate,' says Sue. What's on that phone? Messages? Photographs?

'Well, in that case you go right ahead. It needs a tidy,' says Elizabeth. 'That will be fun for Stephen, a team of goons in the flat at the dead of night. He's a fine host.'

'She might even have left it with me,' says Joyce. 'If you want to give my flat a once-over, too? Especially the bathroom.'

'In the absence of the phone for now, can you remember what the message said?' asks Sue. 'The exact words?'

Elizabeth nods, and recites from memory. 'Poppy and I have been moved to 38 St Albans Avenue, Hove. I would be obliged if you would meet me there. There is something I want to show you.'

'So you can remember the exact words of the message,' says Lance. 'But not where your phone is?'

Elizabeth taps her head. 'My palace has many rooms. Some are dustier than others.'

Sue notices that Lance can't hide a little smile. These two are a piece of work, all right.

Sue nods again. 'You poor thing, ma'am, that must be dreadful. And that was the whole message? Nothing else?'

'Well, it also said come alone, but I thought Joyce would enjoy it.'

'Thank you,' says Joyce. 'I did. Up to a point.'

'And do you have any idea of what he wanted to show you?'

Elizabeth pauses. She looks up at the cameras. As she looks back at Sue Reardon, she makes up her mind.

'Honestly, I assumed he wanted to show me the diamonds.'

'You think he had the diamonds with him?'

'What else could it be?' asks Elizabeth.

'That's assuming he stole the diamonds in the first place,' says Lance. 'And we have no evidence of that.'

'Well,' says Elizabeth, 'and I realize I probably should have passed this on before now, but I know he stole them. He told me.'

'When did he tell you this, Elizabeth?' asks Sue, still calm.

'Oh, a few days ago, perhaps,' says Elizabeth.

Sue is unsurprised. Of course Douglas told her. He trusted her. He loved her. 'But he didn't have the diamonds with him at the safe house, Elizabeth. He'd been searched. Before he got there. While he was there. And after someone blew his head off. So what else might he have wanted to show you?'

'Perhaps he wanted to show Elizabeth a key, or a code, or a riddle,' says Joyce. 'To let her know where the diamonds were? I can't do riddles at all. What's the one about the man who can only lie and the man who can only tell the truth?'

Sue realizes that Joyce is waiting for an answer, so gives her an 'I'm as baffled as you, Joyce' shrug.

'That's very good, Joyce,' says Elizabeth. 'And now, of course, whoever killed Douglas and Poppy, let's assume Martin Lomax, will have that information instead. Riddle or not. So Martin Lomax can get his diamonds back.'

'Perhaps Martin Lomax isn't the only person with a motive for shooting Douglas and Poppy, though?' says Joyce.

'Of course,' says Sue.

'All that money. Twenty million. We'd all like it, wouldn't we?' Joyce adds.

There is a general agreement that they would. It's out there somewhere. But where?

'And, as Elizabeth will tell you, there were two people in the house the night that the diamonds were stolen,' Joyce goes on. 'Douglas and Lance. And I think we're taking Lance's word a bit too easily. I mean no offence by this, Lance, but we don't know you one bit, do we? Who's to say you didn't see Douglas steal the diamonds? And you've been looking for a chance to get your hands on them?'

'Well, I wasn't going to say that out loud,' says Elizabeth.

'But now the cork is out of the bottle. And since we're being filmed, it's worth discussing.'

'Discuss away,' says Lance, 'I have nothing to hide.'

'Almost certainly not,' agrees Elizabeth. 'But you were in the house on the evening of the theft. You knew where Douglas and Poppy were being kept. You probably appointed Poppy to this job in the first place, an unusual appointment.'

'So perhaps you were even in league with her?' says Joyce.

'Total conjecture, of course,' says Elizabeth. 'But I trust this will all be investigated?'

'Oh, it will all be investigated,' says Sue. This is more like it. 'Lance will quite rightly be a suspect, and I will add another suspect to the list. Probably the only other person who knew that Douglas was at Coopers Chase and at St Albans Avenue. A confidante and an ex-wife of the dead man. A woman trained in breaking and entering, a woman trained in killing, a woman who has conveniently mislaid her mobile phone. She would be a suspect, too, don't you think?'

'She certainly would,' agrees Elizabeth. 'As would you, of course, Sue. I imagine you have every skill I had, and a few more they've thought up in the meantime. Let's say you suspected that Douglas had stolen the diamonds?'

'Let's say that, yes,' confirms Sue. She's happy now the conversation is opening up a bit. A chance to observe Elizabeth a little better. Start to read her.

'Or let's say you knew already? Let's say you and

Douglas were more than colleagues? You wouldn't be the first person Douglas has seduced.'

'Let's say not everyone would make the same mistake you made?' says Sue. Interesting line of attack from Elizabeth.

'Touché,' says Elizabeth. 'But twenty million pounds suddenly swimming around. And only one man knows where it is? That might be tempting?'

'I should think so,' says Sue. 'Very tempting.'

'And you, of course, would have had ample opportunity to kill Douglas and Poppy. You knew where they were, you would have access, you would have their trust. You were in charge of putting them there and, no doubt, you'll be in charge of cleaning up the mess.'

Sue nods. 'I'm beginning to wish I had thought of this now. Aren't you?'

'I think I might have thought of a way of doing this without killing anyone, though,' says Elizabeth.

'I hope you might extend me the professional courtesy of imagining that I might have, too,' says Sue. 'I worked with Douglas for nearly twenty years.'

'My condolences,' says Elizabeth. 'Now, while we agree that anyone in this room, other than Joyce, might have murdered Douglas, it does feel that a trip to see Mr Lomax might be in order.'

'Under no circumstances are you to visit Martin Lomax,' says Sue. 'We'll be dealing with him.'

'Of course,' says Elizabeth. 'Don't visit Martin Lomax. We must try to remember that, Joyce.'

Joyce nods. 'Understood.'

'Now, Elizabeth,' says Sue. 'You said Douglas wanted to show you something?'

'I did say that.'

'Well, we found this in his jacket pocket.' Sue reaches into an evidence bag and pulls out a silver locket. It has a mirror inside, nothing else. Will it mean anything to Elizabeth? 'I wondered if this was what he wanted to show you?'

She sees that Elizabeth recognizes it immediately. Well, of course.

'It's inscribed with your name.'

Elizabeth picks up the locket. She weighs it in her hand and flicks it open to see the mirror. Sue sees that she is thinking, and she knows what Elizabeth is thinking too.

Sue smiles at her. 'Very touching, Elizabeth. He must have loved you very much?'

'In his way,' agrees Elizabeth.

'You lucky thing,' says Sue. 'The love of a good man. Or a man, at the very least.'

Elizabeth smiles to herself.

'Now, it's midnight,' says Sue. 'And you have beds to get to.'

And Sue still has one more job to do this evening. Not a pleasant one, but an important one. Lance leads Joyce and Elizabeth from the room. Sue will be sticking close to them from now on.

32

Joyce

Have I ever spoken about Maureen Gilks? I suspect not, no offence to her. She lives in Ruskin Court. Her husband was in motorbikes, and she sometimes comes collecting for the British Heart Foundation shop.

I once gave her a blouse and when I was next in Fairhaven I saw it in the shop, which was a thrill. I sent a photo to Joanna but she just replied, 'Well what did you think they were going to do with it, Mum?' Anyway, next time I went down there it was gone, which was also lovely, though I had nothing to take a photo of that time.

Well, Maureen Gilks has a nephew called Daniel or David, and he is an actor. The way Maureen tells it, he is doing very well, though I haven't seen him in anything. Not even a *Morse*.

A couple of years ago now, this nephew had a hair transplant. Have you heard of them? I saw Doctor Ranj talking about them on *This Morning* once. They take hair from the back of your head and put it on the top of your head and hey presto, you're not going bald any more.

Apparently it worked an absolute treat and Daniel looks ten years younger, and there's no way you would ever know. This is all according to Maureen, by the way, so don't take my word for it.

Actually this is probably not where I should have started this diary entry, so let me backtrack a moment. I'm quite tired.

Douglas and Poppy are dead.

Elizabeth and I went to Hove, which, I have to say, was busier than I'd expected for a Tuesday. Does nobody go to work any more? Douglas had wanted to show Elizabeth something. We walked into a house on St Albans Avenue (near the King Alfred swimming pool?) and there they were, shot dead.

Douglas is fair game I think, but how awful about Poppy? I'm afraid it has left me very sad, even though I try not to get too sad these days.

She was in my living room three days ago. How unfair to die in your twenties with all that fun ahead of you. The kisses and the boat rides and the flowers and the new coats. Those poems she will never read to a new lover? You will go completely mad waiting for life to be fair, but whoever killed Poppy took something beautiful.

Poppy's mum, Siobhan, was supposed to visit today, and I was very worried that I was the one who was going to have to tell her about the murder. But as she's Poppy's next of kin she was told straight away, and is going down to identify the body, poor woman.

She sent me a message, and the message ended with emojis of a poppy and a daisy, which was very moving. I sent one back, telling her we would still like to see her, and I tried to add a poppy and a daisy to that too, but

I pressed the wrong thing and sent a poppy and a Christmas tree instead. I hope she will understand.

So we have two murders on our hands. Three if you count Andrew Hastings, but we already know who did that.

Every time I walk into a bedroom these days someone has been shot. I was going to plump up the pillows in the spare room earlier, but got cold feet.

I don't think we will be able to have fun with Sue and Lance the way we have fun with Chris and Donna and the Fairhaven police. It's a shame. I'm sure we'll try our best though. We often wear people down in the end.

Speaking of Lance, that's why I was talking about Maureen Gilks and her nephew! You can see that Lance's hair is thinning, and I kept thinking that I should mention hair transplants to him. You could tell he was exactly the sort of man whose hair was very important to him. I kept waiting for a lull in the conversation, or a bit of small talk, but the right moment didn't come. Every time there was a pause and I thought, Well, here goes, Sue would mention something about Poppy's gunshot wounds, or the blood, splattered behind Douglas's head. I simply didn't get the chance.

So I do hope I see Lance again, because it is best to catch these things as early as possible. That's what Maureen Gilks said. Let me quickly google her nephew.

OK, I'm back. Nothing. I tried *Daniel Gilks actor* and *David Gilks actor* and he was nowhere to be seen. So maybe I have his first name wrong. Also, he may not be a Gilks? So I don't know his first name or his surname, and I'm not good enough at Google to overcome that.

By the way, I messaged Nigella on Instagram about her sausages in black treacle. She has yet to reply, but I know she's here, there and everywhere, so she's forgiven. I also posted my first photo, just of the post box, and someone called @sparklyrockgirl replied 'nice pic' and followed me. So now I have a follower. We all have to start somewhere.

I wonder if Elizabeth is sad about Douglas? I've never had an ex-husband so I wouldn't know. I could see she didn't much like him, though Elizabeth doesn't much like most people, but she doesn't go around marrying them all. Douglas still loved her, you could see that. And he had her locket in his jacket, which was very touching.

So she must be sad. And she can't talk to Stephen about things any more, least of all this. At least I have Joanna to talk to. I will text her in the morning to tell her I've seen three corpses and been blindfolded and interrogated by MI5. Recently my gossip has been 'so and so has cataracts' or 'a fox got into the hen-house'. I hear her drifting, and I don't blame her.

I won't tell her about the twenty million, though. I don't know why. Well, I do know why – she will have an opinion, and I'm not in the mood for Joanna's opinions.

Imagine if we found the diamonds? I'm not saying that we will, I'm just saying imagine. Martin Lomax will probably find them, probably already has. Or MI5 will find them. Or the mafia.

But let's say, for one moment, that Elizabeth, Ron, Ibrahim and I find them. You never know with us.

That would be five million each.

What would I do with five million pounds, I wonder?

I need new patio doors, they're about fifteen thousand, though Ron knows someone who could do it for eight.

I could buy £14.99 wine instead of £8.99 wine, but would I notice the difference?

Give some money to Joanna? She already has plenty. I used to give her £20 when she went out with friends and her eyes would light up. I loved that. Would they light up the same way for a million pounds? Probably not. She'd probably put it in an ISA or something.

So I probably don't really need five million pounds, but, nonetheless, I'm sure I shall dream about it tonight. You would too, wouldn't you?

33

They had told her to pack a small suitcase, that she needed to come with them. It was already packed.

The officers would be expecting tears, but she couldn't make the tears come. Would they judge her? Would they think she didn't love Poppy? That she was a bad mother? Siobhan supposed that they had seen every sort of reaction possible in their time. She should just be herself. Whoever that was now.

The journey seemed long, but Siobhan couldn't sleep. The two officers talked a little in the car. Was she OK? No, not really. Did she need anything? If they meant a drink or a snack, then no, she didn't. Was she up to doing the identification tonight? Well, she honestly had no idea. They repeated their condolences a number of times, and she thanked them each time.

They reached Godalming just after midnight. Despite the lateness of the hour they passed a van on the long driveway. Travelling in the opposite direction, away from the house.

Sue Reardon and Lance James had introduced themselves. They were both polite, but then what alternative did they have? Sue was exactly as she had expected. Exactly the type she had pictured.

And now they are walking down a long corridor in a

building that must once have been stables. Lance is leading the way. You can see he doesn't know what to say. She would be the same.

Sue Reardon has slipped her arm through Siobhan's, which can't be standard procedure, but there was a time for standard procedure, and this was not it. Siobhan is grateful for the gesture. She knows what lies ahead. What must be done.

Lance takes out a key card and opens a large metal door, knocking on it as it opens. A blast of chill air bends around the door and into the corridor. Sue Reardon stops for a moment and looks Siobhan in the eyes.

'Are you ready?'

Siobhan nods.

'I'm here if you need me.'

Sue lets Siobhan walk into the room first, and she shivers as the cold air envelops her.

The room is small and functional. There are two long tables, and a shrouded figure lies on each. The figure on the left must be Poppy, because there is a doctor standing beside it. At least Siobhan assumes it's a doctor. She is wearing a white coat, and surgical gloves and a mask. She has kind eyes, and that almost makes Siobhan cry for the first time. She doesn't need kindness at the moment.

Lance rests against the far wall, a man in a room in which he does not want to be. Siobhan sees that he reflexively starts to rub his hands together for warmth, but thinks better of it, and plants them behind his back instead. Sue's hand is at her elbow.

'This is Doctor Carter, Siobhan.'

Doctor Carter nods at Siobhan, and Siobhan has to look away from the kind eyes.

'I'm afraid your daughter has traumatic injuries. I would ask you to prepare yourself.'

Siobhan nods. Here goes.

Doctor Carter pulls back the pale green sheet covering the body and, as the unruly blonde hair begins to spill out, Siobhan knows she has to shut a part of herself down. A part she may never get back.

There was little of the face left, but enough. Enough for a mother to tell her own daughter. Siobhan turns back to Sue and nods.

'It's Poppy.'

Siobhan starts to cry now. She knew it would come. Nobody should have to do this. Sue places a hand on her shoulder.

'Siobhan, I just need to ask you a couple of other questions. Because of the injuries. Any other distinguishing features you could tell us?'

Siobhan gulps in air. 'She has a long scar on the back of her left calf, barbed wire on the Isle of Wight. And her left wrist has a lump, she broke it playing hockey. And the stupid tattoo.'

Sue looks over to Doctor Carter, who nods.

'Thank you, Siobhan,' says Sue. 'Would you like to spend a bit more time here? No one is in a rush.'

Siobhan doesn't want to turn back to see the body lying there. She has seen enough. Has an image to last her until her dying day.

'Or we can go somewhere warm? Have a cup of tea?'

Siobhan nods through her tears. She turns back to the body. Doctor Carter has pulled the sheet back over Poppy's face. The blonde hair still peeks out. Siobhan gently reaches out her hand and strokes a loose strand.

Lance, Sue and Doctor Carter all stay quiet as Siobhan strokes the blonde hair and weeps.

Traumatic injuries, thinks Siobhan. Well, that's the truth.

Siobhan takes her hand away and Sue puts an arm around her.

'Let's get you out of here,' says Sue.

Siobhan looks over to the figure on the other table. 'And that's the other one? That's Douglas?'

'Yes,' says Sue. 'That's Douglas.'

'And some poor soul has to come in and identify him too?'

Sue shakes her head. 'Fortunately not. No next of kin. So fingerprints, dental records, whatever we have on file.'

'Well, God bless him, I suppose,' says Siobhan, and Sue leads her out of the room.

34

Elizabeth is rearranging some of the ornaments the MI5 team had misplaced during their search of the flat. She prefers everything in its place. The Delft fisherman Stephen had bought from a Bruges flea market, sitting next to Penny's police badge, sitting next to the shattered Soviet shell casing Elizabeth had dug from the radiator of her Triumph Herald after a misunderstanding in Prague in 1973. So many memories.

Her latest memento, Douglas's locket, is in her bag, and will be staying there.

Elizabeth was surprised that Sue had let her take it away. Surely it was evidence?

Though once they'd checked it for a hidden message, she supposes Sue thought it was harmless enough. It was kind of her to let Elizabeth keep it.

She hadn't seen it for thirty-odd years. Could barely remember it if she was honest. When Sue had taken it out, she had tried to remember what was inside it. A lock of hair? A picture of Douglas, smoking rakishly? But no, the mirror, of course.

When had he given it to her? Back in London, she thinks. An anniversary? Or had she caught Douglas cheating? Either way, he had bought her the locket. 'Not inexpensive,' he had revealed. And the mirror was purest flummery. 'It feels unfair,' he had said, 'that I have the benefit of looking at your beautiful face any time I wish. So I wanted you to see what I see.' Elizabeth had scoffed, she was sure of that, but nonetheless was touched.

She had left the locket behind when she had left Douglas behind, and had not thought of it since. Why on earth had he kept it? And why on earth had it been in his jacket when he died? Was this really what he wanted to show her? He was always one for a romantic gesture. Was this a final act of love?

The first thing she had done when she arrived home was, of course, to prise the mirror out with a screwdriver. There would be a hidden message behind it, she was sure of that. The location of the diamonds? Well, that really would be a final act of love, thank you, Douglas.

But there was nothing behind the mirror. No treasure map, no hidden code. So the locket was just a locket after all, and the act of love was just that, an act of love. Douglas never failed to surprise her.

Before she was loaded into the back of the van in Hove, Elizabeth had used Joyce's phone to message Bogdan. Without hesitation, Bogdan had come and looked after Stephen for the night. Had he cancelled something important? Elizabeth has no idea what Bogdan does when he is not at work. Clearly, he spends some time at the gym and at the tattooist but, other than that, he is a mystery.

Elizabeth is thinking about Martin Lomax. It is obvious that he killed Douglas and Poppy, surely? Too obvious? Perhaps they should just pop up to see him? If the secret wasn't in the locket, they were going to have to start their search somewhere.

Stephen is asleep and Bogdan is sitting patiently by the chess board.

'At first he was asleep, you know Stephen,' says Bogdan. 'But then they needed to search your room, so I woke him up.'

'And he was fine about it?' asks Elizabeth. She weighs up Penny's badge in her hand. Her most recent memento.

'Oh, he loved it,' says Bogdan. 'Asking what they are looking for, helping them to look, telling stories.'

'They tidied up very nicely,' says Elizabeth.

'Well, I had to help a bit,' says Bogdan. 'So, what were they looking for? Can you tell me?'

'They were looking for my phone. They wanted to see the message Douglas had sent me. But I'd taken some pictures of the corpses and I didn't want to lose them.' Elizabeth had filled Bogdan in on the deaths of Douglas and Poppy. Bogdan had nodded at length and said 'I see'.

'Yes, you never know when you might need pictures of corpses,' agrees Bogdan. 'But your phone isn't here? They looked in a lot of places.'

'No, it's behind a loose brick in a low wall outside 41 St Albans Avenue in Hove,' says Elizabeth. 'You wouldn't be a dear and go and fetch it for me later, would you?'

'Of course,' says Bogdan.

'And you'll remember the address?'

'Of course,' says Bogdan. 'I remember everything.'

'Thank you,' says Elizabeth.

'And I gave Ron the cocaine by the pier like you asked.'

'You really are a good sort, Bogdan,' says Elizabeth.

'He's a terrific sort,' says Stephen, waking, looking at the board and moving his bishop. 'Giving Ron cocaine by the pier. Quite right, too.'

Bogdan looks down at the board.

'Forgive me, boys,' says Elizabeth. 'I have a call to make. Bogdan, I'll also need you to drive me to meet an international money launderer today, if you're free?'

'I can be free for that,' says Bogdan.

She walks through to the bedroom. The bed is perfectly made. Given that Stephen had gone back to sleep after MI5 had been by, it could only have been made by Bogdan. She picks up the landline and dials Chris Hudson's number. He picks up on the fifth ring. Slow for him.

'DCI Chris Hudson.'

'Chris, it's Elizabeth. Just checking in on Ryan Baird? I wondered if there had been any developments in the case?'

'You wondered if perhaps we'd found cocaine and a bank card in his toilet?'

'That sort of thing.'

'He's been charged with possession with intent to supply, and robbery.'

'Well, isn't that opportune? You and Donna can tell us all about it tomorrow. There's wine at Joyce's.'

'Ah, I can't tomorrow, I'm working.'

'No, you're not, Chris, I checked.'

'How did you che— no, don't answer. OK, sorry, I'm busy tomorrow.'

Elizabeth hears a woman's voice in the background saying, 'Is that Elizabeth?' Well, well, well, this must be the mystery girlfriend. None of them liked to pry, of course, but it had been a month or so now, and they had yet to be introduced. Elizabeth thinks quickly. How to play this? Joyce will be furious if she doesn't get as much information as possible.

'Oh, that's fine, what are you up to, anything nice? Drinks with friends?'

'Just a quiet night . . . wait a moment.' Chris puts his hand over the mouthpiece and she hears him ask a muffled question. It sounds like, 'Are you sure?'

'Hello,' a female voice comes on the line. 'Is this Elizabeth?'

'This is Elizabeth, yes,' says Elizabeth. 'To whom am I speaking?'

'I'm Patrice, Chris's girlfriend. More lady friend, if I'm honest. What age does that change? I'm afraid Chris and I have plans for tomorrow. But another time, perhaps?'

'Well, another time would be lovely, Patrice, how nice to finally speak to you.'

'And you, Elizabeth, I have heard a lot about you.'

'Well, I wish I could say the same. But mystery is very important, isn't it?' Elizabeth is trying to place the accent. South London? It's a little like Donna's.

'Isn't it?' says Patrice. 'We might keep our mystery for a bit longer, if that's OK. Lovely to chat to you though.'

'And to you, dear. Say goodbye to Chris for me.'

'I will do. See you soon, I'm sure.'

Patrice puts the phone down and Elizabeth looks at

the handset for a moment. She has been put in her place, and she approves. This is exactly the sort of woman Chris needs in his life. And if she likes Chris, and if Chris likes her, then Elizabeth would like to meet her. Could Donna help, maybe? Persuade them both to come to Joyce's? Give Patrice a couple of glasses of wine, really get to know her?

Vetting, they used to call it in the Service.

Stephen pops his head round the door. 'A gang of your lot here last night, I meant to say. Spooks all over the place, after this, that or the other.'

'I know, sorry about that, dear.'

'Oh, not a bit of it. It was wonderful. Whatever they wanted, they didn't find it. I told them, "If Elizabeth doesn't want you to find something, you won't find it. Simple as that, don't waste your time, she could hide Christmas presents in a rowing boat." I didn't know where you'd gone, I thought the shops, but it was very late.'

'Joyce and I were up chatting.'

'I told them any time. Open door to spooks round here. What was it? Somebody murdered?'

'Two people murdered.'

'Spies?'

'Yes.'

'Wonderful. Now what was I doing, dear?'

'Playing chess with Bogdan.'

'Oh, good. He made me scrambled eggs. And he gave Ron cocaine. What a champ. I'll get back to him. I'll leave you to your murdered spies.'

Two murdered spies. Two murdered spies. Elizabeth picks up the phone and rings Chris Hudson again. This time it takes him even longer to answer. Seven rings. Just long enough for a whispered argument about whether to answer it. He obviously recognizes her landline now.

'Yes, Elizabeth,' says Chris.

'Oh, hello Chris,' says Elizabeth. 'I'm sorry, could you put Patrice on?'

'Patrice?'

'Yes, please, dear, no offence.'

There is a pause, a hand over the mouthpiece once again, and another muffled chat.

'Hello, Elizabeth,' says Patrice.

'Hello, dear, I'm sorry to bother you again. I don't know what you're doing tomorrow?'

'Agreed,' says Patrice.

'And I don't want to know, of course, your business. But I'm about to tell you something I haven't told Chris yet.'

'I'll give you thirty seconds, Elizabeth. I was being massaged.'

'Oh, good for Chris,' says Elizabeth. 'Here's my pitch, dear. Yesterday afternoon two spies were shot dead in a house in Hove. I was there. It won't be a police matter, it has gone straight to MI 5, but I would love to talk to Chris about it and get his take. And I just thought that, if you wanted to come over with him – perhaps tomorrow evening? – you sound the sort of person who might be interested in the details of two spies being murdered. I have pictures and everything, and there will be wine, and I know everyone would be thrilled to meet you. As I say, I don't know your plans.'

'Well, we were going to Zizzi's.'

Nearly got her, thinks Elizabeth. How to close the deal though?

'And one of the spies who was murdered just happened to be my ex-husband.'

'OK,' says Patrice. 'We'll bring a bottle.'

Elizabeth hears Patrice call away from the phone, 'We're seeing Elizabeth tomorrow, babes,' and hears Chris reply, 'Well, of course we are.'

'Shall we say six thirty?' says Elizabeth. 'And could you ask Chris to invite Donna, too?'

'Donna?' asks Patrice.

'Yes, wouldn't be the same without her. I'm assuming you've met Donna?'

'Oh yes, I've met Donna,' says Patrice. 'Once or twice.'

'See you tomorrow, dear,' says Elizabeth, and puts down the phone. So Patrice has already met Donna? Must be serious.

Right, on to Martin Lomax.

35

Martin Lomax takes the tray of coffee and biscuits down to his home cinema. Twenty leather seats all angled towards the screen, which takes up an entire wall. The most people he has ever had in here was four, when the Azerbaijani cup final coincided with a particularly profitable heroin deal. Martin Lomax had brought them down nibbles and everybody seemed to have a good time. Lomax didn't really understand much about having a good time, but he was good at blending in and not spoiling things for other people. When there was money to be made, at least.

He points the remote control at the screen and brings up his library of movies. Martin Lomax can't see the point in films at all. It's just some people acting, how could everyone not see that? Someone writes some words, some idiots from America say them and it seems to send everybody cuckoo. Lomax had gone to the theatre once, and that seemed marginally better. At least the actors were there. At least you could talk to them when you disagreed. He had been asked to leave, but he certainly wouldn't rule out going again one day.

He scrolls past countless films he will never watch, although he knows lots of the titles by now. He finally reaches another film he will never watch. It is called *The*

Treasure of the Sierra Madre and you can tell by the picture that it is black and white. Black and white? People really were fools. He selects the film and then navigates down through the menu until he finds 'Subtitles'. A list of languages appears, and Martin Lomax scrolls down until he finds 'Cantonese'. He selects it. He immediately hears those three familiar electronic beeps, and the cinema screen disappears up into the ceiling. Painted on the wall behind is a rainbow. Martin Lomax places his fingertips at either end of the rainbow. There are three more electronic beeps and a door slides open. Martin Lomax picks up his tray and walks into the vault.

Martin Lomax often likes to have his coffee and biscuits in the vault. It is lovely and cool so as not to damage any of the banknotes, or the priceless paintings that are rolled up against the far wall. He has just received his first Banksy, and he is unimpressed. It is a rat looking at a mobile phone. Why would a rat be looking at a mobile phone? Modern art is beyond Lomax, but he bets that Banksy would be delighted to know his work was now valuable enough to be used as a down payment on an international arms deal. The man who had dropped it off, a Chechen, had said that Banksy's real name was a secret, but he told him what it was, regardless. Lomax has already forgotten it. Art was a racket; give him gold any day of the week. You didn't have to understand gold.

The vault is also very quiet, thanks to the six-foot-thick walls surrounding him. You could easily kill someone in here and, in fact, that did happen once. It caused quite a kerfuffle at the time.

Lomax dunks a chocolate-chip cookie in his coffee. The Open Garden week starts today. What will people think of the grounds? Too ornate, too cultivated? Not cultivated enough? Would it rain? Google says there is a zero per cent chance, but how could it possibly know? Would people come? Would they buy his brownies? Would anybody try and get into the house? They would soon discover it was impossible, but what if they got close enough to see all the lasers and the tiny cameras in the hanging baskets? He will leave a comments book outside the pagoda, and he can spend Monday looking through it. Will people write their names? Perhaps he will leave a space for people's addresses too. If anyone leaves an unpleasant comment he can send someone to pay them a visit.

Lomax sips at his coffee, noticing a couple of cookie crumbs floating on the surface. The coffee is Colombian, as was the man who was shot in the vault with a bolt gun that time. The man's boss – who had done the shooting, and presumably had his own reasons – had asked Lomax if he might bury the body in the gardens, but Lomax had quite enough buried there already, and so had politely said no. The boss had been understanding, and Lomax had helped drag the body out to his helicopter by way of an apology.

If Lomax sells all of his brownies then he thinks he will be able to raise seventy pounds. He wonders what he will spend it on.

On the whole, Martin Lomax enjoys his job. It is lucrative, and while money isn't everything – far from it – Martin

Lomax has been poor and he's been rich, and he prefers rich. There is variety, no two days are the same, and that is psychologically healthy. One day will run smoothly, you'll return some gold bullion to a Bulgarian and everyone is smiles and handshakes, then the next day there's a car bomb in Kabul and person Y is cutting off person X's fingers, and everyone wants their money or their paintings or their racehorse, and Martin Lomax is rushed off his feet. It certainly keeps his mind active. Best of all, though, he gets to work from home. Everyone knows that. Martin Lomax won't come to Monte Carlo or Beirut or Qatar or Buenos Aires. Martin Lomax won't even travel to the Winchester M&S if he can avoid it. No, you come to Martin Lomax, whether you're a warlord, whether you're a trafficker, or whether you're Ocado.

But sometimes — not often, touch wood — the job is stressful, and this is one of those times. He flips open his laptop and rings the number he has been sent on his encrypted phone. Frank Andrade Jr, the second-in-command of one of New York's leading crime families. Lomax knows that if the conversation goes badly, the next person he will be speaking to is Frank's father. Who, from memory, is also called Frank. And if that happens, then Martin Lomax really would have to travel. Probably against his will, in the hold of a private jet.

The Americans want to know what has happened to their twenty million pounds' worth of diamonds. Of course they do, that's natural. Martin Lomax doesn't suppose the value matters all that much to them — they can afford to misplace the odd twenty million every now and again – it is more the issue of trust. Martin Lomax has provided an invaluable service for a long time now, and he has provided it with skill and discretion. He has been a well-oiled cog in the wheels of these huge organizations, beyond reproach and above suspicion. But now?

Andrade's face fills the screen, suddenly, and he immediately begins to remonstrate with Lomax, his arms windmilling. He brings a fist down on his New York desk.

'Frank, you're on mute, I think,' says Martin Lomax. 'You need to click on the little microphone. The green button.'

Frank Andrade leans into his screen, mouth open and eyes scanning for the button. He presses it.

'Can you hear me?'

'That's perfect, Frank,' says Martin Lomax. 'What were you saying? When you were banging your fist on the desk?'

'Ah, nothing,' says Frank. It always disappoints Martin Lomax that Frank doesn't have a thick New York accent like in the films. He just sounds like a normal American. 'I was just creating a mood.'

'No need to create anything with me, Frank,' says Martin Lomax.

'Listen, Lomax,' says Frank. 'I like you, you know that. My dad likes you. You're English, we respect that.'

'I sense a "but" coming, Frank,' says Martin Lomax.

'Well, sure,' says Frank. 'If we don't have our diamonds back by the end of next week, we'll kill you.'

'OK,' says Martin Lomax.

'Maybe you stole them, maybe you didn't, we'll deal with that another day. But I will fly over to see you, and if you don't have them then we will conclude our business with you.'

Martin Lomax nods. This and worrying if everyone will be able to park later. What a day!

'I will do it myself,' says Frank. 'It'll be quick, I promise you that. That's the least I can do.'

'Do you never get tired of all this?' says Martin Lomax. 'You know I didn't steal them, but there always has to be melodrama. I know you have a boss, but really, you should listen to yourself sometimes. You don't always have to kill everyone, Frank. Douglas Middlemiss stole the diamonds from me . . .'

'You say,' says Frank.

'Yes, I say,' says Martin Lomax. 'And you've worked with me long enough to trust me when I do. I am tracking him down as I speak, and soon I will have news for you.'

'I don't need news, Martin, I need the diamonds, and I need them the second I see you. Or . . .'

'Or you'll kill me, yes,' says Martin Lomax. 'I've got it. Nice and quickly as a mark of respect.'

'Get my diamonds,' says Frank.

'Right you are,' says Martin Lomax. 'Love to Claudia and the kids.'

Frank shouts off camera, then returns to the microphone. 'Claudia says hi back. See you soon, Martin.'

36

When Bogdan was ten years old, his friends had dared him to jump off a bridge. The drop was, perhaps, forty feet, straight into a fast-flowing, rocky river. A boy had died a few years before making the same jump. For a while the local authorities had put barbed wire along the parapet to stop anyone being quite so foolish again. But by this time the barbed wire had rusted and buckled and fallen into the river below. No one had thought to replace it, because money was tight and memories were short. Also, the boy's mother had killed herself shortly after-wards, so it very quickly began to feel like the whole thing hadn't happened at all.

Bogdan remembers looking over the side of the bridge, down to the furious white water and the jagged grey of the rocks. There were three main ways he could die if he jumped. The simple impact of his body on the water from this height might kill him instantly. He could easily avoid the rocks he could see, but there were plenty of rocks hidden just below the surface, and if he struck one of them he would die for certain. And if he avoided both of those deaths? Well, the current was fierce and unforgiving, and he would need strength and luck to make it to either bank.

His classmates were goading him, calling him *tchórz*, a

polecat, which is what they called being chicken over here. But Bogdan wasn't listening, he was staring at the drop. What would it feel like? Flying through the air? He bet it would feel pretty good.

Bogdan knew, even back then, that he was not an especially brave person, and he certainly wasn't fool-hardy. No one would ever accuse him of that. Bogdan is not a risk taker; he is never driven by testosterone or by insecurity. Nonetheless, he remembers taking off his sweater, one his mum had knitted him, and climbing onto the parapet, to the horror of his suddenly fright-ened friends.

It was a long way down.

'Do I present the football?' asks Ron from the back seat. Bogdan is suddenly brought back to the here and now. Driving Elizabeth, Joyce and Ron to visit an inter-national criminal.

'No,' says Elizabeth.

They hadn't been able to agree on a radio station, and so they were playing Twenty Questions, trying to guess the identity of famous people. Ron had guessed Joyce's one, Noel Edmonds, after getting a 'yes' to the question 'Do I shout at the TV when he comes on?' They are cur-rently at a dead end trying to guess Elizabeth's.

'Am I . . . who's the man I'm thinking of, the actor?' says Joyce.

'No,' says Elizabeth.

'Can we give up?' says Ron.

'You'll kick yourself,' says Elizabeth.

'Go on,' says Ron.

'I was the murdered Russian oligarch Boris Berezovsky,' says Elizabeth.

'Oh,' says Ron.

'Denzel Washington!' says Joyce. 'That's who I was thinking of.'

Bogdan has a bag of sweets, and every twelve minutes he passes them round, because he knows it will keep everyone quiet. He also knows he won't need to save any sweets for the journey home later, because these three will be fast asleep.

They had talked a little about the murders. Ron thinks that Douglas and Poppy were killed by the mafia. He asked Bogdan if he had ever seen *Goodfellas* and Bogdan agreed that he had, and Ron said, 'Well then.' Joyce thinks that some doctor is involved somehow, and Joyce is usually right. Although, Bogdan thinks, looking down at the friendship bracelet on his wrist, she can't knit.

What does Elizabeth think? Who knows? She will wait until she's spoken to this Martin Lomax.

Bogdan would have driven much faster if it was just him. But the combination of Ron's Daihatsu and Bogdan's respect for his passengers meant he kept to a steady eighty miles an hour the whole way. Elizabeth would occasionally tell him to put his foot on it, and then Ron would say, 'Slow down a bit, Bogdan, this isn't Poland.' Which suggested he had got it about right.

He sees the signs for Hambledon at around one thirty. As he knew he would. Not satnav either, he refuses to use them. Bogdan turns right or left when Bogdan chooses to turn left or right. You don't need to tell Bogdan that he's approaching a roundabout.

Hambledon is a pretty English village, though as they drive through Bogdan spots a few roofs that could do with a bit of attention.

'This is where the first-ever game of cricket was played,' says Elizabeth.

'Probably still going on, knowing cricket,' says Ron.

They pass a primary school, a pub called The Bat and Ball and even a sign to a vineyard before the first signs to Martin Lomax's 'Open Garden' appear. Soon they reach a broad entrance off a small country lane, iron gates wide open, and welcome notices nailed to trees. Bogdan drives in and parks next to a hedge the size of a house.

As ever, it is taking his three passengers a while to 'get their things together'.

'I see you back here, OK?' says Bogdan. 'You take as long as you want.'

'Thank you, dear,' says Elizabeth. 'It is very unlikely we're about to be murdered, but if we're not back in two hours then come looking for us, and kick up a fuss.'

'Gotcha,' says Bogdan, and checks his watch. Saying 'Gotcha' always makes him feel very English.

'And the leaflet says there's loos, if you need,' says Joyce, zipping up an anorak and manoeuvring her way out of the car.

'I won't need the toilet,' says Bogdan.

'Lucky sod,' says Ron.

And with that they are gone, and there is blessed silence.

Bogdan thinks back to the parapet and the raging river. His friends were begging him not to jump. The sweater his mother had made was yellow, and he sees it now, neatly folded up beside him. He was always good with creases.

He took one last look down. Three ways to die, sure, but we all die someday. To the screams of his friends, Bogdan jumped.

What a feeling, just magical.

He broke three ribs, but they soon healed. It was the right choice, as he had known it would be.

People love to sleep, and yet they are so frightened of death. Bogdan has never understood it.

37

Joyce

What a long day. We've just got back from seeing Martin Lomax and now there's this meeting at Ibrahim's to go to.

Luckily, I slept all the way back. I woke up with my head on Ron's shoulder. He has a reassuring shoulder, though no one will hear that from me.

Lomax was not what you would expect at all. Or not what I would expect at all. If you met him in the street, you would think he was a solicitor, or a man who owns a dry cleaner's, but doesn't work in it. I would say I found him attractive, except he turned out to be a bit boring, and I can't find boring men attractive. Believe me, I've tried. Wouldn't it make life simpler?

Although perhaps he isn't really boring, if everything you hear is true? Killings and gold, and helicopters and whatnot? Though if you need killings and gold and helicopters to make you interesting then I suppose you are still boring at heart. Gerry never needed a helicopter.

And, regardless, I wouldn't date somebody who killed people.

But all I'm saying is that he looked a bit like Blake Carrington, so don't blame a girl for looking.

Elizabeth was on to him in a heartbeat, of course. Oh,

you must be Mr Lomax, what beautiful gardens, what a beautiful house, is that a pagoda, have you been to Japan, Mr Lomax, you must, you simply must. She is a terrible flirt.

Poor Martin Lomax looked half scared to death, though perhaps that was the point?

Ron was next up. He nodded to the house and said, 'How much did that set you back?' Lomax had no answer, and when Ron added, 'You've got effing turrets, mate, effing turrets,' Lomax pretended to see someone in the crowd and said he must be off.

Elizabeth linked her arm into his and said, 'Well, let's walk together, what a day, glorious,' and Lomax tried, very politely, to shake her off. But no such luck for him.

Elizabeth wondered if she might ask him a few questions, and Lomax said everything she needed to know about the gardens was in the leaflet we'd picked up at the entrance. And Elizabeth said, 'Well, I doubt very much the information I need to know is in the leaflet, I doubt that very much indeed, Mr Lomax.'

Slight worry crossed his face at this point. People really don't buy that Elizabeth is a harmless old woman for very long. With me it lasts much longer, but Elizabeth doesn't have that gift. So Lomax wrenched himself away and said he wished Elizabeth good day and he had plants to attend to.

Elizabeth let him get a couple of metres away before saying, quite quietly, 'I just wondered, before you're far enough away that I have to raise my voice, did you kill Douglas and Poppy yourself, or did you send someone else to do it again?'

Well, that got his attention all right. He turned – and honestly he really does look a bit like Blake Carrington – and he said, 'Who are you?' and Elizabeth said, 'Wouldn't you like to know?' and told him they really should chat, because they were both looking for the same thing.

'And what are you looking for?' he asked, and Elizabeth said, 'Let's talk about that, shall we?'

So, arm in arm, she led Martin Lomax away from the crowds, and around to the side of the house, and introduced herself, and me and Ron. Bogdan had driven us, but he stayed in the car. He is learning Arabic from a tape.

Elizabeth asked Lomax if Douglas had told him where the diamonds were before he'd shot him, and Lomax said he had no idea what she was talking about, and Elizabeth rolled her eyes and said, 'Look, let's just be honest with each other, we're both old hands.'

I felt I should say something. I don't know why, it just seemed about time, so I said, 'We were very fond of Poppy,' and he said, 'Who's Poppy?' and I said, 'She shot your friend Andrew, remember? And then you shot her, yesterday.'

At this you could sort of see he gave up. Perhaps I don't seem harmless any more? That will be annoying if it turns out to be the case.

He confronted Elizabeth and said I don't know who sent you, and she said we sent ourselves, and he looked at us and said he could believe that. Then he said, 'Cards on the table, can I trust you?' and Elizabeth said, 'Not really, but if you didn't kill Douglas, and if you want your diamonds back, we're probably the best bet you've got.' And then he told his story.

Yes, the diamonds had been real, and yes, they had been stolen. I think we all knew and agreed on this point already. Yes, he had found out Douglas was responsible, and yes, he had threatened him. Ron said, 'I would have done too, to be fair,' and Lomax thanked him for that.

You could smell the last of the honeysuckle in the air; it climbs up the side of the house. A west-facing wall is best for it, I learned that on *Gardeners' Question Time*. Gerry was the gardener in the family, not me, but I still listen to it because it reminds me of him.

Lomax then admitted that he had sent Andrew Hastings to Coopers Chase. The way he told it, he had just wanted to give Douglas a scare. To force Douglas to tell him where the diamonds were. Then Poppy stepped in, shot Andrew Hastings, and Lomax was left a man down and none the wiser.

Elizabeth asked how he knew they were at Coopers Chase, and Lomax said that MI5 were very leaky, and I asked Elizabeth if that was true and she said it certainly used to be.

Poppy and Douglas were then whisked away, and Martin Lomax said he had no idea where to, so had given up the chase. Elizabeth asked if he hadn't tried MI5 again, and he said of course he had, but no information was forthcoming. Presumably far fewer people knew about the new safe house.

Lomax then asked if we knew where the diamonds were, and we confirmed that we didn't. And then he said he was likely to be driven out to sea and shot dead if they didn't turn up sharpish. And you could tell that was the truth.

This is my point about boring men and exciting men. Gerry would never be driven out to sea and shot, but he was a hundred times more exciting than this Lomax. And Gerry didn't look like Blake Carrington, but perhaps if he had then he might not have ended up with me? Which is not a thought I'm comfortable entertaining. In certain lights he looked like Richard Briers though.

Ron asked if he could use the toilet, and Lomax said there was one in the stables, and Ron said couldn't he use one in the house, and Lomax said no chance. Nice try, Ron. I don't think he wanted to go snooping or anything, I think he just really needed the loo.

Elizabeth gave Martin Lomax her card (when did Elizabeth get a card? She kept that quiet) and told him that if what he said was true then we had a shared interest in finding the killer. Lomax agreed, and Elizabeth said to ring her if anything cropped up, and she would do the same in return.

I took my chance and went into my bag and pulled out a friendship bracelet. Lomax looked horrified, which I am getting used to, but I explained it was for charity, and Elizabeth assured him I wouldn't leave until he'd bought one. I had one that was gold and green and I thought quickly and said the green was for the garden and the gold was for the sun. I was going to say that the sequins represented the diamonds, but I decided not to push my luck.

I asked him which charity he wanted his money to go to, and he shrugged, and I said to just pick a favourite charity. He said he didn't have one, and asked who people normally gave the money to and, because I was standing with Elizabeth, I suggested Living With Dementia. Then he asked me how much they were and I told him that was up to him, and he didn't seem to understand that, and I said, you just give what you can afford. I was looking at the house when I said that.

He nodded, reached into his jacket and pulled out a cheque book. A cheque book! Even I don't use cheques any more, and I'm seventy-seven. He wrote his amount on the cheque, then folded it up. He handed me the folded cheque and I handed him the bracelet.

He seemed meek as a lamb at that point. But then he said, 'Are you all finished?' and when we said we were, he looked at each of us in turn, like a butcher sizing up a cow. It was quite unnerving.

'I bet they all lap it up, don't they?' he said. 'The three of you. Harmless little gang. The police, MI5, they buy this act?' Elizabeth agreed that people do seem to buy it, yes, and Martin Lomax nodded and said, 'Doesn't work with me, I'm afraid. I don't care if you're eighteen or eighty. I'll kill you regardless. You understand that, don't you?'

It was quite frightening, if I'm being honest. I have to remind myself sometimes that this is not a game.

Elizabeth said that of course we understood, and that he was being 'admirably unambiguous'.

Then Lomax said, 'Charm doesn't work on me,' and

Ron said, 'More power to you,' and then Lomax said, 'If you find my diamonds, and you don't bring them straight to me, I will kill you. If you even *suspect* where they are without telling me, I will kill you.'

He doesn't hold back, I will say that for him. In a way it's refreshing, because at least we know where we stand.

Then he said he would kill us one by one. He pointed at Ron and said he would start with him. Ron gave us an 'it's always me' gesture. And he's right, it always is.

'We'll be sure to let you know then,' Elizabeth said. 'If we find them.'

And this is how it ended. Lomax said, 'I don't *want* to kill you.' Ron said, 'Sure.' Lomax said, 'But I will, without a second thought,' and Elizabeth said, 'Message received and understood.'

By this time Ron really, really needed the toilet, so we said our goodbyes.

We did actually have a quick turn around the garden after that, because it was very lovely, and then Bogdan drove us home. I asked him to do some Arabic on us, which he did. Just one to ten.

Elizabeth believes Lomax, that he didn't kill Douglas and Poppy. I told her I thought he was unconvincing and she said well, that was just the thing. Liars like Lomax always sound at their most unconvincing when they're telling the truth. They're simply not used to it.

So who did kill them? She has a theory, and she has invited Sue Reardon down to the village to test it out. I know not to ask by now.

By the way, earlier, when I said Elizabeth is a terrible

flirt, I didn't mean she's a terrible flirt like I'm a terrible flirt. I mean that when she flirts she's terrible at it. Really all over the place. I like to see things Elizabeth is bad at. There aren't many, but at least it levels the playing field a bit for the rest of us.

As I say, we slept all the way home, so it wasn't until I got in that I remembered the cheque, and got excited.

I opened it up and it said 'five pounds only'. Well, thank you ever so much, Martin Lomax; lucky old Living With Dementia.

38

Ibrahim had suggested they hold the evening at his place. He feels pressured at the moment to get out of the flat. To do things. Ron has suggested they go for 'a walk' sometime. Ron! They are worried about him, and Ibrahim isn't enjoying the feeling. Ibrahim likes to be no trouble. Ibrahim feels like he is beginning to melt away and, right now, that's fine by him.

'Do you know I have a theory?' says Elizabeth, already three glasses of wine to the good.

'You surprise me, Elizabeth,' says Sue Reardon. Sue has a glass of wine too, despite this, officially speaking, being business for her. Perhaps she is oiling the wheels? She will be no match for Elizabeth, regardless.

'Some people in life, Sue, are weather forecasters, whereas other people are the weather itself.'

Elizabeth had rung Sue on the way back from Hambledon, and wondered if she might be free to pop over for a chat? Sue had been delighted to, and had driven straight down. Ibrahim had ordered in Domino's pizza.

'My favourite weather forecaster is Carol Kirkwood on the BBC,' says Joyce. 'I always think we'd get on.'

Joyce had popped round half an hour before the rest, and she and Ibrahim had looked at dogs on the internet. Joyce is on Instagram now too, and was trying to engage him in that. He was losing interest, but then Joyce showed him some videos of a woman solving cryptic crosswords.

'The weather forecasters,' continues Elizabeth, 'and here that's me and Ibrahim, we always have our fingers in the air trying to feel which way the wind is blowing. We never want to be surprised or caught out.'

True, thinks Ibrahim.

'You'll feel the way my wind is blowing in a minute,' says Ron, lounging back on one of Ibrahim's armchairs, finishing a slice of pizza before dunking a chocolate digestive into his red wine.

'Whereas Joyce and Ron, you are the weather,' says Elizabeth. 'You move as you choose, you act as you feel. You make things happen without fannying around worrying about what those things might be.'

'You can't predict things,' says Ron. 'Why try?'

'But you can predict things,' says Ibrahim. 'The tides, the seasons, nightfall, daybreak. Earthquakes.'

'None of that is people, though, mate,' says Ron. 'You can't predict people. Like you can guess what they'll say next, but that's about it.'

Ibrahim is back in the gutter for a moment, tasting blood. He tries to shake it off.

'There's no point overthinking anything,' says Joyce. 'I agree with Ron.'

'Well, of course you agree with Ron,' says Elizabeth, finishing her glass. 'The two of you are peas in a pod.'

'How many times do you ring me, Elizabeth, first thing in the morning, and say, "Joyce, we're going to Folkestone," or, "Joyce, we're going to an MI5 safe house"? "Joyce, pack a flask, we're going to London"?'

'A lot,' admits Elizabeth.

'And do I ever ask why?'

'Well, there's no point, darling, I would never tell you.'

'So I just pack my bits and bobs, look up the train times and off we go. I always know it's going to be fun. No overthinking.'

'Yes, but it's always fun because I plan it,' says Elizabeth. 'You just have to worry about whether to put on a big coat.'

Ibrahim sees Sue risk a peek at her watch. When are they going to get to the good stuff? That's what she's thinking. What does Elizabeth know? Does she know where the diamonds are? That's why Sue had driven down through the dusk. Good luck to you, Sue.

'Let me tell you this,' says Elizabeth to the room, clearly not planning to talk about diamonds any time soon. 'The first trip I ever went on with Stephen was to Venice. He wanted to look at the art and the churches for a weekend, and I wanted to look at him for a weekend.'

'That's romantic,' says Joyce.

'Looking at a man you love isn't romantic, Joyce,' says Elizabeth. 'It's just the sensible thing to do. Like watching a television programme you like.'

Ibrahim nods.

'Anyway, on the way over Stephen had said, let's do the whole weekend without guide books, let's just wander, let's get lost, let's turn a corner and see magic we didn't know was there.'

'OK, well, *that* is romantic,' says Joyce.

'No, that's not romantic either, that's deeply inefficient,' says Elizabeth.

'Agreed,' says Ibrahim. Look where spontaneity has got him.

'I know Stephen. I know Stephen won't be happy unless he sees Tintoretto's *Golden Calf*, and Bellini's altarpiece at the San Zaccaria. Unless he finds a beautiful hidden bar serving cicchetti and spritzers to locals. He doesn't want to turn left and find a local government office, or turn right and find an alleyway full of heroin addicts who steal his watch.'

'I'm sure that wouldn't happen,' says Joyce.

'Well, of course it wouldn't happen,' says Elizabeth. 'Because I'd spent the previous two weeks studying every guide book under the sun. So off we strolled, arm in arm, wandering aimlessly, me with a perfect map in my head, and we were lucky enough to stumble across the San Francesco della Vigna, what a pleasant surprise! And then we were fortunate to pass in front of a beautiful little bar I'd seen Rick Stein in on BBC2 . . .'

'Ooh, I like Rick Stein,' says Joyce. 'I don't like seafood, but I do like him.'

'And then, lo and behold, we turned a corner and found ourselves in the Madonna dell'Orto, and we're up to our ears in Tintorettos and Bellinis. It was the perfect trip and, as far as Stephen was concerned, the whole weekend was one magical accident. And that's because he is the weather, and I am the weather forecaster. He believes in fate, while I *am* fate.'

'Gerry and I never used to plan our weekends away,' says Joyce. 'And we always had a wonderful time.'

'That's because Gerry planned them and never told you,' says Elizabeth. 'Because things are more fun for you when they're not planned, and they were more fun for him when they were planned. It's best to have one of each in every relationship.'

'That's not true,' says Ron. 'Marlee and me were both weather.'

'You got divorced twenty years ago, Ron,' says Ibrahim.

'True,' says Ron, raising his glass a touch.

'I don't wish to be a party pooper,' says Sue Reardon. 'But are you going somewhere with this, Elizabeth?'

She is trying to hurry things along a bit, thinks Ibrahim. But Elizabeth will go at her own pace.

'Why would I be going somewhere with it?' asks Elizabeth.

'Because you asked me down here this evening. And now you've taken me by the hand, you've led me left and right. And I just wondered, where are we going? What's around the next corner? Why do I feel I'm being led into an alleyway full of heroin addicts?'

'Well, you're not,' says Elizabeth. 'You're eating pizza in a room full of doddery pensioners, what harm could possibly come to you? I was only making conversation.'

Joyce snorts, and she and Ron roll their eyes at each other.

'Out with it,' says Sue.

'Well, it really is nothing, except, we went to see Martin Lomax today.'

'Did you now?'

'I'm afraid so, yes,' says Elizabeth. 'And we are minded to think he didn't kill Douglas and Poppy.'

'I see,' says Sue.

'Although I wasn't there,' says Ibrahim. 'On account of my bruising. I would love to have been otherwise.'

You liar. He didn't want to go out. He didn't want to stay in. What was left for him? He was enjoying this evening, at least.

'And it all started me thinking about Douglas in a little more detail. I don't know if you knew him all that well?'

'Well enough,' says Sue.

Elizabeth nods. 'Well, you would think he was the weather, wouldn't you? The way he just blows through people's lives. Having affairs and divorcing people, left, right and centre. But he's not. Douglas was a weather forecaster. Douglas planned everything. If Douglas sent me a message saying he had something to show me, then he had something to show me. And if he was going to show me it at five, he'd be damned sure he was still alive at five. Douglas was very, very careful with words.'

'What are you saying?' says Sue.

'I'm saying, what if Douglas showed me exactly what he wanted to show me? He wanted me to see his dead body?'

'Just like Marcus Carmichael,' says Joyce.

'Who's Marcus Carmichael?' asks Ibrahim.

'Well, quite,' says Elizabeth, wiping orange fingers on a white serviette. 'Sue, can I ask you something? I imagine you'll have thought of it already, but regardless?'

'Anything you like,' says Sue. 'Who is Marcus Carmichael?'

'Look him up, there'll be a file,' says Elizabeth. 'How was Douglas's body identified?'

'Oh, here we go,' says Ron, and takes a swig of his red. 'I knew you had something up your sleeve.'

'Meaning, was the body definitely Douglas?' asks Sue.

'Meaning precisely that,' says Elizabeth.

'You think he faked the whole thing, and took off with the diamonds?' says Ron.

'I think it's a possibility,' says Elizabeth.

'You must have faked some deaths over the years, Sue?' says Joyce.

'One or two,' agrees Sue. 'Douglas was wearing the clothes he was last seen in, he had his wallet, all his cards and so on, but of course he would.'

'Of course,' says Elizabeth.

'But these days it's all done on DNA matches if there's no next of kin. The doctor took a swab, the lab matched it to his file. It was Douglas.'

Elizabeth drinks and thinks. Eventually she nods. 'Those two statements don't follow, Sue, you know that. If Douglas had a plan, he had a plan. If he needed the DNA to match then it would.'

'True,' agrees Sue.

'So who there could have tampered with the DNA? Anyone?'

Sue thinks. 'I could have done, Lance could have done, at a push, the doctor could have done – she wasn't our usual, but she's very experienced. I suppose someone in the lab? We do it all on-site now.'

'Forty years of nursing teaches you it's always the doctor,' says Joyce, reaching for the white wine to top up her glass.

'So it's possible it's not Douglas?' asks Elizabeth.

'It's possible, yes. It would take an unlikely chain of events, but it's possible,' says Sue.

'But that's what good plans are, isn't it?' says Elizabeth. 'A trail of events so unlikely it throws you off the scent. Who would go to all that trouble? That's how I would get away with something, that's how you would get away with something, and that's how Douglas would get away with something. Make it . . . complicated.'

'He was probably having an affair with the doctor,' says Joyce. 'He had affairs with everyone, Sue. No offence, Elizabeth.'

Sue drums her fingers. 'OK, let's say for a moment that you're right, Elizabeth.'

'That usually saves time,' says Ron.

'Why would Douglas want you to see the whole thing? To see his body? If I was faking my own death, I'd keep you as far away from the scene as I could.'

'I agree with Sue here,' says Ibrahim. 'You would be the first to work it out.'

'Something to do with the diamonds?' asks Sue. 'He needed your help with them?'

'Who knows?' shrugs Elizabeth. 'Although if I'm right that he is still alive, then he didn't *need* my help, he *needs* my help.'

Sue nods.

'Joanna has bought me Netflix,' says Joyce, finishing her last slice of pizza. Where does she put it all, Ibrahim wonders. 'There's all sorts on it, but I can't work out what's on when. It doesn't have the times anywhere.'

'And will you help him?' Sue asks Elizabeth.

'No,' says Elizabeth. 'I will try to find the diamonds, of course, but Douglas is on his own, I'm afraid. Don't you agree? If he's done what I think he's done? If he killed poor Poppy, and faked his own death?'

'That's a big "if",' says Ron.

'I do agree,' says Sue. 'So, if you're right, then what? He's left you a clue? I know you wanted to look inside that locket we gave you. But something less obvious than the locket? Some*where* less obvious?'

'I mean, who knows?' says Elizabeth. 'But, yes, I am working on that assumption. I wanted to make sure you didn't think my theory was too outlandish first.'

'It's outlandish,' says Sue. 'But there's no such thing as too outlandish in this job. I'm going to head straight back and have a quiet look into the process, without ringing any alarm bells. I can keep the investigation ticking along for a few days, while we have a think about all this.'

'I think Douglas has hidden the diamonds some-where,' says Elizabeth. 'And I know at some point he has told me exactly where. I just have to remember how and when he told me.'

'Then we both have a job to do,' says Sue. 'I can probably buy you about three days.'

'I still say the mafia and Lomax did it,' says Ron. 'Size of that geezer's house.'

'I still say the doctor,' says Joyce.

'Do you know,' says Sue, 'if you'd told me three months ago I'd be working with Elizabeth Best, I would never have believed you. And now here we are.'

Joyce reaches for a bottle and refills Sue's glass. 'Welcome to the Thursday Murder Club!'

They clink glasses. The rest of the evening passes very pleasantly. A few war stories are told, Sue changing names and dates where necessary and Elizabeth not bothering to. Sue is wearing the friendship bracelet Joyce had given her – always good to curry favour when you're looking for information, Ibrahim supposes. Joyce gives Sue an envelope to give to Lance. Eventually, Sue yawns the yawn of someone looking to leave.

'You'll tell me if something occurs to you?' asks Sue.

Elizabeth nods vigorously. 'You'll be the first to know when I do. He might want me to help him, but, on the whole, I would rather catch him.'

Douglas faking his death? Ibrahim likes the theory. He can see that Sue does too. It was implausible, but possible. The perfect combination.

'Right, I'll be making tracks,' Sue says. 'You know where I am.'

'And look into the doctor, please,' says Joyce.

'I will,' says Sue.

As Sue leaves, the four friends settle again. Wine glasses are refilled. Ron nips to the loo.

'Talking to Sue was a good thing to do,' says Ibrahim to Elizabeth. 'I know you usually like to keep these things close to your chest.'

'I needed to hear about the identification process,' says Elizabeth. 'See if it was watertight. And it wasn't.'

'Ooh, she reminds me of you,' says Joyce. 'Twenty years younger, no offence.'

'None taken,' says Elizabeth. 'She reminds me of me, too. Not *as* good, but not bad.'

'So you think she'll be able to work out where Douglas left his clue?' says Ibrahim.

'Oh, I know where he left it,' says Elizabeth. 'I realized this morning.'

Ibrahim nods. But of course.

'I knew you were hiding something,' says Ron, coming back into the room. 'Poor Sue.'

'I didn't want to bother her with it,' says Elizabeth.

'Elizabeth, you are wicked sometimes,' says Joyce with a smile.

'And besides,' says Elizabeth. 'What if my hunch is wrong? Wouldn't I look a fool then?'

'When are your hunches ever wrong?' says Ron.

'Actually, quite often,' says Joyce. 'She just says them with confidence. She's like a consultant.'

'Absolutely, Joyce,' says Elizabeth. 'Could be right, could be wrong. But I wonder if anyone fancies a walk in the woods to find out for sure?'

'Oh, here we go,' says Ron, rubbing his hands.

'Right now?' asks Joyce. 'Yes, please.'

'You can't go into the woods in your flip-flops, Ron,' says Ibrahim.

'Oh, stop being such a weather forecaster,' says Ron, putting on his coat. 'Off to the woods we go, old friends.'

39

Joyce

It is tomorrow morning, if you know what I mean, and I have just got back from the shop. More of that in a moment. My bag and umbrella are ready, waiting, on the hallway table. More of that in a moment too.

Elizabeth thinks that Douglas faked his own death. It is, apparently, not uncommon in her line of work. Killed someone, had the body identified as his own and ran off with twenty million. Who's to say, but certainly nice work if you can get it.

We were all round at Ibrahim's last night, as Elizabeth wanted to run the theory past Sue Reardon. Ibrahim is moving better, by the way, but he looks sad, which is not like him at all. I mean, he has always looked melancholy, unless he's writing a list, or explaining something, but you very rarely see him looking sad. I need to get him out of his flat somehow. Get him back behind the wheel of his car. Or Ron's car, but you know what I mean.

We had a very nice evening. It was nothing special, but it doesn't always have to be, does it? Having someone from MI5 there might have felt unusual a year ago, but I am growing to expect such things. Sue Reardon looked a bit sad too, I thought. I imagine she is in trouble at work after everything that happened.

I am learning that it is important to stop sometimes, and just have a drink and a gossip with friends, even as corpses start to pile up around you. Which they have been doing a lot recently.

It's a balancing act, of course, but, by and large, the corpses will still be there in the morning, and you mustn't let it spoil your Domino's.

We didn't really talk too much about the case until Elizabeth started going on about Douglas and the weather. That was Sue Reardon's cue, and then Elizabeth let everything spill. Douglas faking his own death, the full works. It does sound a bit complicated to me. How would he have done it?

Though I suppose if you don't put a bit of effort into stealing twenty million pounds then when will you put in some effort?

You could see that Sue didn't dismiss it out of hand. She knows Elizabeth has her head screwed on, and, also, she probably wanted to believe it too. If you are investigating something, you want all sorts of things to be true if they help you out.

I was proud of Elizabeth for sharing, and after Sue left, I was going to tell Elizabeth that she was showing real maturity, not keeping everything to herself for once, but then she told us she had something to show us, and suggested a walk in the woods. Oh, Elizabeth!

Bear in mind, also, that this was gone ten and I had already said, 'Well, this has been lovely,' more than once.

We packed up our things, Ron went to his for a torch and Ibrahim wouldn't come, but wished us luck. I gave him a kiss on the cheek and told him he looked well. He will know I meant the opposite, we are good friends like that.

As we were walking up the hill Elizabeth got into the details of how she'd worked it out.

She had been walking this way with Douglas when he was at Coopers Chase, Poppy trailing behind them with her headphones on. Poor Poppy, I don't think I mind any of this, except for her. Andrew Hastings being murdered was fine by me. Easy come, easy go, that was his job. If you work in a fishmonger's you're going to smell of fish. And Douglas? Well, if he's dead then he probably had it coming too. But Poppy should have been in a different story, and I'm sorry she ended up in this one.

Elizabeth and Douglas had stopped by a tree, and we stopped by the same tree last night. You could see a big hole in it when Ron shone his torch. He was in his element. Gerry was the same if you ever gave him a torch.

Have you ever heard of a 'dead-letter drop'? It's a thing for spies. A place, somewhere public and accessible, where you could hide something, and no one would ever stumble across it accidentally. Spy A would drop off something for Spy B, maybe a microfilm or something like that? Spy B would wander along the canal towpath, that's just an example, lift up a loose fencepost, that's just an example, too, and there you'd have it.

When Elizabeth and Douglas were standing by the tree, he had said to Elizabeth that it would make a good 'dead-letter drop', and it reminded him of one they had used before, and Elizabeth had agreed, and had thought nothing more of it.

Well, that's not strictly true, Elizabeth never stops thinking, does she? She had now convinced herself that Douglas had drawn her attention to the tree for a reason. That he had hidden something in there for her.

And, as so often, she was right.

She asked Ron to shine his torch down into the hole, and guess what we found?

Now, I know what you're thinking. You're thinking we found the diamonds? No such luck, I'm afraid. I promise if we'd found the diamonds I would have started this account very differently. I would have started it 'We just found twenty million pounds' worth of diamonds' or something like that. I wouldn't have gone on about Ron's torch or Ibrahim looking sad. I would have been straight in. In like Flynn. It would have been all diamonds.

But we found the next best thing.

Elizabeth pulled out a letter, on crisp white paper inside a clear ziplock bag. To keep it dry, of course. Honestly, there is nothing those ziplock bags can't do, I've got a drawer full of them. The letter was folded over and her name was handwritten on the front. According to Elizabeth, it was written in Douglas's handwriting. We used to know each other's handwriting, didn't we?

She took the letter out of the bag and unfolded it. It was expensive paper, you know the type, nothing you'd get from your bank or the council, say. Does expensive paper come from more expensive trees, or do they just make it differently?

Elizabeth read the letter, first to herself and then to us. And when you hear what is in it, you'll know what we're going to be doing today. You will know exactly why my flask and my umbrella are on the hallway table.

The reason I've just been to the shop, by the way, is that they have a photocopier there, so that's what I've just been up to. One copy each of the letter for the four of us, and two more in case we decided Chris and Donna might be interested further down the line.

It is 30p a copy! That seems hard to justify. And I had to do extra copies as well, because the first two times I had the letter in the wrong way up. What a racket. You have to wonder where all that money is going. I told Ron on my way back and he was up in arms about it.

I dropped off the original with Elizabeth and she looked rather tired, which is not like her. Though we had been up very late, I suppose. Anyway, she was finally wearing the friendship bracelet I made her, so that was nice.

I have my copy of the letter in front of me now. This is what it says.

Dear Elizabeth,

Never doubted you for a moment, you clever thing. I knew you'd find the letter.

Cards on the table, I should probably apologize for stealing the diamonds, and starting this whole parade. Everyone has their price, and it turns out that mine is twenty million pounds.

Twenty million, darling, just sitting there, and me a dinosaur nearing retirement? Resistance was futile. You understand, don't you?

Dinosaur that I am, I still have a few tricks left in me. Elderly as I am, I still have a few years left in me too. A few years I intend not to waste. Retirement is not for me.

Of course I shouldn't have stolen them, that's a given. You wouldn't have, for example. But I hope you don't begrudge me the adventure of the thing. Not with all the adventures you've been having? It has had my blood pumping for the past weeks at least, and that's a lovely feeling to get back.

Enough of my bunk, let us get down to business.

If you are reading this then I suppose one of two things has happened. I have been killed perhaps? Someone tortured the location of the diamonds out of me then disposed of me? Not impossible. I wouldn't put up with too much torture, adventure or not. Besides, I can simply send them on a wild goose chase. By the time they realize they've been duped I will have been buried in woodland somewhere.

If I have been killed then I do hope there is a part of you that will miss me, and that you will forgive my many sins. I forgave yours long ago. I don't know who would be in charge of a funeral, there is not really anyone around who I have a particular connection to. A couple of bits on the side, but aren't there always with yours truly? I haven't picked up too many friends over the years, and those I had I've shed. If they ask you, and who knows, they might, my mother and father are buried in Northumbria. Please ensure I am buried as far away from them as possible. Rye, perhaps? Remember that weekend we spent? The cottage?

There is a second option, of course, which would be much more fun. And that is that I have got away with it.

Martin Lomax wants me dead, the New York mafia wants me dead, and the Service wants to wash its hands of me. Just at this moment I can't quite work out how I can get away with it, but I have always been resourceful, and perhaps something will come to me? I have a couple of little thoughts ticking over in my brain.

So I am either dead or rich, and I have an easy way for you to find out which.

The diamonds are in a left-luggage locker. You know I requested to be housed at Coopers Chase, and so I left them nearby to make them nice and easy for me to get back. Or for you to get back, if it came to that, which it may well have done.

Darling, the diamonds are in locker 531 at Fairhaven train station. You could break into it, I'm sure, but I have left the key inside this bag.

You go and try your luck. If you open the locker and the diamonds are there, then you will know I am dead. If you open the locker and the diamonds are gone, then you'll know I found a way out. I will be straight over to our old friend, Franco, in Antwerp, cashing the lot in.

On that note, if you don't find the diamonds, it will not escape your notice that I will be roaming free, a very rich man. And if that should interest you at all then rest assured at some point I will find a way to get back in touch. You know I will find someone to share my life with, but it would make me the happiest man alive if that person was you.

You can't blame an old fool for trying.

*God bless you, Elizabeth, and no doubt Joyce, Ron and
Ibrahim too. I am guessing you will keep this between the four
of you. No need to tell Sue and Lance and the gang?*

*I wonder how long it took you to find this letter. Not long is
my guess. If I am dead, then thank you for your speed and
wisdom, and if I am alive then at least I have something of a
head start on everyone.*

*Well done on finding this dead-letter drop, I knew you
wouldn't have missed the clue, you always were, and always will
be, the very best.*

*Locker 531, Fairhaven station. If the diamonds are not there
then I am free. If the diamonds are there then I am dead.*

*So, is this another letter from a dead man? Who knows? But
I imagine your blood is pumping too?*

My love, always,
Douglas

Lovely handwriting, I will give him that. Elizabeth and
I are going to get the minibus down to Fairhaven in a few
minutes. I don't know Fairhaven station at all, but it's
fairly big because you can go to Brighton and to London.
According to the website there is a Costa, a WHSmith
and a place that does sausage rolls and pasties. There's a
First Class lounge, which looks very swish in the pictures,
and a big Travel Centre. And then, of course, there are
the left-luggage lockers.

So maybe we're about to find twenty million pounds'
worth of diamonds. Elizabeth won't let me keep them, I
know, but it will be nice to have them for a bit. Will we

take them to Sue and Lance? Or will we take them to Chris and Donna? I'd love to show them to Donna, that would be my choice, but there are probably protocols to follow.

Or maybe we'll find nothing? Maybe Douglas has out-foxed us all and is out there, on the run? An old man, giddy with freedom, awash with cash, wishing Elizabeth was still in love with him.

Only one way to find out, and that's to get on the minibus.

40

Lance James yawns and scratches. To Sue Reardon, in her office, door open, it will look like he is working. Checking intelligence reports, cross-referencing aircraft manifests? The sort of thing they pay him to do. When he was in the Special Boat Service, life was more exciting. But he was also shot at more often, and these days he doesn't really have the knees to be shot at every five minutes.

Lance is online, looking at houses he can't afford. A country house in Wiltshire? Don't mind if I do. You could convert that stable block into a games room. A penthouse apartment overlooking the Thames? Great views, but look at the floor plan. Where would you put the private cinema?

He is daydreaming. Unless. Unless.

The twenty million would change the picture, wouldn't it? And it's out there.

Lance supposes that even people with twenty million pounds in their hands still look at houses they'll never be able to afford. A hollowed-out volcano, maybe. No one ever buys a house without secretly wanting one ten per cent more expensive.

Money is a trap, for sure. But, to Lance's mind, there are worse traps you could find yourself in.

He looks over and sees Sue Reardon through her open door. She's engrossed in something. Working? He doubts it. Who starts working before eleven these days?

She is frowning at her screen. Does she know something? Is she in there, cracking the case?

More likely she'll be ordering shrubs, or arranging care for an elderly relative, or watching pornography. Nothing about anyone ever surprised Lance any more. Twenty years working with the security services and he has seen it all. Those two women in their seventies? What was the story there? The smaller one, the less scary one, had kept looking at him as if she had something to say. The other one, Elizabeth Best – Sue seemed respectful and wary around her. Was there some history?

Lance glances up at Sue again. She seems deep in thought. Though she's probably just looking at that same house in Wiltshire and working out what she'd do with the stable block. Thinking about the twenty million.

Lance currently lives in a one-bedroom flat in Balham. There is an argument with his ex about buying her half of the property. He can't afford to buy her out, he can't afford to move, and she doesn't much care. He was a poor boy who bought a flat with a rich girl, which was romantic and hopeful at first, but is less fun now their only contact is letters from her dad's solicitor. For now he is paying rent to her. That's the temporary compromise. Paying rent he can't afford to someone who doesn't need the money. To someone who, until six months ago, would tell him every day how much she loved him. Not so much of that in the solicitor's letters. No arm across his chest and sleepy morning kisses from Roebuck Harrington & Lowe.

Had she fallen out of love with him, or had she never been in love? Either way she had slept with their builder, and was now dating an investment banker called Massimo.

Lance's mum had loved her. Everybody loved her. And so now Lance doesn't see his mum so much either. He bets they're still in touch.

Balham was, at least, handy for Millbank, where Lance usually works. But it definitely wasn't handy for this ridiculous set-up in Godalming where he was seconded until this investigation was over. It was all well and good to be investigating two assassinations. But not if you have to stand all the way on the 8.21 train from Waterloo to Godalming in order to do it.

And, to top it all, he is losing his hair. The superpower that had served him so well over the years, the hair that would dance over his eyes, that he would effortlessly run his hand through on dates, knowing that wherever it sprang back to it would look great. It was on its way out. It was thinning, it was greying, it was receding. Just when he was single again.

Sometimes, when they let Lance have a gun, he thinks about just shooting himself in the head.

He should probably do some work.

Lance shuts down the Rightmove property page and opens his emails. He has worked for both MI5 and 6, so he gets all sorts of rubbish. The emails were always a mix of security briefings and the results of the in-house bake-off competition held by the China desk.

Sue has emailed him. She's ten feet away, through an open door, but OK. Can he check on the credentials of Doctor Carter from the mortuary the other night? Send her a report? Of course. Sue is stressed, he can see that. She is under pressure to get this whole mess cleared up.

Grey men have been ghosting in and out of her office for the last few days. About the same age as Sue, he guessed, early sixties perhaps, but more male and more senior. That was still the way it went, despite what all the glossy brochures told you. Lance is aware that he is about as unsuccessful as it is possible for a forty-two-year-old man to be in MI5. But there was time to change that, and he should probably start now.

After reading that the competition to name the MI6 canteen has been won by Priya Ghelani from counterterrorism, with the entry 'Would You Like Spies With That?', he sees an alert about a flight from Teterboro Airport in New Jersey. Lance clicks it open.

Sue Reardon's reputation was high. If there was trouble, she found it, and then she would find the troublemakers making that trouble. She was hard, she could be brutal, that was what the job did to you. But this investigation had been a disaster. Two operatives shot dead in a safe house? Including the chief suspect in the original investigation? No doubt that's why so many grey-haired men were in and out of Sue's office.

A flight has been flagged. On the passenger list is the name Andre Richardson. The flight, on a Gulfstream G65R, takes off from Teterboro and is due to land at

Farnborough Airfield on the morning of Monday the eighth.

Lance closes the email, walks over to Sue's door and knocks. She looks up and closes whatever it was she'd been looking at. ASOS? Paintings of horses?

'Lance?'

'Flight leaving New Jersey on Sunday week. Under the name "Andre Richardson", a known alias of Frank Andrade Jr. Landing at Farnborough, not a million miles from here, not a million miles from Martin Lomax's home.'

'So the man whose diamonds have been stolen is visiting the man they were stolen from?'

'Mmm,' agrees Lance. He is wondering if Priya Ghelani is still single. He has to get back out there, hair or no hair. 'Perhaps I should join the surveillance team for the next week, ma'am? Make sure we don't miss a trick?'

'Good idea, Lance. They're stationed up in Andover. You OK to stay up there?'

A whole week away from the Balham flat. A week away from the commute, and from this office. Maybe some glory and some diamonds at the end of it?

'Yes, ma'am,' says Lance, then raises his hand to push it through his hair, before thinking better of it.

41

Elizabeth is not the sentimental type, but even so.

She is about to find out if her ex-husband is dead. She knows – or knew? – Douglas well enough to know he wouldn't have revealed the true location of the diamonds to anybody else. Whatever false trail he laid would have been a good one. No one else knows about locker 531. That was a secret hidden in a hole in a tree high above Coopers Chase.

If the diamonds are not in this locker, then Douglas has them.

If the diamonds are there, that means Douglas hasn't been to collect them. And that means Douglas is dead. Quite the day she is having.

If Douglas is alive then he is on the run and very rich. And, of course, if Douglas is alive, then he killed Poppy. He killed Poppy, and he faked his own death with a corpse taken from goodness knows where. A fresh corpse, though, there was no hiding that. It wasn't like the corpse of Marcus Carmichael they had pulled from the Thames so many years ago. No one was checking Marcus Carmichael too closely, everybody had their job to do. But Elizabeth had seen Douglas's body. Seen it up close. It was very fresh indeed. So perhaps Douglas had killed two people? That's the only way he could have got away with it.

So, in the grand scheme of things, Elizabeth is hoping that Douglas is dead. No offence meant, but she would rather her ex-husband was a dead thief than a living murderer.

The minibus is full. Carlito, the driver, has a cigarette hanging out of his window. This is not a group who minds if you smoke. And, in return, Carlito doesn't mind if you don't wear a seatbelt. The whole scene might have been from the 1970s, when, if you wanted to die of lung cancer, or in a road accident, then that was your choice.

Joyce is quiet, which is unlike her. It's almost unnerving.

At first Elizabeth thought it was because of Poppy. Joyce and Poppy had bonded, that was for certain. Or perhaps because of Siobhan? Being so close to a mother's grief?

But then Elizabeth realizes that the last time the two of them had been on this minibus together, Bernard had been on the back seat. Just before Joyce and Bernard had become close. Joyce misses him, although they never talk about him. Just like they never talk about Stephen, or Penny. In fact what do she and Joyce talk about? The English countryside passes by outside the minibus window.

'What do you and I talk about, Joyce?' asks Elizabeth.

Joyce thinks. 'It's been mainly murder, hasn't it? Since we met?'

Elizabeth nods. 'I suppose it has. What do you think we'll talk about when there are no murders?'

'Well, we'll find out at some point, won't we?'

Joyce looks out of the window again. Elizabeth doesn't like seeing her friend unhappy. What do normal people say in these situations? Here goes nothing.

'Would you like to talk about Bernard?'

Joyce turns to look at her and gives her a tiny smile. 'No, thank you.'

Joyce returns to her view and, without turning, puts her hand on Elizabeth's.

'Would you like to talk about Stephen?' asks Joyce.

'No, thank you,' says Elizabeth. Joyce gives her hand a squeeze, and leaves it there. Elizabeth looks down at her friendship bracelet. A very ugly thing that means the world to her. Elizabeth's life has been one of classmates and cousins, of professors, of colleagues and of husbands. She has always found friends harder. What did friends want from you? What did they expect you to do? Her great brain hadn't worked it out.

Last night, awake with Stephen at around 4 a.m., he had been showing off about some mountain or other he had climbed when he was a young man. She had then invented an even bigger mountain she had climbed – 'without a single Sherpa, darling' – and he then upped the ante and was climbing Everest without Sherpas or oxygen, and then she was climbing Everest carrying a grand piano, and the two of them were in fits of giggles. It was love, of course, but it was also friendship. Stephen was the first person she had ever met who refused to take her seriously.

Joyce doesn't take her seriously, Ibrahim doesn't take her seriously, Ron certainly doesn't take her seriously.

They respect her, she thinks, they know they can rely on her, they *take care* of her – shudder – but they refuse to take her seriously. Who knew that was the secret all along?

Now she really thinks about it, Chris and Donna don't take her seriously either. First Stephen, then the Thursday Murder Club, now Chris and Donna? Why this sudden wave of people who refused to be taken in by her casual brilliance and brusque efficiency?

She knows the answer, of course. After meeting Stephen she took *herself* less seriously. The moment she had done that, a door was opened, which true friends could walk through. And in they walked. She squeezes Joyce's hand back.

'You know, I *would* like to talk about Stephen. I just don't know how yet.'

Joyce turns away from the window and smiles at her friend.

'Well, the kettle is always on at mine.'

The minibus pulls to a stop outside Ryman's, and everyone starts gathering their belongings. Carlito swivels himself in his chair.

'I see you back here in three hours. No shoplifting, no graffiti.'

Elizabeth stands, then ushers Joyce to the exit in front of her. As she passes, Joyce says, 'Before we talk about your current husband, let's find out if your ex-husband is dead.'

'Yes, let's,' says Elizabeth. That's what friends were for.

The station was a ten-minute walk from Ryman's, down towards the seafront. As the shops peter out, Fairhaven gets a bit grittier. They pass by the end of a road full of lock-up garages, teenagers on bicycles skidding up and down. Fairhaven in autumn is beginning to hunker down, to prepare for winter, no day trippers, no tourists, everyone having to find different ways to make their money. Elizabeth knows that if you opened up all of those garages you would find a thing or two.

Should Elizabeth have told Sue Reardon about the letter? Well, yes, of course she should, that was a silly question, but Elizabeth wanted to be the one to open the locker. Sue would understand that. And if she didn't understand, then they would cross that bridge in time. Elizabeth suspected there would be few complaints if she handed Sue a bag of diamonds.

As they approach the station they pass Le Pont Noir, which used to be the Black Bridge. Ron's son, Jason, had told them many tales of the Black Bridge. They haven't seen Jason for a while. He is dating Gordon Playfair's daughter, Karen, and is very happy by all accounts. The more love the better as far as Elizabeth is concerned these days.

They reach Fairhaven station. It is much as Joyce had described it. Morning rush hour has passed, but it is still lively. Everyone living their own story. Students with backpacks trying to find platforms, men in suits running for connections, pre-schoolers in pushchairs wailing for raisins.

And, standing, looking up at the station signs, a silly old spy and her friend, looking for twenty million pounds' worth of diamonds stolen from the New York mafia.

Elizabeth sees the arrow pointing to 'Left-Luggage Lockers'.

42

Ron sits on the back seat of the taxi, next to his grandson, Kendrick. He always asks for the same cabbie, Mark, because Mark supports West Ham and has a 'Vote Labour' sticker in his back window.

Ron has just picked Kendrick up from the station. Suzi, his daughter, didn't stop, because she was going on to Gatwick. Ron managed to ask her how she was, but all she managed was 'Don't worry about me' before the train started moving again, and he and Kendrick waved it into the distance.

Kendrick is currently hugging his backpack and looking out of each window in turn, excited at every new house, every new road sign and every new tree.

'Grandad, a shop!' says Kendrick.

Ron looks. 'You're right there, Kenny.'

'Call me Kendrick, Grandad,' says Kendrick.

'I've always called you Kenny,' says Ron. 'It's quicker.'

'Uh, it's the same, Grandad.'

'Nah, it's quicker,' says Ron.

'It's not really, is it?' asks Kendrick, straining forward against his seatbelt to get the taxi driver's attention.

'Not my business,' says Mark, 'but yeah, it's got the same number of syllables, I'm afraid, Ron.'

Can't even get back-up from a West Ham fan. People

were so soft around kids. 'I'll call you Ken, then. That's quicker.'

'Just call me Kendrick, maybe? Daddy calls me Ken.'

'Kendrick it is then,' says Ron. Ron's son-in-law was not his favourite person in the world. Safe to say Danny didn't have a 'Vote Labour' sticker on the back of his BMW.

'Can I ask you a question, Grandad?'

'Fire away,' says Ron.

'Do you have a smart TV?'

'Um, I don't think so,' says Ron. 'I doubt it. I only just got a microwave.'

'You do, Ron,' says Mark over his shoulder. 'Your boy Jason brought it round for you. A friend of his had found a hundred of them in a field. You were trying to sell me one.'

'I do have a smart TV then,' says Ron to Kendrick. 'Is that good?'

'It's really good, I think,' confirms Kendrick. 'I've got my iPad, and I know I'm lucky because not everyone has one, but with a smart TV we can all play *Minecraft* together. Do you know *Minecraft*, Grandad? Also, does anyone have cats where you live?'

'There's a few cats who pop in.'

'Oh, I'm really happy about that.'

'One of them killed a squirrel the other day and tried to bring it through my patio doors.'

'Oh, no!'

'Yep. I wasn't having any of it, he was out on his ear.'

Kendrick thinks about this for a while. 'But that's just

cats, they're not trying to be mean. It's sad for the squirrel, though. I hope I can see squirrels. So do you know *Minecraft*?'

'Afraid not, son.'

'That's OK, because you can learn. You get to build new worlds and create all sorts of things, and sometimes you can talk to people, but it's important to be careful. I built a castle and it had a moat but it didn't have a drawbridge, so no one could get in, but also no one could get out, so it was good and bad. Uncle Ibrahim can play too.'

'Uncle Ibrahim's not feeling too clever at the moment,' says Ron. 'Go easy on him.'

'Oh, that's fine; he can still play though,' says Kendrick. 'What would you like to build, Grandad?'

'What is it, use your imagination? Or are there instructions?' asks Ron.

'Imagination,' says Kendrick, throwing his hands into the air.

'Well, I don't know about imagination. Is there fighting?'

'You can fight, but I don't like to.'

'I'd build a unicorn farm, Kendrick,' says Mark, from the front seat. 'But with outbuildings that could bring in commercial revenue. Like a farm shop?'

'Yeah, that's so good,' says Kendrick. 'I'll do that. And maybe slides?'

'Slides and ice cream, perhaps?' says Mark, and Kendrick nods vigorously.

'Why don't you and Uncle Ibrahim build it, and I'll just watch,' says Ron.

Kendrick nods again. 'It's really fun to watch too. And then you can say if you see a cat, and we can stop.'

Mark flicks on the indicator and turns left into the drive for Coopers Chase.

'Here we are, Kenny, home sweet home.'

Kendrick looks up at Ron, one eyebrow raised, legs jiggling. He tries to look out of all the windows at once.

'Do you remember Joyce?' asks Ron.

'Uh huh,' says Kendrick. 'She's nice.'

'She says she's made you a cake if you want to come and see her?'

'Just for me?' asks Kendrick.

'So she says.'

Kendrick nods his approval. 'You can all have some though, I only need one bit. Mark, you can have some too.'

'Love to, but I've got a pick-up in Tonbridge,' says Mark.

Kendrick thinks, then looks at his grandad. 'I haven't got a present for Joyce though, so I'll do a drawing. Have you got paper?'

'They've got paper at the shop,' says Ron.

'We'll go to the shop,' says Kendrick.

'Speed bump,' says Mark, and the car bunny-hops in the air.

Kendrick reaches up and puts his arms around Ron's neck. 'Grandad, we're going to have a fun time.' He starts counting things off on his fingers. 'We can go swimming, we can go for a walk, we can see Joyce, we can say hello to everyone.' He points outside the window, 'Grandad, the llamas!'

Ron looks at the llamas. Ian Ventham's idea when he ran the place. Not his cup of tea, but, seen through a child's eyes, not without charm. If you ended up living somewhere with llamas then perhaps not all is bad.

Kendrick settles back into his seat and shakes his head in wonder. 'Oh, Grandad. You're lucky to live here.'

Ron puts an arm around his grandson and looks out of the window. You're not wrong there, kid, he thinks.

43

The Left-Luggage Office is attended by a bored-looking teenage girl wearing headphones. Elizabeth holds up her key as she and Joyce walk past, and the girl nods them through.

'I don't think you should be allowed to wear headphones at work,' says Elizabeth. 'You miss everything.'

Joyce nods. 'Lovely hair though.'

There are five rows of lockers, grey metal frames and chipped blue doors, stacked three lockers high from floor to ceiling. Elizabeth leads Joyce to the fifth row, and they begin the walk down it.

'I hope it's a middle one,' says Joyce. 'No bending or reaching.'

Elizabeth stops. 'You're in luck, Joyce; middle locker, 531.'

They both look at the locker: 531 is written in sloping white numerals against the blue door. Elizabeth looks at the key. Small and flimsy. Anyone could break in. The girl on reception wouldn't exactly stop you. What a place to hide twenty million pounds.

'Well, here goes nothing,' says Elizabeth and slides the key into the lock. At first it meets resistance, so Elizabeth pulls it out and tries again. But there is resistance once again, and she frowns. She lowers her eye to the keyhole.

'Lock must be damaged. Hairpin, Joyce.'

Joyce searches through her bag and pulls out a hairpin. Elizabeth inserts it into the keyhole very gently, pushing, then twisting, then pushing again. The metal door swings open, to reveal the fate of Douglas Middlemiss.

To reveal nothing.

Well, not nothing exactly. Three grey walls, and a discarded crisp packet. The diamonds are gone.

Elizabeth looks at Joyce. Joyce looks at Elizabeth. They are both quiet for a moment.

'It's empty,' says Joyce.

'Up to a point,' says Elizabeth, and pulls out the crisp packet.

'Is this good news, or bad news?' says Joyce.

Elizabeth stays silent for a moment, then nods herself back into action.

'Well, it's news, certainly,' says Elizabeth. 'Time will tell whether it's good or bad. Joyce, put the crisp packet in your bag.'

Joyce obediently folds the crisp packet and puts it into her bag. Elizabeth shuts the locker door and inserts the hairpin once again. She twists it until the door locks with an unconvincing click.

Joyce leads the way out and they nod to the girl on reception as they leave.

'Excuse me,' says the girl. Elizabeth and Joyce turn back and the girl takes her headphones off. 'A couple of things. First off, there's nothing on these headphones, I only wear them because it stops the manager of Costa coming over and chatting me up, if he thinks I'm listening to something.'

'Well, I apologize,' says Elizabeth. 'What's the second thing?'

The girl looks at Joyce. 'I just wanted to say thank you for being nice about my hair. It's my first post-break-up haircut, so you've made my day.'

Joyce smiles. 'Plenty more fish in the barrel, dear, you take my word for it.'

The girl smiles back and makes a head gesture towards the lockers. 'I hope you found what you wanted today.'

'Yes and no, apparently,' says Joyce, and the girl slides her headphones back on.

As they leave the station Elizabeth sends a text, then plunges into the warren of alleyways behind the station. Joyce has no idea where they are walking now, but they are certainly walking somewhere as Elizabeth leads her expertly through the back streets of Fairhaven.

They take a left and then start down a small footpath. Are they headed for the police station? Why would they be headed for the police station? To give Chris and Donna a crisp packet? Joyce rarely questions Elizabeth, but one of these days she will lose it, surely? Perhaps today is that day?

They are crossing a small park now; there are children on a climbing frame, trying to get the attention of parents looking at mobile phones. They are definitely going to the police station. Joyce is trying to remember if there are toilets there. Surely there must be? But what if they're just for prisoners?

Soon Joyce sees the police station in the distance, and sitting on the stone steps outside is Donna. That must have been who the text was for.

Donna pushes herself up as Elizabeth and Joyce approach. Donna gives Joyce a hug. Elizabeth waves a hug away. 'Hello, dear, no time for hugs. Did you bring the light?'

Donna holds up something that looks like a small pen. 'What's that for?' asks Joyce.

'Can you take the crisp packet out of your bag?' asks Elizabeth.

Joyce knew it. There was no way Elizabeth was making her put an old crisp packet in her bag without a good reason. Joyce takes out the packet and hands it to Elizabeth. Elizabeth tears down the side of the packet, exposing the foil inside. She then flattens the foil on one of the steps. Joyce cocks her head, so Elizabeth explains.

'Tradecraft, Joyce. If Douglas had wanted the locker to be empty it would have been empty, but it wasn't.'

Donna shows Joyce the light. 'This is an infra-red light. I used to use it when we found stolen bikes. Sometimes the owner would have invisibly marked them.'

'And, of course, Donna doesn't have to track down stolen bikes any more, thanks to us,' says Elizabeth.

'For which I've thanked you many times,' says Donna.

'Now she investigates murders,' says Elizabeth.

'Elizabeth, you think perhaps it's a sign of my gratitude that I'm standing on the steps of the police station about to help two old ladies shine an infra-red light at a crisp packet?'

'You know we appreciate you, dear. Now let's get to it.'

'Old ladies,' giggles Joyce. 'I always find that funny.'

Donna kneels and switches on the light. Joyce thinks about kneeling, but really, kneeling over the age of sixty-five is a pipedream, so she sits on the step above instead. Elizabeth kneels. Is there nothing she can't do?

The red light plays across the foil and Joyce sees letters appear. There is clearly a sentence written on it.

'What now, Douglas?' says Elizabeth with a sigh.

Donna moves the light to the top right corner of the foil and starts to read words as she reveals them.

'"Elizabeth, darling . . ."'

Elizabeth mutters, 'I'll darling you.'

'"Elizabeth, darling, we both know that things are never in the first place you look. This was just an extra layer of security, in case somebody else found the letter. But you know where the diamonds are, don't you? If you really think about it?"' Donna stops reading and looks up at Elizabeth.

'That's it?' asks Elizabeth.

'Well, then it says "from your ever-loving Douglas" and three kisses,' says Donna. 'But I didn't want to hear the tut if I read that out.'

Elizabeth gets back to her feet and reaches out a hand to help Joyce up too.

'So we still don't know if he's alive or dead?' says Joyce.

'Afraid not,' says Elizabeth.

'But he says you know where the diamonds are?' says Donna.

'Well, if he says I know, then I know,' says Elizabeth. 'I have some thinking to do.'

Talking of thinking, something has been bothering Joyce, but she hasn't mentioned it. She had never been a spy, so what did she know? It was probably silly. But the sun was out, and she was with two of her favourite people, so where was the harm?

'Didn't you think it was strange that the lock was damaged?' she says.

'Strange how?' says Elizabeth.

'Well, he gave you the key, so presumably it was working when he locked it up? And no one would have been there since. So how did the lock get damaged?'

'That's a good question,' says Donna, and Joyce beams.

'It's a very good question,' says Elizabeth.

Even better! What a lovely day Joyce is having.

'Donna, there was CCTV in the locker room,' says Elizabeth. 'You don't think you could possibly get hold of it? Just for the last week?'

'I could get hold of it, but I'm not going to sit through a week of CCTV footage just because Joyce has a hunch. No offence, Joyce.'

'Oh, I never take offence,' says Joyce. 'Such an effort.'

'If you can get it, Donna, Ibrahim has plenty of time on his hands at the moment. And he loves to be useful.'

'OK, I'll see what I can do,' says Donna. 'But if there's any way we can get involved in this case, then you promise you'll let us?'

'I think that sounds fair,' says Elizabeth. 'Any more news of Ryan Baird?'

'Court case next week, I'll let you know.'

'Are you working on anything fun?'

'Staking out a local drug dealer. Connie Johnson. Nasty piece of work.'

'They often are,' says Elizabeth. 'And I believe we are seeing you later?'

'Looking forward to it very much,' says Donna.

'Any intelligence you can give us on Patrice, before we meet her?' asks Elizabeth.

'She's OK,' says Donna. 'Bit mumsy for me.'

Joyce looks at her watch. They still have an hour before they have to meet the minibus. Time for an almond-flour brownie and a cup of mint tea. Today was one of those days when everything was just falling into place. Perhaps she should buy a scratch card.

44

'They were both shot in the face, so it was a terrible mess,' says Joyce. 'More Battenberg, Patrice?'

'Nowhere left to put it,' says Patrice, holding up her palm. 'I'm half Battenberg already.'

'Murder suicide?' asks Chris. 'Or double murder?'

'Double murder,' says Ron. 'No gun left lying around, eh? Some geezer's walked in –'

'Or woman,' says Donna, and gets an approving nod from her mum.

'Some geezer, or some bird, granted, has just walked in, and opened up, kablammo. Heads blown off. You wouldn't wish it on anyone.'

'More women are murdering people these days,' says Joyce. 'If you ignore the context, it is a real sign of progress.'

Donna tucks her feet up beneath her. How was this all going then? Upside: the look on Elizabeth's face when she realized that Patrice and Donna were mother and daughter. That she had managed to keep it secret. Elizabeth hated other people having secrets. Downside: having to watch her mum and Chris putting on a show for the Thursday Murder Club. Sitting knees together on the sofa. Touching, kissing, cooing. Donna wants them both to be happy, but she doesn't need to watch them being happy.

She doesn't even particularly want to hear about them being happy. So long as they *are* happy, that's all she needs. And they do *look* happy, don't they? What if this relationship was actually going to work? What if Donna had performed a miracle?

'And they'd tried before? They'd tried here?' asks Chris.

'Someone tried to kill Douglas, yes,' says Elizabeth. 'Made a rotten job of it and Poppy took his head off. May she rest in peace.'

'I was hoping you and Donna might come and investigate,' says Joyce. 'But they sent Sue and Lance from MI5 instead.'

'Not that we would ever reveal the names of MI5 officers, Joyce,' says Elizabeth.

'Oh, I'm only telling Chris,' says Joyce. 'Don't be a fusspot.'

'I'll just check the Official Secrets Act, Joyce, and see if that's in there.'

'Anyway, they're not a patch on you two,' says Joyce. 'Sue is a bit of a cold fish. Like Elizabeth, but without the warmth. But you can see she respects her.'

'Senior, were you, Lizzie?' asks Ron.

'And then there was Lance. Balding but quite handsome, and there was no wedding ring. Anyway, I could get his number for you, Donna?'

'A date with a balding spy? Well, that sounds a treat,' says Donna. She had been on a date on Monday. His profile had said he was a diving instructor, which had sounded suitably alpha to Donna. Of course, she had misread the profile, and so had ended up having very disappointing sex with a driving instructor. She had also made the mistake of telling her mum and Chris about it, and they had a field day. Mum had made a number of jokes about his gearstick, and Chris had said, 'Did he look in his mirror before pulling out?' Donna downs her glass of wine.

'Would you like to see photographs of the crime scene?' asks Elizabeth.

'Yes, please,' says Chris.

'I'll need something in return,' says Elizabeth.

'Here we go,' says Chris.

'We just want to know the following. One, how long have you two been dating?'

'None of your business,' says Chris.

'These photos are from every possible angle. Entry wounds, exit wounds, items disturbed in the room.'

'Six weeks,' says Patrice.

'Thank you,' says Elizabeth. 'Two, where do you think this is going to go? I think I speak for all of us when I say that you seem an adorable couple.'

Donna mimes being sick as Joyce and Ron nod.

Patrice smiles. 'Well, let's take it one day at a time, shall we? I enjoyed yesterday, I'm having fun today, and I'm looking forward to tomorrow.'

She had given the same answer to Ibrahim, when she, Donna and Chris had visited him in his sick bed before coming over. He was intently playing *Minecraft* with Ron's grandson, but had looked up long enough to say, 'Theoretically, I know a thing or two about love. And that sounds like a very healthy answer.'

'Any gossip from you four in return?' asks Donna, keen to change the subject. 'Apart from three people being shot?'

'Well, Joyce had Gordon Playfair around for lunch one day last week,' says Elizabeth.

'He was rebooting my Wi-Fi,' says Joyce.

'I'll bet he was,' says Ron, another glass of wine down now.

'Photos?' reminds Chris.

Elizabeth holds up her finger, then fishes into her bag. 'I lost my phone, briefly, but Bogdan found it for me.' She scrolls through her photos and passes it to Chris. 'Here, you two lovebirds can take a look.'

Chris holds the phone in front of him, and angles it slightly towards Patrice. He flicks through a couple of photos, pinching the screen occasionally to enlarge details.

'Professional job,' says Patrice.

'I was about to say that!' says Chris.

'Great minds think alike,' says Patrice and kisses Chris on the lips. Donna rolls her eyes and mutters 'get a room' loud enough for only Joyce to hear. Joyce giggles. Donna gives her a discreet high-five.

'What a mess, though,' says Chris.

'Let me look,' says Donna, and holds out her hand.

'She was always impatient,' says Patrice. 'Wouldn't ride a bike with stabilizers, wouldn't wear armbands in the pool. We were in and out of A&E.'

Donna takes the phone from her mum and begins to scroll through the photos. As she stares at the two bodies, the young woman and the old man, she zones out of the conversation around her. Joyce is asking about Donna as a child, Ron is asking for more wine, her mum is asking about Gordon Playfair. Was all as it seemed in these photos? Something wasn't right. On her date with the driving instructor, he had shown her a tattoo in Chinese script on his upper arm, and she had asked him what it meant. He had had no idea, he had just liked the look of it. To try and make conversation before they had sex again and she could finally ask him to leave, Donna had taken a photo of it and put it through a translation app. It turned out that the tattoo read 'Sample Text – Your Message Goes Here'.

Sometimes things were just for show, they only looked right. Until you changed the way you looked at them. Donna puts down the phone.

'I know you'll have thought about this, but are you absolutely *sure* this is Douglas?'

'Yes,' says Elizabeth. 'I have thought of that. Now, where are we with that CCTV?'

'What CCTV?' asks Chris.

There is a buzz. Somebody is at Joyce's door.

45

'He called it ham-fisted,' says Stephen. 'Ham-fisted!'

'I know, dear,' says Elizabeth. It is 2.30 a.m.

Many years ago, a man named Julian Lambert had written a review of one of Stephen's books, *Iran – Art After the Revolution*. It had not been a good review. Mean-spirited. They were rivals.

'I'll knock his block off. How dare he?' Stephen slaps both palms against the hallway wall, with some force. Stephen is a big man still. Elizabeth has never had to fear his physicality. Might she have to one day? Every day he slips further away.

'Don't give him the satisfaction, darling,' says Elizabeth. Julian Lambert died in 2003, a hosepipe fitted to his car exhaust, in the garage of a house he was renting after an expensive and self-inflicted divorce.

'I'll give him more than satisfaction,' says Stephen. 'Let's see how clever he looks on his arse, shall we? Where are my keys?'

Keys to what, wonders Elizabeth. Car keys, long gone. Keys to the flat, hidden many months ago. Stephen no longer has any keys. How to calm him down though?

'I've just had a rather wonderful idea,' says Elizabeth. 'I wonder if you'd like to hear it before you head off?'

'Don't talk me out of this, Elizabeth. Lambert has had

this coming a long time.' Stephen is checking through drawers. 'Damn and blast, where are my keys?'

Stephen has never been a vengeful man or an angry man. Never been ruled by his pride. Never had those traits you see in weak men. Never felt the need to prove himself at the expense of others.

'I wouldn't talk you out of anything,' says Elizabeth. 'I agree with you entirely. Anyone who insults your book insults you. And anyone who insults you, insults me.'

'Thank you, darling,' says Stephen.

'It's just I was thinking you might take Bogdan with you? He could drive you up.'

Stephen considers this for a moment, then nods. 'He'd scare the living daylights out of Lambert, wouldn't he?'

Elizabeth takes out her phone. 'I'll ring him, dear.'

It is nearly 2.30 in the morning, but Bogdan answers on the first ring.

'Hello, Elizabeth.'

'Hello, Bogdan, Stephen wanted to ask you a favour.'

'OK, hand me over,' says Bogdan. Elizabeth would love to know why Bogdan is wide awake at 2.30 in the morning. He is infuriatingly opaque. She hadn't even heard any background noises, despite her well-trained ear.

'Bogdan? Is this you?' says Stephen.

'Yes, Stephen. What can I do?' says Bogdan.

'There's a fella. He's in Kensington, or Camden, and we need to duff him up.'

'OK, now?'

'Soon as you can get here.'

'OK, I be maybe an hour. Get some rest before, OK? Put me back to Elizabeth.'

Stephen hands the phone back to Elizabeth.

'Thank you, Bogdan,' says Elizabeth. 'You are a good friend.'

'You are, too,' says Bogdan. 'I hope you get him back to sleep.'

'Thank you, darling. What are you up to?'

'Bits and bobs,' says Bogdan.

'What's that I can hear in the background?' she asks.

'I don't think you can hear anything,' says Bogdan.

Elizabeth rolls her eyes. 'Night, night, Bogdan.'

Elizabeth leads Stephen back to bed, and he is already much calmer. Bogdan does that to people. She can't persuade Stephen to undress, but she persuades him to get under the covers beside her.

'You found out who shot your friends yet?' he asks.

Elizabeth seizes on the change of subject. 'Not yet, but I will.' She knows she already has the clue. But what is it? Where is it?

'Of course you will,' says Stephen. 'You always get your man.'

Elizabeth smiles, and kisses her husband on the cheek. 'I certainly got you, didn't I?'

'No, no, I got you, darling,' says Stephen. 'Had it planned from the moment I saw you.'

They had met when Stephen had handed her a dropped glove, outside a bookshop, in an act of tactical chivalry. Elizabeth has never told him that, actually, she had spotted him from a distance earlier that day, sitting on a bench, looking like quite the most beautiful man she had ever seen. As she walked past the bench she had dropped the glove on purpose. He had picked it up, as she knew he would. The dropped glove, a romantic cliché no man could resist. So, yes, Elizabeth always got her man, even when they didn't know it. You should always have a plan.

'He left me a note,' says Elizabeth. 'Telling me where to find the diamonds. Joyce and I followed the trail, and it just led to another note, telling me I knew where the diamonds were if only I were to think about it.'

'Telling you to pull your finger out?'

'That's the long and short of it.'

'How did you find the first note?'

'We were by a tree, up in the woods, and he talked about dead-letter drops.'

'Bit obvious for you,' says Stephen.

Elizabeth laughs. 'In retrospect.'

'He say anything else? Anything in the note?'

'Shall I get it?' says Elizabeth. 'We can look through it together?'

'Yes, let's, what fun. Shall I put the kettle on?'

'No, you stay where you are, darling. Perhaps slip your shoes and jacket off though, make yourself comfortable.'

'Right you are,' says Stephen.

Elizabeth swings her legs out of bed and walks over to her desk. Stephen's shoes fly across the room as she retrieves the photocopy of the letter and gets back into bed. She smiles at her husband, still wearing his tie.

They read through the letter together, Stephen making the occasional comment of 'Northumbria', 'remember that weekend in Rye', 'mafia, of all things' and 'my love always? Well, you lost out there, Chief.'

Perhaps the clue is hidden in plain sight, Elizabeth thinks. There was a very simple technique she and Douglas would use for fun. Spelling out a message with the first letter of successive sentences. They would write huge sweeping love letters to each other, where the initial letters would spell out 'DON'T FORGET WE NEED EGGS AND TOILET ROLL'.

Would Douglas try so simple a trick here? For old times' sake? Surely not?

'I'd say they are at the cottage in Rye, darling,' says Stephen. 'Wouldn't you? Funny to mention it otherwise?'

They are not at the cottage in Rye. It was the first thing Elizabeth checked. It was bulldozed in 1995 to make way for a bypass. Elizabeth picks up the letter again, and looks to see if Douglas has left her a message in the first letter of each sentence. She scans the opening paragraphs.

Never doubted you for a moment, you clever thing. I knew you'd find the letter.

Cards on the table, I should probably apologize for stealing the diamonds, and starting this whole parade. Everyone has their price, and it turns out that mine is twenty million pounds. Twenty million, darling, just sitting there, and me a dinosaur nearing retirement? Resistance was futile. You understand, don't you?

Dinosaur that I am, I still have a few tricks left in me.
Elderly as I am, I still have a few years left in me too. A few
years I intend not to waste. Retirement is not for me.

Elizabeth smiles. You win that one, Douglas. Sometimes, if she thought really hard, she could remember why she'd married him.

'Darling,' says Stephen. 'Do you remember Julian Lambert, he just popped into my head.'

'Never heard of him,' says Elizabeth.

'I might put in a lunch with him. He's just had the most awful divorce. Be nice to check he's all right.'

Oh, stay with me, Stephen, thinks Elizabeth. Stay with me, stay with me, stay with me.

46

Joyce

I am typing quietly because I have someone in the spare room.

The spare room is always made up, in case Joanna comes to stay unexpectedly. Which happens sometimes, if not often. Since her company took over the development on top of the hill she has popped down a few times. She took me up to the site last time, and I had to wear a hard hat. I put it on and knocked on Elizabeth's door so she could have a good laugh at me, but she wasn't in, so I knocked on Ron's door and fortunately he was there. Joanna took a picture of me with Ron. I'm wearing my hard hat, and he's pointing at it. It's on Facebook somewhere if you'd like to see it. I should put it on Instagram!

The pillow in the spare room is one that Joanna bought me for Christmas, because she said my pillows were too thin. She actually said that one pillow was too thin, but two pillows were too thick, as if that had been my plan all along. As if I had gone to British Home Stores and sorted through pillows until I found the perfect ones to annoy my daughter. There is also a White Company candle in there that she bought me for Mother's Day. If I fill the spare room full of things she bought me then she can't complain. That's the theory at least, but she'll always find something.

Last time she was down she told me off for having the slats of my venetian blinds angled upwards instead of downwards. That was the straw that broke the camel's hump for me. I said to her, I'd wanted to say it for ages, that I felt I could never get anything quite right, and she said well she felt the same, and I said that's nonsense, and asked her what she meant, and she said, well Mum, I'm always too fat or too thin, or with the wrong man, or just split up with the right man, or I should wear my hair up or down or I work too hard or I have too many holidays, or I shouldn't have painted my kitchen that colour. That actually struck a nerve, I *can* be a bit like that, but I decided to dig in, so I stood my ground and said Joanna, that's because I care, that's because I love you, and she said so you show me you love me by telling me I'm too fat? And I said well I know you're happier when you're not overweight, and so I just gently tell you, and she said, perhaps she was well aware of when she was overweight, and perhaps her mum pointing out the obvious made her unhappy? Which was also true, so I said well I don't see you often enough, so I have to say everything all at once, and she said well is that what this is all about? That I don't see you often enough? And by that stage we were both in an argument we had no way out of, and so I told her that I loved her unconditionally, and she said well of course I loved her unconditionally, I was culturally hard-wired to love her unconditionally, but that sometimes she wished that I actually liked her. And I said darling I do like you, you don't like me, my life is too small for you, I remind you of the things you've had to change to be a success, and she said, oh so I'm a fraud, is that it? And I said not at all, I was very proud of her, and she looked at me and said she was very proud of me too, and I asked what for, and she said I was kind and wise and brave, and I said she was clever and beautiful and had achieved things I would never be capable of, and we both started crying, and then we hugged and I told her I loved her and she told me she loved me. We wiped our eyes and dusted ourselves down, and then she pulled the cord on the venetian blinds so the slats angled downwards and went and made me a cup of tea.

I am glad I had a daughter instead of a son, though. At least I see her.

So we met Chris's girlfriend this evening. She is Donna's mum, if you can believe that? Anyway, she's lovely, as you might expect, and a teacher, so she's on half-term. I have high hopes, but then I'm a romantic, and I always have high hopes. It's much more fun that way.

We were all chatting about Douglas and Poppy's deaths. Donna agrees with Elizabeth. Are we absolutely sure the body was really Douglas? I mean, I was there, and I saw him, and I would swear it was, but it is an inter-esting question. Unfortunately, it was a question that will have to wait for another day, as at that moment my door buzzer went, and it was Poppy's mum, Siobhan.

She had been in Godalming – 'snap', I told her and had identified Poppy's body. Which doesn't really bear thinking about. She has been there for two days, talking to funeral directors and HR people and lawyers, all quite complicated, and they were going to drive her home, but she asked to come here instead. I think that because Poppy had given me her number she knows that Poppy trusted us. And perhaps she wanted to talk to someone who Poppy trusted. She had spent a lot of time with Sue Reardon and Lance James, and perhaps she had questions that they couldn't answer. Or perhaps she didn't believe their answers.

You could tell she was shattered, so we agreed to reconvene in the morning. She got a hug and kind words from everyone while I made up a hot water bottle.

I can hear her tossing and turning; I don't expect she will sleep well. I forgot to ask her what she likes for breakfast, so I will head up to the shop first thing and get everything, just in case.

Speaking of half-term, Ron's grandson is with us for a few days. Ron's daughter, Suzi, works in travel and is going to a conference in the Caribbean. If you can have a conference in the Caribbean?

Her husband, Danny – he takes offence if you say Daniel – is going with her, taking a break from his busy job of no one quite knows what. He wears suits, but not ties, if that's a clue? Ron jumped at the chance of some time with Kendrick. When we last saw him, he was delightful, so one hopes he still will be. It's round about twelve that the charm wears off with boys, though most of them get it back sooner or later.

47

'Uncle Ibrahim, what's better, a monkey or a penguin?'

'A penguin,' says Ibrahim, and pats the seat next to the bed. Kendrick sits down.

'Oh, OK, Grandad didn't know. Why is a penguin better than a monkey?'

Ibrahim puts his paper down. 'Kendrick, do you know why I like you?'

Kendrick shakes his head. 'I don't even know at all.'

'You ask very good questions. Not many people do.'

'Why don't they?' asks Kendrick.

'Well, there you go again,' says Ibrahim. 'Now, penguins are better than monkeys, because "penguin" is a very specific term, and "monkey" is very unspecific. If we say "monkey" then different people see different things, maybe a mandrill, maybe a little marmoset, whereas if you say "penguin" then we all picture the same thing. Words are very important, most people don't know that, and the more specific a word is, the better it is.'

'But is an actual penguin better than an actual monkey?'

Ibrahim thinks. 'No animal is better than any other animal. We are all just a collection of atoms smashed together. Even people. Even trees.'

'Even tigers?'

'Even tigers.'

Kendrick blows out his cheeks.

'Even hippos?'

Ibrahim nods. He goes back to his crossword.

'What are you doing?' asks Kendrick, hopping. 'Is it a puzzle?'

'A crossword puzzle,' says Ibrahim.

'Is it boring or interesting?'

'A bit of both,' says Ibrahim. 'That's why I like it.'

Ron stands and stretches. 'I'm just going to nip down to the shop. Ibrahim, would you like an ice cream?'

'No, thank you, Ron,' says Ibrahim.

'No one wants an ice cream, righty-ho,' says Ron and turns to go.

Kendrick clamps his lips together and lets out a small noise. Ron turns back.

'You all right there, Kendrick?'

Kendrick keeps his lips together, and murmurs an uncertain 'mmm hmm'.

'Nothing you want? Some eggs? Washing-up brush? Toilet cleaner? Sardines?'

Kendrick shakes his head.

'You sure? I'm going to the shop anyway. Bottle of whisky? A cabbage? I can get you a cabbage, if you want?'

Kendrick looks down. 'No, thank you, Grandad.'

Ron smiles and picks his grandson up. 'Maybe an ice cream though?'

Kendrick looks at him. 'Really?'

'You're on holiday, Kenny. It ain't a holiday without an ice cream.'

'Were you just teasing?'

'I was just teasing.'

'Could I get a Twister? I had one when I stayed at Grandad Keith's.'

Grandad Keith. That old fraud. You don't buy a house that big from selling used cars. And a Millwall fan too. Also, when had Kendrick stayed at Grandad Keith's? Suzi had kept that quiet. Something wasn't right with Suzi and Danny.

'I'll tell you what, you can have two,' says Ron, and puts Kendrick down as he wriggles with delight.

'I have *never* had two Twisters before.'

Out of the window Ron sees Joyce walking with Siobhan. Poor Poppy's mum, she turned up last night. Ron knows he should be feeling nothing but sympathy for Siobhan, but really he's thinking what a good-looking woman she is. Give it a week though, he thinks. He really wouldn't mind chancing his arm. After the funeral, maybe?

He leaves Kendrick with Ibrahim, both happy. As he slips on his coat he can still hear Ibrahim.

'What's another word for "parallelogram"? Seven letters?'

'I don't think there is another word,' says Kendrick.

'Maybe you're right,' says Ibrahim.

Ron opens the front door and smiles. How did he end up with a grandson and a best mate like these two? Lucky fella.

48

Patrice left this morning. There was a cab to the station, there were tears. Even the odd one or two from her. The flat feels very empty, and Chris feels empty too.

Elizabeth and the gang had liked Patrice. On their way out, Joyce had whispered, 'Oh, Chris, she's a dream,' and Ron had given him a thumbs-up and said, 'Give her one from me, son.'

Chris is hungry.

Earlier this week he had been chopping up peppers, just like he had seen people doing on *MasterChef*. He had a red pepper, a green pepper and a yellow pepper. He has always known that you can buy them in packets of three from the supermarket. He has walked past them thousands of times in his life. Mocking him with their healthiness, as he made his way to the pies and pasta aisle.

He's back in work tomorrow. Trying to catch Connie Johnson. There's a team down from London to 'help out'.

Chris has always fantasized about being the sort of man who might buy the red, yellow and green peppers. The sort of man who would buy broccoli or ginger or beetroot out of choice. To Chris, the fruit and veg aisle at the supermarket was where he bought bananas and occasionally a bag of spinach to put at the top of his basket in case he bumped into anyone he knew. People always look into your basket, don't they? Chris wanted to pretend he shopped and ate like a grown man. Slip the KitKats under the spinach and no one's any the wiser.

Chris thinks back to the day a cashier in Tesco's was scanning his shopping. As she swiped through the chocolate, the crisps, the Diet Coke, the sausage rolls, she had looked up with a kind smile and said, 'What is it, dear, a child's birthday party?' Chris has used self-service checkouts ever since.

He and Patrice had gone food shopping. Patrice asked him if he ever cooked stir fries, and Chris had lied and said that he did, and Patrice said she hadn't seen a wok anywhere, so Chris had admitted that, no, he didn't actually cook stir fries, but that he had always wanted to.

They went to the market, not the supermarket, but the actual *market*, and they bought a bit of this and a bit of that. As Patrice asked a man in an apron where his raspberries were from, Chris felt like a proper human being. It was like they were a couple from an advert. Chris kept hoping people would see him. 'What, this? Oh, it's just me and my girlfriend buying beansprouts.'

This place was empty without Patrice. Without her falling asleep on the floor in the living room while doing an online yoga class on her laptop. It was all very good in theory to have a girlfriend who did online yoga classes, but even better to have a girlfriend who was happy to have a nap in the afternoon.

Chris hadn't wanted this week to end. On Monday Patrice will be back to school in south London. They'll be back to Skype calls, and watching the same TV shows in different rooms.

His heart sinks, though, at the thought of the lock-up, and the thought of surveillance food. Would he go back to his old ways the moment Patrice was gone? He thinks back to last night.

Chris had circled coconut oil into a wok. They had had to buy coconut oil. And they'd had to buy the wok. And, once he had completely come clean to Patrice, they had had to buy the chopping board, the sharp knives and the sea salt and black pepper too. What a heady ride that shopping trip had been.

A fifty-one-year-old man, tossing peppers and beansprouts and spring onions and tofu (which was a whole other story) into a wok and hearing the sizzle so familiar from television. He had started to cry. Where had that come from? From the years of late-night take-aways by himself? The snacks, the numbing release of empty fat and carbs, the long nights, the long years, on his sofa with no one to put his arms around? And now this, the colours, the smells, the sheer, everyday normality of it.

Chris hadn't looked after anyone in a long time, and that included himself. He let the tears run down through the steam and into the pan.

As the first tear sizzled, arms had encircled his waist. Patrice had woken up. He had turned and she tilted her head up to kiss him.

'You have to stand back from the wok if you don't want your eyes to water.'

'Good tip,' said Chris. 'How was yoga? You get it all done?'

'Mmm,' says Patrice. 'Intense though.'

She had pushed herself up and sat on the worktop. Chris was aware that he had seen women blithely sitting on worktops in films, but he didn't think it was ever something that would happen in his own kitchen. This lovely, sleepy woman, perched on his worktop, happy to be there.

'So, have you fallen in love with me yet?' Patrice had said with a laugh.

'Of course,' said Chris, smiling, and gave her a kiss.

'I should hope so, too,' said Patrice, and hopped down from the worktop. 'I'll get bowls.'

Chris had turned back to the wok. He angled his head away from Patrice, now busily rooting through a cupboard. The tears came again then, heavier this time. What was wrong with him? It was just a stir fry, Chris. It was just a stir fry, and a woman sitting on a worktop.

It was then he realized. Realized? Understood? It doesn't matter which, it only mattered that, in the instant he knew that, yes, he *had* fallen in love with her.

Oh, God, yes, and oh, God, no.

At some point, would he really have to tell Patrice? Perhaps she could just work it out.

Chris had wiped a tear from the corner of his eye. The pain from a stray chilli flake on his finger was immediate, and all thoughts of love and happiness and shame and vulnerability and fear and excitement had to take second place for the moment.

At least he didn't have to explain why he was crying any more.

Being healthy was easy when Patrice was here; it seemed so simple. Eat fruit, drink slimline tonic, don't have a KFC.

But the evenings were longer when she wasn't here. And Chris Hudson wasn't about to steam broccoli for himself, that seemed weird. Was it OK to have a biscuit, if it was just one biscuit? Perhaps he could have some chocolate if it was just that dark chocolate you could buy in health-food shops? It tasted awful, so surely that made it OK?

Ibrahim had once told him that walnuts were very good for you, so now Chris is eating a lot of walnuts.

Where to draw the line?

Everywhere delivered now. Not just the restaurants, that was bad enough, but the local shops. Chris could have Pringles and an Aero brought to his door within ten minutes.

He eats another handful of walnuts, chewing begrudgingly. Perhaps he would have a herbal tea? Or just order a Twix. What harm would that do? Or two Twixes, because they were so small?

Maybe a curry? But with a vegetable side dish instead of poppadums?

Stop thinking about food, Chris. Think about work. Ryan Baird's hearing is coming up. That should be an easy win. Think about Connie Johnson. Has she made any mistakes? He doesn't like the thought of her being driven around Fairhaven in that Range Rover like she owns the place.

Chris's entryphone starts to ring. 9.45. Late for a visitor.

49

Strictly speaking, it is not a date.

She and a DCI from London had been on surveillance all evening, keeping an eye on Connie Johnson's lock-up. Donna would rather have been on the stakeout with Chris, and now her mum has gone back to south London she'll get her wish soon enough.

There was nothing to report at the lock-up: a few lads on bikes, coming and going. No new faces, no Connie. Donna had half-expected to see Ryan Baird cycling up to the door at some point, but perhaps he is lying low until his court appearance?

Connie had their number, that was for sure. But if she and Chris could find a way of nailing her, then medals and promotions would surely follow.

The DCI was one of a crew down from London for a couple of weeks. Connie Johnson was being taken seriously, and reinforcements had been brought in. He is currently sitting opposite her drinking beer from the bottle ('I don't need a glass, it's already in glass'). He was the only single man in the whole bunch, if Donna's extensive Facebook investigations were to be believed.

The DCI is called Jordan, or maybe Jayden. With desserts on the way it was probably too late to ask which now. She has just been calling him 'sir' all evening and he doesn't seem to mind. So far she has found out that he has never watched *Bake Off* because it is 'mind-numbing rubbish' but, nevertheless, he thinks that 5G phone-masts are a government conspiracy, and something to do with cancer. Something we should be keeping an eye on, at the very least.

He must be thirty-five or forty, it's so hard to tell with men at that age. He looks like he has strong arms, and that was enough for Donna to agree to dinner at Le Pont Noir after their shift. God, she is lonely.

She is nearly thirty, with friends pairing off and disappearing. Carl, her ex, was engaged already, he'd wasted no time. And this a man who 'needed space' and 'wasn't ready for commitment, babe'. His fiancée is a shoe influencer, rather than a police officer, and they are getting married in Dubai.

So Donna is the new girl in a new town. A black girl in a seaside town, where she feels unwelcome or a novelty, and has no interest in feeling either. 'Where are you from then?' 'South London.' 'No, where are you *really* from?' 'Oh, I see, I'm really from Streatham.'

A town where Boots doesn't have your shade of foundation, and the nearest person you can trust with your hair is in Brighton. None of this will kill her, but none of it helps her feel any less lonely.

But you have to make the best of things. And you also have to hang out with people under fifty every now and again. Hence this too-obvious man, whatever he might actually be called. Best foot forward, Donna

'I can't believe you haven't caught her yet,' says the DCI with the possibly strong arms.

'Connie's smart,' says Donna.

'Smart for a small town, I suppose,' says the DCI. 'Not smart for London. Lucky for you lot, me and the cavalry have arrived.'

'You haven't caught her either,' says Donna. Not unreasonably, she thinks.

'London has different rhythms, love. A different heartbeat.'

'I know,' says Donna. 'I'm from London.'

'You have to live it, really. You breathe it in. The big, bad city.'

'As I say, I was born there. Where are you from?'

'High Wycombe,' says the DCI.

'The mean streets,' says Donna.

'Is that a joke?' asks the DCI.

'No, it's just conversation,' says Donna. 'You can join in.'

Does he have nice eyes? Well, they're a nice colour. That's something.

'I'm staying at the Travelodge, by the way,' says the DCI, looking at his watch, a fake Rolex, no doubt 'borrowed' from an evidence store.

Donna nods. So she is going to have to have sex in a Travelodge this evening if she doesn't want to be alone? So be it. Let's get the bill, get a bottle of wine on the way and get it over with. A bit of oblivion, while her mum and her boss are falling in love.

'Your guv'nor, then?' says the DCI. 'Chris Hudson? He seems a bit hopeless?'

'I wouldn't underestimate him if I were you,' says Donna. Be very careful now, Jordan or Jayden.

'He wouldn't last a second in London,' says the DCI.

'Would he not?' asks Donna.

'Nah, he couldn't catch Covid, that one.'

Well, there it was. Donna wasn't going to have to have disappointing sex in a Travelodge this evening after all. Wasn't going to have to boost the ego of this nondescript man. What was she even doing here? What was she looking for? The waiter brings over the bill and the mediocre DCI, who just made the mistake of insulting her best friend, takes a look.

'You OK going halves?' asks the DCI. 'Also, you had wine, so . . . ?'

'Of course, sir,' says Donna, reaching for her bag. She is going to have to do something about her life. In fact, she knows just the man she should talk to. Ibrahim.

She's just sent him the CCTV from the station. Would he mind if she came to see him sometime?

Donna doesn't need therapy, but she wouldn't mind a nice long chat with a friend who happens to be a therapist.

Her phone pings. It's a message from Chris.

50

Chris Hudson pads over to the handset on the wall and picks it up.

'Hello?' Perhaps it's Donna on her way home from a disastrous date with an ice-cream salesman?

'Hi, Chris, it's me,' says a disembodied female voice. Not Donna.

'OK,' says Chris. 'Any other clues?'

The voice on the phone laughs. 'I told you I knew where you lived, silly!'

Chris freezes. Connie Johnson.

'Are you going to let me up? I have something to discuss with you. Won't take long.'

Chris curses beneath his breath and buzzes her in. What is this going to be? He quickly types out a text message to Donna.

Connie Johnson at flat. If I don't ring in 15 mins, send squad car.

Chris looks around to see if the flat is in any way presentable. And, of course, it is, because he'd made it presentable for Patrice, and hasn't had enough time to ruin it yet. There is a knock at the door. Chris takes a deep breath and opens it.

'Hello, Chris,' says Connie Johnson.

Chris refuses to respond, but ushers her in.

'Well, this is nice, isn't it?' says Connie, surveying the flat. 'Small, but nice.'

'Well, it's all I can afford without selling cocaine to children,' says Chris.

'All right, Mother Teresa,' says Connie, and sits on Chris's sofa. Chris takes a dining chair, places it opposite her, and sits.

'You know you're on thin ice?' says Chris. 'Coming round to a police officer's home?'

'Mmm,' says Connie. 'You're probably on thin ice inviting me up. Do you have anything to drink?'

'No,' says Chris. Which is, actually, pretty much the truth.

'Be like that then,' says Connie. 'I'll just get straight to it. What do you know?'

'About you?'

'Yep,' says Connie.

'I know you killed the Antonios. I know you've got a Range Rover. I know you're clever, but not quite clever enough to get away with what you're doing, so I'll just keep plodding on.'

'Mmm,' says Connie again. 'Well, firstly, no comment, and secondly, I think you're pretty smart too. That's what people say.'

'I'm not smart,' says Chris. 'I'm smarter than you, but I'm not smart.'

Connie nods. 'Maybe. It was certainly easy to find out where you lived.'

Chris shrugs. 'It's quite easy to follow someone home, Connie.'

'It is,' agrees Connie. 'It was easy to follow you here, and it was easy to follow Donna De Freitas to 19 Barnaby Street too. She's on a date tonight, by the way. Pont Noir.'

Chris laughs. 'This isn't the school playground. We're Fairhaven police officers, we live in Fairhaven. It's pretty easy to track us down. But if you're trying to scare me, try harder, you wouldn't touch a police officer, and you know it.'

'I do,' says Connie.

'So what do you want?'

'Well, nothing really, I just wanted to say that, as a businesswoman, there's a limit to how much I'm going to tolerate you poking into my affairs.'

'Is there?'

'There is. Taking photographs of my customers and so on. I'm approaching my limit now, so, just between friends, I'm telling you to tread very carefully.'

Chris nods. 'Sure, because you know my address, and you know Donna's address? Terrifying.'

'It's just a friendly warning,' says Connie, pushing herself up off the sofa. 'If you're not worried, you can just ignore it.'

'I will, thanks,' says Chris, showing her to the door.

'Sorry I called so late,' says Connie. 'I keep funny hours. She's gorgeous, by the way.'

Chris had been about to shut the door behind her, but has stopped in his tracks.

Connie laughs. 'You've done very well for yourself, if you don't mind me saying. I bet you're missing her already? You here, and her up in south London?'

'Don't even think about this, Connie,' says Chris.

'Think about what?' asks Connie. 'Just saying Streatham's a long way away, eh?'

'Connie, I'm not kidding, you're not smart enough to pull this off. Let it go.'

'I might not be smart enough,' smiles Connie, 'but I'm quite dangerous. Or unpredictable, that's the nicest way of putting it. I followed you home, but someone else followed Patrice home for me.'

'Get out,' says Chris.

'I'm already out, silly,' says Connie. 'I promise we'll keep an eye on her for you. Make sure she's not up to mischief. She's really very pretty. Bet she keeps you on your toes. Like all the best women.'

As Connie blows him a kiss, Chris slams the door and slumps back against it. Think quickly, assess the risk. Tell Patrice that Connie has just threatened her? Ask her to be careful? Look out for Range Rovers? Terrify her? For what? For some amateurish bluff? Jesus! Was it a bluff? Just how unpredictable was Connie Johnson? Could he –

Chris's phone rings. Donna. His fifteen minutes are up. He knows he has to pick up.

'All clear,' he says.

'What did she want?' asks Donna.

Tell Donna the truth? Chris makes an instant decision. He hopes it's the right one.

'She just wanted to threaten me. And you. Just letting me know she had our addresses. Telling us to ease off.'

Donna laughs. 'She thinks we'll be scared of her?'

'I laughed her off too. Told her to do her worst.'

'And that's all?' asks Donna. 'Just some amateur intimidation?'

'Yep, sorry if I worried you.'

'Don't be silly. You OK? You want me to pop over? We could watch another episode of *Ozark*?'

Chris opens a kitchen drawer and looks at the take-away menus, neatly tidied away by Patrice.

'No, I should get some sleep. You had a good evening?'

'Surveillance with that guy from the Met. Jayden? Jordan?'

'Jonathan,' says Chris. 'I'll see you in the morning.'

'Night, skipper,' says Donna.

Chris looks at the menus again. He would kill for a curry. He slams the drawer shut.

If you don't love yourself, who's going to love you?

51

Ibrahim is propped up in bed. He has a cigar and a glass of brandy on his bedside table, and his laptop open in front of him. He clicks on the CCTV file Donna has sent him. You will go a long way to find someone else in Coopers Chase who knows as much as Ibrahim about IT. A long way.

'Now, I need you to listen carefully,' says Ibrahim. 'Douglas and Poppy were murdered sometime before five p.m. on the twenty-sixth, so we only need to watch the footage from then until Elizabeth and Joyce check the locker on Thursday. Just the next three days or so.'

'OK,' says Kendrick, and leans his head on Ibrahim's shoulder.

'Why don't I look through the twenty-sixth on my laptop, and you look through the twenty-seventh on your iPad?'

'Brilliant,' says Kendrick.

'And if you see anyone trying to open locker 531 then just shout.'

'OK,' says Kendrick. 'Well, I won't shout, I'll just tell you.'

'That's a good plan,' agrees Ibrahim. 'And let's talk while we're watching.'

'So we don't get bored!' says Kendrick.

'Exactly,' says Ibrahim, and presses play on the CCTV footage. The fastest he can play it is at 8x speed. The facility opens at 7 a.m. and shuts at 7 p.m., so it will take him ninety minutes to get through the day. With Kendrick he can cover two days in that time. Perhaps it's not the perfect job for an eight-year-old, but children were far too mollycoddled these days.

'I'm watching mine now,' says Kendrick. 'What should we talk about?'

Ibrahim is looking at the black-and-white feed on his screen. The camera shows the whole aisle of lockers. Even at 8x speed, not a soul has come or gone yet. 'How is school?'

'Ummm, it's OK,' says Kendrick. 'Do you know Romans?'

'I do,' says Ibrahim. A backpacker has just stuffed her bag in a locker further down the aisle.

'Who's your best?' asks Kendrick.

'My best Roman?'

'Mine is Brutus. There was just a cleaner, but she didn't steal anything.'

'I think I like Seneca the Younger,' says Ibrahim. 'He was the greatest of the Stoic philosophers. He was very good on the theory of the whole thing, but also always looked to give practical advice. He believed philosophy was not a sacred text, but a medicine.'

'Oh, great, we haven't done him,' says Kendrick. 'What's the best dinosaur? Stegosaurus?'

'Yes, we agree there, Kendrick,' says Ibrahim, and takes a swig of brandy.

'Does it hurt where they kicked you?' asks Kendrick, his eyes still clearly glued to the CCTV.

'I tell the others it doesn't,' says Ibrahim. 'But it does, very much.'

'They probably know,' says Kendrick.

'They probably do,' says Ibrahim. 'But you're the only person I'm telling for sure.'

'Thanks, Uncle Ibrahim,' says Kendrick. 'Someone just took a box out of one of the other lockers, but just boring. Did you feel it when they kicked you? Were you frightened?'

'Those are very good questions,' says Ibrahim, as a man in a suit puts his briefcase in a locker, then takes off his tie and puts that in too. Lost his job and hasn't told his wife yet. 'I remember being very scared, and I remember feeling like I was in a washing machine. That's silly, isn't it?'

'Not really,' says Kendrick. 'If that's what you felt.'

'And I knew I might die, I remember that. And I thought about that, and I thought it was OK, but perhaps unfair that this was how it was going to happen. And I thought, I wish I'd known.'

'Uh huh,' says Kendrick.

'And I thought about your grandad, and I thought about Joyce and Elizabeth too, and I knew I would miss them, and I knew they would miss me, and I thought, I hope I don't die, I hope this ends up OK.'

'I'm happy that you didn't die, because then we wouldn't be doing this.'

Ibrahim lights his cigar.

'If I was being killed I would think of Grandad too, and now I would think of you. And I would think about Cody at school, and Melissa and also Miss Warren. And I would think mainly about my mum. Wow, that's a big cigarette! You shouldn't smoke, did you know that?'

Ibrahim takes a puff. 'Mostly I do what I'm told, life is easier that way. But sometimes I don't do what I'm told.'

'Like me,' says Kendrick. 'Sometimes I stay awake, but Mum doesn't know.'

'You wouldn't think about your dad?' asks Ibrahim. 'If you were being killed?'

Kendrick considers this for a moment. 'I think maybe he'd be angry about it.'

Ibrahim nods and tucks this away. 'I didn't think about my dad either.'

'You don't have a dad, Uncle Ibrahim. He would be a thousand.'

The boys settle to their work for a while. Ibrahim sees seven or eight people walking up the aisle, always to other lockers, and Kendrick sees about the same. No one has yet touched locker 531. The occasional conversation is very easy, and Ibrahim discovers that Kendrick's favourite number is thirteen, because he feels sorry for it, and Kendrick sets him a quiz about the planets. Biggest, Jupiter, best, Saturn. ('Not Earth?' 'You can't count *Earth*!') The clock on the screen ticks on, eight times faster than the clock on his bedside table. Another cleaner comes in at the end of the day, and they are done.

'That was so good,' says Kendrick. 'Can we do the other day together now?'

Ibrahim agrees that they can. He receives a text from Elizabeth – *Any news?* – and he replies *Yes. I am concerned about Kendrick's relationship with his father.* Elizabeth replies back with a rolling-eyes emoji. She has really taken to emojis.

After a toilet break, considerably quicker for Kendrick than for Ibrahim, they settle down for the footage from the day Elizabeth and Joyce opened the locker, and so they will stop as soon as they see them.

The fast-forwarded black-and-white images zoom by once again. Neither Ibrahim nor Kendrick tires, because who tires when they are having fun? Ibrahim asks if Kendrick likes books and Kendrick says he likes some of them but not others, and Kendrick asks if Ibrahim ever lived in another country, and Ibrahim replies Egypt, and Kendrick spells it for him.

Ibrahim is looking at the video when, around lunch-time, he sees Elizabeth and Joyce, and slows the footage down to normal speed. He can't hear what they are saying, but you can always pretty much guess with those two. He sees them having trouble opening the locker, sees Joyce go into her bag, then sees Elizabeth try again, and the locker door pops open. The picture quality is not great, but you can make most things out. Elizabeth takes out the crisp packet, the one she showed Ibrahim this morning, then Joyce puts it in her bag, and they leave.

Kendrick wants to see the footage of Joyce and Elizabeth, and says, 'Oh my goodness, it's really them,' when he does. But they find nothing else and admit defeat. So no one had visited the locker? No one had tried to open it until Elizabeth and Joyce arrived.

'I wish we'd seen a baddie,' says Kendrick.

'Me too,' says Ibrahim. 'Elizabeth won't be pleased.'

'Let's do the day before,' says Kendrick. 'Just for fun and in case?'

Ibrahim agrees, because the moment this task is over Kendrick will be heading back to his grandfather's.

They watch the footage from the twenty-fifth, the day before Poppy and Douglas were murdered. Or just Poppy, if you believed Elizabeth. Had Douglas really faked his own death? Hmmm. They are a little quieter this time, both comfortable in the silence. Kendrick makes Ibrahim guess how fast a rocket is, but that's about it.

As they are watching together, they both see the figure at the same time. Walking down the aisle like the hundred or so others they must have seen before. But this figure is wearing motorcycle leathers and a closed helmet. And this figure stops dead in front of locker 531.

'What have we here, Kendrick?' says Ibrahim.

'Maybe a baddie?' says Kendrick.

'Maybe a baddie,' agrees Ibrahim, and takes another puff on his cigar. Who needs the outside world?

52

Lance James settles into a huge white sofa next to Sue Reardon. The whole house smells of white fig and pomegranate. He knows that smell well. Or used to before Ruth moved out, taking her candles with her. He will sometimes light a match after he has been to the bathroom, but that's as new-age as Lance gets.

'Do you have a cleaner, Mr Lomax?' Sue Reardon asks. 'A white sofa is a very bold choice.'

'A woman from the village has done it for years,' says Martin Lomax. 'Margery, or Maggie, something like that. Thank you so much for popping in, I don't like to travel. I get car sick.'

'It's no problem at all, Lance was only at the bottom of your drive taking photos,' says Sue. 'And I'm not busy, just investigating the deaths of a couple of colleagues.'

'Investigating?' says Martin Lomax. 'I assumed you killed them? Did you not?'

'Believe it or not, no, we didn't. We assumed that you killed them,' says Lance.

Martin Lomax juts out a lip and nods. 'Well, we can't both be right. They're dead, though, that's the main thing.'

'Yes, that's some common ground,' agrees Sue. 'How does it work with you having a cleaner? Aren't you worried she'll stumble across something?'

'I always tidy up before she comes round. Don't you?'

'Well, I'll tidy away some magazines and do the washing-up,' says Sue.

'I'm like that, too. Always hurrying around half an hour before she arrives, I've always left something out, a brick of cocaine or some such. I've got so lazy with tidying up my things over the years.'

'Hence leaving the diamonds lying about, of course,' chides Sue.

'Well, quite,' agrees Lomax. 'Anyway, then I put Radio 4 on for her, and away she goes. How many people have you killed, do you think?'

'Eight or nine,' says Sue. 'You?'

'Same, pretty much,' says Martin Lomax.

Lance looks around. They are in a conservatory with beautiful views of the gardens. There is some stray bunting hanging from a eucalyptus tree. They must have had an event. Martin Lomax has yet to offer them a coffee, or even a glass of water. It doesn't seem to be a power play, it just seems not to have occurred to him.

'I know this is boring,' says Lomax, 'and I know I bang on about it, but I really do need to find those diamonds.'

'Likewise,' says Sue.

'Well, you don't really *need* to find them, do you?'

'I'm afraid we do,' says Lance.

'Not really, though. Obviously, you'd look good if you found them. Obviously, people would be pleased with you. But they're not your diamonds, Sue, are they?'

'Well, they're not yours either, are they?' says Sue.

'I read a book once where the mafia had somebody

ripped apart by tigers,' says Lomax. 'At a private zoo. Can you imagine?'

'Well, I'm afraid we don't have the diamonds,' says Sue. 'And we have no idea where they are.'

'Rats,' says Martin Lomax. 'In my head you killed them, some big cover-up. You hear about it with your gang, don't you? Tortured the information out of them?'

'We didn't,' says Lance.

'Can you not just give Frank Andrade his twenty million pounds?' says Sue. 'Just give him cash and call it quits?'

'My assets tend to be illiquid. And they also tend to belong to someone else. I could steal from the Mexicans to pay the mafia, then steal from the Serbians to pay the Mexicans. I'd be the old lady who swallowed the fly, and where would that leave me?'

'Dead, of course,' says Sue Reardon.

53

The gang are all crowded around Ibrahim's bed. Elizabeth has brought a notebook, Joyce has brought chocolate fingers and Ron has brought a copy of *Rocky III* ('the best *Rocky*') for Ibrahim to watch with him later.

But there is another film for them to watch first. Elizabeth is drumming her fingers and Ron is pacing as Ibrahim gets everything ready. He gets the footage up on his screen. Kendrick is on the balcony playing *Pokémon*.

'So,' says Ibrahim, 'here is today's question. Who is this?'

Ibrahim presses play, and they all watch as the figure in the motorcycle helmet walks down the row of lockers and stops in front of 531. The figure inserts a key.

'Looks like he's having trouble with the lock too,' says Joyce.

'Or she,' says Ron. Ibrahim notes that Ron is getting much sharper on his gender neutrality.

The figure has trouble with the lock but eventually it pops open. The camera angle doesn't show the inside of the locker, but they know precisely what the figure is seeing. They watch as the biker takes the crisp packet out of the locker, then tosses it back in. The biker stares at the empty locker for quite some time before locking it back up and leaving.

Ibrahim stops the footage and it becomes a still image. 'And there we have it,' he says.

'So this was the day *before* Poppy and Douglas were shot?' says Joyce.

'Yes, we weren't even going to check the day before. Kendrick suggested it.'

'Kendrick?' says Elizabeth.

'Yes, Ron's idea,' says Ibrahim.

'Thought he might enjoy it,' says Ron.

'If this was the day before, then how did somebody else know about locker 531?' asks Elizabeth.

'Douglas must have told somebody else,' says Joyce.

'Douglas probably told everyone,' says Ron. 'All his ex-wives. Stuck it on Facebook.'

'Unless it *is* Douglas,' says Joyce. 'I mean, it could be, couldn't it?'

'It could be anyone, Joyce,' says Ron. 'It could be Elizabeth, for all we know.'

'Douglas was in protective custody the whole time, it couldn't possibly be him,' says Elizabeth. 'And, besides, he was the one person who knew the locker was empty.'

'But who else would he have told?' asks Joyce.

They stare at the figure on the screen. Dark leathers, dark helmet, dark gloves.

'What are we missing?' asks Elizabeth. 'Let's watch again.'

They sit through the footage again. And again. And again. But nothing. Elizabeth slumps back.

'We can't tell the gender, we can't tell the age, we can't even tell the height because of the angle of the camera.'

Kendrick walks in from the balcony. 'That was really good orange squash, Uncle Ibrahim. Did you all see the clue?'

'The clue?' asks Elizabeth.

'Hello, Elizabeth,' says Kendrick. 'Yeah, did you see it? I bet you did.'

'I mean, I read certain things into posture, and into stride patterns, if that's —'

'No, the clue. Did you see it, Joyce?'

'I didn't spot a thing,' says Joyce.

'We made cupcakes earlier, and I did the icing,' says Kendrick. 'Would you like one?'

'No, you have mine,' says Joyce.

'OK,' says Kendrick. 'Grandad and Uncle Ibrahim, I bet you saw it?'

'I saw it,' says Ron. 'But in case it's not the same clue you saw, why don't you say yours first?'

Kendrick leans forward into the screen. 'OK, watch the bit where he's opening the locker.'

Ibrahim speeds the footage through and pauses it. The four of them are all looking at each other. Ron shakes his head a little and shrugs.

'You see when he reaches up to the lock?' says Kendrick.

They do see.

'And you see a little gap between his jacket and his glove?'

They lean forward. There *is* a gap as the jacket slides down towards the elbow.

'And there's the clue!'

The short-sighted lean further forward, and the long-sighted lean further back.

'What is it, dear?' asks Elizabeth.

'He's wearing one of Joyce's friendship bracelets.'

Coiled around the wrist of the figure opening locker 531 are some inexpertly woven strands of wool, studded with sequins.

Everyone in the room looks down at their wrists, and then at Joyce.

Joyce looks down at her bracelet, then back up at her friends. 'Well, that narrows things down nicely.'

54

Joyce

You will never guess what?

Kendrick had been looking at the security footage from the Left Luggage Office. This is Ron and Ibrahim's idea of an appropriate project for an eight-year-old. Anyway, he spotted that the figure in the motorcycle helmet was wearing one of my friendship bracelets!

You really could tell it was one of mine. I don't think anybody else makes them quite like me.

You can imagine the fun we had next.

Who was our biker? Ibrahim made a list on his computer of all the people I had given friendship bracelets to. No one from the mafia, for starters, so that was Ron out of the water. He came up with an elaborate scenario in which I had been seduced by an elderly Italian-American on the minibus and we all had a good giggle. Chance would be a fine thing. You can see he's disappointed though.

The four of us were on the list, of course, and Kendrick. Imagine if it was Kendrick? In a book it would be. Wouldn't it be fun to be in a book? I bet my hip wouldn't hurt so much in a book.

Then a few more interesting names. Sue Reardon has a bracelet. Could it have been her? Might Douglas have told her where he had left the diamonds? Elizabeth says she would have taken the crisp packet though.

Lance? Less likely that Douglas might have told him, but more likely he'd have missed the crisp packet.

Siobhan, Poppy's mum, has one. Had Douglas told Poppy, and Poppy told her mum? Siobhan seems very quiet and unassuming, but don't we all?

Martin Lomax? But I didn't give him a bracelet until after the CCTV was taken. Also, I know I'm not one to blow my own trumpet, but I am fairly sure his went in the bin the moment we left. I did pay in his five-pound cheque to Living With Dementia by the way. Even the woman at the bank looked like she hadn't seen a cheque for years.

So, who else? A few people from around the village, Colin Clemence, Gordon Playfair, Jane from Larkin who is having an affair with Geoff Weekes, and don't we all know it? In fact, she gave hers to Geoff Weekes, so I suppose we have to count him too.

And then Bogdan, of course. I nearly forgot him.

We talked for an hour or so. Who, why, when, what? Then Mark arrived in his taxi, time for Kendrick to go home. We had a big cuddle.

Ibrahim fell asleep – he's still not at his best – so Elizabeth and I left. Ron said he'd be back to watch his film once he'd dropped Kendrick off.

Now, here's the thing, just between you and me.

The moment I said goodbye to Elizabeth, I had a

thought. About how to identify the biker for certain. I was going to call after her, but I thought, no, Joyce, for once in your life why not fly solo? You don't always need Elizabeth.

And so this morning I took the minibus down to Fairhaven. I did the same walk, along the same streets, to Fairhaven station. A bit slower than last time, because Elizabeth is a strider. I know she doesn't mean to be, but she is.

I made straight for the Left-Luggage Office and, as I'd hoped, the nice girl with the hair and the headphones was on duty. She even recognized me, which made my day. No one ever recognizes me.

She took off her pretend headphones, and I asked her how she was, and she said she was fine, thank you. And I asked her if she was still having trouble with the manager of Costa, and she said that, if anything, it was getting worse, and he had even offered her a lift home on his motorbike. I told her that, for what it was worth, my experience of men with motorbikes was really very poor, and we laughed like the women of the world neither of us really is. She asked if I needed something from my locker, and I told her I needed something from her, and that it was funny we were talking about motorcycles, and that got her attention.

You see, the thought I'd had, when I left Elizabeth last night, was that the girl at the Left Luggage desk took her job seriously, and did it properly. I thought there was no way she'd let someone walk into the locker area willy-nilly wearing a motorcycle helmet. And it turns out I was right.

She apologized that she didn't remember the day in question – her job is quite boring, the way she was telling it – but confirmed that she would never let anyone into the lockers without seeing a key, and without seeing a face. So anyone wearing a helmet would have to take it off. I asked if there was CCTV in the desk area, and she said there was because her predecessor had been fired for watching pornography on his laptop while he was working. She said she didn't blame him, as the days can start to drag.

I thanked her, and she asked what it was all about, and I said I couldn't tell her, because it was government business. Well, the look on her face. Imagine me saying that if Elizabeth was there, though? I don't think so. I should do more things by myself.

Then I made the same trip we did last time, through the streets to Fairhaven Police Station to tell Donna about the CCTV. Of course, I forget that Elizabeth always seems to know when Donna is on duty, and Donna wasn't there. So perhaps I shouldn't do more things by myself? It is a tightrope.

When I got home, I told Elizabeth what I had done, and she was delighted by my ingenuity, but also annoyed that she hadn't thought of it. 'Why didn't you tell me, Joyce?' she said, and I said that I'd only thought of it on the minibus. Then she told me I was a terrible liar, which, of course, I am. I promised her I wouldn't do things by myself in future, but she told me never to make a promise I couldn't keep.

Elizabeth has sent Donna a message about the CCTV, so perhaps we shall soon find out who opened the locker. And, presumably, that might tell us who killed Douglas and Poppy?

55

Coopers Chase looks beautiful in the late-autumn sun. As Donna walks up towards the village a llama tilts a quizzical head towards her over a white fence. Donna nods a good morning to it. On the lake to her right, a goose misjudges a landing, inelegantly belly flopping into the water. She swears the goose looks round to make sure none of the other geese were watching.

Up ahead a woman with a cane sits on a bench, her face raised to the sun. Donna wonders if the woman might be lonely, until a man in a panama hat sits down next to her, with sandwiches and two newspapers. The *Daily Mail* for him, the *Guardian* for her. How had they made that work over the years, she wonders. The heart wants what it wants, of course.

She passes another couple, hand in hand, and they both smile and wish her a good morning. They are walking down the path to sit by the lake.

When will Donna get to walk down a path, hand in hand, and sit by a lake?

The path broadens out as it reaches the village, the first building being Willows, the nursing home. Last time she had visited had been when Elizabeth took her to meet Penny, former cop and Elizabeth's best friend. No longer there, of course. Some other poor soul in her bed.

Would Elizabeth be in there one day? Would Joyce? Would Ron? Surely not Ibrahim? The thought of any of them so diminished upsets her, and Donna keeps walking past Willows with her head down.

Ibrahim's block lies ahead to her left, through a pretty garden still bursting with colour. A lady using a walking frame moves to one side to let her through and says, 'Cheer up, my darling, it might never happen.' Donna gives her a small smile in return.

It might never happen. Well, yes, wasn't that just the problem?

Walking up the stairs, Donna wonders again what she is doing here. Everybody goes through tough times, don't they? Everyone feels low? They don't go bleating all their troubles to a psychiatrist, do they? Not where she's from. You don't have psychiatrists in Streatham. You have mates with shoulders to cry on. To tell you to pull yourself together.

But Donna doesn't have mates in Fairhaven, and so here she is.

Ibrahim's door is open as Donna reaches the top of the stairs. The man himself moves gingerly, and is able to give her only the gentlest of hugs.

'Sit down, sit down,' says Donna.

Ibrahim braces himself against the arms of his chair and manoeuvres himself with awkward grace into it. Donna settles herself opposite him, in a beaten-up armchair beneath a painting of a boat. Just a regular police officer, paying a regular visit to a friend who just happens to be a psychiatrist. She won't say anything though, it feels silly now she's actually here. They can just look at the CCTV. She's OK, just a bit down.

'Nice to see you out of bed,' says Donna. 'How's the pain?'

'It's getting better,' says Ibrahim. 'It only really hurts if I breathe.'

Donna smiles. 'Shall we take a look at this CCTV? I thought you might enjoy it?'

Ibrahim nods. 'In good time, in good time. But first, how is *your* pain, Donna?'

'How's my pain?' asks Donna, with a laugh. Oh, OK, is this how it's going to work? Is this how therapy starts?

'Yes,' says Ibrahim, tilting his head to one side, reminding Donna of the llama. 'How is your pain?'

'I hurt my wrist in the gym, but that's the best I've got,' says Donna. She shouldn't be here, wasting Ibrahim's time.

'Is that so?' asks Ibrahim. Well, it's more of an observation than a question.

Donna sees that Ibrahim has a large writing pad on the table beside his chair. He reaches over for it and takes a pen from his shirt pocket. OK.

'I have no interest in putting words in your mouth, Donna,' says Ibrahim. 'But you really could have just looked at this new CCTV by yourself. Or sent it to me. Or arranged to meet all of us. But you asked to see me alone?'

'I wanted to see how you are,' says Donna.

'That's very kind of you,' says Ibrahim. 'Which is not unexpected, because you are a very kind woman.

As luck would have it, I wanted to see how you are, too. So how about we have a little chat, and we see how we both are?'

She can't fool Ibrahim, so here we go. She is now Gwyneth Paltrow or something. Donna sits back in the beaten-up old armchair, nods, and closes her eyes. 'OK.' It's not really therapy, is it? If you're just talking to a friend?

Ibrahim looks down at his watch. 'Where do you want to start? Leaving London? Your mum and Chris?'

Donna tips her head back and breathes in deeply through her nose.

'Perhaps we should start with loneliness?' suggests Ibrahim.

Through Donna's closed eyes, tears begin to escape.

'Does it hurt?' asks Ibrahim.

'Only when I breathe,' says Donna.

She wonders how Chris is getting on this morning.

56

The three men sit around a concrete table outside Maidstone Crown Court. The building itself looks like a 1980s Travelodge at a motorway service station.

It is Chris Hudson's duty to be here, but he would have come to watch Ryan Baird in court anyway for sheer pleasure.

Chris has seen quite enough of Maidstone Crown Court over the years. His very first case here had involved a local councillor who had exposed himself on a train, and blamed his hay-fever medication. That councillor was now their local MP. His most recent case was a Paralympian who had been caught stealing rare birds' eggs. She wore her bronze medal in court but was convicted nonetheless.

But he wouldn't miss this for the world. Ryan Baird. The case was deeply unsafe, of course. The cocaine and the bank card found in the cistern of his toilet? The anonymous tip-off? But needs must, sometimes. Chris has never done anything like this before. The Thursday Murder Club leads him further astray almost daily.

Revenge for Ibrahim, that was the only goal. Last time Chris had seen Ibrahim, he had been battered and bruised, and the fact he was so stoic and uncomplaining had just made it worse. Ryan Baird behind bars would do no one any great harm.

So the trial will be a pleasure, but Chris has another, far less happy, reason for being here.

Connie Johnson. What was she capable of? Would she really harm Patrice? It was unthinkable.

What could he do to stop her? Who could help him?

He couldn't call Elizabeth. Elizabeth would tell him to tell Patrice, and he wasn't going to do that. Although it was almost certainly the right thing to do, the brave thing to do, he simply couldn't. You didn't get to be a fifty-one-year-old man by tackling things head-on.

And so he called Ron.

A pigeon is currently trying to steal Ron's chips. He had insisted on a trip to McDonald's on the way to court. Ron shoos the bird away, but it just stands its ground on the table, staring at him, then staring at his chips, waiting for him to drop his guard.

'Don't even think about it, mate,' says Ron to the pigeon, then turns to Chris. 'I reckon all pigeons are Tory.'

'That's a theory,' says Chris.

'She sounds like a nasty piece of work, then?' says Ron. 'This Connie Johnson?'

Bogdan, the third man around the table, nods.

'Fit, though, I heard?' asks Ron.

'English fit, maybe,' shrugs Bogdan. 'Not Polish fit.'

Bogdan had been Chris's next call. During their surveillance of Connie Johnson's lock-up, they had seen Bogdan pay Connie a visit and leave with a package.

Chris had decided he would need to confront Bogdan at some point, ask him a few questions. But after the package had been found in Ryan Baird's cistern, all his questions had been answered. Bogdan clearly knew Connie Johnson, though, and that could be useful, so Chris had invited him along – 'Meet me in Maidstone, bit of fun, don't tell Elizabeth.'

'It's probably nothing,' says Chris. 'It's just intimidation, don't you think? She won't do anything to Patrice?'

Bogdan grimaces. 'I don't know. She's done worse things than that.'

'Worse than killing the woman I love?' says Chris.

'She killed the Antonio brothers, you know that? Did it herself, too, sliced them in two in front of each . . .'

'Jesus,' says Chris. 'By the way, if you have any evidence of that, you know what I do for a living.'

Bogdan laughs. 'You must never talk to the police. It's the law.'

'That's a vote of confidence,' says Chris. 'Thank you, Bogdan.'

'We will fix it,' says Bogdan. 'Ron? We will fix it, yes?'

Ron nods.

'It's a diabolical liberty,' says Ron. 'I won't have a diabolical liberty taken.'

'Don't do anything illegal, though,' says Chris.

'Well, define illegal,' says Ron.

'Against the law,' says Chris. 'It's pretty simple.'

'Chris, my old son,' says Ron shaking his head. 'You couldn't be more wrong. Legal, illegal. It's a fine line. It's nineteen eighty-four, and we're protesting outside Manton

Colliery in Nottinghamshire. Fighting to protect the jobs of fifteen hundred men, fighting to save an industry.'

'You had coal mines in England?' says Bogdan.

'The government, Thatcher, passes emergency legislation, saying you can't picket outside someone else's pit. But we do it anyway, we stand our ground. Matter of principle. The police come at us with batons and shields, but we don't move. We don't fight back, but we don't move. Each and every one of us carted off to some nick or other, a good beating in the back of the van for our troubles. Next morning we're in court, breach of the peace, two hundred quid. Criminal record and concussion for weeks. Now, forgive an old lefty, but I don't think what I did was illegal, I think it was right.'

'Well, different times, Ron,' says Chris.

'Now, a week later,' continues Ron, 'one of the boys goes to the library and finds the address of the Chief Constable of Nottinghamshire. He was made Lord something or other shortly after this. Anyway, he gets the address, and the next day some brother-in-law of someone's brother-in-law goes round with a bulldozer and drives it into his extension. Now that, I grant you, was illegal. So there's your fine line.'

'Hmmm.'

'And when Jason was on *Celebrity Bargain Hunt*,' continues Ron, 'he found out where the auction was going to be and got two of his mates to bid against each other for everything he bought. Gary Sansom, you won't know him, he's an armed robber, but from up north, he ends up paying a hundred and sixty quid for a silver cigarette lighter Jason bought for a tenner, and he won the whole show. Is that illegal? When all the money went to Multiple Sclerosis?'

'Well . . .' says Chris.

'What we're saying,' says Bogdan, 'is you're in safe hands.'

Chris nods. 'Look, just don't kill anyone. But if you can find a way to stop her, you know, all help gratefully received.'

The men nod. Even the pigeon seems to nod, and Ron gives it a chip.

'And not a word to Donna, and not a word to Elizabeth?' says Chris.

'Elizabeth will know already,' says Bogdan. 'There will be a bug under the table.'

'I'm going to have to tell Joyce something though,' says Ron.

'Nothing to *anyone*, Ron,' says Chris. 'The conversation stays here.'

'Sorry, old son,' says Ron. 'Joyce reckons you're in love with Patrice, and I said, no, they're just banging, and who wouldn't, with respect, she's a beautiful woman.'

'Thank you, Ron,' says Chris.

'So I'm going to have to tell her.'

'Tell her what?' says Chris.

'I'll just say we were having a chat, something about the police, I don't know, and Chris called Patrice "the woman I love". She'll be tickled pink.'

'I don't think I did say that, Ron,' says Chris. Had he said that?

'You did,' says Ron.

'Yeah, you did,' says Bogdan. 'Elizabeth will have it all on the tape.'

Well, thinks Chris. Sitting at a concrete table with two friends, a pigeon enjoying a McDonald's, and being in love. That was something to protect, wasn't it?

57

'I just remember there used to be much more dancing,' says Donna. 'You know? Not so long ago. What happened to all that?'

'I don't dance,' says Ibrahim. 'I don't have the fast-twitch muscle fibres for it.'

'And the drugs, and the friends, and the laughs. I miss it all.'

'They don't let you take drugs in the police,' says Ibrahim. 'You are unlucky there.'

'Spoilsports,' says Donna. Her eyes are still closed, but Ibrahim makes her smile.

'Frowned upon, I bet,' says Ibrahim, and then looks at his pad. 'Dancing, drugs, friends, laughs. Which one of those do you imagine I'm thinking is most important?'

'I'm guessing not drugs,' says Donna.

'Friends, Donna, that's where it all comes from. You dance with friends, you do drugs with friends, you laugh with friends. That is what's gone. The friends. Where are they?'

Where have they gone? Where to begin? 'London, America, having babies with men I don't like, found religion, got proper jobs, one of them joined UKIP. No one's got time, everyone's busy. Except Shelley, and she's in prison.'

'So no one's dancing any more?'

'If they are, they're not dancing with me,' says Donna. 'Who are my closest friends? Chris, who's sleeping with my mum. My mum, who's sleeping with Chris. You lot, and, back me up here, my best friends shouldn't be in their seventies.'

Ibrahim nods. 'Agreed. Maybe one would be OK, but four of us seems a bit much.'

'The only person my age I've met down here who I actually like is Connie Johnson, and she's a drug dealer. I bet she dances though.'

'And she certainly does drugs, I imagine,' says Ibrahim.

Donna smiles again. Her eyes have remained shut. This is peaceful, this is helping. Just saying things out loud. Was this therapy? It didn't feel like it. It just felt like finally telling somebody the truth.

'Open your eyes now, Donna, I want to talk to you in a different way.' Donna does as she is told and Ibrahim looks deeply into her eyes. 'You know that time is not coming back, don't you? The friends, the freedom, the possibilities?'

'You're supposed to be cheering me up,' says Donna.

Ibrahim nods. 'Let it go. Remember it as a happy time. You were at the top of the mountain, and now you're in a valley. It will happen to you a number of times.'

'So what do I do now?'

'You climb the next mountain, of course.'

'Oh yeah, of course,' says Donna. Simple. 'And what's up the next mountain?'

'Well, we don't know, do we? It's your mountain. No one's ever climbed it before.'

'And what if I don't want to? What if I just want to go home and cry every night, and pretend to everyone that everything's OK?'

'Then do that. Keep being scared, keep being lonely. And spend the next twenty years coming to see me, and I will keep telling you the same thing. Put your boots on and climb the next mountain. See what's up there. Friends, promotions, babies. It's your mountain.'

'Will there be other mountains after that one?'

'There will.'

'So I can leave babies until another mountain?'

Ibrahim smiles. 'You do whatever you want. But looking forward, not back. And I'll be here as you climb. That armchair is yours whenever you need it.'

the corners of her eyes. breathes out and blinks tears from

'Thank you, I've felt a bit stupid recently.'

'Loneliness is hard, Donna. It's one of the big ones.'

'You should do this for a living, you know?'

'You are simply a little lost, Donna. And if one is never lost in life, then clearly one has never travelled anywhere interesting.'

'And you?' asks Donna. 'You seem sad.'

'I'm a little sad, yes,' agrees Ibrahim. 'I'm frightened, and I can't see a way through it.'

'Up the next mountain would be my advice,' says Donna

'I'm not sure I have the energy,' says Ibrahim. His eyes

start to fill with tears in turn. 'My ribs hurt, and that makes me feel like my heart hurts.'

'I'll be here as you climb,' says Donna, and takes Ibrahim's hand. She has never seen Ibrahim cry before, and she never wants to again.

'Don't tell the others,' says Ibrahim.

'They already know,' says Donna, and Ibrahim nods.

'Even Ron,' he agrees.

Donna squeezes his hand. 'And if you ever breathe a word of this conversation, I will taser you.'

'Quite right,' says Ibrahim. 'Now, shall we solve a murder?'

'Yes, let's,' says Donna.

Ibrahim indicates the underneath of his eyes to Donna, and she goes into the bathroom to fix her make-up. When she returns, Ibrahim has loaded the footage she brought with her onto his computer. Who is the mystery person in the motorcycle leathers?

Donna sits on the edge of his chair, and Ibrahim presses play.

58

Elizabeth has read the letter again and again. What was Douglas trying to tell her? And if the clue wasn't in the letter, then where was it? The locket? She'd checked again, and nothing.

'And you checked the cottage in Rye?' says Sue Reardon, the letter in front of her.

'First thing I did,' says Elizabeth. 'And I wonder if you noticed the first two paragraphs?'

'Nice try, dear,' says Sue. 'Very Douglas.'

It had taken Elizabeth a lot longer to spot that. Sue Reardon was quick. Which was why they were there, of course.

They are having an early lunch in Le Pont Noir. Elizabeth had come to a dead end, and thought it might be time to share the letter with Sue. Their minds were alike. Sue had grumbled a bit about Elizabeth keeping the letter to herself, but hadn't taken it as badly as she might have. The lack of a big fuss had saved them both a bit of time. Sue filled her in a little. A mafia boss is about to fly over, either to claim his diamonds or to kil' Lomax. All the fun of the fair. Elizabeth is glad to ! back in this world. A last hurrah.

'Any old haunts he might have hinted at?' says 'It's clear he wants you to find the diamonds. The l his life, and so on. So something only you and he would know?'

'Nothing springs out. But I hadn't seen the man in twenty years,' says Elizabeth.

'You lucky thing,' says Sue.

'Sounds like you've had a few run-ins with him?'

'He's of a certain generation, isn't he?' says Sue. 'I'm glad you trusted me with this letter, Elizabeth. It would have been deeply unprofessional if you hadn't, but I appreciate it all the same.'

'Sometimes we have to stick together, don't we?' says Elizabeth. 'I am learning to be more trustworthy as the years go by.'

'Well, I hope that epiphany comes to me one day,' says Sue. 'But I trust you, for what that's worth. I wouldn't put it past us to find the diamonds together.'

'We are peas in a pod,' says Elizabeth.

Sue raises her glass. 'Let's drink to that.'

59

'Ready for the show?' asks Ibrahim.

'Best seat in the house,' says Donna, and puts her arm around the old man's shoulders.

The recording starts a few minutes before the time the locker was opened. They can see the back of the young receptionist's head, and a few people hurrying through the frame in front of her. A balding man in a Costa Coffee uniform saunters over wearing sunglasses. A few words are spoken, mainly by the receptionist, and he walks away again, a little less jauntily. Another twenty seconds or so, and then the biker walks into view. Same leathers, same helmet, same person who came looking for the diamonds.

There is no sound, but the sequence of events is clear. The figure walks out of shot, towards the lockers, and is summoned back by the receptionist. The figure then fishes around in a pocket and shows the receptionist something, and is then asked to take the helmet off. The face is as clear as a bell, and neither of them has the slightest doubt.

They have no ready explanation, either, but they have no doubt.

It is Siobhan.

It is Poppy's mum, opening a locker, looking for diamonds, the day before her daughter is shot dead.

They even see Joyce's friendship bracelet as Siobhan puts the helmet back on and walks towards the lockers.

'I think perhaps we need to call Elizabeth,' says Ibrahim.

60

Time is ticking on outside Maidstone Crown Court. Ron's chips are long gone and Chris is starting to feel concerned. Why hasn't the case been called yet?

His phone buzzes. A message from Donna. She was on a day off, but hadn't wanted to come along. She'll be doing a kick-boxing class or pressure-washing her patio.

He is about to open it when he sees Ryan Baird's solicitor walking towards them. He is wearing a new suit, actually quite sharp. Donna's fashion advice strikes again. As the solicitor reaches the table he shakes his head.

'Sorry,' says the solicitor.

'Sorry, what?' asks Chris, but he knows what's coming.

'Nowhere to be seen. Phone disconnected, your boys have been round to his flat. Nothing.'

'He's done a runner?' asks Ron.

'He has,' replies Chris.

'Or he may be lying injured somewhere,' says the solicitor. Adding, after Chris's dubious look, 'I'm his solicitor, give me a break. Right, I'm going to follow your lead and have a McDonald's.'

'You let us know if he gets in touch,' says Chris. 'From the hospital?'

The solicitor shrugs apologetically and waddles off to eat chicken nuggets in his new suit.

'Jesus Christ!' says Chris. 'What are we going to tell Ibrahim?'

'We tell him nothing,' says Ron. 'Until you catch him.'

'I don't want to break your heart, Ron,' says Chris. 'But we won't catch him. He'll be up north, or in London. Somewhere he can stay quiet until this all gets forgotten.'

'But this ain't going to be forgotten,' says Ron. 'Is it? I've done my bit. Conning my way into someone's flat, planting cocaine in their lavvy. Now you do your bit.'

'I'll do what I can, Ron. You know that.'

'Chris will find him,' says Bogdan to Ron. 'And we will find a way to stop Connie Johnson for Chris. We are clever men.'

'And if we can't?' asks Chris.

'We will find a way,' says Bogdan. 'You have my guarantee.'

'Right, who's for a McDonald's?' says Ron.

'You just had one,' says Chris.

'That was breakfast,' says Ron.

Chris's phone buzzes a reminder. The message from Donna.

Get over to Coopers Chase as soon as you can. Something very weird. Hope they've banged Ryan Baird up.

'Anyone interested in something very weird at Coopers Chase?' says Chris.

Yes. Everyone is.

61

There were two lakes at Coopers Chase. One was man made, dug by Tony Curran's construction team during the first phase of building work at the development. Ron loved this lake. It was manicured to within an inch of its life, and it had a beautiful paved path all the way around. The fish loved it, the swans loved it and Ron loved it. It was even sparkling blue, because of a chemical they mixed into it once a week. Exactly what a lake should look like.

You had to hand it to Tony Curran, God rest his soul. He was a terrible human being, and there were probably bales of cocaine buried somewhere under the water, but he knew how to dig a lake.

The other lake had been there for centuries; it was surrounded by reeds and wildflowers, and skimmed with lily pads and algae. At best it was a greeny-brown. The insects adored it and Ron didn't see the point of it at all.

Colin Clemence from Ruskin Court used to swim across it every morning. Absolutely swore by it, until he caught Weil's disease and they'd had to put up signs.

He can see one of the signs now. They really could be having this meeting indoors, but Ron had wanted Ibrahim to take a walk and to get some air. If he wasn't going to leave Coopers Chase, at least he could leave his flat. So Ron had suggested they meet by the lake. He had meant the other lake, of course, but Ibrahim looked happy, and so he couldn't really complain.

They took up two benches. Both looking out over the disappointingly untamed lake.

'So beautiful,' says Sue Reardon. She had been at lunch with Elizabeth. They'd kept that quiet.

'Isn't it?' says Joyce. 'So wild.'

Even Joyce likes this stupid real lake?

Ibrahim hands around a printout of the CCTV image. Siobhan, helmet off, hair down, sequined bracelet glinting off a strip light.

'Siobhan!' says Joyce.

'Siobhan,' says Elizabeth.

'Well, now,' says Sue Reardon.

Bloody typical, thinks Ron. The second I start fancying someone.

'I know that now isn't the time or place,' says Joyce, 'but how lovely she's wearing the bracelet.'

They continue to stare in disbelief, trying to work out what has happened.

'This is the woman who turned up at yours, Joyce,' says Chris Hudson. Chris and Donna are on the third bench.

'Poppy's mum, yes,' says Joyce. She squashes a tick on her neck. How do you like the lake now, Joycey?

'And this footage is from the day before Poppy and Douglas were killed,' says Donna.

'The evening before,' says Elizabeth. 'Before the shootings, and before any of us knew where the diamonds were supposed to be hidden.'

'So how did Siobhan know about the locker before we did?' asks Joyce. 'That doesn't make any sense?'

Sue Reardon picks up the picture of Siobhan. 'Elizabeth, I suspect you might be thinking what I'm thinking? That only one person could have told her?'

Elizabeth nods. 'It could only have been Poppy.'

Sue nods. 'Would Douglas really have told her though? I doubt that.'

'I doubt that too,' says Elizabeth.

'Maybe they were in it together?' says Ron. 'They were both at the Lomax robbery, right?'

Donna nods. 'Douglas knows he's going to be locked up a while longer, so he tells Poppy about the locker. Poppy gets her mum to go and collect the diamonds for them.'

'Can you spot the slight flaw in that, Donna?' says Elizabeth.

'Douglas hadn't put the diamonds there in the first place,' says Ibrahim. 'If they were in it together, then why send Siobhan on a wild goose chase?'

'But if Douglas didn't tell Poppy about the locker, then how on earth did she find out?' asks Sue. 'The only place it was referred to was in the letter?'

There is silence all around and everybody tries to think of any possible solution. Donna notices that the only person not deep in thought is Joyce. Joyce is simply looking at Elizabeth, with a kind smile on her face. As if waiting for something. But Ron is the first into action.

'OK,' says Ron. 'I got it. I read the mafia have got listening devices, and they can point them at lightbulbs, and there's some science or other, don't ask me, it's on Google, and the glass vibrates, and they can hear what's being said in any room. They had it on talkSPORT the other day. So the mafia show up here, in a hired car probably, and —'

'Oh, for goodness' sake,' says Joyce.

Ron stops, and all eyes are on Joyce.

'Two spies, and you can't work it out? Two police officers and a psychiatrist? And none of you can work it out?'

'What about me?' says Ron.

'Well, at least you tried,' says Joyce.

'And I suppose you have worked it out?' says Elizabeth.

'Elizabeth,' says Joyce, shaking her head kindly. 'For the cleverest person I know, you can be very dim sometimes.'

62

Ryan Baird is a genius, plain and simple. The court case was a stitch-up, that was obvious. Someone had it in for him. Who knew who? Who cared? All it proved was that Ryan was a face, that Ryan had enemies. And what was a villain without enemies? Nothing.

He is sitting in his cousin Steven's flat. They are in Scotland. He forgets where exactly, some town near Glasgow. Begins with a C. He'd got the train up the day before the hearing. No ticket or nothing. If you were Ryan Baird, if you were a face, if you had enemies, you didn't have to pay for train tickets. In the event he had actually been caught by a ticket inspector, hiding in the train toilet, and been thrown off at somewhere called Doncaster. He'd then got back on the next train, only to be thrown off at Newcastle, where he had had to sleep, because the last train had already gone. But he had made it up to Scotland eventually and his cousin had come and picked him up. Ryan Baird 1, LNER 0.

His mum had told him years ago that if you learn a trade you will never be out of work, and she was absolutely right. Within two hours he was dealing wraps of cocaine.

And now he's sitting playing *FIFA* with Steven, nice big spliff on the go, KFC done and dusted. Genius.

Who would ever think of looking for him in Scotland? No one. It was miles away. They might look for him in London. Maybe they'd go as far as Luton, but he doubts it. Ryan has never been to Scotland before, and he sees no reason why the police would either.

To be safe, he's calling himself Kirk, a name he has always fancied. Even if the police do make it all the way up here, and ask around, no one will have heard of Ryan Baird. It's foolproof.

Admittedly he has called himself Ryan three or four times today, but only after a few drinks with Steven's mates, and they all seem sound enough.

A bit earlier he had put on the local news to see if he was on it. Kent drug dealer on the run. 'Police say Ryan Baird is dangerous and shouldn't be approached.' But the local news up here was all Scottish. Who gave a toss about all this Scottish stuff? Someone had burned down a leisure centre, but that was the only good bit.

He'd got a job, a roof over his head, and a new name, all in one day. He had watched a programme about Pablo Escobar on YouTube, and this was just what Pablo would have done. In fact, Pablo! That was a much better name. Forget Kirk, from tomorrow he'd be Steven's cousin, Pablo.

Pablo Escobar got shot in the end, of course. But that's because he'd got careless. That won't happen to Ryan.

Scotland! You had to hand it to him.

63

All eyes are on Joyce. She is staying silent for a moment, like a presenter waiting to announce the results on *X Factor*. The silence is filled with the hum of insects strafing the reed beds. Donna can tell she's enjoying the attention. Good for her.

'Oh, stop milking it, Joyce,' says Elizabeth. 'For goodness' sake.'

'I was just giving you a few more seconds to try and work it out,' says Joyce, and takes a sip of tea from her flask.

'I'm loving this,' says Ron.

'What have you worked out, Joyce?' asks Donna.

'Only this,' says Joyce. 'Elizabeth, that walk you went on with Douglas, through the woods? The same walk we did the other night?'

'Go on,' says Elizabeth.

'When Douglas told you he'd stolen the diamonds, and made a point of talking about the tree? The dead-letter drop?'

'I feel like this is going to be Elizabeth's fault,' says Ron approvingly.

'Well, Poppy was with you, wasn't she?'

'But with headphones on, Joyce.'

'Well, who else have we met recently wearing

headphones? The lovely girl at the station. And what was she listening to?'

'Nothing,' says Elizabeth.

'Nothing. So who's to say Poppy was listening to anything on her headphones? Who's to say she couldn't hear every word?'

'Beautiful,' says Ron.

'So she heard Douglas confess, and she heard about the old dead-letter drop,' says Ibrahim.

'And then she put two and two together, just like you did,' says Joyce.

'Then came back up the hill, found the note, read it, and put it back,' says Sue.

'Then told her mum where to find the diamonds,' says Ron.

Everyone is looking at Elizabeth now. Donna sees she is thinking hard. Eventually she looks up, and straight at Joyce.

'Oh, Joyce. You really are annoyingly clever sometimes.'

Joyce beams.

'It seems,' says Elizabeth, 'that Poppy might have been cleverer than she was letting on. A poet, my foot.'

'So where does this leave us?' asks Sue. 'Poppy finds the letter and contacts her mother. Siobhan travels down and finds no diamonds.'

'And the next day Poppy is shot dead,' says Chris.

'I'm sorry, I don't actually know who you are?' says Sue. Then looks at Donna. 'Or you.'

'DCI Chris Hudson, Kent Police,' says Chris. 'And this is PC Donna De Freitas.'

Sue nods, then looks at Elizabeth. 'Do these two know how to keep their mouths shut?'

Elizabeth nods. 'They do, to be fair.'

'Flattered, I'm sure,' says Chris.

'I think I've got it,' says Joyce. 'I think I know what happened.'

'You're on a roll, Joyce,' says Ibrahim.

'It's simple. Siobhan doesn't find the diamonds, and tells Poppy so. Poppy is frustrated, of course, and so spills all to Douglas. "Where are the diamonds, I know you have them?" Douglas is enraged. Poppy has found his letter, she's told her mum, who else might she tell? So he has to get rid of her. He shoots Poppy, he fakes his death, we wander in and see them both, and Douglas is in a taxi over to wherever the diamonds really are.'

'Oh, Joyce,' says Elizabeth.

'What?' asks Joyce.

'This really is an object lesson in quitting while you're ahead.'

'Oh,' says Joyce.

Elizabeth takes out her phone and opens the photos of the house in Hove. 'I knew something didn't look right about the crime scene.'

'I see you found your phone, then?' says Sue.

Elizabeth gives a happy shrug. 'Back of the sofa. The whole thing looked too staged. Too perfect. Which is why I thought Douglas had set the whole thing up. Shot Poppy, but faked his own death, and substituted another corpse for his own.'

'But now?' asks Donna.

'Well, now I wonder if it wasn't the other way around. What if Poppy faked her own death?'

'Not Poppy,' says Joyce.

'Who told us that the body in the morgue was Poppy's?' asks Elizabeth.

They all know the answer, but Sue is the first to say it out loud.

'Siobhan.'

And it all falls into place. For the spies, for the police officers, for the psychiatrist and the nurse. Even for Ron. The mother and the daughter and the diamonds. What did they really know about Poppy? What did they really know about Siobhan? Nothing. They knew nothing at all.

PART THREE

So Many Day Trips for You to Enjoy

64

Joyce

Well, guess who has just been on the Eurostar? Yours truly, Joyce Meadowcroft.

I tried to get Ibrahim to drive us to Ashford International, but he wasn't having it. He blamed his ribs, but you can tell they're a lot better. I saw him get a teapot from a high shelf yesterday. I'll tempt him out at some point though, you see if I don't.

There is a theory afoot, Elizabeth's theory, but everyone seems to have bought into it, that Poppy is behind the murders. She found out that Douglas had stolen the diamonds and she wanted them for herself. So she hatched an elaborate plan, too elaborate if you want my opinion, to get them for herself.

It doesn't seem right to me. Poppy was so gentle. Have I really got that wrong? Perhaps I have, I am quite trusting. There was a nurse at the hospital once who kept stealing morphine. And she wouldn't say boo to a goose. Also there's an actor in *Emmerdale* who I love. I follow him on Instagram, and there are always pictures of his wife and his baby and his dog, and I always like them. Anyway, Jason was on *Celebrity Tipping Point* with him, and said he was a nasty piece of work. He didn't go into details but he said he knew one when he saw one, and that's true with Jason, so I took his word for it. I still follow him on Instagram, but it's not the same. He really does have a gorgeous kitchen though.

So maybe I was wrong about Poppy too. Maybe she did it. Twenty million pounds is a lot of money after all.

The idea is that she got Siobhan involved. Got her mum to identify the wrong body, and throw us off the scent. Which is possible. If Joanna asked me to pretend a dead body was hers I probably would. When it's your child, you act first and ask questions later, don't you? She once asked me to tell a boyfriend of hers that she'd moved to Guernsey, so I have some form. He was one of my favourites too. I follow him on Instagram now, and he has two lovely kids with a doctor. I think they are in Norwich, but don't quote me. Also, don't tell Joanna I follow him.

Where was I?

Eurostar! Yes. The seats are very comfortable, there is free tea, and you can plug your phone in. When we were in the Channel Tunnel I texted Joanna and said *Guess where your mum is?*, but she didn't reply until this evening, and by that time I was in the taxi home from Robertsbridge station.

Have you ever been to Antwerp? I doubt it, but you never know. It is very pleasant. It has a cathedral, and we must have walked past eight or nine Starbucks. We had an appointment at two, with a man called Franco. Franco is a diamond dealer, and his workshop is in a long row of houses beside a canal, with steps leading up to them.

There are small brass plaques by the doors. I thought there would be windows and windows full of diamonds, but no such luck. There was a cat in one window, but nothing more exciting than that.

Franco was gorgeous. I don't think I really had an idea what Belgian people looked like before today, but if Franco is anything to go by I will keep my eye out in future. White-haired, tanned, blue eyes and half-moon glasses. I asked him if his wife worked with him and he said he was a widower. I put my hand on his, purely for comfort, and Elizabeth rolled her eyes.

Perhaps Poppy was murdered, perhaps Douglas was murdered, perhaps they both were? No one knows for sure, and that's the point. But this is where the killer would have come to cash the diamonds in. Either to Franco, or to someone Franco knew.

He offered us both a glass of milk. I said yes, because I don't remember the last time I had a glass of milk. Do you? As I drank it I was thinking, well, this might be the last glass of milk I ever drink, mightn't it? I can't see another situation where I will be offered one. Unless I were to marry a handsome Belgian. Which I am refusing to rule out.

Imagine if I married Franco? Imagine the ring! Imagine Joanna's face. She is currently dating the chairman of a football club. He is always in the gym, and she has a spring in her step. I would walk down to the market and buy food for tea. Franco would be sitting there, glass of milk in hand, and I would ask how many diamonds he'd sold today (or something more technical once I'd got used to it all) and he would look down over those glasses and say something in Belgian. Yes, please. I wouldn't mind that one bit.

I was glad I was wearing my new green coat from ASOS.

I'm waffling on, aren't I? Though you would be too if you'd met him. Elizabeth asked him if Douglas had been to visit him, and Franco said he'd had a call about a month ago, telling him to expect a visit, but he hadn't heard from him since. They are all obviously old pals from some escapade or other.

Then Elizabeth asked if anyone else had been to see him, with twenty million pounds' worth of diamonds. He said no again.

To be on the safe side we described everyone we could think of. We described Poppy, we described Siobhan, we described Sue and Lance, we described Martin Lomax, we mentioned the mafia and the Colombian cartel, but nothing doing. No one like that had come to see him in the last two weeks.

I had another glass of milk, just to eke things out, but eventually we had to say goodbye. Franco kissed me three times, and I thought well, here we go, but then he kissed Elizabeth three times too, so that must just be what they do in Belgium.

We had to head back to the station, but, on the way, I bought some chocolate for Ibrahim and some beer for Ron. The shop even wrapped them nicely.

I thought we might sleep on the train back, but honestly we were talking. If Poppy was behind all this, then she would have come to Franco. There are very few places in Europe where you can cash in twenty million in diamonds with no questions asked. If Poppy has the diamonds, then perhaps she is lying low? And if she doesn't have the diamonds, then she will still be looking for them. But where are they? Somewhere in Douglas's letter is the answer. But we've read the letter, and Poppy has read the letter. Who will be the first to work it out?

It was quite a long journey back, so somewhere in northern France I unwrapped Ibrahim's chocolates and we ate them, and then I unwrapped Ron's beers and we drank them.

So, we need to find Poppy before she finds the diamonds. Elizabeth says she has a plan to flush her out.

I can see in the distance that her light is still on. That means she is thinking about Poppy.

May your light always be on, Elizabeth.

We are not telling Ibrahim for now that Ryan Baird has disappeared. We're just saying the case is delayed. I hate to lie, but I can see the point.

Ron says Chris is in love with Patrice. Well, I should think so, too. I predict a happy ending there.

I am going to bed now. I know I should be thinking about Poppy and the diamonds. But instead I'm going to think about a big house by a canal, with stone steps, and brass plaques by the door.

You have to keep dreaming. Elizabeth knows that. Douglas knew it, too. Ibrahim has forgotten, but I'm here to remind him when the time is right.

65

The game of chess has finished, and the real work of the evening has begun.

Elizabeth still feels a little woozy from the Belgian beers on the train. And the glass of wine at the station as they waited for their taxi. And the gin and tonic Bogdan had waiting for her when she walked through the door. And the second gin and tonic she is currently drinking.

Bogdan and Stephen had ground out an attritional draw. Bogdan had called Stephen all the names under the sun and Stephen had smiled and said, 'Let it out, old boy, let it out.'

The three of them now sit in the living room. Elizabeth and Stephen on the sofa, hand in hand, and Bogdan on the armchair, legs spread wide. It is 1 a.m. But no one much minds. Bogdan is drinking Red Bull and Elizabeth wonders, once again, what time he normally goes to bed.

Bogdan has filled her in on the trial. Ryan Baird has done a disappearing act. Don't tell Ibrahim. They will soon find him, though; they still have the file that Poppy put together.

Poppy? Now, what was happening there? What signs had Elizabeth missed?

Everyone was capable of stealing. She once knew a vicar who had stolen, and melted down, a crucifix from

330

his own church because he had lost money on the horses. But not everyone was capable of killing. Was Poppy? It seemed so unlikely, but Elizabeth has been fooled before, not often, but she has. She watches Bogdan, pouring himself an energy drink, looking as innocent as the day is long.

And Poppy had shot Andrew Hastings. She had been shaking afterwards for sure, but anyone could fake that. Involuntarily, Elizabeth starts to shake.

'You cold, dear?' asks Stephen.

You see, it was easy. Stephen puts his arm around her and she settles her head on his shoulder. What a man. Also, Poppy's generation were used to generating fake emotion, weren't they? A whole generation, outraged at the slightest thing, sensitive to the slightest criticism, honestly, whatever happened to . . . wait a minute, she realizes she doesn't really believe that, she had just read a *Daily Express* someone had left on the train. Most young people were like Donna, fighting new fights. Good luck to them.

She nestles further onto Stephen's shoulder. The thought crosses her mind briefly, what if *neither* of them is dead? What if they're in it together?

What if Poppy and Douglas were lovers?

Elizabeth wouldn't put it past Douglas. He liked nothing more than a woman he couldn't have. Or shouldn't have. Would move heaven and earth to get her, promise the world.

But Poppy? Honestly, she found it more likely that Poppy would kill Douglas than would fall in love with him. Though it was often a fine line, wasn't it? Especially with Douglas.

Bogdan has just polished off another Red Bull. 'So Poppy says, "I kill you, Douglas, unless you tells me where the diamonds really are."'

'The nerve,' says Stephen.

'Mmmm,' says Elizabeth. She is sleepy and comfortable. There is no way Poppy and Douglas were lovers.

Bogdan continues the theory. 'Then Douglas tells her, "I buried them under a tree, by a fence, don't kill me," but she shoots him anyway.'

'Joyce any nearer buying that dog?' asks Stephen.

'What, darling?' says Elizabeth.

'Your pal, Joyce. She was after buying a dog?'

The things Stephen remembered.

'No, dear, on hold while everyone's being shot, I think.'

'Time and a place,' agrees Stephen.

'Douglas would lie, of course,' says Elizabeth. 'He wouldn't tell Poppy where the diamonds were in a month of Sundays.'

'I should think not,' says Stephen. 'Pointing a gun in his face, asking him about diamonds? The cheek of the girl.'

'So Poppy is out there still,' says Bogdan. 'Looking for the diamonds.'

'Furious, no doubt,' says Stephen. 'Would anyone like dinner, by the way? There's a lasagne?'

'Maybe later, not now,' says Bogdan.

'So what would you do, if you were Poppy?' asks Stephen. 'What are the options?'

'Is obvious,' says Bogdan.

'Oh, good,' says Elizabeth, deciding she should probably rouse herself from Stephen's shoulder. There was work to do.

'I would just keep an eye on Elizabeth,' says Bogdan. 'Sooner or later she knows you find the diamonds.'

'Oh, Elizabeth will find them all right,' says Stephen. 'She'll waltz back in, pockets jingling with them.'

'And when Elizabeth finds them, Poppy will be watching and waiting,' says Bogdan.

'So to find Poppy I need to find the diamonds?' says Elizabeth. 'Which is proving impossible.'

'No such thing as impossible, dear,' says Stephen. 'There'll be a clue you've missed somewhere. Read the letter again.'

'It's not in the letter,' says Elizabeth. 'We've been through the lot.'

'You'll figure it out,' says Stephen. 'It'll be that ex-husband playing silly buggers.'

'We just need a trap,' says Bogdan.

'With the diamonds as bait,' says Stephen. 'Get the brain in gear, old girl.'

'I'm afraid my brain has had a long day,' says Elizabeth. A long day of thinking, a long life full of thinking. So much thinking. Just to find that all she was looking for was this. A Polish man too big for the chair he is sitting in, and a lovely white-haired man who thought he could explore Venice without a map.

Elizabeth rests her head on Stephen's shoulder once more and shuts her eyes. The last thing she sees before they close is the mirror on her far wall. Who is that old woman looking back at her? Lucky thing, whoever she is. She sees the reflection of her husband, still in his tie and his smart shoes, and the reflection of Bogdan, his shaved head, his muscles, and the NIKE logo on his T-shirt, reading EKIN in the mirror.

She opens her eyes again.

66

'Well, he'll kill me,' says Martin Lomax, as if talking to an idiot. 'Chop my legs off, you know the mafia.'

'Agreed,' says Sue Reardon. 'That's why we're here. To protect you.'

'Good luck,' says Lomax, and turns to Lance James standing by the window, looking out over the gardens. 'Good luck, eh, Lance?'

'If they want to kill you, they'll kill you,' says Lance. 'We can probably delay them a bit. But you know the mafia.'

'Don't I just,' says Lomax. 'They don't even take their shoes off when they come in.'

Lance has taken to visiting Martin Lomax every morning, at around eleven. Staking out a house was boring, especially as Lomax never left it. So they had come to an arrangement.

Lomax lets him charge his phone and use his Wi-Fi. And in return he would ask Lance questions about the Special Boat Service.

Nothing classified, obviously, but Lomax is a military history nut, and Lance has plenty of good stories. Lance had been based down in Poole for fifteen years with the SBS, been on operations that everyone had heard of, and he'd been on operations that nobody would ever hear of. Certainly not from him.

'Frank Andrade will be landing on Monday, in a private jet, at Farnborough airfield,' says Sue. 'I'm guessing he'll come straight here.'

'What time does he land?' Lomax asks.

'Eleven twenty-five a.m.,' says Lance.

'Well, he'll hit traffic,' says Lomax. 'The A3 will be snarled up.'

A lot of the work the Special Boat Service would do came through the Security Service, or the Special Intelligence Service, MI5 and MI6. As he got older, Lance spent a bit less time chasing al-Qaeda and a bit more time at a desk. He would come up to London every now and again to give briefings. He would consult on operations. Before you knew it, he had been taken aside and asked to join MI5 permanently. Keeping his hand in on operations, of course. Overseeing the raid on Martin Lomax's house, for example. That sort of thing. Lance could break into anything, and kill anyone. The builder who'd slept with his ex didn't know how lucky he'd been.

'We will have a team here on that morning,' says Sue. 'Commanded by Lance.'

'SBS?' asks Lomax.

'I can't say,' says Sue.

'But yes,' confirms Lance.

He knows he is still seen as a foot soldier. Looked down on a bit by some of the public-school kids. And he knows he is in danger of getting stuck where he is unless he can make some sort of impact.

This case would be a good place to start. A nice calling-card.

'We wouldn't need all this fuss if you simply found the diamonds,' says Lomax.

'I guarantee that's our plan,' says Sue.

'Well, it seems you only have a few days left,' says Lomax.

'I am confident we'll find them,' says Sue.

Lance doesn't share her confidence. Perhaps Elizabeth Best will find them? That's the only hope. But, either way, Martin Lomax will never see them again. That's not how this will work.

How will it work? Lance supposes he will have to wait and see. But Martin Lomax is a dead man.

67

Elizabeth and Joyce are in the minibus, on their way down to Fairhaven. Joyce has flapjacks and Elizabeth has news. Joyce intends to share the flapjacks, but Elizabeth is keeping the news to herself.

'Just tell me,' says Joyce.

'In good time,' says Elizabeth.

'You're such a bully,' says Joyce.

'Nonsense,' says Elizabeth. 'Are you getting a dog, by the way? Stephen wanted to know.'

'None of your business,' says Joyce. She is beginning to think she might not offer Elizabeth a flapjack, but she has made them with coconut oil, and is desperate for someone to try them. So she is in a bind.

Elizabeth had sent her a message first thing.

We are going to Fairhaven this morning. Wear something that goes well with diamonds.

However, she has been no more forthcoming than that. Joyce is wearing another new cardigan. Navy blue. It had better be worth it.

'What are we going to do about Ryan Baird?' asks Elizabeth.

'You tell me,' says Joyce. 'You always have the answers.'

'Are we having a row, Joyce?' asks Elizabeth. 'How novel.'

'Friends don't keep secrets,' says Joyce.

'It's a good secret though, so don't get crotchety,' says Elizabeth. 'I just want to surprise you.'

The minibus pulls up outside the Ryman's in Fairhaven and Carlito bids them all farewell. He is vaping, and Elizabeth tells him to smoke a proper cigarette for goodness' sake.

'So where are we going?' asks Joyce.

'You know where we're going,' says Elizabeth, and sets off towards the seafront.

'You're so infuriating,' says Joyce, setting off behind her.

'I know,' says Elizabeth. 'I honestly can't help it. I have tried.'

The shops peter out, and they find themselves on a familiar route. They pass the rows and rows of lock-up garages. They pass Le Pont Noir. Elizabeth striding, Joyce hurrying to keep up.

'Are we going back to the train station?' asks Joyce.

'By George, I think she's got it,' says Elizabeth.

'Why are we going to the station?' But Elizabeth is hurrying ahead.

The walk continues, until they find themselves inside Fairhaven train station. No need to follow the signs this time. They stop at the Left Luggage Office and the receptionist takes off her headphones and smiles.

'Welcome back!'

'Thank you,' says Elizabeth.

'Do you need anything?'

'No, thank you, dear,' says Elizabeth, and holds up the key to locker 531.

Elizabeth and Joyce enter the rows of lockers, and Elizabeth stops by the first one.

She takes something out of her handbag, and passes it to Joyce. It is the locket that Douglas gave her.

'You found something in the locket?' asks Joyce. 'Is that why we're back here?'

Elizabeth holds up a finger to stop her. 'Joyce, you solved this for me.'

'Oh, good,' says Joyce.

'Well, you and Bogdan.'

'I don't mind sharing with Bogdan,' says Joyce.

'You worked out that Poppy overheard my conversation with Douglas. Which made me really think about the conversation. I've told you, there's never a word out of place with Douglas. He is meticulous. Even in our wedding vows I noticed he put the slightest question mark after "I do".'

'Ooh,' says Joyce.

'When we were by the tree, he reminded me of a dead-letter drop we had had in East Berlin, only, you see, the dead-letter drop was in West Berlin. I put it down to old age. It hits men harder, as we know.'

'But it wasn't old age?'

'Open the locket, and what do you see?'

Joyce opens the locket. 'Nothing, just the mirror.'

'Just the mirror, precisely. The worthless mirror that Douglas was so keen to give me. But what does a mirror do? It turns East Berlin into West Berlin. It turns NIKE into EKIN. And?' Elizabeth holds up the key.

Joyce almost squeals. 'It turns 531 into 135!'

Elizabeth nods, and motions along the line of lockers. 'Would you like to do the honours?'

Joyce follows behind her. 'No, you.'

They reach locker 135, and Elizabeth slides the key into the lock. It is a perfect fit. She turns it, and the door swings open. Inside is a blue velvet bag, with a drawstring around the top. Elizabeth motions for Joyce to take it. Joyce lifts the bag and loosens the drawstring.

Diamonds sparkle inside. Thirty or so. Big ones.

She was wearing exactly the right cardigan.

'You're holding twenty million pounds, Joyce,' says Elizabeth. 'Slip it into your bag, will you? And promise not to get mugged on the way back to the minibus.'

Elizabeth reaches into the locker again and pulls out a note. It is from Douglas. She reads it, then shows it to Joyce.

Darling Elizabeth,

So you found them? Sorry for the wild goose chase, but it was fun, no? Did you get it from East Berlin, or did you need the mirror? Belt and braces, I know. I didn't want to make it too easy, but I wanted to make sure you would get there eventually. I hope you didn't go down to the cottage in Rye? They built a bypass through it years ago.

In any event, congratulations. Aren't they beautiful? What will you do with them? You really should keep them. Go on, you know you want to?

On a slightly more sombre note, it goes without saying that if you've found this note then I am dead. So it is swings and

roundabouts, isn't it? Though life is always swings and
roundabouts, so I don't see why death should be any different.
I wonder if I'll be heading upstairs? I doubt it, don't you?
I will love you always,

Douglas

Joyce hands the letter back to Elizabeth. Elizabeth folds it up and returns it to the locker. Joyce looks down into her bag, at the diamonds. They are tucked away under a Kate Atkinson.

'So what are we going to do with the diamonds?' she asks. 'I don't suppose we could just keep them?'

Elizabeth slips her arm through the arm of her friend. 'We're going to use them as bait to catch Poppy and Siobhan.'

Joyce nods. 'It will be nice to see Poppy again, even if she murdered Douglas.'

'And maybe bait for a few more people who deserve catching, too,' says Elizabeth.

'Perhaps we could just keep one or two of the diamonds?' says Joyce. 'I don't think anyone would notice?'

'I think,' says Elizabeth, 'that we need to convene an emergency meeting of the Thursday Murder Club.'

'Wonderful,' says Joyce. 'I'm sorry I was angry earlier.'

'Don't mention it,' says Elizabeth. 'I'm infuriating.'

Joyce smiles. 'You certainly are. Would you like a flapjack?'

'Finally,' says Elizabeth.

68

Donna is drinking whisky on Chris's sofa. They have just been watching *Succession*, her favourite show. Billions of pounds, family rows, people in and out of helicopters every five minutes. She could handle a bit of that. Chris has never seen it, because he is nearly fifty-two, and never watches anything new unless he is forced to. She knows he would happily watch repeats of *The Inbetweeners* and *Ramsay's Kitchen Nightmares* until the day he dies.

Chris is currently on FaceTime with her mum.

'Wish you were here, Patsy,' he is saying.

Patsy? Christ! Also, 'Wish you were here'? My company not up to scratch?

Patrice replies, 'I'm coming down on Sunday, Big Bear.'

Donna can't help but smile. Let them enjoy themselves. The chat with Ibrahim has done her good. Life was not running away from her. Just the opposite, she was running away from life. So onwards and upwards. All that nonsense.

There is a ring on her mum's doorbell and she says, 'Hold on, gorgeous, let me get that.'

'Leave it,' says Chris quickly. Donna looks up. That doesn't sound like him. But Patrice ignores him, of course; it runs in the family.

'Leave it?' asks Donna.

Chris dismisses her with his hand. 'I was just enjoying chatting.' His eyes flick back to the screen. Patrice is still not there.

Donna tilts her head. 'Is something up?'

'Stop being such a police officer, Donna,' says Chris.

'What a mentor you are,' says Donna. 'Every day I'm learning.'

Patrice is still not back. Chris starts to whistle. But his leg is jiggling up and down at speed. Something isn't adding up here.

'So did you enjoy *Succession*?' Donna asks.

'Yep, yep,' says Chris, but his eyes don't leave the empty screen. The top of a sofa, a dying pot plant and an old school photo of Donna with a missing front tooth.

'You looking at an empty screen instead of me?'

'Sorry,' says Chris, and gives Donna the briefest of glances before looking back at his computer. What was going on here? Perhaps he's in love? He'd better be.

'You're not hiding anyth—'

Donna is interrupted by the return of Patrice. 'Sorry, dear, it was the Lib Dems at the door. I had to put them straight on tuition fees.'

Chris's leg has stopped jiggling. And he has sucked his stomach in again.

Donna's phone buzzes. A message from Elizabeth.

You are cordially invited to a meeting of the Thursday Murder Club, tomorrow at eleven in the Jigsaw Room. I recommend attendance.

69

Chris could live without this. Two spies had been shot. Or one spy had been shot by another spy. Or no spies had been shot, and the whole thing was one big magic trick? But, whatever the truth of it, it wasn't something he could get involved with. He could catch and handcuff the killer himself, but no one would ever get to hear about it. This was one for the Security Services.

It was interesting, sure, murder and diamonds, and if he was in a better place he could enjoy it. But all he can think about is Connie Johnson. Connie Johnson and Patrice. When Patrice's doorbell rang last night, he had feared the worst. And had hid it badly from Donna. Perhaps Ron and Bogdan could work a miracle?

But here he is regardless. Out of politeness. In the Jigsaw Room, with the Thursday Murder Club in full flow.

Dominating the room are three huge boards, each covered in a sheet of perspex. Beneath the perspex sit half-finished jigsaws of *The Haywain*, Sydney Opera House at Sunset and a 2,000-piece puzzle of the wedding of Prince Charles and Lady Diana. So far only the borders of that jigsaw, and the eyes of the happy couple have been completed. During the opening pleasantries, Chris had been looking into Diana's eyes. The future was there for all to see. Poor Diana, he thought, I hope you had a bit of fun along the way.

But now Elizabeth has dropped the bombshell, and she has Chris's full attention.

'So you have twenty million pounds' worth of diamonds?' asks Chris Hudson. 'In your possession?'

'Yes, give or take,' says Elizabeth.

'And where are they?' asks Donna.

'Never you mind where they are,' says Elizabeth.

'They're in my kettle,' says Joyce.

'Do your spy friends know you've got them?' asks Chris.

'Not yet,' says Elizabeth. 'I'll tell them, but I need a plan in place first. I thought you could help?'

'If we help, can I see the diamonds?' asks Donna.

'Of course, dear, I'm not a monster,' says Elizabeth.

'What can Donna and me do?' asks Chris.

'Donna and I,' says Elizabeth. 'If I tell you, you have to promise not to get angry.'

'Oh, here we go again,' says Chris.

'I want to organize a meeting with the mafia. In Fairhaven.'

'Of course you do,' says Chris. 'Any reason? Or was bridge cancelled and you had a slot in your diary?'

'You know I don't like humour, Chris,' says Elizabeth.

'We want to drag Poppy out of hiding,' says Joyce. 'Get her to break cover.'

'She'll still be looking for the diamonds,' says Elizabeth. 'So she'll be keeping track of me somehow. Or she'll be keeping track of Sue Reardon, or Martin Lomax. So I want us all together in the same place, with the diamonds. Monday afternoon. Say threeish?'

'I don't understand what you need from Donna and I?' says Chris.

'From Donna and me, this time,' says Elizabeth. 'I need you outside, keeping those keen eyes peeled for Poppy.'

'None of this is my business, Elizabeth,' says Chris. 'I can't just suddenly get involved. Donna, back me up. It's not our case.'

Donna agrees. 'The killings are not our case, Martin Lomax isn't our case, the mafia's not our case. Unfortunately. I'd love it if the mafia was my case.'

'And even if we were there,' says Chris. 'What's your plan while we're waiting outside? Give a load of diamonds to the mafia?'

'I haven't worked out that bit of my plan yet,' says Elizabeth. 'But I will.'

'You can be sure she will,' says Ibrahim.

'Sorry,' says Chris. 'I've done all sorts for you, and I've always wondered where I'd draw the line. And I think that line might be keeping watch as you hand over twenty million pounds to the largest crime syndicate in the world.'

They are at an impasse. Until Ron clears his throat.

'I've got a suggestion. A good one, if anyone's interested?'

'Ron, I love you dearly,' says Elizabeth. 'But are you *sure* it's a good one?'

'I was just thinking,' says Ron. 'Seeing as it's not Chris's case. Why don't we *make* it Chris's case?'

'This does actually sound like it might be good,' says Joyce to Elizabeth.

'Chris,' says Ron. 'You and Donna have been chasing that drug dealer, haven't you? The woman?'

'Connie Johnson?' says Donna.

'Is that the one? Yeah, I don't know nothing about her,' says Ron. 'But it's your case, right?'

'It is,' says Chris.

'Well, what about we get her involved? We tell her we're some big gang, down from London. Tell her we've got a diamond trade set up with the mafia. We've got a meeting locally, and we've heard good things. Does she fancy getting involved?'

Chris could kiss Ron. He won't but he could.

'So Sue and Lance and that mob can swoop and catch Lomax and the mafia geezer. And you and Donna can catch the woman. Remind me of her name again?'

'Connie Johnson, Ron,' says Chris. Actually, he will kiss him. First chance he gets.

'If you say so,' says Ron. 'What do you reckon?'

Chris looks at Donna. 'If we got a tip-off that Connie Johnson was doing a deal. And we had a time and a place? We'd go and investigate, wouldn't we?'

'We'd pay it a visit, I reckon,' says Donna.

'Ron,' says Elizabeth. 'This isn't bad at all. But how do we convince Connie Johnson that we're a big London gang?'

Ron motions to himself, offended. 'I just show up, don't I? Whack on a suit. Tell 'em I'm Billy Baxter or Jimmy Jackson, down from Camden. Flash the tattoos, flash the diamonds.'

'Hmmm,' says Elizabeth.

'I'm not sure that gangsters have Chairman Mao tattoos,' says Joyce.

'All right, I'll take Bogdan with me,' says Ron.

'Well, this is beginning to feel like a plan,' says Elizabeth. 'We'll go and pick up Frank Andrade from Farnborough airport on Monday morning, tell him the good news, we have the diamonds, do come with us. We'll get Lance to bring Lomax down with him. Get them all over here to meet Connie Johnson. We'll have Sue listening in a truck, and, no doubt, Poppy loitering nearby. Everybody gets arrested, everybody gets medals, and we're home in time for *Eggheads*. Where should we have the meeting? I need somewhere we can control. Somewhere without escape routes?'

Donna pipes up. 'There's a manager's office above the arcade at the end of the pier. I had to visit it once because of all the underage kids on the machines. The manager tried to bribe me with a grand in 10ps.'

'The end of the pier sounds perfect,' says Elizabeth. 'Oh, and Ibrahim, I'm going to need you to drive us up to Farnborough and back.'

'Not on Monday,' says Ibrahim, shaking his head. 'My ribs, and my eyesight. Maybe in a few weeks. I would love to, but I'm afraid I can't.'

Donna looks at Ibrahim. 'I think you probably can, though. Don't you? Just a little mountain?'

Ibrahim thinks. Then shakes his head at her and mouths 'sorry'. Chris looks at Donna. What was *that* about?

'Splendid,' says Elizabeth. 'Everyone has a job to do.'

'Except Joyce,' says Ibrahim.

Joyce smiles. 'Oh, I have a job to do. A secret for now though. Ron, do you fancy walking me over to mine afterwards? I have an idea for you. And, Donna, why don't you wander over with us too, and I can show you the diamonds before you head off?'

70

Joyce

I didn't want to say I had found Ryan Baird in front of everyone. Least of all Ibrahim, who doesn't even know he's missing.

I had the file that Poppy had given us, all of Ryan Baird's information, big photo, and lots of details, and I had been looking through it, trying to find a bit of inspiration.

Can I say, by the way, that Poppy had put a Post-it note on the front of the file, and had put a little kiss and a smiley face on that Post-it note? And I just wonder if that's really the sort of thing a murderer would do?

Perhaps cold-blooded murderers are endlessly drawing smiley faces on Post-it notes? I was going to say I don't really know any murderers, but of course I do these days.

I know we can all pretend to be all sorts of things. Gerry once pretended to be Dutch when we were camping in the Dordogne. He did the accent and everything. That was just for a bit of fun, to make me laugh, he wasn't planning on shooting anyone.

I *think* it's a fact that Poppy must have found the letter in the tree? Nothing else makes sense otherwise. And I know it's a fact that Poppy's mum opened locker 551, and that, the next day, someone shot someone in the safe house on St Albans Avenue. So all fingers point to Poppy.

But still I come back to the smiley face and the little kiss on the Post-it note.

So, yes, the file.

I had looked up Ryan Baird on Instagram before, of course. There were twelve of them, but only one in Kent. BigBairdWolf2003. But the account was private, and I am not a computer hacker, and I don't know any computer hackers, so I didn't take it any further. Someone from BT came round to fix my broadband last week, and I asked her if she knew how to hack into private Instagram accounts, but she didn't.

I still don't know how to get into my @GreatJoy69 private messages. There are now over a thousand. How frustrating.

Anyway, then I had a bright idea, even if I say so myself. In Poppy's file is a list of Ryan Baird's friends and family members, and so I started looking them up on Instagram too. I thought, Well, he's gone *somewhere*, hasn't he? If I was ever on the run, there's a woman I used to work with – Sandra Nugent? – who retired to the Isle of Wight, and I would probably go and stay with her. She says it's the middle of nowhere, but you can still get a Tesco delivery, so that would suit me down to the ground. Sandra can get a bit much sometimes, but if you're on the run you can't be too picky.

Ryan Baird's mum is in Littlehampton, but I couldn't find her on Instagram. I couldn't even find her on Facebook, so she may very well be dead. He has an older sister, Leanne, and I think I found her, but she never posts anything except rainbows in support of various different things. Good for her, but no help to me.

Then we got on to cousins, of which there were plenty. This was a long job, by the way. I'm making it sound quick, but it wasn't. There were so many people to check, and I also kept getting distracted by new posts from people I follow. I watched Joe Wicks do a new workout, for example.

The file got on to Steven Baird. Born in Paisley, which I know is in Scotland, so I had a little search, and there are lots of Bairds in Scotland, and lots of Stevens too. So I scrolled through a few. Then I stumbled across StevieBlunterRangers4Eva.

He had a look of Ryan Baird about him, something unfortunate around the eyes, so I thought I would explore a little. It didn't take long. Two days ago Stevie Blunter had posted a series of pictures of a party. It was in a small, messy flat, and, even in photographs, it looked loud.

Then I found the photograph I was looking for. The caption read:

Bluntin of ma nut wi ma cuz Pablo

I couldn't really make head nor tail of it, but the photo showed Steven Baird, arms around Ryan Baird, both smoking roll-up cigarettes. Clear as day. So there he is. In Scotland.

After the Thursday Murder Club meeting I asked Donna and Ron to come over.

First things first, I showed Donna the diamonds. She held the biggest one on her ring finger and walked up and down like a model. Then she made Ron do the same and they were both laughing. I took the opportunity of an empty kettle to make us all a cup of tea.

I showed them both the photo, and they both said I'd done a wonderful job. Ron hugged me. I will say this for Ron, he is not my type, but he is a very good hugger. He will make a very specific type of woman a very good husband one day.

It is a shame about Siobhan, because she might even have been that woman. I wonder who she actually is?

Donna translated the Instagram caption for me. It means 'smoking cannabis with my cousin Pablo'. Pablo must be Ryan Baird's nickname.

Donna said she would get straight on to Strathclyde Police and have him tracked down and arrested. But then I told her my plan instead. She and Ron both listened, and then agreed that my plan was much more fun.

They've just gone, the two of them, and the diamonds are back in the kettle where they belong.

Ron is off to see Connie Johnson tomorrow. I'd like to be a fly on the wall, I really would. You can see he feels ten feet tall at the moment, and I have every faith in him.

I can see the Post-it note in front of me still. Poppy's smiley face. I don't know at all, I really don't.

Perhaps she'll turn up on Fairhaven pier on Monday, or perhaps she really is dead, and this is a wild goose chase.

But I suspect that Elizabeth is right in one thing. If we get everybody together at the end of the pier, diamonds out in the open, then surely we'll find out exactly who shot who and why.

71

Connie Johnson has changed three times already this morning. The summer dress was too obvious, the jumpsuit was not obvious enough, and the trousers she'd bought from Whistles were perfect, but she hadn't been able to comfortably hide her gun in them.

In the end she had a brainwave, and she is dressed in her Lycra gym kit. This sent a number of messages. Firstly, 'Oh, this meeting is not a big deal, I'm just fitting it in on the way to the gym,' but, more importantly, 'Here you go, Bogdan, this is what's on offer,' but in a healthy, rather than a slutty way.

And her gun is in a handy bumbag.

There is a large bag of MDMA on her desk, which she tidies into a drawer, before checking her watch. They are due any minute. Bogdan had slipped a letter under the lock-up door – a letter, swoon. He was bringing a man called Vic Vincent with him to discuss some sort of deal. Vincent being some major player in London.

She had googled 'Vic Vincent', of course, and nothing had come up, which was all the reassurance she needed. She was dealing with a pro.

There is a baseball bat covered with barbed wire leaning up against the photocopier, and Connie nudges it out of sight. She checks her hair once again. Perhaps Bogdan will be wearing a singlet? Those glorious arms rippling, ready to —

There is a loud bang on the metal door. Here we go, Connie. As she gets to the door she notices a large bloodstain under one of the coat hooks. Too late to clean it up now, they'll just have to take her as they find her.

She opens the door, and in walk Bogdan and Vic Vincent. They shake hands. Bogdan is not wearing a singlet, but he is wearing sunglasses, so she still has plenty to work with. Vic Vincent looks familiar, but she can't place him. Have their paths crossed before? He looks the part, face admirably busted, but his suit is a little too tight, and is that a West Ham United tie?

Nobody wants coffee — 'You mustn't drink coffee before the gym,' Bogdan says, and, yes, of course, she should have thought of that. They sit.

'I've heard good things about you, Connie,' says Vic Vincent. 'From Bogdan here.'

He's heard good things from Bogdan. Bogdan has been talking about her. 'I see, and does Bogdan work for you?'

Vic Vincent laughs. 'Bogdan don't work for no one. But now and again I ask him to help out. He gets a job done with no fuss. You understand?'

'I understand,' says Connie. She looks over at Bogdan, sitting there silent in his sunglasses like Mr Darcy. She just bets he gets a job done with no fuss.

'I've got something you might be able to help me with. You interested in diamonds?' asks Vic Vincent.

Where does she know him from?

'Not really,' says Connie. 'I'm interested in money, though? If that's involved too?'

Vic Vincent nods. Bogdan is looking around the room. She is glad she tidied away the bag of MDMA and the baseball bat. You can tell he likes tidy.

'You ever dealt with the mafia?' asks Vic.

The mafia? Well this is getting interesting.

Connie shakes her head. 'I tried to cancel Sky Sports once, that's the closest I've got.'

'A gentleman is coming down to Fairhaven on Monday, he's called Frank Andrade. I want someone to meet him. We've got a room on the end of the pier. Manager's office.'

Connie nods, she knows the room well. She once threatened to burn down the arcade. Perhaps Bogdan will be at the meeting? What will she wear then? The mafia *and* Bogdan?

'I need someone I can trust, and Bogdan says that's you, to give Mr Andrade these.'

Vic Vincent hands her a blue velvet bag. She opens the drawstring. Diamonds, he wasn't kidding.

'What are they worth?' Connie asks.

'Let's just say they're worth doing the job properly,' says Vic Vincent. The buttons on his shirt are straining. That face is so familiar. What's going on here?

'And why can't you hand them over yourself?'

'We don't get on, I killed his brother.'

Connie nods. 'Been there. And why at the end of a pier?'

'A lot of people want these diamonds. I can't tell you

why, but they do. We need somewhere we can keep an eye on everyone who's coming or going.'

'And what's in it for me?' asks Connie.

'There'll be another geezer there. Called Lomax. Andrade trusts him. Sells a lot of coke in south London and looking for a new wholesaler.'

'What happened to his old wholesaler?'

'Accident with a cement mixer,' says Vic.

'Clumsy,' says Connie.

'So I told him to check you out. Buy fifty grand's worth from you, check the quality, see if you might be what he's looking for.'

Connie nods.

'And for that introduction, you hand over the diamonds to Andrade for me. Sound fair?'

Vic Vincent gives her a little smile. Connie knows this guy, she swears. Knows his face. Talk about too good to be true. Is this the copper, Chris Hudson, setting her up?

Connie fiddles with her bumbag for a moment, and then pulls out her gun. She points it straight at Vic Vincent. If that was really his name. Vic and Bogdan both raise their eyebrows a little.

'Sorry, mate, no offence, but I know you. I've seen you before.' Connie keeps the gun pointing straight between Vic Vincent's eyes. Vic scratches a tattoo on his arm. It says 'Kendrick'. Without taking her eyes off him, she addresses Bogdan. 'Who is he, Bogdan? Just tell me. Just tell me, and you boys can walk out and we'll say no more about it.' Can she kill Vic Vincent and still go for a drink with Bogdan? She doubts it, but she'll have a good go.

'He's Vic Vincent,' says Bogdan. 'I worked for him a few times, never any trouble.'

'Keep going,' says Connie. Vic Vincent looks cool as you like. But a bead of sweat drops down his neck, across a faded West Ham tattoo.

'He called me, few weeks ago, says, "Bogdan, you know anyone I can trust?" I said Connie, because I trust you.'

God, this is hard, thinks Connie. But focus.

'He asks if you deal coke, and I say of course, everybody does. So he tells me, buy coke from her, let me see.'

'That ten grand the other day?' asks Connie.

'That was Vic's money.'

Connie starts to laugh, she puts down the gun and gives Vic Vincent a hug. He is sweatier than she expects.

'That's where I know your face from! I've got someone who follows everyone when they leave here. Checks they're not cops, rivals, whatever, takes photos. Bogdan took the coke to you, by the pier.'

Connie opens a drawer and flicks through some photos. She pulls out one of Ron and Bogdan by Fairhaven pier.

'Dressed as a plumber, I like it. I knew I knew your face. Sorry, Mr Vincent, I didn't mean to point a gun at you.'

'No problem,' says Vic Vincent, and scratches his Kendrick tattoo again. 'And bring that gun with you on Monday. Just in case.'

'So, I'm in,' says Connie. 'Fifty grand of coke, and the diamonds.'

'Monday, three p.m.,' says Vic Vincent.

Connie looks at Bogdan. 'And will you be there?'

Bogdan takes off his sunglasses and looks straight at her. 'Yes, we can do it together.'

Jesus Christ, that was an intense look. 'Maybe we could all go for a drink?'

'You are going to the gym,' says Bogdan, putting his sunglasses back on.

Damn!

'I need one more favour, Connie,' says Vic Vincent. 'If you don't mind. Nothing difficult.'

'Go on,' says Connie.

'My wife's niece lives down here, and she's got a boy looking for an opportunity. Just thinking you might need a driver on the day, wondered if you'd give him a chance?'

'I've got a driver,' says Connie.

'I'd rather have someone I know I could trust too,' says Vic Vincent. 'Family. He's done a bit of work for you before, the way he tells it. He can drive the three of us to dinner afterwards, if you fancy?'

Connie does fancy.

'Sure, what's his name?'

'Ryan Baird,' says Vic Vincent, and slips a piece of paper over to Connie. 'He's up in Scotland at the moment; that's the address. You think you could send someone up to bring him down for Monday?'

'Of course,' nods Connie, thinking about where to go for dinner.

Monday on the pier was going to be a lot of fun.

72

Elizabeth had explained again and again to Joyce that Farnborough wasn't an airport like Heathrow and Gatwick, and that there wouldn't be shops. But her friend is crestfallen nonetheless.

'But there's not even a WHSmith's,' says Joyce, looking around the arrivals terminal.

'What did you want to buy, for goodness' sake?' asks Elizabeth. It is eleven thirty in the morning, and Frank Andrade Jr should be walking through the arrivals doors very soon.

'Well nothing, it's just the principle,' says Joyce. 'Once you've used the toilet there's nothing else to do.'

'I'm so sorry if I'm boring you, Joyce, bringing you to meet a mafia boss so we can drive him to a diamond swap where we're going to catch a murderer.'

'I'm just saying,' says Joyce, and settles into a chair.

Elizabeth hadn't been able to persuade Ibrahim to drive them to Farnborough, so Ron's friend Mark has driven them up in his taxi. It would have been more fun with Ibrahim but, for a friend of Ron's, Mark was actually rather good company. She was worried about what radio station he would want to listen to, but it was Radio 2, so she had got off fairly lightly.

Joyce is sulking, Elizabeth knows what will cheer her up

'That really was a terrific idea. Ryan Baird as the driver. And to find him in the first place, well, that was first rate.'

'Stop trying to cheer me up,' says Joyce. 'I should be looking at travel toiletries in Boots.'

'Righto,' says Elizabeth. Everything was in place. The pier would be closed for maintenance as soon as the meeting began. Chris and his team would be there. They had received a tip-off that Connie Johnson would be on the end of the pier at 3 p.m., with cocaine and a gun.

A group of Japanese businessmen walk past. A driver is pushing their luggage on a trolley. Elizabeth would love to open every single bit of luggage that came into this airport. Private jets flying in from all directions. She had briefly worked as a luggage handler at Heathrow, stitching tracking devices into the suitcases of trade delegations.

Sue would be there this afternoon, too. That had been a tricky conversation. Yes, Elizabeth had found the diamonds, no, she didn't have them right now, yes, they were in the hands of a south coast drugs baron, yes, she understood this wasn't best practice. Where had she found them? Well, that was a story for another day. On and on it had gone, threats and name-calling. 'I thought we had an understanding?' Why did people always get so angry? We'll all be dead soon enough.

Sue had calmed down eventually, and she will be tucked away somewhere, watching and listening.

Lance will be there, too. He is staking out Martin Lomax's house, so will be driving Lomax to the meeting. That had worked out very nicely.

'Can I say something?' asks Joyce.

'Not if it's about why there are no shops here, no,' says Elizabeth.

'I don't want you to get annoyed with me,' says Joyce. 'I just . . . I'm just not sure that Poppy is behind all this. I know I've got a soft spot, I do know that. Ever since she trusted me with her mum's phone number, I've felt very protective of her. More fool me, perhaps.'

'I meant to ask. Did she make eye contact when she put the number in your pocket?' asks Elizabeth. 'Flutter her eyelashes? Poor me?'

'No, I just found it when I got back. But, also, I haven't told you about the smiley face on the Post-it no—'

The arrivals doors swish open in front of them, and through them walks a man dressed for all the world as if he's heading off for a game of golf. Polo shirt, beige slacks, sunglasses pushed up into his hairline. Mid-forties perhaps? All by himself, one small briefcase. He is looking around for the car-hire desk, as Elizabeth and Joyce step into stride on either side of him.

'You must be Mr Andrade,' says Elizabeth.

Andrade stops and looks at Elizabeth.

'Nope,' he says.

'I'm Joyce,' says Joyce. 'And this is Elizabeth.'

'I'm happy for you,' says Frank Andrade. 'Now if you'll excuse me.'

Off he strides again, with Elizabeth keeping pace alongside and Joyce hurrying to catch up.

'You won't need a car, Mr Andrade,' says Elizabeth.

'I hate to disagree,' says Frank Andrade.

'Mark from Robertsbridge Taxis is driving us,' says

Joyce. 'We worried the boot wouldn't be big enough for your luggage, but look at you with only the one bag. It's a Toyota Avensis.'

Andrade stops again. 'Ladies, forgive me, I don't know who you are. I don't care who you are. I got somewhere to be, and someone to see.'

'We know,' says Elizabeth. 'We're here to help. You're off to see Martin Lomax.'

Andrade gives Elizabeth a hard stare.

'About your diamonds,' says Joyce.

Andrade gives Joyce an even harder stare. Elizabeth sees Joyce blush. For goodness' sake, is there no one Joyce doesn't find attractive?

'OK, ladies, I've had a long flight. I want to get in my car, I want to visit Martin Lomax, I want to get what I came for, and I want to come straight back here and fly home.'

'Well, Martin Lomax doesn't have your diamonds,' says Elizabeth. 'I do.'

'You got my diamonds?'

'I *have* your diamonds, yes,' says Elizabeth.

'OK,' says Frank Andrade. 'And you think I won't kill you because you're an old woman?'

'Oh, I'm sure you would, Frank,' says Elizabeth. 'I don't doubt it for a moment. But, equally, I would kill you without hesitation. So shall we stop the grandstanding and get down to business?'

Frank Andrade laughs. '*You* would kill *me*?'

'She would,' confirms Joyce. 'I don't think she will, but she would.'

'OK,' says Andrade. 'So where are my diamonds?'

'They're in Fairhaven,' says Elizabeth. 'At the end of the pier.'

'And where is Fairhaven?' asks Andrade.

'Well, you see how useful we can be to you already?' says Elizabeth.

Elizabeth sees that Mark has driven around to the front of the terminal building. He gives her a quick honk on the horn. You shouldn't really honk at the mafia, but she supposes Mark is not to know that.

'You come with us, you make up with Martin Lomax, and my representative will give you the diamonds. We'll have you back here by nine p.m. at the latest,' says Elizabeth.

'With my diamonds?' asks Andrade.

'With your diamonds,' says Elizabeth. She points out Mark's car. 'So shall we?'

'And why am I trusting you?'

'Well, just use your judgement,' says Elizabeth. 'And look at Joyce's face. Who wouldn't trust that face?'

Joyce smiles. 'If you want, you can sit in the front. I was in the front on the way up, but I don't mind going in the back. I'll probably sleep anyway.'

Mark is out of the car and has the boot open. He holds out his hand to Frank Andrade.

'That all you've got then? I'm Mark, nice to meet you. Are you really from the mafia?'

Frank Andrade hands over his bag. 'Uh, yeah.' He looks at the car and he looks at his three companions.

'Now,' says Joyce. 'It's at least a two-hour drive, so do you need the toilet before we set off?'

73

Donna and Chris are parked in a side street outside a shop selling candy floss, models of Tower Bridge and international phone cards. They are facing the sea, grey and unhappy like the sky, and have a clear view of the entrance to Fairhaven pier away to their left.

Donna has an ice cream. She offers some to Chris, but he declines, and looks down at his bag of sunflower seeds.

Connie Johnson is the first to arrive. Her Range Rover pulls over onto the broad pavement in front of the pier, and she steps out and looks around her. She is carrying a large holdall, and Donna hopes it has five kilos of coke in it. The five kilos of coke that will hopefully see Connie arrested before the afternoon is through.

Donna can't see the driver behind the tinted windows, but she is looking forward to rearresting Ryan Baird too. She had to hand it to Joyce there.

Suddenly Bogdan appears, though Donna can't figure out from where. They had been watching the pier for half an hour already and hadn't caught a glimpse of the big man. The big, taciturn man with the deep blue eyes. Donna swears that her ice cream starts to melt faster. She watches him walking up the pier with Connie

Johnson, carrying her bag of cocaine for her like a gentleman.

'He's a good guy,' says Chris.

'Mmm hmm,' agrees Donna.

A black Lotus sports car pulls up next, and two men, one older and one younger, step out. Donna sees Chris look down at a picture on his phone.

'That's Martin Lomax,' says Chris. 'The other one must be the spy?'

'Lance,' says Donna. Joyce had told Donna she might like Lance, but he's too old. And the hair? Not a bad try though, Joyce. Ten years ago maybe.

Lance James and Martin Lomax begin the walk along the pier, leaving the car where it is. Donna thinks it must be nice to work for MI5 and be able to park anywhere you want. Donna had once wrestled a man wielding a sword in the Streatham Lidl, only to find her car had been clamped outside for parking across two bays.

It is five minutes to three. People seem to be punctual where diamonds and cocaine are involved. A Toyota Avensis with 'Robertsbridge Taxis' stencilled onto the driver's door arrives next, pulling up behind the Lotus.

The driver, whom Donna doesn't recognize, steps out and makes his way to the boot. From the passenger seat steps a man who can only be Frank Andrade Jr.

Martin Lomax and Frank Andrade Jr are none of Donna and Chris's business today, but it's interesting to see them nonetheless. MI5 will be dealing with the two of them, while Kent Police deal with Connie Johnson and Ryan Baird. And no questions asked by either side. Elizabeth had brokered that deal.

And speak of the devil, here she is now. Elizabeth and Joyce exit the back seats. Joyce looks like she has just woken up.

The driver hands Frank Andrade a briefcase and the two men shake hands.

Bogdan has returned, and he motions to Frank Andrade to come with him. Andrade looks at Elizabeth, who nods. Elizabeth doesn't shake Andrade's hand and neither does Joyce. Which is very unlike both of them.

Bogdan gives Frank Andrade a small smile. Has Donna seen Bogdan smile before? She doesn't think so, but she would like to see it again. 'Climb your next mountain,' Ibrahim had told her. As she watches him walking up the pier with Frank Andrade Jr, Donna wonders what it might be like to climb Bogdan? She eats her chocolate flake whole, then starts on the cornet.

'So the gang's all here,' says Chris. 'You ready?'

'Ready,' says Donna.

She sees Elizabeth walking along the promenade now, Joyce behind her, trying to brush creases out of her skirt after the journey. They pass the Lotus and they pass the Range Rover. Joyce looks over, spots them and gives them a big wave. It will be a while before Joyce makes an effective undercover officer. Donna waves back and Joyce looks thrilled.

Joyce and Elizabeth reach a nondescript white van, parked by the promenade railings, cordoned off by safety

368

tape. On the side of the van it says 'T. H. Hargreaves – Railings. All Jobs Considered'.

Elizabeth steps over the tape, followed by Joyce. Someone inside the van opens the back doors and they both climb in.

74

It is a nice enough office for one man, overseeing the day-to-day running of a slot-machine arcade on an award-winning pier.

It is a little cramped just at the moment, however. Connie Johnson sits behind a desk, with Martin Lomax opposite. Frank Andrade Jr is perched on a windowsill. Lance James leans against a wall and Bogdan stands in front of the door.

The introductions had been swift. Mainly 'Who are you?' and 'None of your business.' Frank Andrade Jr had greeted Martin Lomax with a handshake though. 'Looks like I won't have to kill you today, Martin!' 'Looks like it, Frank. How is your wife, did she get the muffins I sent?'

No one is quite sure how to begin. Because, of course, no one in this room has actually arranged this meeting. It has been arranged by a seventy-six-year-old woman currently sitting in a white van, four hundred metres away, listening to every word they are about to say.

And so it falls to the alpha character in the room to kick things off.

'OK then,' says Bogdan, 'we start.'

OK then, says Bogdan, *we start*.

Inside the white van Sue Reardon is wearing headphones

and watching the monitors relaying pictures from the cameras her team had installed in the office over the weekend.

Elizabeth and Joyce are having to share headphones, one ear each. Cutbacks.

'You're sure she's still got the diamonds?' asks Sue.

'I left Bogdan in charge of that,' says Elizabeth. 'So, yes, I'm sure.'

'And what the hell's in that bag she was carrying?' asks Sue.

Elizabeth shrugs. The drugs are for Chris and Donna's benefit, Sue doesn't need to know about them. She looks back at the crowded office on her screen. The pictures are so much clearer than in her day.

Frank Andrade, sitting on his windowsill, addresses Connie Johnson.

So you got my diamonds?

I've got diamonds, says Connie. *I'll take your word they're yours.*

How'd you get 'em? asks Andrade.

Fell out of my Coco Pops, says Connie. *Are you really from the mafia?*

He's a businessman, says Martin Lomax. *Very well respected.*

Yeah, I'm from the mafia, says Andrade. *Now, show me the diamonds.*

Well, here we go then, thinks Elizabeth. They are *not* going to like what happens next. Good luck one and all.

Connie reaches into her holdall. When are they going to talk about the drugs? She wants her fifty grand, and she wants to do more business with these people. She had been worried, she has to admit, about this whole thing.

Cautious. But it was all going the way she'd been told. The way Vic Vincent had explained. There was a guy from the mafia, there was some old posh guy, there always is, and there was Bogdan. All very reassuring, and she is keen to make a good impression. There's another guy, bored and balding, but he's probably just a bodyguard. Bogdan knew him, and that was enough for her.

She puts the blue velvet bag down on the desk in front of her.

'Well, hallelujah,' says the old posh guy.

'Show me,' says Andrade. 'Pour the diamonds out on the table. Don't spill any.'

Don't spill any? That's a weird thing to say, thinks Connie, but this guy's American, and they say weird things.

She loosens the drawstring, and carefully tips the diamonds onto the table.

'There you go,' says Connie. 'Didn't spill a thing. Both the diamonds, safe and sound.'

There is silence. Andrade, the old posh guy, even the bodyguard are staring at the diamonds on the table. Connie senses there is suddenly an atmosphere.

'You got two diamonds?' says Andrade.

'Yeah,' says Connie. 'These are the diamonds. What were you expecting?'

What were you expecting? says Connie Johnson.

'Where are the rest of the diamonds?' says Sue Reardon, looking frantically at Elizabeth.

'Oh, I only gave her the two,' says Elizabeth. 'Just enough to flush out the killer and liven things up a bit.

Any news on whether your gang have spotted Poppy lurking about yet?'

'Jesus Christ!' says Sue. 'Can't you play anything straight?'

'Only when it suits my purposes,' says Elizabeth. 'And it didn't suit my purposes today.'

'So where are the diamonds?' asks Sue.

'They're safe,' says Elizabeth. They are now in Joyce's microwave, because she uses it far less than her kettle.

On screen they see Frank Andrade pull a gun.

'Christ almighty!' says Sue. 'What the hell have you done, Elizabeth?'

Lance sees Frank Andrade pull his gun, and so pulls his own. Andrade's is pointed at Connie Johnson and Lance's is pointed at Andrade.

'Where are my diamonds?' asks Frank Andrade. 'All of them.' He sounds calm, but, in Lance's estimation, he does not look it. Lance doesn't blame him. What scam is being pulled here?

'These are your diamonds,' says Connie Johnson. 'Put your gun down, you drama queen.'

'Where are *the rest*?' says Andrade. He doesn't sound calm any more.

'The rest?' says Connie. 'This is all I was given.'

'Given?' says Andrade. 'Given by who?'

'Some old guy, Vic Vincent,' says Connie. 'Don't you dare shoot me for this. This guy gave me the diamonds, told me this posh guy wanted five kilos of coke and said meet you on the pier. This is between you and him.'

'What coke?' says Frank Andrade. 'And who's Vic Vincent?'

'This coke,' says Connie, reaching into her bag. But instead of pulling out cocaine, she pulls out her gun. She points it at Andrade.

'This is a lot of guns in a small room,' says Bogdan, and sighs.

'That is such an English gun,' says Andrade. 'What did he look like? Vic Vincent?'

'Old, like a boxer or something,' says Connie. 'Lots of tattoos, West Ham tattoos, all sorts.'

Martin Lomax slams his fist on the desk.

'I know him,' says Lomax.

'I'll bet you do,' says Andrade, and points his gun at Lomax. 'What have you set up here?'

Well, isn't that just the question, thinks Lance. Connie Johnson's gun is aimed at Andrade. Andrade's is aimed at Lomax. Lance supposes he should aim at Connie Johnson, just for a sense of equilibrium. How does this play out now? It's going to end badly for someone. He just needs to ensure it's not him. What a place this would be to die. The seagulls calling overhead and the empty slot machines beeping down below. At least if he's shot he won't have to deal with the kitchen wall at his flat. All the same, try not to get shot, Lance.

'I'm as baffled as you, Frank,' says Lomax. 'As I live and breathe. But there will be a perfectly simple –'

'Enough,' says Frank Andrade. He pulls the trigger and shoots Martin Lomax in the chest. Lomax doubles forward in his chair, blood spreading through his suit.

Andrade aims the gun at Connie Johnson now, even though he was raised to shoot all the men first. He is too late, however. Connie Johnson squeezes off a single shot, which passes through Frank Andrade, through the window and out towards the grey sea.

Martin Lomax looks up, as if to comment on the noise. But whatever comment he has will have to go unsaid. He topples over to his left and hits the floor.

Frank Andrade slides off the windowsill, leaving a smear of thick, scarlet blood trailing down a plastic radiator. His feet end up in the crook of Martin Lomax's arm. Two men sleeping. Dreaming of guns and drugs and money, of always taking and never giving.

What now? thinks Lance. There are two corpses on the floor, there are two diamonds on the table, and a bag full of cocaine under the desk. He and Connie have their guns pointed at one another, neither quite sure what to do.

Bogdan steps between the two guns.

'Connie, you have no business with this guy and he has no business with you. He's just here for dead guys and diamonds. Get your bag and run.'

Outside on the pier are members of the Special Boat Service, their eyes peeled for Poppy. They know not to touch Connie Johnson. Their orders are clear. She will reach her car.

Connie grabs the bag, slides over the desk and makes for the door. Bogdan opens the door for her. She reaches up to his face and kisses him.

'Call me, yeah?' she says, and then disappears at speed, holdall full of cocaine swinging as she goes.

Lance surveys the scene. The big Polish man next to him is blushing. The blood of the two corpses on the floor is starting to intermingle.

Sue had raced from the van as soon as the two shots had gone off. Elizabeth hadn't felt the need to follow, and so Joyce has stayed where she is too.

'Well, I never,' says Joyce.

'I don't really like anyone being killed if one can avoid it,' says Elizabeth. 'But no great loss here.'

Joyce thinks about this. As soon as Elizabeth had decided to give Connie Johnson just the two diamonds, something like this had been inevitable. Elizabeth could be brutal sometimes. She was a very bad enemy to make.

The world was better off without Frank Andrade Jr, that was for certain. Mark from Robertsbridge Taxis had wanted to talk to him about baseball, but had been told to 'shut the hell up'. Except Andrade hadn't said 'hell'. Mafia or no mafia, what a dreary, inadequate man Frank Andrade Jr is.

Was.

And Martin Lomax? With his house and his millions, and his work. The things he had helped to fund. The weapons, the gangs, the warlords. The smell of honeysuckle covering the stench. She thinks about his cheque for Living With Dementia. Five pounds. She looks at the screen, sees his body and feels nothing.

Joyce has seen so many good people, innocent people, unlucky people, die over the years. Sometimes she would go home and cry, and Gerry would hold her, knowing there was nothing he could say.

But she would shed no tears for these two. 'Good riddance,' Gerry would say, and Joyce quite agrees. Still, to *make* it happen, as Elizabeth has just done? Was that worse? Or just more honest? A question for someone cleverer there. She would ask Ibrahim.

She watches the monitors and sees Lance approach each camera in turn and switch it off. The last thing she sees each time is her friendship bracelet. The final screen goes black.

'What now?' she says to Elizabeth. 'I don't suppose they found Poppy?'

'Oh, Poppy's dead, Joyce,' says Elizabeth. 'I worked it all out in the car on the way down here. It all clicked while the Jeremy Vine show was on.'

'Oh,' says Joyce. 'So what now?'

'Well,' says Elizabeth, looking at her watch. 'I'd give it half an hour or so, but then, I hope, a trip back to Godalming in a coroner's van with the person who killed Douglas and Poppy.'

Connie is running at full pelt along the pier. She has shot a mafia boss, she has kissed Bogdan and she still has her cocaine, so it is hard to judge how that went. She needs to get back to the office. Regroup. It honestly feels like she might come out of it all pretty cleanly. She trusts Bogdan, and the other guy seemed to have no interest in her.

The Range Rover is up ahead. The driver, Ryan Baird, was deeply unimpressive. She remembered he had done a few jobs for her before, and not particularly well. He stunk of weed and didn't know how the heated seating worked. And he tried to talk to her, which was unforgivable. When she sees Vic Vincent again she will have to tell him the truth about his nephew, family or no family.

Connie risks a look behind her, but no one is giving chase. No one is even looking in her direction, which is strange. A blonde woman in a business suit running down a pier with a sports bag? Surely someone would turn their head? But the pier was quiet, just a few couples in dark clothing walking arm in arm.

She reaches the door of the Range Rover, throws it open and dives in. Straight into the lap of DCI Chris Hudson. She is cuffed before she can speak.

'Hi Connie,' says Chris. 'You're under arrest. You do not have to say anything, etc.'

In the front, Connie sees Ryan Baird, handcuffed in the passenger seat. Behind the wheel is Donna De Freitas. She turns to Connie.

'I've never driven a Range Rover before, Connie, so forgive me if I'm a bit stop-start. I've put Fairhaven Police Station in the satnav though, so we won't go far wrong. What's that scent you're wearing? It's gorgeous.'

'So we just need another word for a horse,' says Ibrahim, crossword propped up on his laptop.

'Horsey?' says Kendrick, bouncing his way in and out of the FaceTime screen.

'Too many letters,' says Ibrahim.

'I think it's the only word though,' says Kendrick. 'So maybe they got it wrong?'

Ibrahim nods. 'Perhaps, yes.'

He should have gone today. Should have driven Joyce and Elizabeth to the airport. Should have driven them down to the pier. Should be there now. Ron has texted. Two more people dead, but the right people, so everyone seems happy.

Mark from the taxi company is driving Ron home, and he's bringing fish and chips with him. Elizabeth and Joyce still have a long night ahead of them.

'Do you still hurt?' asks Kendrick.

'I do,' says Ibrahim. 'But not when I'm talking to your grandad, and not when I'm talking to you.'

Through the windscreen of the Range Rover, Donna sees Elizabeth and Joyce climbing out the back of the white van. Elizabeth sees Donna behind the wheel and gives her a hopeful look. Donna responds with a thumbs-up, and Elizabeth nods and mouths 'well done'.

Ron now appears at her open driver's window.

'Oh, they're all here today,' says Donna. 'Pensioners' outing?'

'That's Vic Vincent,' says Connie, lunging forward as far as her cuffed hands will allow. 'These are his drugs. Arrest him.'

Ron looks at Connie. 'Never heard of him, love. Sounds like a right wrong 'un.' He then looks at Chris. 'What she do, then?'

'Murder,' says Chris. 'All on camera. Plus a big bag of coke.'

'That's her dealt with then, eh?' says Ron. He then looks over at Ryan Baird.

'You all right there, Ryan?'

Ryan Baird is quietly crying.

'You have a good cry,' says Ron. 'And I'll tell you a story. Couple of weeks ago, you nicked a bloke's phone. My sort of age, the bloke, but looks older, losing a bit of hair. You gave him a nasty little kick to the back of the head, do you remember? No reason I can make out. I've seen him cry too, you know, since you done that, and I don't like it, Ryan. I know you don't care, old son, but he's my best mate, this fella. I want you to remember his name for me. Will you do that? Ibrahim Arif. You remember that name every night you're locked up. No one messes with Ibrahim Arif.'

Connie leans forward again, getting as close to Ron as she possibly can. She hisses, 'When I get out, you're a dead man.'

Ron looks back at her. 'Well I'm seventy-five, and you'll be doing thirty years so, yeah, agreed.'

Donna sees Bogdan approach. Oh boy. He walks up behind Ron and pulls him away from the window.

'Time to go,' says Bogdan, and Ron nods, giving the weeping Ryan Baird one final look.

'Ibrahim Arif,' says Ron. 'Don't you forget now, Ryan.'

Bogdan looks at Donna. 'You are Donna?'

'Yes,' confirms Donna.

'I am Bogdan,' says Bogdan.

'I know,' says Donna.

Bogdan nods. 'OK.' He then looks into the back seat, and says, 'Hello, Connie.'

'You're all dead,' says Connie. 'Every single one of you.'

'Sooner or later, for sure,' agrees Bogdan, and Donna watches him walk away, his arm around Ron.

Elizabeth has been a fool, but at least she knows why.

It was all Marcus Carmichael's fault, really.

Right from the very beginning. The dead man by the River Thames who never was. The unclaimed body collected from a London hospital and dressed up by her operatives. That reminder of the grand illusions of her trade. Making people believe exactly what you wanted them to believe. Making things *complicated*. Taking pains.

Elizabeth had been a master of it. Douglas had been a master too. Somewhere in a drawer is a photograph of their wedding day. Elizabeth and Douglas with smiles so broad you would swear it was the happiest day of their lives.

Nothing was ever how it seemed.

Except, Elizabeth realizes now, sometimes things are exactly how they seem. At least she has realized this in time.

She is sitting on bench seating in the back of the coroner's van. They are heading to the morgue at Godalming. The same morgue where Douglas and Poppy's bodies had been identified.

Next to her is Joyce. She is doing a word search on her phone. Elizabeth knows she should listen to Joyce more often. Of course, Poppy hadn't done it. Poppy hadn't murdered Douglas, then murdered some poor young woman and had the body identified as her own.

Poppy hadn't hatched a plot with her mother to steal the diamonds. There was another explanation for Siobhan.

Who on earth would ever believe that Poppy had done it? Only someone very stupid. Or someone too clever by half.

Elizabeth is coming to understand that perhaps, just sometimes, things are exactly what they seem. When Ron gives her a hug, or Joyce bakes her a cake, or Ibrahim laminates a document for her, they are not playing a game. They don't need anything in return other than her happiness and her friendship. They just *like* her. It has taken Elizabeth a long time to accept the truth of that.

On the bench opposite her is Sue Reardon. Sue Reardon has a mind like hers. They had laughed about it. Peas in a pod. Elizabeth hadn't realized the half of it.

Between the benches, along the length of the van lies the corpse of Martin Lomax. Frank Andrade's is being dealt with by MI6. His is in a different van, travelling down a different motorway.

Poppy and Douglas were both shot dead. There were no fake corpses, there was no grand cover-up. They were both shot dead by Sue Reardon. For a very obvious reason. And Sue Reardon had spun Elizabeth a line she knew she wouldn't be able to resist.

How to prove it though?

Elizabeth looks over at Joyce, tongue sticking out as she circles words with her finger. Like butter wouldn't melt. She is recording everything on her phone. Just as she has been told.

The first part of the journey had been the expected barrage of questions from Sue about the diamonds, and who on earth was Connie Johnson, and why did she have a bag full of cocaine with her? Elizabeth had answered all the queries as politely as she felt able. But now it was her turn to ask the questions.

'So,' she begins, leaning forward and smiling at Sue over the draped corpse of Martin Lomax. 'We didn't find Poppy then?'

'No,' says Sue. 'Nowhere to be seen.'

'Curious,' says Elizabeth. 'Perhaps she really is dead. Do you think, Sue?'

'Perhaps,' says Sue. 'But we still can't explain her mum looking for the diamonds.'

'You nearly had me, you know?' says Elizabeth.

'I'm sure I don't know what you're talking about,' says Sue.

'You killed Douglas and Poppy. You knew where they were, you walked in, you shot them, and you walked straight out again.'

'Sounds very simple,' says Sue.

'It was simple. But you knew simple wouldn't be interesting enough for me. So you led me on a piece of string around all sorts of wonderful theories. Just to buy yourself a bit of time to find the diamonds. Or for me to find the diamonds for you. Keeping me interested.'

'Well, now it sounds outlandish,' says Sue. 'What an imagination you have, Elizabeth.'

Elizabeth shakes her head. 'My imagination was my downfall here, I'm afraid. As soon as I realized it was you who slipped Siobhan's phone number into Joyce's pocket, the whole thing fell into place.'

'Oh, I wondered why you asked about that,' says Joyce.

Sue Reardon's phone buzzes. She opens a message and smiles.

'Well, speak of the devil – there's Poppy's mum now. With some good news.'

'Do tell,' says Elizabeth.

'I'm told we've found the diamonds. In Joyce's microwave of all places. How pleasingly suburban. But I suppose the gloves are off at least.'

Sue Reardon presses an intercom button and talks to the driver. 'A change of plan. Coopers Chase retirement village. It's not far.'

An echoing electronic voice replies. 'Postcode?'

Sue thinks for a moment, takes a gun from her bag and points it at Joyce. 'Joyce, what's the postcode?'

76

Chris Hudson munches on a carrot baton. When you got used to them they actually weren't so bad. Well, they were, but it seemed to matter less. Connie Johnson is in her cell. Her interview had been terminated fairly quickly. It consisted almost entirely of threats to kill him, Donna, Bogdan and whoever she imagined Ron to be. Bogdan came in for some particularly graphic abuse. No mention of Patrice though, that particular threat forgotten. He will never mention it to Patrice or Donna. And he knows Ron or Bogdan won't either.

Ryan Baird's interview had been a quieter affair. Eight minutes of silent, shoulder-shaking sobbing, before his solicitor suggested they might reconvene in the morning. Perfect. An evening off for Chris.

Ryan Baird's solicitor, Chris couldn't help but notice, was still dressing better, now had a nicer haircut and was even starting to lose some weight. He was doused in Lynx Africa, but, as Chris well knows, you can't change everything all at once. After the interview the solicitor had taken Donna aside and asked her out for a drink. His wedding ring in his pocket, no doubt. Donna had told him she would love to, but that they should probably wait, so as not to jeopardize the ongoing investigation. Even at the end of a long day, Donna was a quick thinker.

Chris's mind goes back to the table outside Maidstone Crown Court. The promises Ron and Bogdan had made him. They had come good, thank you, gents. Patrice will come down to Fairhaven again next Sunday and this time Chris will tell her that he loves her. Sometimes the universe turns your way. He hopes that Elizabeth and Joyce got what they wanted from today too.

A man voluntarily eating carrot batons. That really was someone to be.

77

Now it is Elizabeth who is staring down the barrel of Sue Reardon's gun. How many gun barrels had she stared down in her career? Twenty? Thirty? None of them had killed her yet.

The basic rule is, if they don't kill you immediately, they're not going to kill you. There are always exceptions, but no point worrying about them for now.

The coroner's van is heading towards Coopers Chase. How had Siobhan found the diamonds at Joyce's? Someone had told her exactly where they were. Ibrahim? Stephen? Been *forced* to tell her? Please no. She has to keep calm.

'Can I tell you what I think happened?' asks Elizabeth. 'Just to pass the time. Or is that all a bit "James Bond" for you?'

'Please do,' says Sue. 'I can't tell you how delighted I was to fool you.'

'Poppy found the letter,' Elizabeth begins. 'Just as Joyce said. But she didn't go after the diamonds, and she didn't give it to her mum. She gave it to you, because that's what Poppy would do. She did her job. So you read the letter, you read Douglas's confession. But the confession part wasn't news to you, you'd known all along. You and Douglas had planned the whole thing together. Yes?'

'A little retirement plan, yes,' agrees Sue.

'I had a brief, awful thought at one point that Douglas and Poppy were lovers,' says Elizabeth. 'But I was wrong, wasn't I? You and Douglas were lovers.'

'Ooh, yes,' says Joyce. 'I can see that.'

'Have I got that right?' asks Elizabeth.

'You have,' says Sue.

Joyce looks between the two of them. 'He definitely had a type, didn't he?'

'I see the appeal, I promise,' says Elizabeth. 'I was almost ten years older than him, you ten years younger. He very neatly spanned our generations, didn't he?'

'He was very handsome,' says Joyce. 'Not my type at all, no offence to either of you, but very handsome.'

Elizabeth looks straight into Sue's eyes. 'So you were reading the letter, saw the key, the locker number and what have you. I assume he hadn't told you where he'd hidden them?'

'He told me they were safe,' says Sue.

Elizabeth nods. 'So, it was interesting information to you. Lucrative at the very least. But the big news came further down in the letter, didn't it? When he said he still loved me? That he would wait for me if needs be. That must have been the moment you realized the two of you weren't in this together? That you and Douglas weren't about to head off into the sunset with the twenty million? That was the moment you realized you would have to kill him?'

Sue shrugs. The barrel of the gun shrugs with her.

'He wanted it all for himself,' says Elizabeth. 'Or worse,

he wanted it for him and me. Though you're bright enough to know that would never happen. Originally the two of you were just going to see out the investigation, let it fizzle down to nothing and cash in. So now you needed a change of plan.'

'Perfect so far,' says Sue. 'Too late, of course, but perfect.'

'So you decide you want the money for yourself,' says Elizabeth.

'I don't blame you one bit,' says Joyce.

Joyce is still doing her word search. You had to hand it to Joyce sometimes. Even with a gun pointed at her best friend, Joyce trusts her to get out of this situation. Does Elizabeth trust herself? That's a very good question. What is going to face them back at Coopers Chase? Is Stephen safe? Is Ibrahim safe?

Elizabeth keeps thinking as she talks. 'So how to kill him? Well, first attempt, you tell Martin Lomax where Douglas is, which is as good as signing Douglas's death warrant. Cowardly, but you need him out of the way if you're going to escape with the money yourself, and you're angry. Lomax sends his man, Andrew Hastings, to kill Douglas, but poor Poppy gets in the way and shoots Hastings. Douglas very much still alive, a bump in the road, but never mind. You are still determined, and that's understandable. We all fall out of love, don't we?'

'We most certainly do,' says Sue.

'Not me,' says Joyce.

'Nonsense, Joyce, you're in and out of love monthly,' says Elizabeth, then returns to staring into Sue Reardon's gun. 'So you still need Douglas out of the picture, and you realize you are going to have to do it yourself. You know you can move Douglas and Poppy to Hove. To a house you have used before, a house you can access easily. So killing him yourself will be easy. But how to get away with it? That was your question.'

'It was,' agrees Sue Reardon. 'I didn't need to get away with it for long. Just until I found the diamonds.'

'And perhaps,' says Elizabeth, 'you were worried that I might work things out?'

'I was,' says Sue. 'I just needed you to find the diamonds before you worked out I was the killer. And you didn't let me down.'

'She worked it out eventually, to be fair,' says Joyce.

'But I still get to the diamonds,' says Sue. 'As soon as I've picked them up, I'll be off. I can disappear easily, Elizabeth, as you'll know. So that's what I'll do. Feel free to tell everyone what I did. They won't find me.'

'You're not going to shoot us?' says Joyce.

'Not if you behave yourselves,' says Sue.

'Not really our speciality,' says Joyce.

'I knew you wouldn't be able to resist a clever little mystery, Elizabeth,' says Sue. 'I knew I'd have you chasing your tail. You were having lunch with the killer, talking tactics, without even knowing. Isn't that a hoot?'

Elizabeth nods. 'Your plan forms, and you realize you are going to need help with it. So you call Siobhan. Now this is where I'm hazy. Who exactly is she? An old friend, I imagine? An old colleague who owed you a favour?'

'Guess again,' says Sue Reardon.

'No matter,' says Elizabeth. 'She agrees to whatever terms you present her with. Help me with a double murder and . . . what?'

'A million pounds,' says Sue Reardon.

'That would do it,' says Elizabeth. 'You come to Coopers Chase to take Andrew Hastings's body away, and on your way out you slip a note into Joyce's cardigan, simply saying "RING MY MUM", with Siobhan's phone number.'

'Wait,' says Joyce, 'Siobhan isn't Poppy's mum?'

'Keep up, Joyce,' says Sue.

'Don't speak to Joyce like that,' says Elizabeth.

'Oh, I don't mind,' says Joyce.

Elizabeth feels the coroner's van take a sharp left turn and slow down. It crosses a cattle grid. They are at Coopers Chase.

'You send Siobhan to check the lockers for the diamonds. You'd been in before, I presume, to make sure there were security cameras?'

'I had,' says Sue.

'Trusting that I would eventually check the recordings. And be led to Siobhan. And put two and two together?'

'Which you were, and which you did,' says Sue. 'I knew you wouldn't be able to resist it! The idea of Poppy faking the whole thing. So unlikely. I knew you were just clever enough to fall for it.'

Sirens go past them at speed. Sue pauses, then visibly relaxes. Ambulances, not police. Elizabeth goes cold. Driving at speed from Coopers Chase. Who was in the ambulances? Stephen?

'You even thought Douglas had faked it at first, didn't you?' laughs Sue. 'That was a delightful surprise. Not my plan at all, but I was happy enough to go along with you for a few days. You were my useful idiot, Elizabeth, if you don't mind me saying?'

Elizabeth tries to take her mind off the ambulances, their sirens now faint in the distance. 'Siobhan comes back to you, empty-handed. The next day you enter the safe house on St Albans Avenue. You shoot Poppy first, I'm guessing?'

'Correct,' says Sue. 'A shame, but needs must sometimes. She'd seen the letter.'

'And helpful in encouraging Douglas to let you know where the diamonds were? What did he tell you? Before you shot him? He obviously didn't let on?'

'He just said, "Stick close to Elizabeth, she'll find them." I thought that sounded true enough, and the best I was going to get, so I shot him.'

'And you did stick close to me, I'll give you that.'

'And you did find them. So thank you,' says Sue. 'As I say, a useful idiot. I'll be out of your hair very soon, I promise.'

The van pulls to a halt. Sue puts her gun hand into her handbag, but keeps the gun pointing at Elizabeth. The driver opens the back doors.

'After you, ladies,' says Sue, and the driver helps Elizabeth and Joyce climb down. Sue follows, needing no help.

'We won't be long,' says Sue to the driver. 'Just need to spend a penny.'

It is 5 p.m. The sky is darkening, and lights are coming on across Coopers Chase. The normal business of a normal day. Quizzes on the TV, books being read, grandchildren on the phone, a few tardy birds flying to their roosts. Elizabeth sees Colin Clemence taking in a garden chair from his patio. Miranda Scott from Wordsworth Court is posting a letter. She enters competitions, and last year won a lifetime's supply of washing powder. Persil must have rubbed their hands with glee when they discovered she was ninety-two.

All is quiet in this happy place. Another day done, family safe and sound, curtains closed and heating on. Nothing you'll ever see on the news, but something you should really pay more attention to, just the gentle hum of contentment.

Take a look out of the window, and there is nothing to see except two old women taking an evening stroll together. It's Joyce and Elizabeth, isn't it? Thick as thieves, those two. There is a younger woman walking a few steps behind. Heading over to Joyce's, I think.

'As soon as the shooting on the pier had finished, I was on the phone,' says Sue. 'Three men Martin Lomax put me in touch with a while ago. Men who could do a few jobs off the books. Ex-special forces, armed to the teeth. They were standing by, so I sent them straight here with Siobhan. I knew someone would know where the diamonds were. Your friend with the broken ribs, or that husband of yours, Elizabeth. Though from what I read you could tell him anything and he wouldn't remember.

Poor thing.' She sees Elizabeth stiffen in front of her and she smiles.

'My God, this was harder than it was supposed to be. "The perfect crime," Douglas had said to me. No victims. How many deaths now? Five? Although we all heard the ambulances, so who knows? Maybe a couple more.'

Elizabeth's phone starts ringing in her bag.

'Don't touch it,' says Sue.

Elizabeth does as she is told. But she doesn't need to touch it. She has recognized the personalized ringtone.

They reach the front door of Joyce's building. Elizabeth looks up at her best friend's window. The curtains are shut. They were not shut when she picked Joyce up this morning. Joyce keys in her security code and the three women enter the building.

The lift doors are directly in front of them. Elizabeth presses the button and the doors open. Sue Reardon smiles.

'If you try anything in that lift, I've got three armed men upstairs.'

'We've given up, Sue,' says Elizabeth. 'Don't you get it? Just get your diamonds and go.'

The doors close and the lift jolts upwards. Sue stands behind Joyce and Elizabeth, the gun at their backs. As the lift doors open on the first floor, her view is obscured.

'Joyce, hit the ground!' shouts Elizabeth.

Elizabeth and Joyce throw themselves to the floor, giving Bogdan a clear shot. He hits Sue exactly where he aims, through the shoulder. Sue drops her bag and her gun, her eyes wide in surprise.

Bogdan kicks Sue's gun away, then helps Joyce and Elizabeth to their feet.

'Come in,' says Bogdan. 'I've put the kettle on.'

78

'You've never seen anything like it,' says Stephen, sitting on Joyce's sofa. 'I was having forty winks in my chair, when I hear a noise. I open my eyes. Three fellas pointing guns at my head. "Hold your horses," I say, "what's this about? I'm imagining you're looking for Elizabeth?" You know, all dressed in black, guns and what have you. "Not a bit of it," says the fellow in the middle. "Tell us where the diamonds are."'

He is interrupted by a low moan. Joyce is tending to Sue Reardon's shoulder while she sits on a kitchen chair.

'Stop moaning, you big baby,' says Joyce, tightening a bandage.

'So I play the innocent Frenchman as it were, "What diamonds?" all this caper, and they don't like it one bit. Then madam here . . .' Stephen nods to another kitchen chair, where Siobhan sits, hands tied behind her, 'walks in, friendly as you like, "Just tell us, Stephen, tell us and we'll be on our way." Anyway, I stall for time, I couldn't remember where you'd gone, Elizabeth, but perhaps you'd be getting back soon. So here's me, "Oh, I don't know about diamonds, I'm afraid, not my area, you need the boss, she'll be back presently," and this lady – I'm sorry, I've forgotten your name?'

'Siobhan,' says Siobhan.

'Beautiful name. She's saying, "Elizabeth won't be back any time soon, and she won't be back at all if we don't get the diamonds." Well, I think, then you don't know Elizabeth like I know Elizabeth. One thing you can rely on with Elizabeth is she'll be back. Never let me down yet.'

'Never will, darling,' says Elizabeth.

'Tensions start to run high. "Where are the diamonds?" "What diamonds?" A couple of the fellows start ripping the place apart. Becoming a regular occurrence eh, dear?'

'Not even worth tidying the drawers these days,' agrees Elizabeth.

'And then I hear a key in the lock and think, well, here she is, but the door opens and it's the man himself.' Stephen motions over to the figure in the corner of the room.

'Ron had gone home to watch snooker and I thought Stephen would like to hear about the shootings,' says Bogdan.

'Before you know it, the three chaps all have their guns pointing at Bogdan, the poor bugger, and I'm thinking, get out of this one then.'

Bogdan takes up the story. 'Stephen says these guys are looking for the diamonds, and I say, "Well, you came to the right guy, follow me, they're at Joyce's. If I show you, I get to keep one?" and they look at Siobhan, and she's like, sure. "So come with me, but hide the guns when we get out the front door, I don't want you scaring the old people." So they're grumble, grumble, but OK, and out we go.'

'Immediately, I hear the most terrific noise,' says Stephen. 'Twenty seconds or so. Then in walks Bogdan and asks me to give him a hand clearing up.'

Elizabeth: 'So, the ambulances?'

'That was the three guys, yes,' says Bogdan. 'So I say to Siobhan, look, who's behind all this, and she's looking at the guys with the guns on the floor, and thinks maybe she should tell the truth. She says she works with Sue, OK, I get it. So I say send message to Sue, tell her you have the diamonds. "Where shall I say they are?" she says. And I don't know, so I look at Stephen.'

'And I say, "Tell her the truth," no reason not to. "They're in Joyce's microwave."'

Elizabeth looks over at Sue. 'I hope that's agony, dear.'

'We had a good laugh about it, didn't we, Elizabeth?' Stephen continues. 'She had to move them because she kept forgetting, and making cups of tea.'

'Oh, I'm the figure of fun now?' says Joyce. But she is smiling.

'The ambulances came, they had a lot of questions, understandably.'

'I told them to talk to Chris Hudson,' says Bogdan. 'He owes me a favour.'

'Oh, does he?' says Elizabeth.

'And then we toddled over to Joyce's to wait for you.'

'I saw you through the curtains,' says Bogdan. 'Gave you a ring to let you know I was here. Then I shot Sue.'

'And that's us up to date,' says Stephen.

Elizabeth walks over to Joyce's microwave and pulls out a green felt bag. It was usually full of Scrabble tiles, but now is full of diamonds. She pours them onto the kitchen table in front of Sue Reardon.

'Here you are, Sue. This is what it was all for. Poppy, Douglas, Andrew Hastings. Lomax, Frank Andrade. And this is the closest you'll ever get.'

'To be fair,' calls Joyce from the sofa, 'Martin Lomax and Frank Andrade weren't really Sue's fault. That was you.'

Elizabeth nods, conceding the point. She turns to Siobhan.

'And how did you get roped in, Siobhan? What's your connection here?'

'I'm easily led,' says Siobhan. 'Always have been. And it's not really Siobhan. It's Sally, Sally Montague, if you remember that name?'

Douglas's three exes. United.

Sue Reardon groans again, a guttural cry. 'Please, I need to go to the hospital.'

'I think Bogdan might have used up all the ambulances,' says Elizabeth.

'We'll give it a couple of hours,' says Joyce. 'I'll make sure you don't die. It'll be much more fun to see you in prison. Would you like some painkillers?'

'Yes, please,' says Sue, the anguish etched onto her face.

'Shame,' says Joyce. 'I don't have any.'

79

Patrice looks at the clock, sighs and pours herself another glass of wine.

Nine thirty, dark outside, and she is only halfway through marking the Jane Austen homework. She thinks about Chris. She thinks about him more and more these days. Patrice has fallen in love before, and this is beginning to show all the signs. That might just be the wine and the Jane Austen though.

She has always worried about Donna's work, and now she worries about Chris's too. Is that something she could get over? At least they are both in Fairhaven. That felt safer than London. How much trouble could there be in Fairhaven?

There were schools down there, weren't there? Of course there were, Patrice, you idiot, there are schools everywhere. What even made you think about it? It's not like you're going to be moving down there or anything.

She had felt safe and happy there during half term. Safe with Chris, and with Donna nearby. Happy with Chris, and with Donna nearby. They both feel a long way away now, as she sits alone in the house. But the weekend? At the weekend she is driving down to see them.

She thinks about ringing Chris. Maybe tell him how much she's been thinking about him? Maybe. Or perhaps just tell him tomorrow? When she'd had less to drink? Yes. There are certain steps you take in life that you can't easily turn back from. So take them with care. You don't want to make a fool of yourself.

Patrice smiles. How could she ever make a fool of herself in front of Chris? She will ring him. She'll mark three more essays, then she'll ring Chris as her treat. She will be slurring her words a little bit, but if you slur your words with a man you can get away with saying anything. Maybe she will mention Jane Austen, and see where that leads? It will be nice to hear his voice. Do they have darts on TV on Mondays? If they do she is sure that's what he'll be watching.

There is a noise on the street outside. Probably foxes.

She picks up the next essay on the pile. Ben Adams. Patrice suspects that Ben hasn't read a single word of *Sense & Sensibility*. She also suspects he has watched the film instead, mainly because at one point he accidentally calls Elinor Dashwood 'Emma Thompson'. Nice try, kid. Oh God, this is going to take her for ever.

Patrice has said it so many times, marking will be the death of her.

As she picks up the next essay, she hears a knock at the door. Another glance at the clock. That's late.

Patrice knows she should probably ignore it. But perhaps it's a neighbour needing something. And she'll do anything to leave the marking alone for a moment.

Patrice walks down the hallway, glass of wine still in hand. Donna has told her a hundred times to get deadlocks, to get peepholes, 'Never answer your door to strangers, Mum.' How old did she think Patrice was? Patrice will get peepholes and deadlocks when she's older. Patrice isn't even fifty, and she's not going to be frightened in her own home. It's nice that Donna cares, but Patrice can look after herself, thank you very much. She should ring Donna too. She's been a little down. So, ring Chris, then ring her little girl. Or ring her little girl first?

Patrice puts her wine down on the hall table and gives her hair a quick check. She nods her approval. You should always look your best, whoever's at the door.

The knock comes again, a little more insistent. All right, all right. Patrice flicks up the latch and pulls the door open.

Her mouth falls open, marking forgotten, wine forgotten, hair forgotten.

It is not a neighbour. She tries to compute, but there is no time.

'Look,' says Chris, standing on her doorstep, flowers in his hand and tears on his cheek. 'I know it's late, but it couldn't wait. I can't go another minute without telling you. I'm in love with you. I'm sorry if that's stupid.'

Patrice tries to think of something to say. She is so pleased she checked her hair. What would Jane Austen say?

'Can I come in?' Chris asks.

'Yes, my darling. Yes, you can come in,' she says. Patrice takes her wine from the hall table and reaches out her hand to lead Chris inside.

That will do just fine.

80

'I just thought I would come in and have a freshen up,' says Joyce. 'I'll put the hoover round, and a bit of Mr Sheen. I won't go anywhere near your bits and bobs.'

'Thank you, Joyce,' says Ibrahim, sipping his tea. 'I'm sorry to miss all the fun yesterday.'

'I'll fill you in, don't worry.'

'Ron is fuming that he missed it,' says Ibrahim. 'Especially as Siobhan was there.'

'It won't do Ron any harm to keep it in his pants for now,' says Joyce, dusting the sideboard. 'How are you feeling? In yourself?'

Ibrahim slides back into his armchair. He gives a small smile and a shrug.

Joyce nods and gets to work. 'I need your help today.'

'I'm sorry, Joyce, I can't. Not today.'

'You don't even know what I want yet.'

Ibrahim laughs. 'Of course I do. It's the first day of peace we've had for weeks, Joyce. You want me to drive you to the animal rescue centre? To pick up your dog?'

'Well, yes, please, that is what I'd like. Why don't you finish your tea, and we can head off? Lovely drive?'

'I'm afraid not.'

'You seem to think I might take no for an answer?' says Joyce. 'How long have you known me?'

Ibrahim leans forward and puts his tea back down on the low table. 'Joyce, look at me.'

Joyce puts down her duster and does just that.

'I know what you are trying to do, and I am moved that you are trying. You know I am frightened, you know I don't want to leave this flat, and I certainly don't want to leave this village. You know that is unhealthy, and you want to look after me. You are too clever to come over and tell me to pull myself together. You know I am in too many pieces for that. And so your tactic is different, your tactic is cleverer. "Ibrahim, please help me," is your tactic. "Ibrahim, I need you." But, Joyce, you don't need to go to the rescue centre today, Alan isn't going anywhere, I've seen his picture, you are the only person in the world who would choose him. And when you do go to the rescue centre you won't need me to drive you. Get a taxi, or get someone else to drive you. Gordon Playfair has a Land Rover, which would be perfect for dog transportation. Your kindness is welcome but it is transparent. I am not leaving this village again. I have made my peace with that.'

Joyce nods.

'You read people very well, Joyce, don't think I don't spot that. I see how you do it too, coercion through kindness. But understand this. Behind me, in these files, there are people I couldn't help, people beyond reach, problems I couldn't fix, whichever way I twisted and turned. You like to fix things, too, Joyce. You can't bear it when something is out of place. And so you come in, and you smile, and I know your affection for me is genuine, and you ask me to drive you to the animal rescue centre. How could I resist? And before you know it I'm back behind the wheel of that car, I'm outside the village, and I'm soon surrounded by lost, stray dogs and, while I don't like dogs – quite the opposite – I am sure to feel a kinship with these animals lost and alone. Lost and alone and waiting for Joyce to make things better. It is a terrific plan, you are a very good and clever friend. But, and I need you to really listen to this, it's not going to happen. I am too scared. There are times when a wise man admits defeat, and I hope you agree I am a wise man. I have many certificates. So, thank you, from the bottom of my heart, but, just for once, Joyce, this is a problem you cannot fix.'

Ibrahim leans back in his chair.

'I understand,' nods Joyce, and places the duster over her shoulder. 'I wonder, though, if I might just say this . . .'

Around forty-five minutes later Joyce spies the first sign for the animal rescue centre and Ibrahim takes the exit.

'I just love to see a horse in a field,' says Joyce. 'When you can tell they're happy. Happiness is what life is all about, don't you think?'

Ibrahim shakes his head. 'I can't agree. The secret of life is death. Everything is about death, you see.'

'Well, recently, yes,' agrees Joyce. 'But surely not everything? That seems a bit much?'

'In essence,' says Ibrahim. 'Our existence only makes sense because of it; it provides meaning to our narrative. Our direction of travel is always towards it. Our behaviour is either because we fear it, or because we choose to deny it. We could drive past this spot once a year, every year, and neither the horse nor ourselves would get younger. Everything is death.'

'That's one way of looking at things, I suppose,' says Joyce.

'It's the only way,' says Ibrahim. 'Will there be a toilet at the rescue centre?'

'You would think so,' says Joyce. 'And if not, there will be a staff toilet.'

'Oh, I can't use a staff toilet,' says Ibrahim. 'I always feel I haven't earned it.'

'Surely, if everything is about death, then also *nothing* is about death?' says Joyce, applying lipstick in the passenger mirror.

'How so?' asks Ibrahim.

'Well, just say that everything was blue. You, me, Alan, everything?'

'OK.'

'Well, if *everything* was blue then we wouldn't need the word "blue", would we?'

'I accept that,' accepts Ibrahim.

'And if we had no word for blue then nothing would be blue, would it?'

'Well, death is an event, and so . . .' begins Ibrahim, then sees the entrance to the rescue centre up on his left. 'We're here!'

Which is a relief, because Joyce does sort of have a point.

Perhaps everything isn't about death after all? What a time to find out.

81

Bogdan stares at the chess board, but it makes no sense. He has just made a fatal error, and he never makes fatal errors.

Stephen's lips are pursed. He has spotted the mistake. He looks up at Bogdan.

'Goodness,' he says. 'Quite unlike you, quite unlike you.'

Stephen moves his bishop to capitalize on the error. Bogdan is doomed. He looks down at the board again, but the pieces start dancing, they won't behave. He tries to blink it all away. Get everything back in its place. Everything in order.

'Something on your mind?' asks Stephen.

'Nothing,' says Bogdan. Which is usually true. But not today.

'If you say so, then who am I to question?' says Stephen. 'You killed someone else, perhaps?'

Bogdan looks at the board. Looks at the pieces. He can't see a way out. Stephen was going to win.

'You love Elizabeth?' says Bogdan.

'Too small a word, that,' says Stephen. 'But yes. Where is she, by the way? She did tell me.'

'Antwerp,' says Bogdan.

'Sounds like her,' says Stephen. 'Go on.'

'When did you know you loved her?' asks Bogdan. 'Like, ages?'

'Twenty seconds perhaps,' says Stephen. 'I recognized her the moment I met her. I just thought, Well, there you are, I've been waiting for you.'

Bogdan nods.

'Do you have a little crush on someone?' asks Stephen. 'Is that it? You can resign the game if you want, by the way. No coming back now, surely?'

Bogdan looks at the board. Perhaps there is no way back? But he won't resign just yet.

'How do you know if someone likes you?' asks Bogdan.

'Well, everyone likes you, Bogdan,' says Stephen. 'But I imagine you mean romantically?'

Bogdan nods, and looks down at the board again, desperately searching for a way out.

'A boy or a girl?' asks Stephen. 'I've never liked to ask.'

'A girl,' says Bogdan.

'Well, then I owe Elizabeth twenty pounds,' says Stephen. 'The best thing to do is just ask. How about a drink? If she says yes, then there's the answer.'

'But what if she says no?'

'Then she says no, dust yourself down, plenty more eggs in the omelette and so on.'

Bogdan thinks back to the parapet of the bridge. The rocks and the river below. The yellow jumper his mum had knitted. He looks down at the board and shakes his head. Sometimes the pieces weren't where they were supposed to be. Sometimes you weren't in control. And perhaps that was OK? He will ask her for a drink, and if she says no, she says no.

Bogdan holds his hand out to Stephen.

'I resign.'

'Good lad,' says Stephen. 'Who is she?'

'She's called Donna,' says Bogdan. 'Police officer.'

'Just what you need,' says Stephen. 'Keep you on the straight and narrow. Just ask her for a drink, you ridiculous man.'

Bogdan hears the front door open. Elizabeth is back. She walks in with a bag full of files.

'Hello, darling,' says Stephen. 'Where have you been?'

'Antwerp, darling,' says Elizabeth, and kisses him on the top of the head.

'Sounds like you,' says Stephen.

'You boys having fun?'

'Bogdan was asking when I knew I was in love with you.'

'Oh, really. And when was it?'

'The jury's still out, I told him. Giving her the benefit of the doubt for now.'

'And how did the subject of love come up?'

'Darling, Bogdan and I must have our secrets, mustn't we?'

'You must,' agrees Elizabeth.

Bogdan looks at the paperwork poking out of Elizabeth's bag. 'How was Antwerp? Everything good?'

'Everything good, yes,' says Elizabeth. 'All taken care of.'

82

Joyce

So Alan will be with me next week!

The rescue centre have to come and visit the flat, just to check that I'm a fit and proper person. I certainly think I am, but it will be nice to have it confirmed.

I am glad they didn't come round last week. Sue had bled all over the kitchen floor, there were millions of pounds' worth of diamonds on the kitchen table and Bogdan was storing three guns under the spare-room duvet. I don't know what the rules are for 'fit and proper', but I imagine I would have been breaking one or two of them there.

And, by the way, yes, it is Alan, not Rusty. They let us take him for a walk around the grounds, and Ibrahim read the riot act to me. And it does suit him, to be honest.

We got on like a house on fire. Ibrahim tried to make him sit, but Alan was having none of it, just happily chasing his tail instead. A dog after my own heart.

I took a picture of him while we were there, to show Elizabeth and Ron. They both said he looked like trouble, which I know they both meant as a great compliment.

Anyway, that photo is @GreatJoy69's Instagram profile picture now, so people can judge Alan for themselves.

And, by the by, Joanna solved the mystery of my private messages. She went into my account and searched all of them for me. She told me that if I didn't want to be sent an endless tide of photographs of men's genitals, I should really change my username.

Needless to say, I haven't changed it.

I know I said I wanted something to happen. Do you remember? And it has been fun, for the most part.

Except for Poppy.

We met her real mum yesterday, she actually is called Siobhan, which I suppose was all part of the plan. Elizabeth and I sat with her and talked about Poppy and she and I cried. She had to identify the body, which had already been identified. The scars on the back of her leg had actually come from a car accident when she was very young. Siobhan had lots of photographs, and we looked through them together.

Elizabeth gave Siobhan the poetry book, which had been on Poppy's bedside table in Hove. The bookmark was left where it was, on a poem called 'An Arundel Tomb'.

Arundel is not too far from Brighton. Gerry and I once went antiquing there. This was before there were Starbucks, but we went to a nice tea room.

Poppy's funeral is next week, and we will all be there. Ron is taking flowers for the real Siobhan. Ever the optimist. Ibrahim is driving us.

Elizabeth got a bit upset that Douglas had told Sue to stick close to her if she wanted to find the diamonds. Not that it was any sort of big deal, Elizabeth said, but she couldn't help feeling a bit betrayed. I laughed and asked her if she had not worked it out? Douglas told Sue to stick close to her, because he knew Elizabeth would eventually catch her out. She took my point and cheered up a little.

Maybe a bit of peace and quiet would be nice now. Just for a bit? Joanna is popping down at the weekend. She's bringing the football chairman down with her, and I am making lunch. I have invited Ron over too, because he will know what to talk about.

I asked Ron what football chairmen ate, and he said ham, egg and chips. Luckily I know Ron's games, so I am doing a roast.

I will tell them everything that's been going on, except what happened to the diamonds. That's just between Elizabeth, Ibrahim, Ron and me. We decided together, and it's our little secret. We all need secrets, don't we?

Speaking of which, I have one more secret, which you mustn't tell anyone. I haven't even told Elizabeth. I went down to Fairhaven last Wednesday, and there's a little place near the pier. We must have been close to it when everyone was being shot. I'd booked an appointment. I didn't know if you had to, especially on a Wednesday.

It took the lady a few hours, and it still hurts a bit now, but it was worth it. I never wear sleeveless dresses, not with my arms, so no one will ever see it. Unless I get lucky. It's at the top of my left arm, and ever so pretty.

Just a small tattoo of a poppy.

83

Lance James had kept the leaflet that Joyce had sent him. It was too expensive, but a man could dream, couldn't he? He was very glad he kept it, and he had booked the appointment as soon as the money from the diamonds had come through.

He looks around the room, bigger than his whole flat. Oak-panelled. Carpet, actual carpet. Two huge windows overlooking Dublin Bay.

It had been chaos at the end of the pier. The report had taken him a long time to write. Who shot who and why. Leave a few things out, invent a couple of things that perhaps hadn't happened. The footage from the monitors had disappeared, so all that was left was the word of Lance, Bogdan and Connie. Lance and Bogdan had met for a pint, got their stories straight, and that was that. The report was all true enough in the end. He'd written worse.

The main thing he had left out, of course, was the two diamonds. They were just sitting there on the desk, for heaven's sake, twinkling like pennies in a fountain. He had slipped them into his pocket, because what was the alternative? Where would they go otherwise?

It was the first time Lance had done something illegal, and it would be the last. Well, he had once driven a hire car on holiday with Ruth when, technically, he had been uninsured. But that was about it.

If you are going to commit one major crime in your life, Lance reasons, make it stealing diamonds from the mafia.

They had given him a few days' leave after the shootout on the pier, told him to take some time to relax. Relax? In the tiny flat he didn't own? With the kitchen wall still half demolished? The builder had, unsurprisingly, not returned to finish the job.

So Lance had taken the ferry to Zeebrugge, then the train to Antwerp, then a cab to the jewellery district, and the address he had been given by an arms dealer who owed him a favour.

The diamonds as a whole had been worth twenty million, that much he knew. So what were the two he had slipped into his pocket worth? A million? Dare he dream two or three million? He had been looking through the Rightmove app all the way there.

Sue Reardon had told him about Elizabeth Best when this all began. Her reputation, her bravery, her cunning. A legend of the Service. He had expected – and, in retrospect, Sue must have expected too – that her powers would have deserted her. Sue must have thought Elizabeth Best was an easy touch.

But Sue would have a long time to regret her misjudgement of Elizabeth.

So Lance should have known really, when he was on the train, looking at all the expensive houses.

The jeweller had examined the stones, nodding and

smiling. 'These are nice, these are very nice,' he'd been saying. Where had Lance got them?

Lance told him that a relative had died.

'You have papers?'

'Afraid not.'

The jeweller had shrugged. No matter. Then he had put down his eyeglass.

'Very nice indeed. I can offer you thirty thousand.'

Lance must have looked shocked, because the jeweller had immediately said, 'OK, OK, thirty-five.'

Yes, of course, Lance should have known. He should have known Elizabeth wouldn't have left a million, or two or three, in the hands of Connie Johnson, or whoever else might have ended up with the diamonds in the chaos. She had given Connie the runts of the litter. Thirty thousand pounds, out of twenty million. Lance had started to laugh. He wouldn't have been able to spend a million anyway. The Service does yearly audits, unusual spending, extravagances. Checking the Russians or the Saudis weren't paying you. Or that you hadn't just stolen some diamonds from the mafia. Spending three million would have been virtually impossible.

But spending thirty-five thousand? That had been a breeze. He had bought Ruth out of the flat. Of course, she hadn't asked him where he had got the money, because, to Ruth, twenty-five thousand pounds was insignificant.

And the other ten thousand? Well, that's why he was here, in this grand room in Dublin, with its oak panels, and beautiful windows. With the coffee table, stacked with magazines not to read, while he waits.

He likes to think about what happened to the rest of the twenty million. What has Elizabeth done with it? Maybe she has kept it? Perhaps Sue could have bought her off after all? Lance doubts it very much though. He wonders if, one day, he might be allowed to ask her. He hopes so, he would certainly like to meet her again.

Lance picks up the *Sunday Telegraph* magazine. The cover image is familiar. 'Hidden Treasure – Is This the Most Beautiful Garden in England?' Hidden treasure indeed, he thinks, and wonders what the eventual new owners of Martin Lomax's house might dig up around the place.

As he flicks to the article, the nicely groomed man behind the desk in the corner says, 'Doctor Morris will see you now.'

Lance gets to his feet and, for once, runs his fingers through his hair. It'll be good to remember what it feels like before the transplant.

'Thank you,' says Lance.

Sylvia Finch slips off her suede shoes, still dark from the puddles, and pulls her chair up to the empty desk.

She comes in for two days a week, and has done for around ten years now. Ever since she retired.

She has the odd week off, usually when the kids and grandkids come to visit. She doesn't have her own desk, they just put her wherever they have space. Space is tight, and money is tight, and Sylvia is glad to just muck in. Glad to help the people who helped her.

Wherever they put her, she takes out the picture of Dennis and props it against her computer. To remind her why she's there.

She logs into the online banking system. Today is just cross-checking the accounts. Making sure monies paid in have arrived, and making sure nothing unauthorized has gone out. There is usually the odd anomaly, a promised transfer which hasn't gone through, or a staff member buying lunch on the wrong credit card. Never anything really sinister, but always best to check.

Today, however, as Sylvia clicks onto the main holding account, she spots an immediate error. The error is amusing, more than anything else, the sort of thing that, in happier days, she would tell Dennis about when she got home.

Sylvia rings the bank and gives her details. She runs through the error she has spotted, but is assured that it is not an error. Which is impossible. She asks the lady on the other end, Lisa, very friendly, to double-check, which she does. No error. So she asks for a few more details.

Sylvia thanks Lisa and puts down the phone.

The bigwigs are all in a meeting. Eight of them around a table that is far too small. The bottom half of the glass meeting-room wall is frosted, but in the clear pane above she can see the tops of people's heads and, cramped into a corner, the chief executive standing by a flip chart, pointing out figures.

Sylvia has never interrupted a meeting before, would never dream of it, in fact. She has never liked to draw attention to herself, and she has always been glad that accountants very rarely need to interrupt meetings. But in this instance she probably should.

She checks and double-checks the screen. Then checks and double-checks the information she has written down. She takes a final look at the photograph of Dennis. Her husband, her love. Gone to dementia, then gone for ever. The man who died twice. Courage, Sylvia, Dennis is with you.

As she walks over to the meeting-room door, she hears the noise of the discussion, and begins to feel awkward. She pauses for a moment outside the door. What will she look like when she walks in? A silly, thin old woman? Sylvia, who says good morning, puts the picture of her husband on her desk, then doesn't speak again until she says good evening? Sylvia, who silently holds up his flask every time someone offers her a cup of tea? Sylvia, who doesn't know which jumper goes with which skirt? Well, she supposes she can't change who she is, and this is important. Sylvia knocks.

There is a slight pause, then, 'Yes, come in.'

Sylvia pushes open the door, and the faces around the table and the face at the flip chart all turn towards her. She feels giddy. The flip chart is branded with the logo of the charity. 'Living With Dementia – Living With Love'. They had done all they could for her and Dennis, and she gives everything she can to them in return. She has no money to give, and so she gives her time. She sees they are waiting for her to speak. So here goes nothing.

'I'm ever so sorry to interrupt,' she says. 'But I don't suppose anyone here knows anything about twenty million pounds from Antwerp?'

Acknowledgements

Well, well, well, well, well. And there we have it, *The Man Who Died Twice*.

I hope you liked the ending? I read a book about thirty years ago where the *very last line* was integral to the plot, and I'd always liked that as an idea.

In *that* book we discover in the final line that a package the villain has been carrying throughout the book contains the cryogenically frozen brain of Adolf Hitler. I'm not sure that specific reveal would have worked here, but it certainly stayed with me.

Thinking back, the last line of *The Thursday Murder Club* was about Joyce's gooseberry crumble, so I really feel I am growing as a writer.

OK, acknowledgements. Once again, I have so many people to thank. Despite repeated requests to my publishers, I am not allowed to score people out of ten according to how helpful they have been, so I will just list them instead.

Thank you to my wonderful editor, Katy Loftus, for her crucial combination of wisdom and enthusiasm, and for often asking, 'Would Ron *really* say that?' A great editor is a gift, and Katy is a very great gift. I am so lucky to work with an incredible team at Viking. We've all had such fun together since the release of *The Thursday Murder Club*, and I'm so glad they all stuck around for *The Man Who Died Twice*. Olivia Mead and Chloe Davies, Georgia Taylor, Ellie Hudson, Amelia Fairney and Vikki Moynes, you are very much HASHTAG *TheThursdayMurderClub*Club.

Thank you to the incredible sales team, led by Sam Fanaken, who just kept coming back with steeper and steeper graphs and wider and wider eyes. Richard Bravery and Joel Holland are responsible for the perfect front cover, and special thanks to Richard Bravery for providing me with the ideal pen-name should I ever decide to write an SAS thriller. Thank you also to the DeadGood team, the PageTurners team, the amazing audio team, to Sam Parker from the Penguin UK website and to the unstoppable Annie Underwood.

Final Viking thanks to Natalie Wall and to the master copy-editor Trevor Horwood. Trevor, is it OK that I started a sentence with 'And' just now? Let me know.

Incidentally, Barack Obama is also published by Viking, but you never see him in reception.

I am blessed with an incredible agent, Juliet Mushens. Rarely have I worked with anyone who can be so professional and so excited at the same time. Thank you for everything, Juliet, I couldn't do it without you. And thank you to the brilliant Liza DeBlock, who used to be Juliet's assistant, but gets more senior by the day, and soon won't speak to me at all.

I am also indebted to my American gang, Pamela Dorman, Jeramie Orton, Jenny Bent, Kristina Fazzalaro, Nora Alice Demick and Marie Michels. Pamela told me I couldn't call this book *The Following Thursday* and on this, as on so much else, she was right. Pamela and her team are so smart and supportive and, as soon as it's legally permissible, I will fly over and thank them in person.

I am lucky to have so many brilliant foreign publishers too. I am so happy that you have taken this very British story around the world, and that Joyce is now famous in China. I wonder what she would make of it?

My deepest gratitude to Mark Billingham, Lucy Prebble, Professor Katy Shaw, Caroline Kepnes, Andi Osho, Sarah Pinborough and Annabel Jones. Always on hand for help and advice. There is no question small or stupid enough that one of them won't answer it for me. Any writer, or indeed any human being, with that sort of firepower to call upon is very lucky indeed.

For a number of specific plot points I am also very grateful to HHJ Angela Rafferty QC and the Recorder of London HHJ Mark Lucraft QC. Thank you for answering the question 'But could this actually happen?' with 'Yes, it could.' That was a relief.

Thank you to the amazing booksellers up and down the country who have been so supportive, and so quick with tea and biscuits every time I came in to do signings. City Books in Hove appears in this book, but there are so many more I could have mentioned, and I'm sure I will do in future stories. Please support your local bookshops. 'Use it or lose it' is quite right.

And thank you to all the frontline workers who looked after us during lockdown. What you did will never be forgotten.

Thank you to the amazing Ramita Navai for keeping me sane and safe through a difficult year for us all. I know we will still be best friends when we are in a retirement village of our own. And my gratitude to the whole Navai clan, Laya, Ramin and Paola, for being the best Iranian/Colombian gang any man could wish for. And a special dedication to a very special man, whom we lost in 2020: Kourosh Navai. With your wit and charm, your kindness and strength, your sense of mischief and your sense of loyalty, Kourosh, you will forever be an honorary member of the Thursday Murder Club.

Finally, as always, thank you to my family. To my mum for the love and support, and for the endless supply of material. Thank you to Mat and Anissa, and to Jan Wright, you all mean a great deal to me, and I don't say that often enough. I thanked my wonderful late grandparents, Fred and Jessie, last time and I shall do so again. And will keep on doing so for as long as I write.

And finally, thank you to my children. I know I dedicated this book to you as well, but you're the best thing that ever happened to me. Even better than when Fulham beat Juventus 4–1. Love you.

DISCUSSION QUESTIONS FOR READERS

1. The novel kicks off when Elizabeth is reunited with her ex-husband Douglas, who admits to stealing twenty million pounds' worth of diamonds. Where did you think Douglas had hidden the diamonds? Were you correct?

2. What do you think you and your friends would do if you stumbled across twenty million pounds? How would you split it? What's the first thing you would buy? What do you think your friends would buy? What charities would you support?

3. Ibrahim is accosted by teenagers while out on the town by himself, a traumatic event that lands him in hospital and ultimately results in him completely withdrawing from his friends' outings. As he recovers, Ibrahim thinks to himself: 'They say a man who desires revenge should dig two graves, and this is surely right.' What do you think he meant by this?

4. Once more, Elizabeth somehow seems to be ten steps ahead of everyone else. Did you doubt her instincts at any point? If so, why? What makes her such a good leader for the group? Who would you rather have on your side, Elizabeth or Bogdan?

5. Have you ever been lonely in a new town? How did you overcome it?

6. Did you suspect Joyce's friendship bracelets would play the role they did in solving the mystery of the missing diamonds? What about the locket? When did you know, and why?

7. Who is your worst ex?

8. How do you think the dynamics of the Thursday Murder Club shifted once Ibrahim stepped back after his assault? Did the Club's relationship with Donna and Chris or Bogdan change in any way?

9. Did you guess how the dead-letter drops would be used in the novel? If you had to hide something, what would you use for a dead-letter drop?

10. Who did you think was behind the murders? Were you correct?

11. Would you be happy with a dog named Alan? What is an acceptable name for a pet, and what is unacceptable?

COMING SOON

A NEW
THURSDAY MURDER CLUB MYSTERY!

The Thursday Murder Club faces a new challenge in the third book in the bestselling series.

PRE-ORDER NOW

Scan the QR code or visit your favourite bookshop

The Thursday MURDER Club

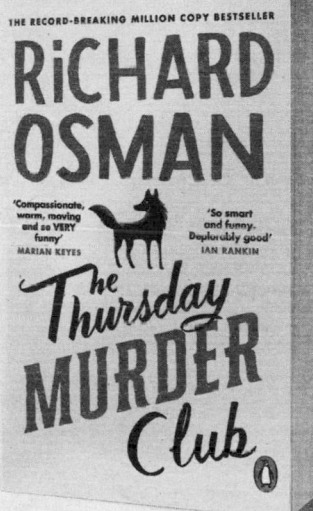

THE RECORD-BREAKING MILLION COPY BESTSELLER

RICHARD OSMAN

'Compassionate, warm, moving and so VERY funny'
MARIAN KEYES

'So smart and funny. Deplorably good'
IAN RANKIN

The Thursday MURDER Club

Join the Thursday Murder Club at the start of their journey, as our four amateur sleuths find themselves in the middle of their first live case.

ORDER NOW

Scan the QR code or follow this link: penguin.co.uk/RichardOsman

TO HEAR THE LATEST FROM RICHARD, INCLUDING EXCLUSIVE GIVEAWAYS AND QUIZZES

The Thursday MURDER Club NEWSLETTER

Sign up now! Scan the QR code or follow this link:
penguin.co.uk/RichardOsman

Join the club!

 TheThursdayMClub 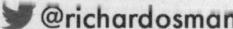 @richardosman  @misterosman